Eagle's Claw

Morgan Jameson

This book is dedicated to the memory of my favorite uncle, Bill Fabens, who gave me a copy of 'The Quiller Memorandum' by Adam Hall, when I was a young boy, and got me hooked on thrillers. Bill not only had a kind word for everyone he ever met, but always was incredibly supportive, no matter how crazy the idea seemed, and was simply one of the greatest men I've ever met. Thank you, Bill, for everything you did for me. March forth, Bill. Lead the way.

Acknowledgments

This book would not exist without the help of the following people:

Mark Gula, Harry Weisberger, and Marianne Horn, who weren't just readers, but editors who kept my commas consistent, my participles positioned, and prevented semi-colons from taking over the text. James Wallis did his usual, exceptional work on the cover, which I just cannot say enough about. Thanks James! Linda Au did a fantastic job as proofreader. Any errors are mine, not hers. We sometimes differ on stylistic points.

Joe Spencer, Scott & Debbie Humberd, Steve Robinson and Larry Osborne were all fans who became beta-readers, as was Pat Cady. They were all incredibly helpful. I'd like to thank my father, Deac Jones for his continued support as well. My good friend, Mike Callahan, again was a reader and gave me valuable insight. Thanks, Weenie!

Jeremiah Horstman, Heiko Effenberger and Nicole Olson Buchanan all helped not only make sure that my German was used correctly, and verified locations, but also contributed little gems to the book, Heiko the bit about Tante Emma ladens, ('Aunt Emma' stores - a sort of early, German convenience store,) and Nicole, the detail of Roemer glass goblets, which I used in a love scene. Jeremiah was not only a reader, but helped me test rappelling on parachute cord to see if it was possible. (It is, but I would *not* recommend it.) Alexandra Caldwell once again was a reader, and took more pictures of yours truly, despite the possible damage to her camera lens from my ugly mug.

Of course I can't forget my best friend, my brother, staunchest ally and most vociferous critic, Robert Allison, who not only is my first 'go-to' reader, but also gifted me with a new printer, rather than just make recommendations when I needed a new one.

Also, a special thanks to Kimberley Cameron, my agent of many years, whose faith in me continues to encourage me in my writing endeavors.

Finally, I want to thank my very good friend, Tracey Burraston, who was not only a reader, but an inspiration: With her permission, I used a thinly disguised, true story about her daughter, Sedona, and her son, Jake, which added levity and a sense of reality to the book. She also advised me that my love scenes needed 'punching up,' prevented me from making a silly mistake with an expletive, and as a result, other female beta readers loved those parts. She was also the inspiration for Marie, although they are different in many ways. She is the epitome of a strong woman, and a heroine in her own right, as are all single mothers. Thanks, Trace.

A few German terms
that may help the reader:

German — English

Achtung! — Attention!

Aufseherin — Female guard or supervisor in prison camps

Bitte — Please

Danke — Thank you

Danke schön — Thank you very much

Doktor — Doctor

Feuer — Fire

Hallo — Hello

Hände hoch! — Hands up!

Herr — Mister

Ja — Yes

Jungs — Boys

Kripo — Kriminalpolizei, responsible for murder investigations, among other
things.

Kübelwagen — German Jeep (Looks like VW 'Thing')

KG76 + KG200 — Stands for 'Kampfgeschwader'—a Luftwaffe battle group

Luftwaffe — German Air Force

Nein — No

Orpo — Regular Police (uniformed)

Panzer Deine Waffe! — Literally, 'Panzer: your weapon!'

Perfekt — Perfect

Raus! — Out!

RLM — Reichsluftfahrtministerium or German air ministry

RSHA — Reich Main Security Office

Scheisse — Shit

Schnell! — Quickly!

Schwanz — Prick

Schwimmwagen — Amphibious Jeep

Streng Geheim — Top Secret

Stück Scheisse — Piece of shit

Verstehen? — Understand?

Was ist hier los? — What's happening here?

Wehrmacht — German Army

Also, bear in mind that 3000 meters doesn't sound impressive as a height, but converts roughly to 10,000 feet.

– Part One –

1

June 2nd, 1944—Obersalzberg, Germany

Despite it being summer, the wind howling through the open floor hatch of the B-24 was cold. The German paratrooper gear felt strange to Donny. This was not the first time he had inserted by parachute, but the first where he was wearing German Fallschirmjäger gear, as he'd much rather be mistaken for a German paratrooper blown off course than for what he was – an OSS agent about to drop into Obersalzberg – one of the most secure areas in all the Third Reich, and Hitler's home in Bavaria. It was also the first time he'd been asked to land on a spot the size of the proverbial dime, near the top of one of the largest mountains in Austria.

The view down through the open jump hatch wasn't encouraging. Spires of rock punctuated by steep, narrow moraines and the occasional hardy pine or scrub was all he could see rushing beneath them. There was a waxing, gibbous moon, threatened by a small, dark front of rain clouds, which made it more likely he'd be seen, but less likely that he'd be killed slamming into a cliff face in the dark. The German parachute had been rejected for a number of reasons, the main one being that the German single point attachment made the damn thing even tougher to steer than the American or Brit models, which were pretty much unsteerable themselves. His chute was the latest design, straight from British MD1 secret labs, known as "Churchill's Toyshop," but it was up to the pilot to drop him exactly on target, which considering the small size of the target and the wind at this altitude, was damn near impossible.

The red light came on and the Brit who was acting as jumpmaster flashed an open hand at him. Five minutes. He wondered briefly who the idiot was who had decided it was better to jump out of a hole in the fuselage where the belly turret gun used to be rather than to go out the side door like a normal commando – even the Germans jumped out the side – then decided it didn't matter. What mattered was the landing, and so far he hadn't seen a decent place yet. Nor would he – they were dropping him onto the biggest mountain in the area: the Kehlstein Hoher Göll.

"Whose damn idea was this anyway?" he said aloud, knowing the jumpmaster couldn't hear him above the roar of the B-24's engines. His ride was via the "Carpetbagger Air Force," a motley volunteer group of some of the craziest, yet most skillful pilots available to the Allies. Using blacked-out, highly modified B-24 bombers, they flew in under the radar, or by 'catching a ride' with a bombing raid, then dropping out, back down below radar, to make their run inland. Donny had done all but two of his airborne jumps out of a C-47 Gooney Bird, and wasn't looking forward to dropping through the small hole in the bottom of the plane. Too easy to catch something on the way through, bang your head on the edge, or…

The green light came on and the jumpmaster screamed at him, but Donny was already on his way. The wind tore at him and he tumbled, then caught himself and straightened out. He saw the top of the Hoher Göll above him, just as the chute jerked him upwards, then he was floating above Berchtesgaden in the moonlight, for anyone to see, totally vulnerable. He was already regretting not bringing a weapon with him other than his Sykes-Fairbairn dagger, but he knew that where he was going, it was a risk to try and take a Sten or a pistol and be caught with it.

He looked down, trying to find his landing area. A patch of rocky ground roughly thirty meters in diameter, on a knoll at the top of a winding stairway leading up from the Eagle's Nest. Hitting it would be sheer luck. If he hit below it, he'd slam into the nearly vertical cliff and likely be killed, and if he pulled too soon, flew over the top and made it all the way to the bottom without a similar result, he'd land somewhere in the middle of the German Army – many of them SS. Neither option appealed to Donny, so he concentrated on getting it perfect. Perfect was the only way down.

The rear windows of the famous Kehlstein house, or "Eagle's Nest" as it was called, built on top of a mountain in tribute of Hitler's 50th birthday served as his bull-seye. The plan was for him to land just above the building in a small open area, strip off his gear and hide it, then hike down the steep, narrow trail to the Nest, where he'd meet his contact. At first he thought he was okay, then he realized he was drifting right, away from the mountain, and if he continued on this course, he'd be carried out past the promontory the Kehlsteinhaus perched on, and out over the valley below – game over.

He pulled desperately on the left riser bundle, spilling some air from the right hand side of the chute, essentially banking him left. There were two problems with this – the best result being that it sent you tearing off in the other direction too far, which in this case might slam him into the cliff, breaking every bone in his body. That was preferable, however, over spilling too much air out of the chute and having it lose its loft and "candlestick" on him, becoming nothing more than a streamer to mark his passing. Although he had a secondary, he was so close to the rock face that he'd have no time to cut loose and deploy it.

He got the chute straightened out somewhat, but still pendelumed from side to side, and he realized to his chagrin that he was too low, and wasn't going to land on the upper crest as planned. In fact, he was headed straight for the Eagle Nest's rear patio. He was about to crash Gretl Braun's pre-wedding party.

The flagstone patio rushed up at him and he realized he was going way too fast. As his feet hit the ground he tried to use them to brake himself against his forward momentum, but they just acted as a fulcrum, spinning him forward as a sudden wind gust yanked him forward again, throwing him straight at the cut stone wall of the Kehlsteinhaus – the famous Eagle's Nest.

He winced at the imminent contact, but another gust swept him up off the ground and up onto the roof. One ankle smacked painfully on the wall as he went over—the pain sudden and sharp, making him nearly cry out—but he had a more pressing problem: he was being dragged along the slate roof toward the other end, which dropped off hundreds of meters into the valley below. If he didn't get stopped, he was dead. The wind intensified into another gust, sweeping him along the roof, which suddenly stabbed him. He realized then it was a bird spike, and finally managed to grab one as he went by, his feet slipping on the smooth, slick slate, finally finding one of the snowmelt dams that ringed the roof. By the time he stopped his legs were hanging off the outer edge, the valley far beneath him – with nothing but air in the middle. He just hoped none of the party-goers came out on the front patio for a smoke and saw him struggling on the roof.

The chute yanked at him again, and another bird spike stabbing him in the left forearm, but he held on grimly, knowing this was not the sort of thing you get a second chance at. With his right hand, he found his Fairbairn-Sykes knife and pulled it loose, then quickly slashed behind him, trying to cut the chute away before it pulled him off the roof.

It was a good thing the knife was sharp, because he had soon cut through most of the shrouds on the right side. He had a bad moment when he had to change hands to cut the other side loose and the chute snapped in the wind a final time like a dying animal, trying to kill him yet again, but it didn't fill completely with so many shroud lines cut. Still, it very nearly tore him off the roof, and one foot came free, sliding out into free air at the edge.

Finally he'd cut enough of the shrouds so the chute deflated completely, but he didn't trust it, and was finally able to pull it back up to him and tuck it underneath him. It wasn't easy one- handed, but he somehow got it under him, then tucked into a canvas bag he had secreted inside his camouflage jump smock for just such a purpose. *"Can't have the bloody Jerries finding a spare, used parachute laying around now, can we?"* Major William Fairbairn, his former Scottish SOE instructor, had told him in a heavy brogue.

Donny slashed the last two riser lines loose, but as he went to put the knife away, he fumbled it with his cold fingers and it went skittering away from him on the roof, clipped the snow dam, and of course bounced over it and dropped off the edge. Now he had no weapon. He cursed under his breath, but there was no help for it. What was done was done. He tucked the parachute under his chin and into the canvas bag inside his smock so as to have both hands free, then began climbing back up onto the spine of the narrow roof, well aware of the staggering drop on each side.

Heights didn't normally bother Donny much, but these weren't normal heights. It took him back to a certain rope bridge in Greece a couple of years earlier. He hadn't enjoyed *that* experience much, either.

Slowly and carefully he crawled back along the roof, straddling the ridgeline, which was covered with a row of six-inch pot metal spikes to keep the birds off. The slate on each side was slick, and his shoes scrabbled for purchase. *If I slip,* he thought, *children are out of the question.*

Finally, he made it to the rear edge—the one over the rear balcony—a sort of narrow patio, and peered over carefully. A young, pretty woman in a thin sweater stood on the flagstones staring up at him, arms folded against the cold. She waved urgently to him to join her. *So much for code words,* Donny thought, as he eased himself over the side, using the bird spikes as handles.

He was almost over with just one boot still on the roof, when the canvas parachute bag caught on another spike. Holding on with his right hand, he let go and used his left to try and unhook the parachute bag. The tin bird spikes, however, had not been designed to hold the weight of a 6-foot, 210-pound man, and he could feel the one in his right hand, the only thing really keeping him on the roof, bending. Somehow, he managed to get the parachute loose, but just as he did, the bird spike snapped and he rolled off the edge.

He expected to land hard, on the flagstone patio, but to his surprise he crashed into a wicker loveseat his contact from the resistance had pushed under him. It knocked the wind out of him, but other than that and a few bird spike punctures, he seemed okay. He rolled upright, trying to catch his breath, only to meet a furious fräulein before him.

"You *idiot*. Do you want to get caught? They'll kill us both!" she hissed at him in German. "Scheisse. Hurry, get out of that uniform," she said, yanking the canvas bag containing the chute out of his jump smock. Donny looked around. They were alone at the moment, but she was right – he could hear voices inside. Despite being June, nights in the Alps were cold, keeping the revelers inside, but some hardy soul might come outside to have a smoke or simply look at the moon at any moment.

With her helping him frantically, in a matter of moments he had the helmet, harness, smock and jump trousers off, which she quickly rolled up in a ball and hid beneath a serving cart – one of the kind with a curtain around it to hide dirty dishes, and from which she produced a pair of men's shoes and a tie, which he quickly put on. She thrust a stamped card at him.

"Your pass, stamped by the RSHA. Show them this and no one will stop you. Take the elevator down to the entrance. Outside the tunnel entrance in the parking area there will be a van waiting. Knock on the left rear door three times and my husband, Karl, will come help you with the cart. He will explain the rest then. The cart goes into the truck with you, understand? This is a tasting party for Gretl Braun's wedding tomorrow. The food on top was rejected and these dishes are going back to our pâtisserie," she said, using the French word. "Now go!" she said urgently, just as two SS officers stepped out onto the patio, one tapping a cigarette on his fist.

Donny took the cart and began pushing it back into the building, his contact at his side.

"I think they should have gone with the lemon cake, myself," she said to him, ignoring the officers. "But it's her wedding, I suppose." They were nearly to the door when from behind them came the command every German was familiar with.

"Halten sie!" They stopped and turned. One of the officers had his hand up and was walking toward them. Donny quickly palmed an ice pick laying on top of the cart with some other silverware and slid it up his sleeve.

"Bitte – these are some of the tastings?" he said, approaching the cart.

"Ja, but for the bride and groom. You are neither, Herr Sturmfuhrer," his contact said disdainfully. The officer smiled at her apologetically, raising his hands.

"Bitte – you are just going to throw all this lovely food away anyway – mightn't we have just a bite?"

"Nein. This is, as I said…" she began.

"Wait. I don't see why we can't give them each something to try," Donny said in flawless German. His contact's eyes flared in warning, then she smiled and conceded.

"I suppose it would be all right… but we are going to be late if we don't hurry."

"Don't worry, Fräulein – I'll be quick. You mentioned lemon cake?"

2

Although it being the beginning of June, it was snowing lightly as Donny pushed the cart out the main gate. Summer in the Alps, he thought, as a sentry held the huge, iron door for him. Donny passed outside where a small Peugeot catering van was parked. He pounded on the back door as ordered, and a moment later it swung open and a black-haired, thin man with dark, brooding eyes looked at him. He didn't say a word, just reached down to grasp the front edge of the cart, which they lifted into the truck carefully. The driver immediately tied it off to a rack inside the tiny truck – obviously he'd done this before.

"Close the door and get in front," he said without looking at Donny.

The truck was clean, but old, and smelled of pastries and bread. It was a pleasant smell – much better than the bomb bay of the B-24 that'd dropped him. Karl made his way forward, dropped into the driver's seat, and handed him a paper bag pulled from a small, galvanized metal, insulated box between the seats; warm comfort on a cold day.

"Croissants. There is a thermos of Kaffee on the floor. We thought you might be hungry," he said.

Donny *was* hungry, ravenous in fact, but hadn't even considered eating. The hot coffee and warm croissants were a pleasant surprise, and he ate as Karl drove, the road steep and curvy, but well designed and well built. *The damn Germans really know how to build things,* Donny thought.

The occasional flurries changed to light rain as they descended, their headlights glowing dimly against the side of the mountain as they slowly wound their way downward. They didn't pass any other vehicles on the way up, the Eagle's Nest area being heavily restricted. They stopped at a checkpoint near the bottom of the hill, and a corporal in the 5/31 SS asked politely for their papers. Karl gave them to him, and offered yet another bag of croissants from the box between the seats for him and the other men manning the checkpoint. The corporal first demurred, then finally accepted the still-warm bag with a smile and a thank you. A little enough bribe, Donny thought, and smart, on a dark, cold night like this.

Their papers were stamped and returned, and Karl pulled out onto the main road to Salzburg after waiting for traffic, mostly military, on the busy thoroughfare. It seemed as though everyone was in a hurry to get somewhere, and Donny wondered what was going on, then remembered just before he got in the plane that the pilot was telling his copilot that he had it from a reliable source that Rome was about to fall.

Everyone knew it was just a matter of time, but Rome being taken was a big deal. Once Italy was defeated, they could base bombers out of Italy and reach pretty much the entire eastern front – including where he was right now.

"I don't see any evidence of bombing," Donny said to Karl to fill the uncomfortable silence. He wasn't much of a conversationalist, it seemed, and Donny got the feeling Karl wasn't thrilled at the idea of risking his skin to help him.

"No. We're out of range, thanks be to God," he said, then sighed. "But it's just a matter of time before they get around to us," he finished, looking at Donny as if he personally had planned all the bombing raids that were decimating Germany. Although there was a large military presence here, it felt very far from the war at the moment. It felt strange to be here, in Hitler's backyard so to speak, and Donny felt oddly safe now that he was on the ground. As long as he steered clear of the Gestapo, he would be fine.

"We found you a room at the Alpenhof, and it was rented in your name. It was the best we could do. Apartments in Salzburg proper are impossible to find. All the officers want to be close to the cafés. The generals just take what they want, but the rest have to pay, and apartments are expensive as a result."

"I'll need a local map of the area," Donny said.

"There is one in the glovebox you may have, but I recommend when you go to the visitor's bureau to sign in that you ask them for a map. There are Gestapo everywhere, and they are trained to notice discrepancies. Do not test them. I hope you know your cover story inside and out, Herr Buschausen," Karl said.

"You needn't worry about me," Donny replied in perfect German. "I've spent quite a bit of time in Germany."

"Your accent – Silesian? What will you tell them when they ask what you are doing in Austria?"

"Why, I will say I was offered a job by a member of my extended family, and have always wanted to spend some time here in the Alps, *Cousin Karl.*"

Karl gave him a look and muttered something unintelligible beneath his breath. It was obvious that neither he nor his wife were happy that he was here, and why should they be? It put them at risk. They would see it through, however, Donny was sure. They had a five-star rating in their file for reliability, and their cautiousness was, in his opinion, a good sign. It meant they were extremely careful, and you couldn't be too careful with the Gestapo always sniffing around. Careful kept you from being shot.

Karl pulled up in front of the Alpenhof and stopped, but didn't shut off the motor.

"Your bag is in the back. We are closed tomorrow, but you must come in and work Monday. We have other employees, and they are not part of this. If questioned, they must be able to back up your story. Take the bus in the morning. I have a bicycle I will lend you so you have some transportation otherwise. We will not speak of this at work. In fact, don't be surprised if we yell at you. You are here for just a short time, and we'll 'fire you' once you leave, 'family' or not. Take some time to familiarize yourself with Salzburg. We'll have you over for dinner Tuesday. We can talk more then."

"Danke, Cousin Karl," Donny said with a smile as he got out. Karl didn't smile back, but instead simply stared straight ahead, hands gripping the steering wheel, a grim look on his face. Donny retrieved the traveling bag that was clearly meant for him from the back of the truck and closed the door, slapping it with his palm, but it was already moving away. He climbed the freshly swept steps to the Alpenhof hostel, wondering what was in the bag, then wondering how he was going to get into Hohensalzburg Castle.

3

As a policeman, I kept a journal for every case, and so I shall for this one. I would have kept one while imprisoned, but of course they don't generally provide paper and pen to prisoners, and if they had, I would have been too tempted to use it for my toilet, such as it was.

Yesterday I was pulled forcibly from my cell by two guards who hustled me through the damp, nearly silent halls of the old building. I was allowed to shower, after another inmate with the quiet, insouciant air of a professional tailor quickly measured me for clothes. He wore the same prison uniform of blue and white ticking I did, but had a primitive, yellow, six-pointed star sewn to his left breast and right arm. It made me sad – whereas I had killed a man, this tailor's only crime was likely being a Jew.

The water was tepid but wonderful. I was given a sliver of soap, and some foul, coal and antiseptic-smelling shampoo, which I made the most of. I used it all, and took my time. What were they going to do, put me in prison?

When I got out I was given a mish-mash of clothes: the trousers and shirt of a working man, held together with the well-made shoes, belt and braces of a burgher or banker. The sport coat and hat were French, from what I could tell, but I was afforded no tie. Apparently, ties are in high demand in the German Reich.

After cleaning up, I was taken to an office and told to sit in a heavy, wooden chair parked in front of an even larger, heavier desk. The guards walked me more slowly this time, thankfully, and never touched or hurried me despite my slow pace due to the injuries to my feet. I left my shoes loose and untied, hoping I could find bandages soon for my feet and hands. I realized that, prior to my cleaning, they had just hurried me to minimize their exposure to the nits I had lived with for the last three months, as well as my rank odor. I really couldn't blame them.

I sat in the heavy chair with relief—my feet were killing me. Many nerve endings end in the soles of the feet, which is why the Gestapo enjoys whipping the bottoms of your feet so much. I just hoped wherever they were taking me, that it involved a minimum of walking.

The desk was the desk of a busy man. I recognized it because it reminded me of my old desk. A flash of nostalgia for a job I despised in some ways, loved in others flushed me. I loved the hunt—the solving of puzzles, felt the pride of the policeman in apprehending brutal animals, as well as empathy for the victims, but I'd hated the tedious, repetitive grind of paperwork— paperwork which had kept me from my family many an evening.

I also hated what the job had done to my soul: to confront evil on a daily basis and witness the pain and suffering it causes sometimes made it difficult to go home and bounce your children on your knee. I take that back – I have met psychopaths who did just that, but for normal people, the weight of what you had seen and done that day could drag you down at times. It was hard to pretend that evil wasn't just beyond the door, as I knew it to be. Now the lunatics had taken over the asylum, and I had lost my bearings completely. My family was simply the best medicine a man could have for that particular ailment. They were my tropical island in tempestuous seas – the importance of friendly smiles and affection of a wife and children cannot be overstated in the treatment of melancholia.

My family. Marie, Anna… little Sascha. Where in God's name had they taken them? My heart physically ached with imagined depredations they may have been exposed to. Warm finally, and clean but miserable, I waited to find out what they wanted.

4

After some time, a man entered the office carrying two thin files, gave me a dour look over his glasses, then sat down behind the desk and pulled his chair in. He was tall and thin, and reminded me strangely of Ichabod Crane in Washington Irving's American horror story, which I read to the children occasionally. He was the absolute opposite of myself. Of medium height and weight, with brown hair and eyes, I am the very definition of unremarkable – the "every man" look having stood me in good stead throughout the years when tailing suspects or having to blend into different neighborhoods.

"Herr Moeller, my name is Reinholdt Gephardt," Ichabod Crane said from behind the desk. "You have been brought here to me because the Reich has need of your services... temporarily. This is not a pardon, but merely a reprieve. You will help us solve a crime, and in return for your efforts, we will release your family."

My heart leapt. Could this be some sort of cruel joke? "Where are they now?" I asked, surprised at the wheezing huskiness of my own voice, which I, of course, hadn't required for months. Ichabod regarded me as a lizard regards a fly.

"They are at the Mauthausen work camp, and are still together. I have been assured they are receiving good treatment. Their future treatment, however, is up to you and you alone."

"What does the Reich require of me, Herr Gephardt?" I asked.

He consulted the two files briefly, then picked one up and dropped it on my side of the desk. "There has been a murder... or rather a series of murders in the Salzburg area – brutal ones. We have reason to believe they are connected, perhaps the work of an enemy agent. Top Secret paperwork is missing. The killer is sly and professional. Your record at catching serial killers is incomparable, despite your crimes against the state. Unfortunately for us, experienced murder detectives are hard to find at the moment, or you would not be here. Find the killer and stop him, and your family will be sent home. Fail us? Well, I'm sure you understand.

"Under no circumstances will you be released or pardoned when this is over. You will have the opportunity to see them one final time, then you will be tried for murder and executed. Until then you will have all the powers of your previous position, with the exception of access to greater assets in order to bring this case to a swift and successful end. This is yours," he finished, handing me a suspiciously heavy manila envelope, which I opened, finding to my surprise my wallet and Walther HsC pistol, the last item notably missing its ammunition.

My old badge was tied to the wallet with a piece of string, and I saw to my surprise that they'd given me new credentials. I was no longer a Kripo murder investigator, but now worked for the SD—the Sicherheitsdienst or the SS intelligence agency—an organization which, prior to this, I'd had nothing but loathing for. Also inside was a thick envelope stuffed with bank notes. I looked at the man I couldn't stop thinking of as Ichabod.

"Five hundred reichsmarks. That should get you quite a ways. You will not be required to do daily paperwork, but you must check in with me every few days," he said, passing me a business card with his number on it. "Failure to do so…" he began, then shrugged. "Du verstehst?"

"Ja, Herr Gephardt. I understand," I said.

"If you need something—say a train ticket—use the letter in the file. If you require something out of the ordinary—say, a plane ticket, or access to a high-ranking individual, perhaps additional personnel—call me and I will determine whether it's necessary or not. That money should last you quite a while, but monies will be deposited in your old bank account each week in the amount of your old salary. This should also help your family once… let's say *if* you are successful, and they are released. Verstehen?"

"Ja."

"Sign here, here and here," he said, indicating lines on three forms he thrust at me. I signed them with the pen he gave me, and with a wave of one hand he indicated that I should keep it, then he took the forms back, placed them inside the second folder without looking at them, then gave me that lizard look again, this time as if he were about to strike. "Herr Moeller, I am but the administrator of your fate. Personally, I do not care whether this crime is solved or not – although the interest comes from the highest levels. Nor do I care whether your family is set free or not. They mean nothing to me – the case does. It may not be solvable, so I am not doing you or your family any favors by involving you. I expect you to do your best only because you are an intelligent man who has just been shown both the carrot and the stick."

I stood with difficulty, my damaged feet protesting. "Danke, Herr Gephardt," I said, very nearly calling him Herr Crane. "I will not let you nor the Reich down," I said, extending my hand.

"That remains to be seen, Herr Moeller," Ichabod said, ignoring my hand. "Now get out of my office; you reek of insecticide and mold."

5

Donny spent the next month working at the pâtisserie, and true to his word, Karl took every opportunity to criticize him, seemingly taking pains to do it in front of their other two employees, and once, in front of a customer, a Gestapo officer who had stopped in for some blintzes. It was the best sort of cover, believable even to the Gestapo, but he couldn't help but feel Karl was enjoying himself a bit every time he took him to task.

On Tuesday night, the week of his arrival, he had dinner as suggested at Karl and Ilsa's apartment behind the shop. They assured him it was okay to talk openly, but ever cautious, they played records on a beat-up crank-style record player, including one of Edith Piaf's first albums, which he thoroughly enjoyed. Every time he heard 'La Vie En Rose' on the radio, he thought of Elena, a young woman he'd met in Prague – a Czech resistance operative. There was nothing between them, but damn, she was beautiful. There was just something about her. Whenever he saw her to use her radio set, it was as if someone had kicked the table the record player was on. She wasn't exotic, like a model, but she took his breath away, and he realized that her beauty came from inside her, shining out through her eyes, her smile like a klieg light.

While he could not discuss the details of his mission, he did tell them that he was going to have to break into a secure building, and that he would be leaving immediately afterwards.

"What building?" Ilsa asked. When she saw the look on his face, she grimaced. "Fine, don't tell us. I just thought we might know something you don't that might be of some help, that's all," she said petulantly, getting up to clear the table.

Donny took a deep breath, deciding to trust them. "The Fortress Hohensalzburg," he said. Ilsa sat back down.

"You must be insane," Karl said. "There is no way you can break into that castle. We deliver pastries there quite—" Ilsa kicked her husband under the table, making Donny smile.

"You needn't worry. I have no intention of putting your position here at risk. Your reports are invaluable, and I would not want to compromise you in any way," Donny said.

"So, how do you plan on getting inside?" Ilsa asked.

"Why, I'm going to walk right in," he said, taking another sip of the excellent Riesling they'd served with dinner. They looked at each other.

"It may require some ugliness, however, and it's better you be surprised. When your cousin, the layabout Herr Buschausen, doesn't show up for work, you'll know I'm gone. I will need some new papers, however, and a few more weeks of your time. I thank you both for everything, and for a wonderful dinner." He raised his glass. "Prosit!"

"Prosit!" they responded as they clinked glasses, Ilsa's demeanor having defrosted for the moment, undoubtedly in relief, knowing their guest would be gone soon. Every minute he stayed here he put them at risk. Donny smiled and sipped more wine. It would take time to set up, but he had a plan. He just needed to find his rabbit...

6

At the base of the hill leading up to Fortress Hohensalzburg, near the Reisszug cable car entrance, was a small café favored by officers stationed at or visiting the castle. They were Luftwaffe mostly, although some Army officers from the nearby "Replacement Army Command," the entity responsible for all replacement troops headed to Italy and the eastern front, could be occasionally found there, as well as a few local civilians. Donny made it his business to spend an hour around lunch time there each day, even though it meant riding the bike across town and then up the damn hill to the café. It was certainly keeping him in shape.

He always brought a newspaper, and while it looked as though he were ignoring the Luftwaffe and Heer officers, in reality he was sizing them up. Occasionally, when he found a likely mark, he would wait until they stood up to leave, then get up to leave himself, making sure to pass by them closely enough to estimate their height in comparison to his own.

He soon had several likely candidates, but since so few Army officers came there, he concentrated on Luftwaffe officers. One, a major, seemed perfect size-wise, except he was a bit flamboyant. He nearly always showed up riding a nearly new motorcycle, wore tailored uniforms, and was obviously well liked and known by a number of people, likely due to his penchant for picking up the tab, even after several rounds or a large meal.

Donny decided that he would be missed too quickly, and after another ten days of visiting the café every day for lunch, instead chose a tall, dour-looking oberstleutnant—a lieutenant colonel in the Luftwaffe, who spent at least three days a week at the castle, ate at the café each day he was there, and every Thursday, apparently his last day of the week there, his supper as well. He was a loner, stingy with tips, and a bit rude to the help, whom he addressed with a superior air. Donny had seen one of the waitresses actually spit in his food, then deliver it with a smile. He would not be missed, and although a bit taller than Donny, he seemed the same size in every other respect. He wore trousers bloused into tall boots, so the extra couple inches would not be an issue. Pants could be hemmed.

His papers would be an issue, however. As well-known as the officer obviously was at the castle, Donny couldn't simply change the photograph— he needed an entire set of similar, forged papers. He discussed it with Ilsa and Karl, but their verdict was not hopeful. They had a man who could forge the forms, take correct photos, even replicate some of the stamps, but the problem was they didn't know which stamps were needed, and Hohensalzburg likely had its own stamps. Also, the stamps were notoriously hard to replicate—the Nazis weren't stupid. Karl said he had an idea, though.

The following Friday, Donny took his normal seat at one of the few outdoor tables on the street, where he was able to observe his mark easily. A man of habit, the oberstleutnant came walking down the hill to lunch, a hand in one pocket of his trousers, the other carrying a briefcase. Donny watched with interest as two attractive young women came walking quickly down an adjoining side street, talking animatedly and laughing, clearly not watching where they were going.

When the brunette bumped into the Luftwaffe officer, it was so natural, that if he hadn't known it was going to happen, Donny would have sworn it was an accident. She seemed horrified at her mistake, her hand on his chest as he steadied her from losing her balance and falling. He never saw her other hand slip into his tunic pocket, the pocket where Donny had told them he always kept his wallet.

The officer was polite, acting as an officer should, clicking his heels and bowing slightly as the two young women apologized. Donny saw his lips move, and though the angle was bad, was sure he was insisting that the fault was his, despite it clearly being hers – the perfect gentleman. He never smiled, however, although his eyes did follow them as they left, waving back over their shoulders and sharing a giggle, heads nearly together. He didn't flirt with them at all, although he did give them a last hungry, wolfish look before sitting down at his usual table. Once again, from what Donny could tell, he would not be missed.

Donny didn't leave – he sat through lunch as usual, waiting for the officer to get up and leave, noting with satisfaction his consternation at not being able to find his wallet, as well as the pissed-off response of the waiter when he couldn't pay his bill.

He decided it was time, folded his napkin and, leaving it on his plate, walked over to the waiter, who was arguing with the now red-faced Luftwaffe officer.

"Yes? What is it?" the waiter said angrily when Donny interrupted.

"I'm sorry—I couldn't help but overhear," Donny said. "This gentlemen has apparently forgotten his wallet?"

"Yes, and now he expects us to feed him for free!" the waiter replied.

"NEIN. I told you that I would return with full payment tomorrow! I'm sure I simply misplaced it…"

"I hear this all the time! Do you know how many meals you Army people have simply walked out on?"

"LUFTWAFFE, Dummkopf! I am *Luftwaffe!*"

"Excuse me," Donny said.

The waiter turned to him, murder in his eyes.

"I'm sure this officer is a man of honor, and is good for it. Tell you what – let me pay his bill. I'll buy him lunch in thanks for his service to the Reich, eh? I see he lunches here frequently, as do I. Perhaps he can simply return the favor and buy me lunch sometime?" Donny said quickly before they could begin arguing again.

The waiter looked at the Luftwaffe colonel and shrugged. "Fine with me," he said, placated for the moment.

"Herr…"

"Strausshind, Carl Strausshind. Nice to meet you," Donny said, offering his hand. The Luftwaffe officer took it, and Donny cringed a bit—it was cool and damp, like shaking a mushroom.

"Herr Strausshind, I deeply appreciate the favor. This man obviously does not know that the word of a Luftwaffe officer is his bond—his honor!"

"How much do I owe you for both meals?" Donny said to the waiter before the argument went into round three. The waiter gave him a figure, which Donny paid, along with a generous tip. Placated now, the waiter thanked him, nodded, and went off to tend his other tables.

"Herr Strausshind, let me introduce myself. I am Oberstleutnant Jakob Fuhrmann, at your service," he said, clicking his boot heels and finishing with a sharp, Prussian bow. Donny wanted to shoot him right there.

"Very pleased to make your acquaintance, sir. Unfortunately, I'm going to be late for an appointment if I don't go. I'm sure you understand?" Donny said.

"But of course. Thank you again for stepping in on my behalf. You must permit me to repay your kindness and return the favor – perhaps tomorrow?" Fuhrmann said.

"Perhaps. My schedule changes almost daily. I usually come here about this time… as time permits."

"Of course."

"Until then?" Donny said. The two men shook hands and parted, Donny whistling as he made his way down the hill to where he'd locked up his bicycle out of sight.

7

July 14th, 1944 (Three days prior to Moeller's release)

Donny didn't return to the café for several days – not only did this give Ilsa and Karl's resistance contact time to duplicate the papers—and most importantly, the correct stamps—but it would also make the Luftwaffe officer all the more anxious to repay his debt. Donny knew his type, and knew he hated being indebted to someone himself.

On the fourth day he rode back to the café on the bicycle, making sure he got there early, where he ate, and timed it so that he was just finishing and paying for his lunch when the German got there. He was finishing his coffee and ostensibly taking one final look at the paper when he saw Fuhrmann approaching. Taking a final sip, Donny stood, emptied the last dregs of coffee, then tucking his paper under his arm, tipped his hat to the waiter and began walking in the other direction.

"Herr Strausshind, bitte!" he heard from behind him. He let a look of puzzlement turn to a smile of recognition.

"Herr Oberstleutnant. A pleasure to see you again," he said, extending his hand.

"The same, Herr Strausshind. I have not seen you the last several days. I had hoped I could settle our debt."

"Oh, you needn't worry about that, Herr Colonel. Tell me, did you ever find your wallet?"

"Nein. It has caused no small amount of consternation, actually. I had some very important papers in it—now they must be replaced. It has been… awkward."

"I can imagine," Donny said, knowing very well the contents of the lieutenant colonel's wallet. "I am, however, late for an engagement… if you would excuse me?"

The officer's face fell. "Perhaps tomorrow I might buy you lunch? Repay your kindness?"

"Ah. Unfortunately, I must return to Vienna tomorrow on business. I will be gone a month, I'm afraid. Tell you what. You can buy me a schnapps this evening before I go. Let's say, seven? At the Zum Nussbaum?"

This brought a rare smile to Furhmann's face, as it was a bar where he usually went on Fridays, where he drank steadily by himself for several hours, then staggered home.

"That would be very agreeable, Herr Strausshind. We shall have *several* schnapps, eh? Of course, I am buying."

"Danke, Herr Colonel. I will see you there at seven."

"Seven," Furhmann replied. They shook hands and Donny walked away, having set the hook.

8

Donny wasn't there at 7:00…or at 8:00. At 9:45 he saw the officer stagger out the door of the 'Nut Tree,' mumbling to himself, hat crooked, clearly inebriated. Donny followed the lieutenant colonel carefully, through a series of side streets, keeping his distance. He had a bad moment when the man turned toward him in an alleyway, but he was far enough behind him that he was able to duck into a dark doorway protected by a small portcullis and watched the idiot pass back by, obviously having taken a wrong turn. He considered taking him right there, but the intersecting street was just too close by, and had too much traffic on it, even at this time of night, to risk it.

Two alleyways down, Fuhrmann turned again, stopping to retch behind some garbage cans, holding onto a decrepit drainpipe for support. Donny let him get nearly to the end of the alley, closing the distance between them in short bursts of speed, the gymnasium shoes he wore nearly silent on the cobbles. He took a deep breath, checked both ways, then came up behind his quarry.

"Herr Oberstleutnant! I missed you at the Nut Tree. They said you came this way…" Donny said as he closed the space between them.

The Luftwaffe officer turned unsteadily, blinking at Donny as if he couldn't quite believe it. An external, caged light from a nearby warehouse that should have been turned off because of blackout illuminated them, but it couldn't be helped. It had to happen here.

"Herr Strausshind? Is that you?" he said, as Donny stepped forward, his face shaded by his hat, his hands at his sides. He let the ice pick he'd stolen from the party slip down into his palm, then in one quick motion, stepped forward, grabbing his victim's right wrist with his left hand, then stabbed him quickly three times in the side of the neck.

Fuhrmann opened his mouth to gasp, but could not, as Donny pushed him back and away to avoid the spray of arterial blood spurting from his neck. He went to his knees, trying to wheeze through his damaged windpipe, grabbing at his neck fruitlessly as his heart, running on pure adrenaline, pumped his life out of him, into the gutter.

Donny looked quickly both ways as the Luftwaffe officer collapsed on his face, the jets now subsiding to a dull pulse, knowing it would stop soon. He bent over the still-warm body and checked the pockets, finding a temporary ID, a small wad of bills in a money clip, and some change.

He took all the money and the temporary ID, then pulled out the colonel's original papers and ID wrapped in a handkerchief—the set the two young resistance women had so cleverly stolen— and threw them at the body with a flip of the handkerchief, the last act of a violent robbery. Some of the papers landed partly in the pool of blood he so carefully avoided. He took a moment to consider the death tableau, then taking a quick glance around him, stepped over the body and ran up the alley, making no attempt to muffle his footsteps. Reaching the next street, he slowed down to a walk and turned south, toward his rented room where the uniform and spare pair of boots he'd stolen earlier from his victim's apartment waited for him. He would go to the Fortress Hohensalzburg now, as late as it was, and be gone from Salzburg entirely before they found the body. He just hoped the forged documents and stamps passed close scrutiny. He supposed he'd find out for sure, one way or another, in about another hour.

9

Friedrich Moeller's Journal, July 18th, 1944 (Four days after the murders)

It pains me to admit that my first act upon my release was to find some decent food. The thin gruel they gave us, which always tasted as if it'd had ashes and sawdust added to it, was barely enough to subsist on, and the richness of the borscht, black bread and sharp cheese I feasted upon in the café across the street from the Vienna RSHA headquarters, though plebeian by pre-war standards, was manna from heaven for a starving man.

I ate slowly, although I wanted to inhale it. Having so little real food for so long, my stomach was unused to such rich fare. I took frequent breaks to consult the murder file, which was fairly unremarkable – the fact that all three victims had been killed with an ice pick or awl the only real consistency.

I found it interesting, however, that two of the victims were found in the same building. It made me wonder if they had known each other, despite one being in the Luftwaffe, the other a civilian scientist. Also, they had both died on the same date, although there were no coroner's reports yet. The third body was found several blocks away, apparently murdered the previous day... or that evening.

The timing seemed odd to me. There must be some connection between the victims, I thought, as the waiter brought me more beet soup, a healthy dollop of sour cream floating in it. I closed the file and tried to concentrate on my meal, but thoughts of Marie and the children intruded. Almost every day for the past month I've been waking at four a.m.—and my immediate thoughts are always the same: I think of Marie. It's a curse, I think, to yearn for her so – in my dreams I hold her in my arms the way I used to, spooning her in my embrace, kissing her phantom neck and the spot just behind her right ear gently.

I can even smell her at times like this – her familiar, lilac scent gnawing at my cerebral cortex. Ghostly hair tickles my nose, and I blow it out of the way the way I always did, and for a moment—just a moment—she's real and I whisper that I love her, even though I can tell she's asleep.

I don't know where she is at the moment, and it makes my heart ache to think of her huddled in the cold on some hard, flea-infested pallet with the children, trying to stay warm, and I weep. Every morning it's been like this… I don't know that I can bear another.

10

July 14th, 1944 2 a.m. (Three days before Moeller's release)

D onny had passed himself off as a German officer before – once as an SS colonel, once as a Wehrmacht major. He had never tried passing as enlisted – too many things could go wrong. Being an officer was bad enough; other officers had a tendency to ask questions of you, such as where you were from, who you knew, where you'd gone to school... such a role was full of pitfalls. It didn't pay to be friendly, therefore he had decided to imitate Fuhrmann's prickly mannerisms.

This was so unlike Donny's true nature that he spent the best part of an hour in his rented room, getting into character: striding across the floor and glaring at the mirror disdainfully. He knew far too well the price of failure. One small mistake and it'd all be over. When they caught OSS agents, they didn't send them to a nice, cozy concentration camp, they gave them to the Gestapo, where sooner or later he'd tell them everything he knew. No one could hold out against torture forever – different people simply had different breaking points. All you could do was delay the inevitable, hopefully giving the people in your immediate circle or "cell" time to escape.

Donny had no intention of getting caught, however. He looked out the window and saw it was raining. *Scheisse*, he thought, shrugging on Fuhrmann's greatcoat and Schirmmütze: the high, peaked cap of a Luftwaffe officer. He glared at himself once more in the mirror, then, peering carefully into the hallway to make sure he was unobserved, he stepped out and locked the door behind him. He would return here to change later, then leave Salzburg on a train with whatever papers he could recover from Dr. Eberhardt's office.

He was fortunate to catch a passing taxi as he left the hostel, and actually managed to stay fairly dry. "Wohin gehen wir?" the taxi driver asked him.

"Die Burg Hohensalzburg, bitte," he replied gruffly, shaking the water from his hat as he imagined a pissed-off field-grade officer would do.

"Ja, Herr Oberstleutnant. Immediately," the driver said, putting the Citroen Traction-Avant in gear and accelerating away through the downpour, up the hill toward Hohensalzburg Castle – the huge, ancient fortress overlooking Salzburg. He checked the ice pick concealed inside his sleeve with a piece of string. As a weapon, it seemed unimpressive at first, but the OSS had learned the effectiveness of a spike-style stabbing weapon from the British Special Operations Executive, and had copied many of their weapons and operational manuals. The ice pick was easily hidden, more so than a knife, and it was effective. Still, he felt a bit like Daniel in the lion's den.

11

The downpour had reduced itself to a measly drizzle by the time they reached the castle. There was a guard station set up at the portcullis, and Donny handed the guard his papers, affecting a bored, slightly annoyed air as he imagined a typical staff officer would. After a cursory inspection, the guard gave him his papers back, thanked him, and reminded him to sign in at the desk. He had originally planned to take the Reisszug cable car, but the heavy rain had changed his mind, and he opted for taking a cab all the way to the top. Donny nodded and the taxi continued on up the hill, into the depths of the fortress, the narrow, curved roadway and high walls on each side reminding him more of an ancient town – which of course, is what it was: An ancient, fortified town.

The walls on the left were smooth and whitewashed, the ones on the right rougher, bare stone formed into a round, crenelated watch tower at the inside end, which Donny supposed may have been the armory or grain storehouse – likely a point of final defense. Once past the tower, the walls opened up into what wasn't simply a courtyard surrounded by walls – it really was an entire town, and Donny realized to his dismay that he may have made a terrible mistake coming here. Could he even find Eberhardt's office in this huge place? And if he did, then what? It would undoubtedly be under guard. Still, he had to try.

The taxi driver had clearly delivered officers here before. He pulled up in front of a lit doorway, outside of which stood another guard, who stepped forward, and out of deference to Donny's rank, opened his door and saluted him.

Lt. Colonel Buschausen of the Luftwaffe high command got out, handling the locked briefcase chained to his wrist casually, as if he were used to it. He paid the driver, then stepped into the lighted entryway: a large, arched portcullis with a smaller brother of an arched, open doorway leading to a heavy, wooden door with huge, wrought iron hinges and a thick, twisted loop of steel that served as a door pull, the finish in the middle silver and smooth from many hundreds of years of use. Donny briefly wondered how many people had actually passed through this door as the guard once more held it open for him.

Almost immediately inside was a young, non-commissioned officer at a desk. He stood and saluted Donny, who saluted back and indicated for him to sit back down.

"Guten Abend, Sir. How may I help you?"

"My name is Oberstleutnant Buschausen. I am here to see Dr. Eberhardt."

The adjutant printed this in a large, bound notebook, thick with names and dates, then turned it to Donny and offered him a pen.

"Please sign the record, Sir. I will ring Herr Doktor Eberhardt's apartment for you," he said, surprising Donny. He figured there was probably a 50/50 chance Eberhardt would even be on site. He took the proffered pen and signed the book. His heart was racing, but he didn't show it. *Into the dragon's lair,* he thought inanely.

After consulting a small address book, the adjutant picked up the receiver of a black telephone and dialed three quick digits, rubbing one tired eye as the phone rang. Donny could hear the ring even on the other side of the desk, with the sergeant's back to him. He heard a click as someone on the other end picked up, then a muffled greeting.

The clerk spoke in a low, practiced tone, appropriate for such a late hour. It seemed he was arguing with whomever was on the other end, and he turned to Donny, the phone against his ear, and gave him a helpless look as the receiver squawked at him. He pulled it from his head as if it had bitten him, and covered the lower transceiver with his left hand.

"Colonel, Herr Doktor asks if you could possibly return in the morning? The hour is late and..."

"The hour is *never* too late for Luftwaffe business!" Donny said imperiously, holding up the briefcase chained to his wrist. "Does this look as though it will wait until later, Herr Unteroffizier?"

The clerk didn't cringe, but he got the message, turning his back to Donny once more as he spoke urgently into the phone. Finally Donny heard him say, "Danke, Herr Doktor." He hung up the phone and stood, placing a folded placard on the desk which had "10 minutes" neatly written on it, and smiled at Donny.

"Herr Doktor recognizes the importance of your visit despite the hour and will meet you in his workshop. I will take you there," he said, quickly putting on a heavy coat, then his Feldmütze service cap and gloves. "Normally we'd have more personnel, but we are a bit short-handed at the moment. I'm sure you understand, Herr Colonel," he said with a quick nod.

Donny rebuttoned his coat against the rain as they passed out into the night again. Summer or not, the rain at this altitude had lowered the temperature to near winter temperatures, the clerk leading him out into the drizzle, turning to say, "This way, Herr Colonel."

He had to walk quickly to keep up with the sergeant, who clearly didn't like the rain and who would likely be running except for the presence of a superior officer. Donny felt like running himself, shivering as the cold water dripped off his hat and down his neck.

They reached another, smaller door on the other side of the courtyard, this one a normal- looking, rectangular door, which the sergeant threw open impatiently, the rate of the rain having increased during their brief walk. "Bitte, Sir," the clerk said loudly against the noise of the rain.

Donny dove inside, the sergeant right on his heels. As the sergeant flipped on a light, Donny could see that they were in a short hallway which tee'd into another, obviously longer one. They took a minute to shake off their caps and brush the water off their coats as best they could, wiping their feet on an expensive-looking area rug, now worn and thin at the center.

"Bitte," his guide said, once more leading the way. Donny followed him as he turned left at the tee, the stone floors and concrete walls reminding him somewhat of a school or hospital. The wooden trim here was far more utilitarian – obviously a newer or remodeled section of the castle, but still excessive by modern standards. Donny kept track of the runs in his head, memorizing the route they took so he wouldn't get lost when it was time to leave, knowing there was a good possibility that he might be running. Finally, they turned right, into an older stone passage with curved walls and a staircase at the end.

"I'm sorry, Herr Colonel, but we must take the stairs. There is no elevator."

Donny waved him on with a suitably impatient look, and they followed the curving staircase up a long flight to the next level, then again up to the third, the combination of altitude and stairs taking their toll on Donny despite his excellent physical condition. Three years of working behind enemy lines hadn't helped. He felt like an old man at times, despite only being in his mid-thirties. He was tired of war.

The third level was brightly lit, and definitely warmer than the lower levels, likely due to convection – the warmer air from below rising slowly to heat the upper floors. They rounded a corner and halfway down the length of the hall was a Luftwaffe airman standing at rigid attention. Donny knew no one stood at attention like that all night, and surmised that the sound of their footsteps echoing off the stone floor and walls had been a sufficient alarm clock to wake the guard, who saluted as they approached.

"Corporal, is Herr Doktor here yet?" his guide asked the guard, as they both returned the salute.

"Nein, Herr Unteroffizier. I have not seen him since coming on duty," the guard replied, still at rigid attention.

"At ease, Corporal," Donny said. It was a bit out of character for the role he was playing, but he wanted the guard relaxed and unaware when it came time to deal with him, not alert, at attention, and full of adrenaline.

"Danke, Herr Oberstleutnant," the guard said, taking a slightly more relaxed stance, but nothing like the way he'd likely been slumped atop the stool, half-asleep, before they arrived.

"Herr Oberstleutnant, I must return to my post. Herr Doktor should be here shortly. Do I have your permission to leave?" the sergeant said, saluting sharply. Clearly he knew his way around superior officers, knowing exactly when to be deferential, and when not to be.

"Ja, Herr Unteroffizier. Danke schön. I will wait inside the lab for Herr Doktor," Donny said.

"I'm afraid that won't be possible, Herr Oberstleutnant. Herr Doktor is one of only two people with a key," the guard said. Donny cursed under his breath. He'd seen the *Eintritt Verboten* sign on the door, but had still hoped to bluff his way in.

He glared at the guard. "Fine, then. I shall wait *here* for Herr Doktor," he said.

"Good luck to you, Herr Oberstleutnant," the sergeant said, "And please remember to come sign out before you leave so I can stamp your pass."

Donny doubted he would be signing out, but he nodded his agreement and returned a desultory version of the sergeant's salute. He'd been right – he could hear the sergeant's footsteps all the way down the steps they'd come up. He turned to look at the corporal, who stared dispassionately forward, eyes fixed on the wall in front of him. Donny hoped Eberhardt wouldn't take long – the more time he spent here, the more likely he was to be found out.

He heard a door open and close from what sounded like a great distance away, then an indeterminate sound which eventually resolved itself into soft, shuffling footsteps, coming closer and closer. The doctor was on his way, obviously having an apartment on the same level. Even in such a large facility, it was clear that Eberhardt was an important man to commandeer such space.

As Dr. Emile Eberhardt turned the corner of the hallway Donny saw that the good doctor was still in pajamas and robe, his slippers scuffing on the granite floor, producing the odd sound Donny had noted. It was clear that he was unhappy at being awakened at this time of night – he had a pinched, unhappy look on his face, and as he looked at the Luftwaffe officer who had demanded to see him, Donny thought he saw a flicker of doubt behind the round glasses he wore. There was nothing to do but bluff.

"Herr Doktor Eberhardt," Donny said loudly, clicking his heels together as he bowed stiffly. "I apologize for the lateness of the hour, but I bring important information from Berlin," he said, holding up the briefcase chained to his wrist.

Eberhardt's brow furrowed. "Berlin? What does Berlin have to do with…" then he stopped himself, seeing the guard, still staring blankly at the opposite wall. "Never mind. Come inside, where we can talk." He pulled a set of keys from the right-hand pocket of his robe and unlocked the door, then led the way inside. Donny followed him in as Eberhardt flipped the lights on, then locked the door behind them.

The room they were in was large, and looked as though it had once been two rooms now joined together. Several high lab tables filled the space, with models of airplanes and what looked like scaled-down engines of some sort. Jets? Donny quickly unlocked the briefcase from his wrist and set it on one of the tables as Eberhardt gave him a sideways look and surreptitiously threw a blanket over a model of something Donny could not identify, then turned to face him.

"Now, what is so urgent that—" he began.

Donny quickly stepped forward, grabbing the back of Eberhardt's head with his left hand, and with one practiced movement, drove the ice pick he'd kept with him right through the doctor's glasses and into his right eye. The doctor's mouth fell open, then he collapsed, knocking over a metal stool, which clanged loudly as it hit the stone floor. Donny pulled the ice pick from Eberhardt's eye socket with some difficulty as the guard began pounding on the door loudly.

"WAS IST HIER LOS?" he yelled through the door, turning the knob futilely. Donny thought quickly, then rose, walked to the door and unlocked the bolt, pulling the door open. The guard stood on the other side, gripping his submachine gun tightly, clearly agitated.

"Quickly – Herr Doktor has collapsed! We need to get him to the infirmary!"

The guard rushed past him into the room, and over to Eberhardt's already cooling body as Donny closed and relocked the door. Blood was pooling beneath Eberhardt's head from the wound.

"What happened?" the guard asked.

"He just fell, knocked over the stool, hit his head on the table on the way down – a heart attack, perhaps?" Donny said. The guard set his submachine gun down on the table—an Mp34 by the look of it—and Donny noted that the bolt was locked back, in the fully cocked position. It wouldn't take long before he noticed the wound in Eberhardt's face.

As the guard bent over the body, Donny quietly picked up the Mp34, made sure the safety was off, and pointed it at the guard's back. He could have easily just killed him with the ice pick, but he preferred not to unless it was necessary. He'd tie the man up, then...

He saw the guard stiffen, undoubtedly noticing the hole in the doctor's eye, then he spun around, lunging for the submachine gun, but it was no longer on the table. Now Donny held it, and the muzzle was pointing directly at the guard.

"You don't have to die. I will tie you up, then once my business is complete, I will—" Donny began, but the guard did something Donny didn't expect: he charged him. Donny pulled the trigger, and the submachine gun stuttered out eight or ten rounds, but they just stitched across the ceiling because the guard already had hold of the barrel, pushing it up and to the right. The man was fast, and obviously well trained, and as Donny took a stumbling step back, he knew he had underestimated him.

Off-balance now, the German drove him backward, into the wall, punching him in the face, the submachine gun trapped between them, knocking the air from Donny's lungs. It's difficult to fight with the breath knocked out of you, but Donny had been trained by a sadistic Scotsman on loan from the British Special Operations Executive, who had made sure the OSS recruits at "Camp X" had plenty of practice at it. Donny brought his knee up between his opponent's legs, and saw the airman's eyes widen in pain. He pushed the man back, but with a sweep of his arm, the German knocked the Mp34 from Donny's grasp, and it hit the floor, firing another short burst.

Donny knew once things went noisy he wouldn't have much time before more guards showed up, and cursed his luck as the airman pulled out his bayonet and smiled at him, a man clearly not new to hand-to-hand combat.

They circled each other as an alarm bell began ringing somewhere in the hall, then the German thrust at him, which Donny avoided by a fraction of an inch. He stabbed at Donny again, coming in low, but this time Donny stepped inside the blow, deflecting it to the left as he brought the ice pick up with his right hand, flipping it around and stabbing it into the side of the German's neck. Three quick blows and it was over – the man's carotid artery doing the rest as blood jetted from his neck, the airman clearly panicked now, trying desperately to stanch the flow with his left hand. He looked at Donny with horror and dropped the bayonet, which clattered on the floor, the bell ringing loudly in the hall.

Donny could already hear running feet, and he quickly moved to the door and made sure it was locked. He wanted to turn the lights out, but he needed them to find what he was after. The German slumped to the floor, unconscious and soon to be dead, as Donny flew around the lab, grabbing what papers he could, then pulled a small Minox camera from the briefcase and took several pictures of the odd contraption Eberhardt had covered when he came in.

He then took pictures of all the models on the worktables, most of which seemed to be heavy bombers or sections of bombers, such as gun turret designs and bomb bay details, but one especially piqued his curiosity: a model of a huge bomber with a small, jet-powered fighter mounted atop it. *Geniuses*, he thought. *Damn Germans are geniuses.*

He found a locked cabinet just as someone began beating on the door, yelling in German to open up. He looked carefully at the file cabinet and noticed a small manufacturer's emblem, boasting the cabinet was feuerfest, or fireproof. A locked, fireproof cabinet? Something important was inside.

The noise at the door got louder as the frustrated guards attempted to break it down. Normally Donny would pick the lock, but he had no time. Grabbing the Mp34 off the floor, he struck the lock hard with the buttstock, then again, but it barely dented the thing. Now it sounded like they were using an axe on the door, and he knew it wouldn't hold forever. Once it went, he was dead.

Donny flipped the Mp34 around and with face averted and eyes closed, fired a burst from the submachine gun into the lock, which shattered. Yanking it open, he grabbed several files without really looking at them, stuffed them into the briefcase, then noticed a heading on a folder marked *EAGLE'S CLAW* with STRENG GEHEIM, (Top Secret) stamped in red on the front, and grabbed it as well.

The inside frame of the door was close to splintering, as heavy as it was, and Donny fired the last of the magazine in a long burst through the door, which quieted things down for the moment. He stopped at the airman's body just long enough to retrieve two more magazines from the blue, three-cell pouch the guard wore on his belt, replaced the empty mag, and stuck the other under his own belt. He fired a few more rounds through the door for good measure, then latched the empty handcuff tied to the briefcase to the back of his belt.

Running to the window, he reached into the depths of the briefcase and pulled out a spool of olive-drab parachute cord – 500 feet, to be precise. It had been carefully rewrapped doubled up, with a loop in the middle, sticking out of the neat bundle, providing a double line of 250 feet in length. He yanked on it now, giving himself about a 2-foot loop as the Germans began pounding at the door again. It was time to go.

He quickly slung the loop around a heavy lab table leg, then stuffed the rest of the spool through the loop, drawing it tight in a simple Prusik knot. He slung the Mp34 on his back, then flung the nearest window open and threw the weighted spool of cord out, hoping it actually unraveled the way it was designed to, and that it wasn't more than 250 feet to the ground. He grabbed the doubled-up line, then climbed up into the big window and looked down.

The window was on the outside wall of the castle, which meant the window was three stories above… a sheer cliff. It was dark, and Donny couldn't even see the end of the rope. Rope? No, not even rope, just doubled up parachute cord – two strands, side by side. They felt impossibly thin in his hands, but he had no choice. He slung them around his back, wound his right arm through the line above him to act as a brake, and leaned out the window, hearing the heavy wooden door splintering as they began going after it with some sort of heavy ram.

Donny leaned back away from the wall the way he'd been taught, and immediately realized a couple of things. First, it was still raining, and the wall of the fortress was slick, so his feet kept wanting to slip out from under him, and second, whatever moron at OSS headquarters had suggested rappelling using a couple strands of parachute cord had obviously never tried it.

The two thin strands of cord were nearly impossible to hang onto, and his hands immediately began cramping. He leaned back further, knowing that if he slipped, the full weight of his body would be held only by the cord wrapped around his right arm, then he was screwed. The weight of the submachine gun on his back actually helped pull him backward a bit. On the other hand, his right arm was taking all the punishment. He brought his left hand up higher, trying to use the friction of the cord against his back as a brake, and to take some of the stress off his right arm, and it helped, but not nearly enough.

He knew he had to hurry, that anytime now the Germans would break down the door and he'd be completely vulnerable. Would they shoot him from above or simply cut the line? He lost footing for a second, but recovered, realizing it was a window from the floor below. One more floor to go, then a cliff... a dark, wet cliff he couldn't see.

Water poured off the battlements above, soaking him faster than the rain itself, hitting him in the chest and face, making it hard to see. *At least it's not boiling oil,* he thought, cackling madly at the thought. Then he felt a tug on the line and knew he had another problem – the Germans had made it into the room. He tried to go faster, but the damn wall was so slick... he was a bit surprised that the German officer's boots he wore gripped as well as they did. Then they began shooting at him – the distinct rattle of an Mp40 from above, the zip and whine of 9mm bullets whizzing past. Donny tried making himself a smaller target, by hunching closer to the wall, but that was a mistake – it changed his point of balance, and his feet slipped out from under him and he fell, his right shoulder exploding in pain as all his weight was suddenly caught by his right arm, still wrapped in the cordage. He screamed into the wall, feet dangling, scrabbling at the wet surface, but he couldn't get his feet back beneath him no matter what he did. His entire arm burned, the parachute cord cutting off blood flow to his hand. When it went numb entirely, he was dead.

He took a deep breath, telling himself that he'd been in worse spots. Trouble was, he couldn't think of any. His shoulder was just a mass of pain. He began sliding downward, releasing the cord little by little, but the parachute cord was cutting into his hands, constricting around his right forearm – the only thing keeping him from falling uncontrollably. Then he realized the shooting had stopped. Did they think his scream was from being shot?

The blow from above hit him in the right ear and shoulder – the sudden flash of pain would have made him scream again had it not dazed him a bit. What? They were dropping rocks now? Then there was an explosion below him and he realized it had been a potato masher grenade the bastards had dropped on him that hit him in the head. Shrapnel from below whizzed past him, and he felt a sudden burn in his left calf, like being sliced with a hot knife. They were really beginning to piss him off.

Donny wasn't sure where he was on the wall anymore, other than somewhere between the first and second stories. Normally this would be good—he wouldn't have too far to fall—but when he looked down he saw nothing but blackness. He knew it was just a matter of time before they got around to cutting the lines and began slipping lower, then lower yet, expecting another grenade at any second. Then they did something Donny hadn't counted on: they began pulling him back up.

Again he screamed. Every jerk on the lines sent pain shooting through his shoulder, which at this point he was sure was dislocated. They yanked him up a foot, then another. There was only one thing to do. Donny let go.

12

For the second time that night, Donny had all the air knocked out of him. He hit hard, but it was a slope, and it could have been much worse. That's what he would tell himself later, but while cartwheeling down the rocky slope in the dark, with the submachine gun smacking him in the head and punching into his side each time he hit, the briefcase smacking him in the back, brush tearing at his face and hands, it didn't feel as though it could get much worse. The only blessing was that he couldn't get enough of a breath to scream and give away his position.

Finally he slid to a stop, whimpering as he rolled off his damaged shoulder, wheezing desperately for air. It seemed every part of him ached, and he could taste blood running down his face into his mouth from a head wound, likely from the grenade, but possibly a rock. Still, he was alive... for now.

He just lay there for a while in the rain, gradually getting his breath back, taking stock of his injuries: a dislocated shoulder, head wound, likely some shrapnel in one leg, a twisted ankle, not to mention various bruises and contusions, plus the terrible friction burns on his hands from that damn parachute cord. Beat up, but still alive. He couldn't help but smile, although it hurt to do so. *I'm still alive, you bastards!* he thought, pulling the briefcase to him. It hadn't come open in the fall, but he needed to get it somewhere dry, before any of the documents he'd fought so hard for were damaged. Goddamn cold rain on top of everything.

He couldn't return to his room – someone was sure to notice his bloody condition and the shredded German uniform he wore, and report him. Donny had planned on simply bluffing his way back out, then onto the midnight train to Prague, where he was to examine the documents, rendezvous with the Czech Resistance there, and turn them over to be smuggled out of the country. Then he would report in by radio and find his own way out of Czechoslovakia, or wait for orders. He realized he had to go back to the pâtisserie. Karl and Ilsa weren't expecting him back, but he had nowhere else to turn.

He struggled to his feet and brushed himself off, but even without a mirror he knew he looked far from presentable. He had no choice—somehow he had to make it across Salzburg—make it to Karl and Ilsa's without being seen. He considered throwing away the Mp34, but decided to keep it. It was all or nothing now. Miraculously, his spare magazine hadn't fallen out in the fall, and was still tucked into his belt. He exchanged it for the partial mag in the weapon, one-handed, although with great difficulty, holding the stock between his knees, his right arm useless.

He made sure the weapon was cocked, then set it on the ground and slid the handcuff holding the soft briefcase around his officer's belt to the rear so it was out of his way, winding it around the belt so it rode snugly at the small of his back. It felt awkward, but he couldn't use his right hand at all. The pain in his right shoulder was excruciating, and he bit his lip as he tucked his right hand under his belt to take some of the pressure off. He stuck the partial magazine back into his belt, picked up the Mp34 in his left hand, and began picking his way carefully down the steep, rock-strewn slope toward Salzburg, the sirens and floodlights from the castle above and behind him.

13

Moeller's Journal, July 18th, 1944 (Four days after the murders)

The cheap room and hot water were as welcome as the food. Every soldier knows that without rest, or food, or a warm bath every now and then, any hero is sure to be defeated, so I rented a cheap room, bathed, cut my hair badly with borrowed scissors, and after a hot bath, bandaged my hands and feet awkwardly, then slept.

It was evening of the following day before I awoke, ravenous, the soup having long since lost its effect. I lay there for a moment, wondering how Marie and the children were faring, and offered a short prayer for their safety. Then I pushed them from my mind and got dressed, knowing that I could not be effective doing the job at hand if I kept wondering about them, my success being directly linked to their ultimate salvation. There was simply no room for failure. I had to find the killer, and quickly.

The black market eggs and ham I got from the same café where I'd eaten the day before weren't bad, but the bread tasted as though it'd been cut with sawdust – a likelihood in my opinion. There was no butter to be had; that was a peacetime luxury, or at least kept for party officials. I felt guilty for a moment, wondering what the children would eat that day, if anything, then turned my thoughts to something more productive: the file.

I found myself slipping back into old habits as I went back over the murder file again – making notations in the margins with a borrowed pen, completely immersing myself in the file. Concentration had always been one of my rare strengths. As I read, however, I wondered more and more why the Gestapo or Kripo were not handling the case themselves.

Time-wise, the first murder was that of a Luftwaffe oberstleutnant; a lieutenant colonel, who'd been stabbed in the neck with an ice pick in a narrow alley near the river.

The other two murders were clearly related, having taken place in the same room at the Fortress Hohensalzburg. I saw that in all three cases, the murder weapon seemed to be some sort of awl or ice pick – an unusual choice, there clearly being other, better weapons available during wartime… or were there? An ice pick in the jugular was certainly a quiet option.

I spread the murder file out on the table before me, to the dismay of the proprietor, who was in the middle of his dinner rush. I ignored him, and looked at the times of death. The oberstleutnant had met his end in the alley several hours prior to the other two victims, who had died about the same time. I looked at the personnel files next: The colonel had been a frequent visitor to Hohensalzburg, and the other two victims worked there, a Doktor Eberhardt and a Luftwaffe feldgendarm: Hans Kohl, a guard. They were both killed at about the same time, approximately one a.m., and both bled out in the same room, Herr Doktor from a wound in the right occipital orb and the guard from several vicious stab wounds to the left side of the neck, indicating a right-handed assailant.

There wasn't much else, just the names of Luftwaffe personnel who'd been on duty at the time and who had shot at the killer as he'd escaped out the window. On the third floor of the Festung Hohensalzburg? I wondered. How did he escape? Did they wound him? Did anyone see him after that? Clearly my first stop should be Hohensalzburg. I will begin there and work my way backward… or should I address the murders in the same order that they happened, beginning with the lieutenant colonel? I decided to go to the castle for the autopsy. I should see the bodies first, while they were fresh, before some idiot disposed of them. I was slipping. Eight months in prison will do that to you.

I put the file back in the folder, tucked it under my arm, and rose, to the relief of the proprietor, who hurried over to clear the table. I rounded up the bill, thanked him, and left, fortunately finding a taxi almost immediately, having decided that since the Reich had seen fit to flay the soles of my feet to the point where I could barely walk, now that they required my services, they could damn well pay for a cab.

14

It took Donny nearly two hours to make it back to the pâtisserie. He had taken a roundabout route in order to avoid patrols, heading straight for the river, then doubling back uphill, limping from one shadowy doorway to the next, the submachine gun at the ready, his dislocated shoulder on fire, his left eye swollen shut, his hair wet with blood from a wound to his scalp.

Every sound sent him scurrying for cover, and several times Kübelwagens and motorcycle patrols with sidecars and belt-fed machine guns passed within just a few feet of him, but his luck held. He made it to the street where the bakery was located, stopping to listen for a moment. There was no cover he could see for at least half the block, until he got to the alley that would take him around back to the service entrance where they received deliveries. Even then he would be somewhat exposed.

He took a step forward and the world exploded with a loud screech. His heart jumped in his chest as the orange tabby he'd stepped on, that'd been cowering on the cobblestones before him, tore off like a crazed banshee and disappeared around the corner.

"Scheisse!" he swore, his heart beating out of his chest.

"You will always revert to your native tongue in times of stress," Fairbairn had told them. *"You must learn to swear in German automatically. If you say 'Bloody hell,' or call someone 'a wanker' in Hamburg or Berlin, well… that'll be the end of ye, laddies."*

Donny had been raised by his maternal grandmother, who had emigrated from Germany just before the Great War and still spoke poor English. As a result, Donny spoke German beautifully, but as his grandmother had rarely used bad words, he still had to train himself not to swear in English. Twice he had traveled with her to Germany as a child, and he was comfortable there.

He also grew to realize that his grandmother understood English just fine, but pretended not to when it suited her.

Donny heard the distinctive whine of another Kübelwagen gearbox up the street, around the corner. He crossed the street quickly and started down the sidewalk as fast as possible while trying to walk somewhat normally, wondering if someone in one of the many upper windows was even now peering down at him from behind their curtains.

Two more shops to the pâtisserie... then one, then he heard the Kübelwagen turn down the long, curved street behind him. He walked faster, but clicked off the safety on the Mp34 with his left hand. Fairbairn had forced them to shoot with their weak-side hands for three days in a row—tying their favored hand behind them to their belt—but Donny'd never been much good at it, receiving many a brogue-flavored harangue when he missed. Like most Scots, his instructor had a sharp tongue, and plenty to say with it.

"Aye laddie, yer det. Ga head an' lie doon onna ground. I'm dun wid ya!" he'd scream in Donny's face when he missed the target, his breath smelling of haggis and pipe tobacco. The ground was often wet and muddy, and it seemed to Donny as if it were always raining there, or about to.

Donny could hear the Kübelwagen coming slowly down the street behind him, and knew it was a matter of seconds before he was seen. He broke into a stumbling run, his ankle a mass of agony, but he bit his lip and drove on. It was more important at this point to get out of sight than to risk looking suspicious. Then he looked down at himself, in a dirty, torn, blood-spattered officer's uniform with a dead right arm, a suitcase chained to his belt and a stolen submachine gun in his left hand, and wondered if he'd make it. Someone was sure to report him, looking like this.

He made it to the alley and ducked into it just as the patrol car came around the curve. He didn't dare ring the night bell and expose Karl and Ilsa, so he ducked down behind a row of foul-smelling garbage cans, laying down on the cobblestones, back against the wall, making himself as small as possible, biting back a scream as his dislocated shoulder made contact with the ground.

The Kübelwagen came to a halt at the entrance to the alley and they shone a spotlight down it, revving the engine to make the light brighter – it obviously being hooked directly to the generator. Donny held his breath and listened.

"I thought I saw something," one soldier said.

"You're dreaming. You're always seeing things," another voice said.

"I'm getting out and taking a look," the first voice said. Donny tensed. This was it.

He heard the sound of the soldier getting out, and the tinny sound of the Kübelwagen's door banging shut. A weaker beam of light began playing around the alley, and he could see the soldier's shadow looming on the ground, backlit from the spotlight. He heard the soldier's companion—the driver who'd stayed in the car to rev the engine and man the spotlight, curse softly—and Donny's finger tightened on the Mp34's trigger. The soldier was just on the other side of the garbage cans...

A scream split the night as another cat—or perhaps the same one—gave the soldier a warning screech and tore off down the alley, making him drop his flashlight, which immediately went out, bouncing into the cans with a bang, then skittered across the cobblestones, nearly right in front of Donny.

"SCHIESSE," the soldier exclaimed, just as Donny had earlier. "Fucking cats!" He picked up the small, square flashlight and shook it, slapping it against his palm. Donny kept his face down against the cold cobblestones despite wanting to look up at the soldier, knowing that faces show up very well, even in pitch black. He heard the soldier at the car laughing at his friend as he smacked the misbehaving flashlight with the palm of his hand, saying "Stück Scheisse"softly. *Don't look down*, Donny thought. *Just don't look down.*

The soldier in the car tired of the game and took his foot off the gas pedal, and the spotlight dimmed as the revs dropped.

"Kommen sie. We have to finish this sector," he yelled to him. The soldier in front of Donny turned and walked back to the open car, still swearing softly, having no idea how close he'd just come to being machine-gunned.

"Damn cats! Can you believe it? I think the bulb is broken," Donny heard him say. He heard the door slam, and the Kübelwagen drove off, the gearbox once again whining in low as they made their way down the street. Donny clicked the safety back on and set the submachine gun on the ground, then slowly rolled left, onto his back, his right shoulder in agony. He'd tried to keep his weight off it, but where he'd been forced to take cover it'd been impossible.

He got his breath back, then got onto his left side and forced himself to his feet, his entire body screaming at him to sit back down. The ground swam in front of him and he knew he was close to passing out. He picked up the Mp34, stumbled the few steps to the pâtisserie's delivery door, then slung the weapon over his left shoulder to free his left hand, his right arm still useless.

He felt in the dark frame of the doorway for the night buzzer, and carefully pressed it twice, then waited, then three times, then once, spacing the rings as he'd been told. Then he sat back down on the cobblestones to wait – unable to stand any longer, fighting the urge to close his eyes.

He heard the door open, and saw Karl looking down at him, a short club in his hand. He hadn't turned a light on, just stood there in the dark for a moment as if considering whether splitting open Donny's head with the truncheon was a good idea or not.

"Scheisse," he heard Karl mutter under his breath, and tried to rise, but Karl grabbed him under the arms and unceremoniously dragged him inside, then took the submachine gun from him and pushed the door shut, locking it.

"Ilsa! Come help me. The idiot is back," Donny heard him say just before he passed out.

The pain in his shoulder brought Donny back to consciousness. He could feel the hard, wooden floor beneath him, then a chill as he opened his eyes. He was on a table, not the floor, and wearing nothing but his boxers. He tried to sit up and pinched off a scream as a spike of pain from his dislocated shoulder stabbed through him. He gasped, then someone was blocking the light. There was a feminine hand on his good shoulder, then Ilsa's voice.

"He's awake."

Another form loomed over him, and Donny could smell pipe tobacco.

"Gut. We need to fix that shoulder – the sooner, the better. Help me get him up," a deeper, male voice said. Not Karl, someone new. Then they were sitting him up and Donny bit off another scream, but couldn't hold back a small whimper. It hurt so bad. He'd been shot, stabbed, had broken bones… but nothing had ever hurt like this. It was like having a couple broken ribs, but a hundred times worse. Damn it hurt.

"Herr Strausshind, can you hear me? Understand me? Verstehen?"

Donny nodded and another spike of pain shot through him.

"We have to relocate your shoulder. It's out of position. It's going to hurt quite badly, but once we're done, you'll feel much better."

"Just fix it," Donny mumbled.

He later learned that Ilsa and Karl held him while the doctor yanked his arm back into position with one hard, practiced jerk, but all he could remember was an incredible flash of pain, and screaming finally, before he passed out again.

15

A section of Hohensalzburg Castle had been set aside as a temporary morgue. The medical examiner had done a preliminary examination and was waiting for me there at my request. He did not look happy. He introduced himself as Doktor Gersten and we shook hands.

"I apologize for the inconvenience, Herr Doktor, but time is of the essence," I said.

"Besides my duties as coroner, I have a full practice, Herr Moeller, so I would appreciate brevity."

I nodded apologetically. There was a time to be harsh, usually with suspects, occasionally witnesses, but doctors expect a bit of respect, and I gave it to him.

"I promise, Herr Doktor. I will keep it as brief as possible."

"As I'm sure you know, there are two bodies," the coroner began.

"Two? There should be three. I requested that the body of Oberstleutnant Fuhrmann be delivered here also."

"Ja. Unfortunately, the body has already been shipped by train to Linz, where he lived with his wife and child. I tried to retrieve it, but to find one casket en route these days is, I'm afraid, impossible. I do have the autopsy record, however – done by a colleague. I assure you, it's all you will need."

"I will decide what I need, Herr Doktor," I said. I hate paperwork with a passion—even paperwork done by others—but autopsy records are undeniably useful to a detective.

The doctor shrugged. "I'm sure I can get the body back eventually, but it will take time, Herr Inspector."

"Tell me about these two," I said.

"I'll start with the older gentleman. He has been identified as Herr Doktor

Emile Eberhardt, formerly of the German Academy for Aviation Research, where he worked alongside Willy Messerschmitt. He has been living and working for the RLM on top secret projects at Hohensalzburg Castle since August 1942. His wife lived with him in a top floor apartment at the castle. She identified the body."

"Cause of death?" I asked, even though I already knew the answer.

The doctor pulled the sheet down, exposing the scientist's face. "A direct blow to the brain through the occipital cavity. Basically, someone stuck an ice pick in his eye and shoved it straight into his brain. It shut him off like a light switch."

"Not a knife? An awl, perhaps?"

"Nein. I peeled back the face and inspected the eye socket. There was no sign of impact to the surrounding bone other than the small puncture wound at the rear of the occipital cavity. An awl produces a similar wound, but isn't long enough to penetrate into the brain. I removed the brain and measured the diameter of the wound as approximately three millimeters. Whoever killed him knew what they were doing."

I looked down at the scientist's ruined face. The top of his skull had been expertly removed to access the brain, then everything stitched back into place. The stitching around his head and neck reminded me of Frankenstein's monster. All he needed were some bolts on his neck.

"And the other one? The guard?" I asked.

"Found nearby in the same room. He died from similar wounds, but I feel it was during a struggle," the doctor said, gently replacing the sheet over the scientist and turning to the second table. He pulled the sheet back.

"Please explain," I said. A struggle made sense, but I learned long ago not to color my investigations with my own theories… not until I was sure.

"First of all, there are minor defensive wounds – bruising here, here and here, indicative of hand-to-hand combat. There is also a large perimortem bruise across the width of his back, as if he'd been thrown against something – a table, perhaps. There is bruising and contusions on the hands— particularly the knuckles—indicating our brave feldgendarm was giving as good as he got.

"I found powder residue on his tunic, indicating that he was close to a firearm that was discharged, but there is no gunpowder residue on his hands, so it was likely fired by his opponent. He wasn't shot, however – although I did find a slight graze on the right side of his head, possibly burned by a bullet."

"Cause of death?"

"Three brutal blows to the left side of the neck, again with an ice pick. Because of the position of the wounds, I would say that his attacker was likely right-handed. The first two blows weren't lethal, though they were undoubtedly painful, but the third blow ruptured the carotid artery and punctured his windpipe. He choked to death on his own blood."

I looked down at the damaged face of the young airman. I had seen plenty of corpses, many of them in the prime of life. All I could think about was how much my damn feet hurt, even wrapped in bandages. I nodded to the doctor and limped to the door of the chamber, turning to him to shake his hand, albeit gingerly, as mine still hurt horribly. The doctor saw the bandages, and his grasp was understandably gentle.

"Danke, Herr Doktor Gersten. A very good summary. It is clear to me that you know your business," I said.

He gave a little nod of thanks, and handed me the autopsy files. How could I have forgotten? I really was slipping.

"You walk like a man in pain. You don't look like a wealthy man to me, so I doubt it's gout. An injury, perhaps?"

"Hmm, yes. The bottoms of my feet are a bit... bruised. I've bandaged them, but..." I shrugged.

He raised his eyebrows. "A very painful condition, I'm sure," he said, knowing as well as I the Gestapo's penchant for beating the soles of the feet of their suspects.

"You've been soaking them in hot water, I suppose?" he said. I nodded.

"I thought as much. Warm salt water is good for open cuts, but bad for bruising. Soak them in ice water instead. Not nearly as pleasant, but it will contract the capillaries and reduce the swelling. The feet are full of nerve endings and very sensitive – as I'm sure you're now aware."

I nodded again. He pulled a pad from his pocket and wrote something unintelligible, at least to me, on it. Signing it with a doctor's flourish, he tore it from the pad and offered it to me. "Take this to the pharmacy and have it filled. It'll help with the pain. Keep any open cuts clean and bandaged, but don't wrap your feet all the time, and then loosely, just enough to pad them. Ice water, remember? You won't enjoy it, but it will help, believe me. Try and stay off your feet as much as possible the next several days."

"Danke, Herr Doktor. I thank you for the prescription, but staying off my feet is not an option. Thank you again for your help."

"Nein, it was my pleasure. May we process the two bodies now?"

I nodded. "Yes, of course. I have what I need."

"Good luck, Herr Moeller, and goodbye," the doctor said, turning back to gather the instruments of his trade.

"Goodbye, Doktor, and thank you again," I said, then turned, closed the door, and fought my way up the wide, stone steps, my feet protesting the whole way.

16

When Donny awoke he was lying on a narrow bed in a room he didn't recognize, with a couple thin blankets over him. Just moving his head to look around hurt. The only window was a small one, set high on the end wall, curved at the top to match the ceiling, with two-piece shutters fit to it. They and the window were open, and he had the feeling it was late morning.

Next to the bed were a side table and chair – nothing on the table but a modest oil lamp with a yellow glass base, a small pitcher, and a glass of water. Water. He pulled himself up and reached for the glass. He could move his right arm again, but it still hurt to do so. He used his left hand instead, managed to get the water to his lips, and drained the glass.

With some difficulty he supported himself on his right elbow so he could pour more water with his left, but although his right shoulder protested, the pain was at least bearable – unlike the previous night. He drank the second glass of water more slowly, then set the empty glass back on the table and lay back on the pillows again.

He should have been in Prague by now, but instead, was stuck here, injured and undoubtedly wanted by the Gestapo. At least he was alive. Thoughts of Prague, one of his favorite cities, brought him thoughts of Elena, the Resistance operative whose radio he'd used a few times. There were other radios in Europe, but he kept returning to Prague, and to her.

It wasn't simply that she was beautiful, although she was. There was simply something about her: a natural radiance that simply filled his heart whenever she smiled at him. Donny knew it was foolish, even dangerous, to mix espionage and romance, yet he couldn't stop thinking about her – she'd pop into his mind at the most inopportune moments.

It didn't help that their cover was as a couple—boyfriend and girlfriend—or that her kiss was so memorable, her lips so soft, her laugh so infectious. Her vivaciousness made him forget at times that there was a war on, and that they were just playing roles, and he was just there to use her radio set. He'd been looking forward to seeing her again; now he was stuck in an attic room in Salzburg. He wondered briefly what she was doing at that moment, then pushed it from his mind. He needed to stay sharp, not be daydreaming foolishly about some woman. In his game, romance was almost sure to get you killed.

He knew he needed to get up, that it was dangerous to just lie there, but it felt so good, and he was still so tired. He looked up at the graceful, curved ceiling and the open, leaded glass window beyond it. He could hear the mutter of people on the street, the clopping of horse's hooves on cobblestones and the intermittent squeak from the wheel of a vendor's cart as it passed by. The vendor was espousing his wares in German – something about tomatoes, he thought, but Donny was fading, and feeling safe for the moment, he let it come, sweeping him back off to oblivion.

17

Moeller's journal July18th, 1944

I dreamt of Marie last night; the simplest, most wonderful dream I've had since this mess started. I was just watching her at the table, after a fine dinner with friends at our house, her face animated, telling one of her stories, her hands painting pictures in the air, then the punchline, and she threw her head back and laughed as the table erupted in laughter and applause. She always was the life of the party, a real social butterfly, who touched everyone merely by her presence.

I stood in the kitchen doorway, a fresh bottle of Riesling in my left hand, the corkscrew in my right, just drinking in the sight of her: her long, aristocratic neck, high forehead and royal cheekbones, light red hair tousled and wild as always, the candlelight illuminating it as if she were on fire, her eyes sparkling with joy, tiny crow's feet crinkling at the edges. God, how I love this woman.

Morning, and consciousness, brought another memory, this one of Anna, twelve, bringing me the omelette with fried potatoes she'd made me for my birthday, her face alight with a proud smile. Despite her using way too much salt and pepper, I think it was the best omelette I'd ever tasted.

Anna, clearly her mother's child, tall and sleek, but slightly more reticent in her show of emotions – more like me, I suppose. Kind, thoughtful, and incredibly patient with her little brother. I think of that omelette, her first, as I sip my meager breakfast of acorn coffee, and it makes me wonder how she is. I miss my family so very badly that sometimes it physically hurts. When you spend each day with them, refereeing squabbles between siblings, sighing at their minor complaints, enduring the occasional poisonous looks from your spouse for some faux pas you felt was no big deal, you forget the simple, wondrous magic of moments spent with them, watching your children blossom, turning into someone new with each passing day. You can't see the forest for the trees at times.

Sascha—such a little man, even though he could be a real monster at times, when he'd come sit on my lap to have a book read to him (usually more than one), or even when he was squirmy and ticklish—the memory of his absolute trust and love fills me now. I look at Anna at the age she is, and wonder what my son will be like in ten years. I only wish he had a slightly older brother to help me usher him into manhood. I used to work far too many long hours… and now that I see this failure clearly, my fate is sealed, even if theirs is not. Who will help him become a man in my absence?

Anna – at that awkward stage of being half-woman, half-girl. I see her now in my mind, tall and smart, with a few of her mother's mannerisms, and oddly, a couple of mine, but altogether her own person, with her own way of talking and moving. She is an artist as well, but a different sort than her extrovert mother – she's a writer, of all things, although God only knows where that comes from.

I think upon how soon she will reach the age where she will meet some young man and leave my house… then I remember that our house has been given to some party functionary and his family, swept clean of all Marie's wonderful, lunatic art, our possessions traded, sold or burned, and I want to cry.

My family in a work camp, I sit in this miserable hotel room and stare at the murder board, praying for an epiphany that will bring me closer to catching the Allied agent so that I may save them. The art, the house, our meager possessions can all be replaced, but the three people in my life I love most cannot. The Nazis can take everything from me, but they cannot take my memories, which are all I own now, and, as bittersweet as they are, give me strength. Love must prevail. I must catch this killer – I must. These memories remind me of my goal, and I drive myself, constantly phoning or visiting all the top secret facilities on the list, over and over, pressing hands and making connections, ensuring that they will remember me and, by extension, the man I am chasing.

It has been a year now since I've seen my family. I use the ache I feel for them to harden my heart so that I might complete my task. At night, however, I dream of them, of their laughter, of their happy, glowing faces, and I live again; a real life, with no war, no horror, just peace and the warmth of our shared love. All right, Friedrich, enough melancholia. Time to get back to work.

18

July 16th, 1944 (One day prior to Moeller's release)

When Donny awoke the second time it was night. The window and shutters had been closed against the high altitude summer night, and the oil lamp was lit, guttering on a low setting. The water glass was full again, and some clothes were neatly folded on the chair beside the bed. This time he was able to sit up and swing his legs out of bed to drink the water, and he found that he was hungry. His entire body hurt, and when he examined his torso and legs he saw that they were a mass of cuts and bruises, which were turning yellow and purple around the edges already.

His left ankle and calf were bandaged, and his eye was still swollen shut. He wondered idly what his face looked like. He wasn't vain, but he couldn't go out in public looking like he'd been in a fight.

Donny dressed with difficulty, the rough, tan canvas pants a little big on him, but there was a belt, and they were well broken in. The shirt fit him perfectly – a dark blue button-down that had been made in Hamburg according to its label. It felt good to be dressed, even if he had no shoes.

He felt a bit dizzy as he stood, the ancient plank floor rough and cold on his bare feet, but the feeling passed. He poured himself another glass of water and drank it, already feeling better, although the weight of his arm was pulling on the damaged shoulder muscles. He needed a sling... and some food.

He opened the door to a small landing. There was another door on the other side, and a set of steep, narrow stairs leading down. He blew out the oil lamp, let his eyes adjust to the darkness, then made his way down the steep stairs, albeit with some difficulty, as the rail was on the right, and he had to reach across with his left to grasp it, crabbing down sideways one step at a time, his ankle shooting pain into his leg every time he put his weight on it.

He was glad now that he was barefoot – if he'd been wearing shoes, he likely would have fallen. As he reached the landing, Donny could hear the clink of silverware and the soft murmur of voices somewhere below him… and the smell of something wonderful. He turned and started down the second set of stairs.

They stopped talking when he entered the kitchen. Karl sat across the table from a man Donny had never seen before, with Ilsa seated at the end. None of them looked particularly pleased to see him.

Ilsa wiped her lips, put down her napkin and came over to him, helping him into a fourth chair, across from her. Donny sat gratefully, feeling as though he'd just climbed the Matterhorn. Before he knew it, there was a big bowl of French onion soup before him, and some bread on a side plate. There was no butter, of course, but amazingly, there was thick, gooey cheese floating in it, melting in the hot soup. The bread was slightly stale, but softened quickly enough when dipped in the soup.

He ate one-handed, resting his right hand on his lap, trying to restrain himself as he inhaled it, stopping only to allow Ilsa to slip a black, cloth sling over his head and gently slip his injured arm into it. He winced, but it took the pressure off the muscles in his shoulder, and he thanked her, grateful for the relief. She said nothing, her body language still showing her anger, yet she brought him more soup.

Karl and the unknown man pushed their bowls away and sat back, clearly finished with their repast, and the man Donny didn't know produced a pipe and tobacco pouch from a pocket on his coat, which hung around the chair behind him, while Karl rose to get a bottle of black pepper schnapps and two glasses. He asked his wife if she wanted schnapps, but she shook her head no as she finished clearing the table, giving Donny a dark look that he was unable to decipher.

His host poured two glasses of schnapps, setting one in front of the other man, who having successfully lighted his pipe, blew the match out, picked up the glass and raised it.

"Prosit," he said, and the two men threw back their drinks. Karl refilled both glasses, then sat as Donny soaked up the last of his soup with a crust of bread, popped it into his mouth, then looked up to see both men looking at him in a less than friendly way.

"Why did you come back here? You are supposed to be on a train," Karl said.

Donny wiped his mouth with the cloth napkin, wincing as he touched the split lip where the German guard had hit him.

"I'm sorry. I had no other option," he said.

"You put us all at risk," the unknown man said.

"And if the Germans had caught me, what kind of risk would there be for you in that?" Donny retorted, getting a little angry now.

"*Exactly!*" Karl exclaimed, hitting the table with his fist. "For you, this is some kind of game. For us, it is our *lives.* If you are caught, we'd all end up in a labor camp, or worse. I have half a mind to shoot you in the head myself and dump your body in the river!"

"KARL," the other man said loudly, a warning. It was clear who was in charge here. He looked at Donny. "Tell us what happened."

Donny told them the entire thing, leaving nothing out. They were risking their lives for him; he figured the truth was little enough compensation. When he got to the part about rappelling out the window on parachute cord, and the guards dropping grenades on him, the two men looked at each other.

"That's what we heard the other night," Karl said, the other man nodding. Ilsa had turned from the sink where she'd been doing the dishes and was listening intently now.

Donny finished quickly, detailing his fall and tumble down the rough slope, but leaving out nearly being discovered by the patrol on their very doorstep. That wouldn't help anything except the odds of him getting a bullet in the ear and a long nap in the river.

"I'm sorry. I expected to simply walk out of there, then take the train to Prague as we'd planned. I had no other choice but to come here," Donny finished. Karl and the unknown man looked at Donny, then at each other again. Karl got up from the table, retrieved two more glasses, filled them, and gave one to his wife and one to Donny. They all raised their glasses.

"Foolish Americans," Karl toasted, and they all drank. The alcohol burned Donny's split lip, but it didn't matter. For now, he was safe.

19

The second murder scene was on the east side of Hohensalzburg Castle, and I decided that it only made sense to visit it first, while I was there. I'd had to cross the courtyard to get there, and I was quite taken with the beauty of the place – the large courtyard or common area surrounded by high, whitewashed walls with windows opening onto it from all sides, many of them with flower boxes sporting begonias and peonies. It did not remind me of a military installation in the least, except for the occasional guard or military vehicle, and of course the flags, always the flags.

Arched doorways and portcullises in the flying buttress style and the large tree growing in the middle of it gave it the feel of a small village or town, which, of course, it really was originally. I had been told that Italian POWs had been held there during the previous war and there were enough guards and officers around even this late to convince me that the old pile of stones now had some hidden purpose... perhaps several.

The room was on the third floor, of course (just my luck), near the end of a series of long hallways, and they'd roped off both ends, with *Eintritt Verboten* signs hanging from the ropes, and a pair of stern Luftwaffe Feldgendarmie with submachine guns to discourage the curious.

A Luftwaffe major by the name of Hess had been detailed to accompany me, more of a leash than a facilitator, and I suspected by his pips and overbearing manner that he was likely military intelligence. He walked us through the outer and inner barricade without a problem – we didn't even have to show our papers, which surprised me. The German military loves paper, even more than the police. It was apparent that it wasn't his first trip to the crime scene. In fact, he'd likely posted the guards himself.

The window in the entrance door had been shattered, the inner security screen battered and bent out of the way. Someone had a hell of a time getting in. The first thing which struck me when I first walked in were the enormous, wooden beams running the width of the room's ceiling, spaced more closely together than any structure I'd ever been in, likely necessary to carry the great weight of the castle above. The room had apparently once been a storage room for salt— the source of Salzburg's early success and continued fortunes—but had recently been converted to a workshop or laboratory, with massive, stone-topped workbenches so heavy that I wondered how they'd gotten them up there.

The blood on the floor had long since dried, and the tracks of many feet led back and forth through it, likely during the initial forced entrance by the guards responding to the call. All the windows were closed, but a double length of what looked like olive drab parachute cord was tied off with a simple prusik knot to one of the stout table legs, the rest of it laying in a jumble on the floor in front of one of the windows, presumably the window the killer had escaped through.

I looked at Hess. "This one?"

He nodded, clearly already bored with my investigation. I limped to the window and unlatched it, swung the double sashes open, then leaned out over the sill to look down. Directly below was a sheer drop of at least 75 meters, with nothing but what looked like possibly another window, closed at the moment, one story below. I knelt down and scooped up the pile of parachute cord with my hands and threw it out.

It tangled a bit, but I was able to shake it out, and I leaned over the sill again to see how far down it went. It was difficult to tell, but it clearly didn't reach the base of the wall. I estimated that the murderer had, at a minimum, a drop of at least 10, perhaps even 20 meters once he'd reached the end of the rope, and that with a landing on a rock-strewn, 80-degree slope.

I estimated the length of the doubled cordage at approximately 70 to 75 meters, and the drop from the window to the ground at about 100 meters. It was a miracle he'd gotten away, and he was almost certainly injured. To have escaped in such a way was nearly superhuman. A brown smear on the right side of the window caught my eye. I scraped a fingernail against it. It was what was left of a bloody handprint.

"Is this really necessary, Herr Inspector?" Hess asked from behind me. I ignored him and began pulling the doubled line back in, more slowly this time, stopping at several points to examine discoloration on the cording. It looked like dried blood to me. Apparently, our killer wasn't superhuman after all.

I dumped the line back on the floor where I'd found it, but left the window open, which apparently offended Hess somehow as he immediately closed it. I washed my hands at a large, deep craft sink in the corner of the room. At the opposite corner was the desk, presumably the good doctor's, but as I walked up to it, it seemed missing the papers and associated detritus the desk of a busy scientist would likely be covered with.

Something was missing, but I couldn't put my finger on it. It was clear that someone, likely Military Intelligence officer Hess himself, had sanitized the room – the workbenches, for example, had tools on them, some of which looked like modeling tools, but no actual projects in progress. It was odd. Then I wondered, as a former, lowly Kripo investigator who would have previously studiously avoided any pissing matches with Military Intelligence, how good my new SD credentials really were.

"What was Herr Doktor working on, Herr Major? Do you know?"

"That is classified information, Herr Inspector."

I looked at him as if he'd killed Eberhardt himself. "I am here under the auspices of the SD, which is *in charge* of these projects, Herr Major Hess. Do not make me work for this."

Hess looked uncomfortable, and pursed his lips. "I will have to make a call first," he said.

"Fine, I'll wait."

20

After further discussion, it was decided that Donny should go back to his apartment, but not right away. It would look suspicious if he left his things behind without checking out – but he needed his "Strausshind" papers in order to really go anywhere. To leave his clothes behind would be inconvenient. To leave travel papers in another name behind would simply be foolish.

His weekly rent was now past due, so he wrote a letter introducing Ilsa as his cousin, saying that he'd been in an accident and was staying with family for now, but would like to keep the room. He enclosed two weeks' rent and asked for her to be given access to his apartment in order for her to bring him some things he needed.

Ilsa would recover his papers and perhaps a few clothes, while leaving enough there to make it seem as though he were coming back, then in a couple weeks, once things had settled down, he could extricate himself from the rental agreement in a normal fashion to avoid raising suspicion.

In the meantime, he hid upstairs in his little garret, reading the papers he'd stolen from the lab, but they left him with more questions than they answered. Most of what he'd grabbed was technical falderal that wouldn't have made sense to him in English, let alone German, but the Top Secret file titled "Eagle's Claw" was interesting. A number of subtopics caught his eye: the first discussing a project called "Mistel" or "Misteltoe" in English, which he determined had to do with the models he'd seen of an He177– type bomber with a small jet aircraft piggybacked to it.

This didn't disturb him much in and of itself, but he noticed several references in the file to the Me264 *Amerika Bomber,* which he did find disturbing. The model had four engines, if he remembered correctly. didn't the Heinkel He177 have only two engines?

He knew the Nazis had been trying to develop a bomber with the range to hit the U.S. and return safely for some time. Had they finally done it? He continued reading – again, a lot of technical jargon, but he found a reference to a Vergeltungswaffe V5 or *"Vengeance Weapon 5,"* which was tied to the Mistrel project in some way. It's code name was Operation Eagle Claw, which sounded ominous. There were several technical drawings in the file, detailing a new bomb rack, designed to carry just one bomb of about 9,700 pounds, which seemed pretty heavy to him for a single piece of ordnance.

The gist of the attached treatise was the advantageous effect of the lighter bomb load on fuel consumption, thus increasing range of the larger He227 from 6,950 km to 9,340 km. He also found a graph comparing the fuel consumption to an He177 with normal bomb load, and something called an He274, but he found nothing else specific to Heinkels.

The attached calculations for the Me264 were unintelligible to him, but he was sure some egghead back home would be overcome with joy when he got hold of them. The document called for further tests and suggested an airfield nearby, but an attached letter from the RSHA specified an airfield called "Krefeld," which Donny was pretty sure was in Eastern Germany, near Cologne. The tests were approved, and recommended final approval for this candidate for *"Amerika Bomber."*

Donny now realized how important the information he held in his hands was, and knew he needed to get it back to OSS headquarters in Bern, Switzerland, and into Dulles's hands as soon as possible. The idea of a fleet of bombers, with the range to reach England or the U.S., perhaps with a small fighter jet attached to each one for final, operational defense, each bomber carrying some sort of new "Vengeance Weapon," chilled him.

One bomb? It didn't make any sense to him unless that bomb was incredibly powerful. Had the Germans made some sort of breakthrough? Had they developed some new, powerful explosive or had they finally cracked the atomic problem? There were references again to "Operation Eagle Claw" and a "Uranprojekt," which seemed to be centered in Prague, although Pilsen and a facility called 'B8' near Sankt Georgen outside of Linz, part of the Mauthausen prison camp complex, was apparently where "primary manufacturing" was being done, whatever that meant. Still, he found it hard to believe.

Donny knew it was up to him to get healed and get to Prague, but he had no idea where to begin once he was there. He heard a door close, and Ilsa's light tread on the stairs. He smiled in greeting as she came through the door to his attic room, but she didn't return the smile.

"I managed to get your papers… but I had to leave your clothes," she said.

"Why? What happened?"

"The SD is looking for you," she said.

21

The second murder scene—or rather, the first, as the coroner was convinced that Oberstleutnant Fuhrmann had been murdered several hours before the other two—was in an alley in a run-down, very old neighborhood near the river. An officer from the Orpo showed me where the body had been found. They'd canvassed the neighborhood, but if anyone had seen anything, they weren't talking.

I walked through it anyway, comparing the photographs in the file with the reality of the scene until I could see it in my head. The police seemed sure it was a simple robbery – the victim's wallet had been found, emptied of money, and his wedding ring and wristwatch were both missing.

I was sure, however, that Fuhrmann's death had nothing to do with robbery and everything to do with the invasion of Eberhardt's laboratory at Hohensalzburg. I just didn't see the connection yet. It would have made more sense if he had been killed for his credentials, but his military ID wasn't taken, and although found in a pool of the victim's blood, it'd been enough to make a preliminary ID. The oberstleutnant who had presented himself at the castle had used a different name and different set of credentials, but shared the same rank. It seemed an odd coincidence.

The one thing I had going for me was an actual photograph of the killer, taken without his knowledge, at the entry desk of Festung Hohensalzburg. Because of the secure nature of the work there, everyone signing in was photographed by a hidden camera. The suspect had moved just as the camera clicked, so it was a bit blurry, but showed a man in his early to mid-thirties, with dark hair and a strong chin, wearing the officer's uniform as if he'd been born to it. I had stared at the photograph until it was burned into my memory, but I had no doubt that, dressed differently, such an experienced agent could walk right past me.

There, I said it. *Agent.* It is obvious now that these killings were definitely not the work of an ordinary criminal or even psychopath, but the handiwork of a skilled, Allied operative – either British SOE or American OSS. Gephardt's analysis was correct, much as I hate to admit it.

I had a final stop before reporting back to Gephardt – the oberstleutnant's apartment, which I hoped had been ransacked less thoroughly than Eberhardt's lab. My feet were feeling a bit better after taking the doctor's suggestion and soaking them in ice water, but they still hurt terribly, so I had Becker—the Orpo police liaison assigned to me—drive me over there. I cursed when I found out it was on the second floor, but struggled with the stairs, showed my SD credentials to the policeman guarding the door to the apartment, and stepped inside.

It was a typical officer's billet: unassuming, but clean and neat, with a small icebox and two-burner stovetop. I made the mistake of opening the icebox door – the ensuing stench told me that the dead officer enjoyed limburger cheese and sausage, and that he hadn't added any ice in several days. Hard to do when you're dead, I suppose.

I verified visually that there was nothing hidden inside and closed the icebox door. I looked at Becker, who looked as discomfited as I felt. "Open a window, why don't you?" I said. He nodded in reply and opened two in response – a good decision, if you ask me.

The bed was neatly made, with a large, embroidered Luftwaffe flying eagle insignia on it at the center. I had never seen such a thing, and doubted it was official – more likely the work of a loyal spouse: either an attempt to provide her husband with a little piece of home, or perhaps a reminder of fidelity while he was away?

A knock came on the door. I looked at Becker, who shrugged, then went to answer it while I continued poking through the lieutenant colonel's meager possessions: a pile of letters bound with string (correspondence from a loving wife), the requisite number of uniforms needed by any good officer for various occasions, and a picture of his family, which I held up to examine.

His wife was a stolid, unsmiling, robust woman, posed with her hands on a boy's shoulders – a boy about twelve years old by the look of it, wearing a Hitler Jugend uniform. Fuhrmann stood beside them, his hands clasped together in front. By the similar unsmiling looks on all three of their faces, I doubted there was much laughter in the Fuhrmann household.

I set the picture back down on the dresser. Something nagging at me. Something…

"Herr Inspector?" Becker said from behind me. I turned, and he was holding out a large manila envelope. "The landlady brought this up. She said it came for Herr Fuhrmann this morning."

I took the envelope from him, opened it, and shook the contents out onto the bed. It was a complete set of new identification and travel papers in Fuhrmann's name. The accompanying letter made it quite clear that lieutenant colonel or not, next time he lost his papers, there would be a fee. I looked at the uniforms hanging from the clothes hook fastened to the top of the cabinet door. There were two empty hangers. Not one, two.

I threw the envelope on the bed and looked in the cabinet, then under the bed. In a small, blue bag, again embroidered with the Luftwaffe eagle, I found a tin of shoe polish and a soft polishing cloth, but nothing else. Typically, officers will keep two pair of boots. Where was his second pair? I got back to my feet with some difficulty, but my exuberance outmatched my pain. I now knew why Oberstleutnant Fuhrmann had been murdered, and I was positive now that an enemy agent had done it.

22

The mood at the table was not a good one. There was no schnapps this time, and Karl had his hands folded in front of him on the table – which, Donny had learned, was a good barometer as to how pissed off he was. Donny's bruises had been turning yellow and brown, and the cuts on his face were healing, but it'd be at least another week or two before he'd be able to travel without drawing attention to himself. The real question was, how much did the SD know? No one was talking, so Donny decided to go first.

"I see no way they could know anything about Strausshind. It must have been a normal security check."

Karl nodded. "I asked around, and they are checking IDs at all hotels, hostels and apartment houses... so, I agree with you that they didn't know about Carl Strausshind. The question is, do they know now? I think there's a 50/50 chance that your landlady didn't report you, to save paying the accommodation tax, but if she did, then they'll be looking for you."

"Our friends Karl spoke with said that they are looking for an injured man," Ilsa interjected. "I had told the landlady just minutes before that my cousin, Carl Strausshind, had been injured in a car accident. I think we can assume your cover is blown. If I hadn't overheard her speaking with them from the stairs and gone out the back way—"

"What Ilsa is trying to say is, you're putting us at risk again. First you show up here in a Luftwaffe uniform, hurt and bleeding, with a damn submachine gun and a briefcase full of secrets, now this. Frankly, I don't like you much, Herr Strausshind, and I want you gone," Karl said. "If it hadn't been for Ilsa, I would have just put a bullet in your ear that night. I want to help the cause, but I don't intend to become a martyr doing it. More importantly, I don't want my wife getting hurt," Karl said.

"So, when things get dicey you're ready to quit? I have news for you, Karl. There's no going back. You're both in it up to your necks now," Donny said angrily. "Now listen. I recovered some critical information on weapons that could change the war for Germany if they are able to deploy them. I have to get to Prague – the sooner the better.

"These papers," Donny said, tapping the soft accordion file in front of him, "need to get to OSS headquarters as soon as possible, along with a message. I suggest we use Aunt Jemma.

"Now, I think we all agree that I can't travel openly on my current papers, so I need either new identity and travel papers, or a hidden way out of Austria. Once in Prague, I should be okay — hopefully the name Carl Strausshind is not on a Reich-wide SD list yet.

"I don't want to put either one of you at risk, but there is risk in what we do, terrible risk. You knew this going in, and I won't apologize for it. I had no other option than to come here. For *that,* I'm truly sorry. Find me a way out of Salzburg and I'll be out of your hair… and for what it's worth, Karl, I'm not too fond of you either," Donny finished.

A small smirk crept onto Karl's face, and he nodded. "You're right – we knew what we were doing when we got into this," he said, looking at his wife, taking her hand. She covered his with her other hand, giving it a squeeze, looking back at him.

"But it scares me to think of how close she came to getting caught. Even now she's not safe. If the landlady gives them a description—"

"Karl," Ilsa said, giving his hand another squeeze. He looked at her, then back at Donny, the smile long gone.

"We'll do what you ask – I want you out of here as quickly as possible."

Donny pushed the accordion folder over to him, a folded letter on top. "This is for the courier packet. I'm sure I don't have to tell you not to look in the file. It's better you don't know. You may read the letter—send it in the clear—there's nothing incriminating."

Karl opened the letter and read it quickly.

Dear Aunt Jemma,

I'm sorry for not writing before now, but we were in a bit of trouble. Our papers were stolen from our hotel and we had to get them replaced.

We are having a wonderful vacation despite the war, however. Thank you again for the tickets.

Prague is our next stop. Hermann has a friend who knows someone with a Skoda automobile for sale in excellent condition which they wish to sell. I'm not sure where we will get the fuel to get it back to Germany – things are such a mess since the invasion, but Hermann is determined to look at it regardless. Hope all is well with you, your loving niece,

"If Ilsa could rewrite it, then sign it with a woman's handwriting, that would help. Sign it with the name Elsie," Donny said.

Karl nodded, refolding the letter. "Okay, I'll get these out, but no guarantee on how long it'll take. I have an idea on how to get you out of Austria, but you probably aren't going to like it. I'll look into it. I want you *gone*, verstehen?"

"Yes, I understand," Donny said, looking at his hosts, knowing there was nothing more to be said.

23

Moeller's Journal, July 21st, 1944

Gephardt was not glad to see me – no surprise, really.
"I told you I didn't want to see you until you had some results," he said curtly, coming around the desk. He'd kept me waiting, very likely on purpose, the schwanz.

"I have some results... but I need some more information in order to go further."

"Don't tell me you already know who the killer is," he said, giving me a stern look.

"As a matter of fact, I do. Now I just need to find him." He raised an eyebrow as I continued. "All three murders, or killings, rather, are obviously the work of one man – either a British SOE or American OSS agent."

He looked at me. "That's your big breakthrough? I told you already that this was obviously the work of an enemy agent." He paused. "I assume you heard about the attempt on the Führer's life yesterday?"

I hadn't, but I hoped he was dead. "No, I've been busy."

"A bomb was set off at the Wolf's lair. Hitler narrowly escaped with his life. The world's being turned upside down," he said, unusually talkative for once.

"It certainly is," I agreed, not sharing my opinion that it was the Nazis who'd turned the world on its ear.

"Now, what are you really doing here? What is it that you want?" he said.

"He took some Top Secret files from Doktor Eberhardt's workshop. I need to know what was in those files, but the Luftwaffe is being less than cooperative."

Gephardt shrugged. "You're surprised? Streng Geheim files? Of course, they're being reticent – rightfully so."

"I suspect he has left Salzburg. The files he took must have led him somewhere else – perhaps another research facility he intends to invade. If you want me to catch him, I need to know what he took from that file cabinet."

"Watch your tone with me, Herr Moeller."

"I apologize, Herr Gephardt," I said, wanting nothing more than to pull out my little pistol and shoot him in the face. "You told me that I would have whatever I needed to solve these crimes and catch the killer. I'm simply telling you what I need."

Gephardt took a big breath and let it out, looking at me critically. "All right. I'll see what I can do, but if you intend to leave Austria, I need to know first. Next time, call me – don't just come by here."

I nodded. "Ich verstehe, Herr Gephardt. Danke," I said.

"You're welcome. Now get out."

I stood, and shrugged on my coat – it was hot in the office. I stopped, my hand on the shellacked wood of the open door. "Herr Gephardt, I hate to ask, but… have you had any word on my family? Are they all right?" I asked.

"They're fine," he said without looking up, reading some paperwork, then signing it. "Why wouldn't they be? They're being held in the bosom of the Reich."

I stood there until he looked up at me, but I couldn't read anything in his eyes.

"I would like you to get this letter to my wife, bitte," I said, stepping forward and setting an envelope containing the two-page letter I'd written the night before on his desk.

"Why would I do that?" he asked.

"Why would I continue this investigation without knowing my family is being treated properly?" I said. It was a gamble, but one I had to take.

Gephardt's eyes narrowed. "All right, I will see what I can do… but no promises. You may go," he said.

I went out and closed the door behind me. *Bosom of the Reich,* I thought. Why did I not find that comforting?

– Part Two –

Late August 1944, Austria

24

It took nearly a month for Donny to heal sufficiently and for Karl and Ilsa to arrange his transport out of Salzburg – much longer than Donny had hoped, but things like this took time. Karl was right – Donny didn't like his ride out of Salzburg one bit, but he had to admit, it was effective. The hidden compartment in the wagon would never be searched, due to the immense, reeking pile of manure atop it. Having limited options, Donny endured, the slow clip-clop of the horse's hooves testing his last nerve, the stench and slow drip of urine from the pile above him nearly unbearable.

They passed through three checkpoints, and at one a soldier actually checked the pile of manure with his bayonet, the other soldiers laughing at him when he got a horse apple stuck on his bayonet, and manure in the barrel of his Mauser. The narrow, hidden compartment with the OSS agent inside stayed hidden.

At Bad Griesbach the wagon stopped, and the manure was shoveled off. It seemed to take forever. By this time, Donny was far past uncomfortable, he was miserable. The compartment had never been meant to hold a human being, and there had been no room to move. The pain from muscle cramps and charley horses was excruciating, but he couldn't make a sound. He'd never considered himself claustrophobic, but he'd had a couple panic attacks in the tight, uncomfortable quarters, and he had to force himself to relax and breath normally – something the stench made nearly impossible.

Finally the wood slats were removed and he stuck his head out gratefully into the chill night air, gulping in huge breaths. The farmer, whose name he'd never heard, helped him out of the tiny space, his body so racked by cramping he could hardly stand, but after a hot bath, and fresh clothes, Donny felt much better.

He ate supper with the farmer's family – nothing extravagant, just a simple but wonderful meal of wiener schnitzel and sauerkraut, but the bread was fresh, and to his surprise, there was butter. No one spoke to him at the table, but their five-year-old boy wouldn't take his eyes off Donny, despite his father cuffing him in the back of the head every time he caught him at it.

After eating he was given a couple blankets, and followed the farmer with his lantern to the barn, where a rude pallet was made up for him in the haymow. The farmer told Donny they would leave early the next morning and he would wake him for breakfast. He made sure Donny knew where the ladder was, then left him in the dark, taking the lantern with him. Donny was asleep almost immediately.

The morning came far too early – it was still dark when the farmer shook Donny awake. Still sore from his ordeal at the castle, and the awful ride in the wagon, his entire body protested as he got up.

Breakfast was a simple porridge, or gruel, served with goat's milk. Donny wasn't enamored of it, but it was filling, and he had no idea when he'd get the chance to eat again. The farmer showed him where they were on a map – outside a village called Bad Griesbach, about 186 kilometers south of Pilsen. Donny noticed that the rest of the family were dressed in their best clothes and looked as though they were going somewhere. He asked the farmer about it, who seemed a little surprised. He told Donny they were going with him to Pilsen. When Donny mentioned that sounded dangerous, the farmer gave him a knowing look.

"Which is more suspicious – two men in an empty truck, or an entire family on a three-day trip to the big city?" he asked. "Besides, Olaf has never seen a real city." Olaf, the five-year-old, gave Donny his widest smile yet as his father told him to get his summer jacket and to be quick about it.

The farmer was right. They were stopped only once, but briefly, in Passau, asked where they were headed, then waved through. Donny sat in the back, surrounded by children and baskets of tomatoes, turnips and fresh eggs – worth their weight in gold in a big city these days. The farmer stopped at the train station to drop him off, and gave him directions, which Donny memorized. He gave the farmer a third of his money – a generous amount, but the man and his family had risked everything in helping him. As they drove off, Olaf and his sister waved. Donny shouldered the small drawstring bag he'd been given and went into the train station, wondering what time the train to Prague left.

25

The train to Prague is a fine memory gone bad. Marie and I took a holiday there once before the children were born, indeed, as young lovers, even before we were married. We cuddled and flirted on the train shamelessly, earning disapproving looks from the dowager across the aisle, but young enough then not to care. The world was our oyster, and that weekend we were devouring it.

I remember the sunshine: hard and flat that September, turning the fields the train sped through as golden as the pilsner beer we drank like water once we reached our destination. Our room, which we'd scrimped and saved for, had partial rock walls from the older part of the building poking through the plaster, the walls whitewashed until they were clean and new. There was an old brass bed covered with a quilt, and a simple washstand with the toilet down the hall. I remember returning from the bathroom in the hall to find Marie sitting up in bed, smoking a cigarette, wrapped in that quilt.

I'll never forget the way she looked at me—appraising me as if I were something she'd bought, something clearly hers now—then she looked me in the eye and pulled the quilt aside to bare her breasts to me: proud and lovely, the nipples erect and expectant... but it was the way she looked directly at me that excited me most.

I leapt onto her, a lion on a gazelle, and she shrieked with laughter. We didn't eat until late that evening, then devoured the best meal of our lives – slabs of carp in a wonderful cream sauce from a workingman's café, washed down with an early Bock from the Pilsner- Urquell brewery, our hands, mouths, and eyes devouring each other along with our food. Now, oddly, I find myself returning to Prague on the business of saving my wife and children.

The train is more crowded this time, and hot – full of human misery. Everywhere I look, I see pain and unhappiness. No one sharing food, no one talking. It's like a microcosm of the war: everyone simply enduring, wishing for it to be over.

The sunny fields with haystacks and working teams of Belgian horses that I remember so well lay grey and fallow, denuded long before of anything they might supply, the horses given up long ago to the Wehrmacht or the butcher. I saw one farmer the entire time, swinging a scythe interminably in a huge field. By my figuring it should take him until the end of the war to harvest it all alone, but I admire his perseverance. One has to try, no?

The weather didn't help – dark and grey, matching my mood. Sure to rain soon, I thought. "At least the Americans haven't bombed us here, yet," I heard one old woman tell another as we boarded – a poor excuse for optimism in a country swollen with it not so very long ago.

My own optimism for the health and well-being of my family has been dulled somewhat by Gephardt's attitude, I must confess, but I have nothing else to hold onto. During the day I follow the few clues I have – the files I'd demanded, each marked "Streng Geheim" on the covers. At first I'd only been allowed to examine them in a hot, airless room at Luftwaffe headquarters, the files having been brutally redacted – entire sentences struck out with a heavy, black pen. It was hard to get anything useful from them, but I'd managed to glean the name of a Czech company— the Skoda Works—and from the next-to-the-last file, the name of what with a little more digging I found out to be an airfield near the Belgian border.

I demanded to see the files without redaction, raising quite a fuss, actually, bullying them with my best police investigator's tone, and after another call to Gephardt, which I'd insisted upon, they finally relented. I made it clear that I would take what files I required, to be returned at a later time. This time the files had more information, and many photographs, and I found the concept of a bomber which carried its own fighter for defense fascinating. The other pictures, mainly detail photos of some sort of oddly shaped bomb rack, from what I could tell, I could not decipher. The term "Eagle's Claw" was mentioned several times, obviously some sort of hush-hush operation that the

Luftwaffe refused to comment on.

So, I will travel to Skoda, then to a number of obscure airfields, and find out what I can there. If I were an Allied spy, that's what I'd do... a spy's greed for information is their greatest vulnerability. I have a photo of him from Hohensalzburg, but it's blurry and indistinct – I need to have it blown up, though that will make it even blurrier. Even then, will I recognize him in civilian dress? More importantly, is my family safe? Are they getting enough to eat? Are they warm? These thoughts keep interfering with my task – I simply can't help it. My heart aches to know the answer.

26

Donny had gotten lucky. The next train to Prague left in less than 30 minutes – time enough to find something to eat. He bought a ticket and left the station, ravenous. He found a vendor working out of a small stall outside the station and spent a few koruna on some watery potato soup and a heel of bread, which actually was not bad – no boll weevils, and he could barely taste the sawdust.

He finished his soup, bought an apple and a small wedge of cheese for the train, then went back into the station to wait. He had a small drawstring bag with a change of clothes, a sliver of soap, and a razor wrapped in a small towel: the traveling kit of a poor farmer and nothing else. Ostensibly, he was going to see a sick cousin in Prague.

Someone had left an old newspaper on a bench, and he picked it up, unslung the bag and set it beside him, then began reading the newspaper as if it were the most fascinating thing he'd ever read, reinforcing the impression of a farmhand in the big city, well aware that he was being watched by two well-dressed men in long coats – obviously Gestapo.

Donny heard the sound of marching troops passing by outside, then the door to the station opened and the sound got louder for a moment. He couldn't help it – he turned to look as any curious person would, only to see German troops pushing into the station, spreading out, running to seal the building as their German officer yelled, "MACH SCHNELL!"

Who'd given him up? Did they know what he looked like? The name on his papers? He knew he couldn't let them take him alive – he simply knew too much. They'd use him to roll up the Resistance. He had no illusions about withstanding torture—he'd been tortured before —had the scars to prove it, but he had been lucky enough to have gotten rescued before he'd told them what he knew. Everyone talks eventually. *Everyone.* Different people just have different breaking points. This time, Donny knew, there'd be no rescue party coming to save him. Hell, Operations didn't even know where he was.

"ACHTUNG," the hawk-faced man in the tan coat said loudly. "All men between the ages of eighteen and forty-eight are to line up against this wall to have their papers checked. Schnell!"

27

As the train pulled into Pilsen, the first thing I saw were soldiers. The conductor told everyone there would be a slight delay as our papers were checked. I could see Gestapo going slowly down a line of about thirty men backed up against the tile wall, inspecting their papers. I realized people were standing up around me.

"Bitte, sir. Everyone must get off the train for a security check," the conductor said. It seemed I was the only one still seated.

"Nein," I said, showing him my new SD credentials, which made him clearly uncomfortable.

"Yes, sir… I mean no, sir. Everyone is required to exit the car temporarily. You may leave your belongings in your seat – it won't take long," he told me.

I thought that if I really made a scene, I could have remained in my seat, but I decided to be proactive. I pushed my way from the car and made a beeline for the officer in charge, pulling my SD credentials to ward off a young, foolish private who got in my way. My feet still hurt badly, I hadn't gotten much sleep the night before, and my family was in a labor camp in Austria. I was not in a good mood.

"Was ist hier los?" I demanded, holding up my badge. The officer did not seem overly impressed with my credentials, but he acknowledged me with a nod and a click of his heels.

"We received a tip – there is someone working with the Resistance who is on this platform, who was about to board this train to Prague, Herr Inspector. We are about to arrest him."

"I am on critical business for the Reich," I said. "How long will this take?"

Suddenly a man wearing a peasant's cap broke from the line, punched one of the soldiers, and grabbed his weapon. Several submachine guns stuttered, jerking his body like a string puppet, then he dropped the gun and collapsed on his face. The officer looked at me with a smile.

"Not long at all, Herr Moeller," he said, then barked orders at his men, telling them to let the others go and to remove the body. He turned back to me. "You may reboard the train now," he said.

I couldn't think of a suitably snide reply, so I got back on the train, wondering what makes a man so foolish? Desperation? Hatred? Perhaps his family in a work camp somewhere?

28

Nobody expected him to run, least of all Donny. When the man on his right dove forward and tackled the guard, grabbing at his weapon, Donny's first instinct was to help him – but the end came quickly, and like the others in line, Donny covered his ears and cringed instinctively against the rattle of the guns and the sudden rain of bullets.

When it stopped, miraculously the only dead man had been the one who'd tried to run. Donny half-expected the Germans to arrest them all, but he was simply asked if he'd known the runner, to which he honestly answered no, then his papers were returned and he was told he could now board his train. He queued up with the other passengers, many of which had already been on the train, but who had been forced off and subjected to the same inspection, and wondered again about the mechanics of it. The Germans would spare no resource to find someone, but once the culprit had been apprehended—or in this case shot—everything would immediately go back to normal. He looked at the soldiers—mostly boys in their teens and twenties—and realized they were like a swarm of bees, just following orders.

Donny gave his ticket to the trainman, who punched it, then he climbed aboard, the steel railing cold against his hand.

He found a good seat near the window, across from an innocuous-looking man in his late forties, dressed like a bureaucrat or salesman, his leather briefcase held across his knees to serve as an ersatz desk, supporting a notebook or journal in which he was writing furiously. "Excuse me. Is this seat taken?"

29

This business is going bad. I wonder how many others see it besides myself? I have never trusted politicians, especially when they offer free soup, but they say a starving man has no politics.

The man seated across from me is dressed like a farmer on holiday. I recognized him when he sat down from the line of men the Gestapo had lined up against the wall of the station. Frankly, with the panic of the last few days—the invasion in France, now Rome surrendering—I'm a bit surprised they didn't simply machine-gun them all. Tempers are running high these days.

Back to Prague. I'm wondering now if I should have stopped in Pilsen and checked out the KG200 lead... no, I shouldn't second-guess myself. As a top Luftwaffe bomber group, KG200 has a top secret classification. I'm sure they'd simply stonewall me, even with SD credentials. What chance would an OSS agent have getting in there? I was told that they actually had a small fleet of captured American B17s they flew on secret missions. No, I'll have to come at the Ju390 from the back side – the Junkers factory in Dessau, where it was built. Of course, their main office is right here in Prague, but again, like KG200, I doubt they'll volunteer to tell me anything useful.

It is likely that the Ju390 is a very large plane – probably a bomber, although it's claimed to be a transport. The Luftwaffe colonel I asked told me that I must have it wrong, that he knew of only Ju290s in use, as long-range bombers or transports, but mostly the latter. He claimed with no little pride that they'd been flown to Japan and Manchuria nonstop, over a polar route, but somehow I doubt it – could we really have a plane that can fly that far?

I am quite positive, however, that the designation Ju390 was not just a typo in the file, as I saw it three times in the same document. It was some technical bullshit about wing-loading vs. take-off weight vs. range that made my eyes glaze over just looking at it, but it seems logical an OSS agent would be highly interested in such a long-range, tactical aircraft.

The Skoda Works angle makes even more sense. I am not completely sure what he actually stole from the file cabinet, because I do not entirely trust that the Luftwaffe gave me everything, but we work with what we have. Skoda is a huge armaments factory, that makes all sorts of weapons, so who knows? Oh, wait. The American OSS agent knows. Ironic, no?

I just heard some whispering behind me that the Germans have taken the Slovakia seat of government by force to quell an insurrection. I must find a newspaper at the next stop, or perhaps borrow one from someone on the train. Not that it would tell me much – everything they print these days seems to be mostly propaganda at this point. It worries me – it seems as though we are spinning toward something we cannot see, simply because we're moving too quickly.

30

Donny could feel the man's eyes on him, and changed his evaluation. The man wasn't in his late forties as he had first thought, but had suffered some terrible deprivation. He limped when he got up to borrow a newspaper, and Donny noticed his shoes were untied – his feet either swollen, bandaged, or his shoes too small. With all the deprivations of the war, the latter was clearly possible, probable even, but his limp led Donny to believe it was the former: he'd suffered some terrible injury to his feet.

The thing that really bothered Donny however, was his gut feeling that despite his obvious injuries, the man was a policeman, likely plainclothes. Not just off-duty; perhaps an investigator of some kind. The man gave him a sharp look as he sat back down, and Donny forced himself to smile. It was the most powerful weapon an OSS agent had – the simple ability to remain calm. He'd taught himself to take it even further, to divert suspicion from himself. Still, he thought, of all the seats he could have chosen…

"Excuse me, can you tell me the time?" he asked his new traveling companion.

The man looked at his watch, then at Donny, as if deciding something.

"Half-past ten," he said. "Going to Prague?"

"Ja. And you?"

The man nodded, putting his notebook carefully inside the thin satchel and buckling it shut. *A minor functionary? Plant manager perhaps?* Donny looked at the man's wardrobe more closely as he snapped the borrowed newspaper open. *No, definitely a cop.*

Donny had grown up on the streets of Baltimore, where he'd learned to hot-wire cars and pick locks – skills that had gotten him a sentence of four years in the service, or four years in jail. Stealing the mayor's Lincoln had been the final straw. "Hell," Donny had told them, "I just had a date and wanted to impress her. We just went on a picnic, for chrissakes – I wasn't going to keep it!"

As it turned out, stealing that Lincoln had been one of the best things that'd ever happened to him. The OSS and its unconventional methods required unconventional thinking and creative solutions, along with a fearless penchant for risk-taking, which described Donny to a T.

So Donny knew cops... and this guy was clearly a cop, no doubt about it. The question was, what kind of cop was he? Definitely not Gestapo – those guys dressed better than this, and not military police, or he'd be in uniform. The question was, was he Kripo, SD, or something else entirely? And what was he up to? The policeman folded the paper once more, then got up with some effort to return it to the owner. "Danke," he said, then sat back down heavily, wincing. No doubt about it – his feet were hurting him.

"Are you all right, mein Herr?" Donny asked, faking concern.

The man gave him another sharp look. "Fine. Why do you ask?" he said, leaning back in his seat.

"You seem in pain," Donny said.

"Ja. A minor accident. Tell me, what is your name?"

Here we go, Donny thought. "Carl Strausshind. Und Sie?"

"Friedrich Moeller, Herr Strausshind. A pleasure to meet you," the policeman said, extending his hand.

He didn't show his credentials, nor ask to see mine, Donny thought. *Was I wrong?* Their eyes met briefly as they shook hands, and Donny knew he'd been right – definitely a cop of some sort.

"You have business in Pilsen?" Donny asked, immediately regretting it. *Now he WILL show you his credentials, you idiot.*

"Ja. A minor paperwork dispute," Moeller said.

Careful, Donny told himself, nodding. They were well into the countryside now, and the train had sped up. Fields encircled by hedgerows and low stone walls flew past.

"And you? May I ask, why are you going to Prague, Herr Strausshind?"

Donny was untying his bag of meager possessions and didn't look up at Moeller, but into the sack instead.

"My cousin is very ill. I am going to visit her," he said casually, as he reached into the sack.

"Oh, that's unfortunate. What's wrong with her?"

Donny didn't reply right away, but instead pulled a large, juicy apple from the bag, along with the small chunk of cheese he'd purchased, then took out the folding knife the farmer's wife had thoughtfully included, and began cutting apple slices onto a clean handkerchief on his lap. He popped a piece of apple into his mouth, speaking around it.

"They don't know, that's the problem. She's very sick. They keep giving her tests, but they still don't know," Donny said, letting a little anger creep into his voice. He looked up at Moeller as if remembering a guest. "Would you like some apple? I have some cheese…" he said, offering the handkerchief to Moeller, who looked at him oddly, his dark eyes piercing and bright, obviously those of an intelligent man. Warning bells went off in Donny's head again.

Moeller smiled. "Danke. One piece perhaps, just to taste it? It's been awhile since I had an apple."

"Nein. You must share my lunch, poor as it is," Donny responded.

"No, just one piece is fine," Moeller said, taking a slice of apple and biting into it as Donny began slicing cheese onto the handkerchief, throwing the apple core and seeds out the open window. Something flickered in Moeller's eyes, but he didn't know what it was.

"The apple… iss gut, no?"

"Ja. Best I've had in years," Moeller said.

"Then please, by all means, take more… and some cheese. It's very sharp, very nice," Donny said, offering the meager meal again with what he hoped was an encouraging smile.

Moeller smiled again. "All right then, I will. Danke schön."

"My pleasure. I am just sorry I have no bread or sausage to offer you."

"Nein, mein Herr. I thank you for sharing your lunch with me," Moeller said between bites.

Donny held up his hand and shook his head. "It is little enough as a snack – hardly even a lunch," he said. They were finishing their meal just as the train began slowing and the conductor came back through the car announcing the Prague main railway station. Donny looked out the window and, to his shock, saw what looked like an entire division of German soldiers waiting on the platform.

31

Moeller's Journal, August 29th, 1944 (continued)

There is no end to a policeman's intuition – no way to turn it off. Take, for example, the man who got on the train at Pilsen and seated himself across from me. At first I took him for a poor peasant from Austria, but when he told me he was traveling to Prague to visit his sick cousin, my antennae went up. First of all, if she were that ill, wouldn't she more likely be in Vienna, at the Medical University of Vienna with its famous medical facilities? Why would they send her to Prague if she were already in Austria? Vienna was nearly 100 kilometers closer. Second, although his German was perfect, his accent was not that of an Austrian. Silesia, perhaps? Those two things were, of course, not enough to convict him, but his responses seemed far too erudite for a farmer, and the way he cut up his meager lunch of apple and cheese (which he so kindly shared with me) spoke of better breeding. Also, his hands seemed soft for a farmer, and he threw the apple seed from the core out the window, rather than saving them as I would suppose a farmer might. But perhaps I'm wrong. I'm sure farmers have plenty of apple seeds, after all.

All my instincts tell me he's up to something, but what? Likely smuggling of some sort. If he were Resistance, he would have given himself away, I think… although I've met some pretty cool characters. No, I will leave him alone, but I will not soon forget Herr Strausshind. Perhaps once Marie and the children are safe, I will look into his background a bit. Scheisse! Just look at all the troops on the platform. Headed for Slovakia, no doubt. Wouldn't they be of better use in Normandy and Brittany fighting the invasion? This war tires me.

32

Once in Prague, Donny's instructions were to go to the brewery at 1:00 p.m. and order two Bocks – a strong, local beer, and to tell the bartender he was meeting a friend. If the bartender responded, *"I hope for your sake the friend is female,"* he was to laugh and say, *"Yes, but she's no pushover."* This was the fourth time he'd used Elena's radio, and he found that he couldn't wait to see her. Thoughts of her made him antsy and uncertain – he hadn't felt anything like this since Peggy… and she'd died in '42 of diptheria. He was overseas when she'd gotten sick, and typical of her, she'd waited too long before going to the doctor. She was gone before he knew it.

It had devastated him. They'd been together since the beginning of the war, and it was because of her that he'd ended up being recruited by the Office of Strategic Services: the OSS. In retrospect, stealing the mayor's Lincoln had been the best thing that ever happened to him. He got the girl, and an exciting new career. A year after she died he'd dated a bit, and had had a few women casually, but other than a brief fling with a female operative in Greece early in the war, it had never felt quite right to him for some reason. He'd simply concentrated on his job, which he was very good at. But the minute he'd met Elena, a Czech Resistance radio operator, he'd been smitten. He wasn't used to the feeling, being both nervous yet comfortable at the same time with her.

As he had a little time to kill, he walked around the ancient city, playing tourist, then went to the Kavárna Slavia with its high windows and restrained ambiance, ordered two beers, and settled in to wait.

"Hello, darling. Did you have to wait long?" Elena said, throwing an arm around his shoulder, and as he turned to her, she kissed him – warm and soft, tasting slightly of cigarettes. It was just a quick, hello kiss, purely to reestablish their cover, but he felt it all the way to his knees. She pulled back and smiled. Donny smiled back. It was too easy. The same woman, and what a woman.

"I got you a Bock," Donny said, but she sipped it, made a face, and told the bartender it was too warm and to get her another. The bartender gave Donny a look that told him he was dismayed that she'd kissed him. She took a sip of his beer while waiting for hers, and Donny had to admire how natural she seemed – as if they had known each other for years and hadn't just recently met. He knew her name but very little else, other than the fact that he found her irresistibly attractive. There was just something about her he couldn't get enough of, and it wasn't just that she was pretty. At times he felt that she was attracted to him, but mostly she was all business, at least when she wasn't pretending to be his girlfriend. He found it maddening. He wanted to know all about her, but of course in their business, information was not shared freely, particularly personal information.

Elena prattled on about this friend or that, and despite not having a clue as to whom she was talking about, Donny found it easy to listen to her. She was very attractive, somewhat pixeish, with brunette hair tied in a simple tail behind her head, blue-grey eyes and a pretty, pug nose, but he realized that her real beauty came from a vivacious spirit that burned brightly within her like a lantern, attracting men like moths.

They spent a pleasant hour talking and laughing, drinking beer, and Donny found that he was actually enjoying himself for the first time in a very long time. To lose yourself in the simple, pleasurable company of a woman. *When will this damn war be over?* he wondered, as she suggested they finish their beers and go back to her place.

It was a beautiful, cool summer night, without the constant drone of bombers as you'd hear most anywhere in Germany. Prague was still far enough from the Allied bases to have avoided being bombed, and for a minute Donny nearly felt like a normal human being – just a guy strolling home with his girlfriend, her arm tucked around his waist possessively, their strides matching as if they'd already slept together, the lights of the city throwing circles of light onto the cobblestones at their feet. *No blackout here?* Donny wondered. He knew the Czech underground literally *was* underground – there was an entire level of an ancient, secret city beneath their feet, beneath the streets and buildings of Prague—but he had never been invited there; it was Resistance only. He was only allowed to use the radio set and the cryptography unit at her apartment to send coded messages as needed. Even that had to be approved through Resistance high command because of the danger—the Germans ran radio triangulation cars around Prague nightly.

It was her trade craft that brought him back out of it, as she whispered, "Stop and kiss me. I'll check behind us." Donny did so, but the moment was lost – her kiss a dry well. They took a roundabout way back to her place, establishing once and for all that they weren't being followed, and once inside the foyer she was all business. The locked foyer and stairway were dimly lit. Several fixtures were missing light bulbs, impossible to get at this stage in the war. Elena led him up an ancient, creaky staircase to the next floor and unlocked the door to her apartment quickly, then stepped inside, holding the door for him, waving him inside urgently with one lovely hand.

Donny stepped into the darkness, and as she closed the door behind them and locked it, he heard movement inside the room and realized he'd made a mistake. A floor lamp was switched on, but before his eyes could adjust, one of the two men in the room stepped forward and punched him in the stomach, knocking all the air out of him.

"Search him," the man sitting in the chair said as Donny knelt down on one knee, trying to get his breath back. He knew that whether Gestapo or Resistance, it was useless to resist, but it pissed him off. He thought again about what that damn Scotsman had told him at Camp X and what he had to say about fighting with the wind knocked out of you, and when the guy who'd sucker-punched him grabbed his shoulder, he came off the ground like a coiled spring, giving him a surprise uppercut that snapped the man's head back. His eyes rolled up and he fell back against the wall, then slumped down to the floor, shaking his head like a dog; not knocked out, but clearly shaken.

Donny looked at the man in the chair coldly. He was finally getting air, his lungs aching with the effort. "Hell of a welcome," he said in Czech.

The seated man raised an eyebrow. "You can't be too careful these days," he replied as his bulldog pushed himself to his feet and glared at Donny. Donny saw him clench his fists and knew he was in for it. Well, fine. He had his breath back now and he was pissed. The guy was bigger than he was, but

Donny was Irish – he just didn't have any back-down in him.

The bulldog took a step toward him and Donny stepped back onto his right foot and brought his hands up in the loose defensive stance William Fairbairn taught all the Jedburghs and Joes – OSS agents such as himself.

"STOP. Let him be, Anton." The bulldog took another step.

"I MEAN IT. Leave him alone. You both got one shot in, that's enough. Save it for the Germans," the man seated in the chair said sharply. The bulldog took a step back, but pointed his finger at Donny as if to say, *Later.*

Donny relaxed somewhat, abandoning his defensive posture as the man in the chair stood, coming forward to meet him, offering his hand.

"Jan Moravek," he said. "And you are?"

"Carl Strausshind," Donny told him as they shook, giving him his current alias.

"Are there many Strausshinds in America?" Moravek said in English, letting Donny know he wasn't fooled.

"I'm sorry, I don't speak English," Donny replied in Czech. The Germans would often switch to English to trip up suspected spies. The OSS and SOE spent a lot of time doing the same to inure their agents to such tactics.

Moravek smiled. "Then perhaps we'll speak in German, eh? Your 'native' tongue?" he said in German.

"My Czech is passable, but weak. Yes, German would be better," Donny said, lapsing back into Deutsch.

"May I see your papers?"

"May I see yours?" Donny replied – the only correct response. Jan Moravek laughed, clapping him on the shoulder. "All right, you're clear. I have to ask you, though – why do you want to see Albert Göring?" he said, suddenly serious again. Donny looked at the bulldog, then at Elena.

"It's all right, you can speak freely. They're cleared for this."

Donny took a deep breath. "I want to ask him if he's heard of Operation Eagle Claw. As far as I can tell, it's something to do with long-range bombers."

Moravek shook his head. "I don't know specifics, but I know Junkers and Messerschmitt are both building some very large planes right now. There are rumors..."

"Yes?"

He shook his head. "No, it'd be better for you to hear it directly from Albert. He's at his country house outside Brno at the moment. He's heard some things firsthand from his brother. We weren't sure if it meant anything, but we decided to pass it along."

Donny didn't like the idea of Dulles being ahead of him on this – it made him feel like an errand boy. Moravek was already at the door, which the bulldog prepared to open for him. "We'll go out the back. I have a car – we can be in Brno in three hours. Let's go."

The bulldog pulled the door open, and Jan Moravek led the way, and Donny followed, but before he could pass through, Elena grabbed his hand. He turned to look at her and she smiled. "Come back and have another beer with me, eh?" she said.

"Perhaps when this is all over," Donny said, and she raised up on tiptoes to kiss him primly on the cheek. Donny smiled. "This damn war..." he began.

"Let's go," the bulldog said, roughly slapping Donny on the back. Donny turned and got in his face. His breath smelled of onions.

"Perhaps I'll see *you* after the war as well, eh?" he said to the bulldog, who just smiled at him and nodded enthusiastically. Donny noticed he had a tooth missing on one side, likely from a previous altercation. Moravek was waiting impatiently on the landing. "Let's go, it's nearly curfew," he said, as Donny passed into the hall, the softness of Elena's kiss still in his mind.

33

They crammed themselves into a small, odd-looking car whose front end reminded Donny of a 1938 Chrysler Airflow – curvy and futuristic, but odd. It was his first time riding in a Skoda. He wasn't all that familiar with Prague, having been there just a few times, but he knew when they left the city. Heat lightning flashed silently on the western horizon, then he realized that it was lightning of a man-made type: bombs being dropped somewhere in Germany, and he couldn't help but wonder about the people beneath them.

God knows he had no love for the Nazis, but his German grandmother had raised him, taught him to be a good man, and he'd spent many happy vacations in Germany, unaware that his grandmother's frequent trips were missions to deliver food and money to her relatives and loved ones starving in the post-WWI fatherland. Donny was exhausted, and fell asleep propped up shoulder to shoulder between Jan Moravek and the bulldog, relying on them to awaken him when they got there. In his line of work, you slept when and where you could.

Jan shook him awake seemingly minutes later, but nevertheless Donny felt refreshed. They were on a dark, narrow road that wound back and forth between tree-lined, ancient fieldstone walls stacked by farmers centuries earlier.

"Where are we? I thought we were going to Brno?" he said.

"We're outside Brno now. Don't worry, it's safe," Jan replied.

They turned left down a long, narrow drive, which led to a large country manor built of finely cut stone, with a steeply pitched roof and a chimney at each end, and Donny wondered idly how old it was.

Lights were on downstairs, but otherwise it was dark, and the grey stone seemed foreboding – the same color as a Tiger tank, which Donny knew

Skoda helped build as well. They climbed out of the tiny car with difficulty, and the door was opened just as they reached it by a tall, aristocratic man with Valentino hair wearing a smoking jacket. He welcomed them even as he hurried them inside and shut the door.

As the aristocrat turned back from locking the door, Jan Moravek said, "Albert, this is the man I told you about. Herr Strausshind, meet Albert Göring."

Göring offered his hand and Donny took it, the firm grip showing surprising strength from a man with such a cultured, almost effete exterior. Göring seemed to be sizing him up shrewdly, as if deciding something.

"Your reputation precedes you, Herr Strausshind," he said.

"As does yours, Herr Göring. I must say, however, your true allegiances are still a matter of some debate in our organization."

Albert sighed, nodding as he let go of Donny's hand. "I can't say I blame them. Trust the brother of Reichsführer Hermann Göring? One would have to be a bit mad, wouldn't you think? Would you care for a drink, Herr Strausshind?" he said calmly, as he led them out of the hall and into a room that Donny would label as a parlor or sitting room, filled with expensive antiques. *Pretty tony,* he thought. *Clearly he's not hurting for money.*

Göring went to a sideboard fairly covered with cut glass decanters of various types, as well as a few American whiskey bottles and some expensive French brandy Donny had only heard of. Far too rich for his blood.

"So? May I offer the OSS a drink?" he asked Donny, turning to him with a smile, holding a decanter he'd just uncorked.

"Bourbon if you have it," Donny said.

"Ice? Water?"

"Just neat, thanks," Donny said.

"Jan?"

"American whiskey? Yes, thank you."

Donny noticed Albert didn't ask the bulldog – either he didn't drink, or as security he wasn't supposed to.

Albert Göring poured him a healthy three fingers out of the decanter and brought it to him with a smile, gave Jan his, and raised his glass. "To the

Nazis' defeat," he said in English, surprising Donny. The three of them clinked glasses and drank.

Albert sighed theatrically, holding his glass up to the light, perhaps to admire the color. "Damn good booze, I have to admit. You Americans certainly know how to make whiskey. Now, how may I help you?" he said, waving Donny into a comfortably overstuffed chair as he leaned back against the sideboard, crossing his arms.

"We've come across an interesting program, called 'Mistel' or 'Mistletoe' in English," Donny said. "It involves piggybacking small parasite fighters on the backs of bombers for defense. Our analysts believe the Germans are preparing another air offensive against the United States or Britain. I understand Skoda is building one of the parasite fighters," Donny said.

"The SkP.14.02, yes. The German High Command however, decided the Messerschmitt 328 was a better design, so they've canceled the program. There were… production delays with the Skoda fighter," Göring said, earning a smile and a wink from Jan Moravek. Obviously the Resistance had something to do with the delays.

"So the 'Amerika Bomber' program isn't a threat?"

"Well, it's true that the 'Amerika Bomber' program was designed to turn New York City specifically into a smoking ruin, and a Junkers 390 actually flew within just twelve miles of New York – close enough to take photographs before returning. The program has recently been put on hold for now by Albert Speer… although it has not been completely abandoned. Der Führer wants to bomb America in the worst way, but the Luftwaffe needs more fighters to protect Germany against your bombers.

"To that end all money and resources earmarked for the '*Amerika Bomber*' project is going into a number of new jet interceptors: the Me163, which is operational, but dangerous due to its hydrogen peroxide fuel mixture; the Me262, of course, which is a superior fighter in every way, and the He162, the 'Volksjager' or 'People's Fighter.' If they can get them into the air in sufficient numbers, and if they can find enough pilots to fly them, they could potentially decimate the bomber formations. They are simply faster than anything the Allies have, you see."

"They'd need a squadron of bombers to level New York," Donny said.

Albert was shaking his head. "Nein. They would need just one or two. They have an entire squadron of bombers waiting in Norway – moved there because of expectations that you might invade. Of course, you invaded in the wrong spot. Made it very inconvenient for my brother and his cronies," Albert said with a smile, pouring himself more whiskey. "More?" he asked, holding up the decanter.

Donny shook his head. "No, thanks, I'm fine. I don't understand what just one or two bombers could do against New York... and if they have the bombers, why not use them?"

Albert looked at him seriously. "It's a matter of range. They can reach the U.S., but it's impossible to return, especially when carrying a bomb load. It's even more problematic now that the French coast is in allied hands and they've lost the airfields there. They've been working on refueling the bombers while in flight, however..."

"*What?* How the hell would you do that?" Donny said.

"I don't know the specifics, but apparently they have not one, but three or four designs they've been playing with. Once they are confident in the new technology... of course, being bombed day and night has made development of *anything* problematic. Well, that is, other than the atom bomb."

Donny looked at him, trying to decide if he was serious. He'd heard of atom bombs of course – he'd been briefed on the possibility of their existence; they'd even been in the papers, both in London and the U.S., but they were still hypothetical. Sure, there had been several references to one in the Eagle Claw file, and it was being whispered that the Germans were working on one, and likely the U.S. and England as well, but that information was way above his pay grade. He simply found the whole idea fantastical.

"You look skeptical, my friend. The Germans *invented* nuclear physics, Herr Strausshind. They have no less than five separate development programs, from what I understand. These are very smart, committed people. It is quite likely that they will succeed. If they do? Well, one or two atomic bombs dropped on New York or Washington would certainly get the Americans' attention, would it not?"

"Bullshit."

"Nein, Herr Strausshind. Not bullshit at all. For some time there have been rumors of a vengeance weapon unlike anything used so far. A single, large bomb that could level a city using the power of the sun. There is talk that smaller ones could be fit into the V2 rockets. Imagine the use of even a small one on a battlefield. Didn't you get the information we sent? I thought that was why you were here."

Unfortunately, Donny knew that it was likely the Czech Resistance's report was languishing in a pile on someone's desk, as it had been pretty much decided that any report from Hermann Göring's brother could not be trusted.

"The parasite fighters are just another small part of the entire picture. The idea, of course, being each bomber could carry one or even two such small fighters to help defend them during the attack. Junkers, Heinkel, and Messerschmitt are all developing huge, long-range bombers which they hope will have the range to reach America and still return. As I said, fuel consumption is the main problem. The invasion has made long-range bombing more difficult... fortunately for you," Albert finished.

"Can they do it, do you think?" Donny said.

"It's hard to say what they can accomplish. Fanaticism has its own energy. Plus, the bastards have a huge pool of slave labor. Hundreds, if not thousands, of Jews and other 'undesirables' are dying in the camps and secret factories every day."

"You know, I've had briefings and have heard the same rumors everyone else has – they even wrote it up in the London *Times* and the Washington *Post*... but I can't believe the Germans actually have an atomic weapon."

Göring didn't falter. "I've overheard my brother, who as you know is not only head of the Luftwaffe, but head of Reichswerke Hermann Göring, of which Skoda is only a part, speaking about this. From what I overheard, they are very close. They will test this weapon soon, perhaps this fall. They are positively frantic about it. A Junkers 390 has already flown a polar route to Japan, and as I said, within twenty kilometers of New York City – close enough to take photographs of the skyline. They are very close to pulling this off."

A low whistle came from the front hall where the bulldog had stationed himself. Jan frowned and set down his drink, ducking quickly into the hall. Just as quickly, he was back.

"A car just pulled up in front. Two men – they look like Gestapo."

"Come with me," Albert Göring said, setting down his drink and striding quickly into the hallway. Approaching the stairs from the side, he touched something on the trim of the wainscoting that Donny couldn't see and a small, triangular section of panel popped open. He swung it wide to reveal a dark hole. Donny could hear car doors slamming, then footsteps scuffling on the walk outside.

Albert held a finger to his lips, then in a low voice said, "There are electric torches at the bottom of the ladder. Follow the tunnel to the end. The door opens inward – like a garden gate, and comes out on the river. Go downstream and stay off the road. Parallel the road back to Brno and catch the bus to Prague. I'll bring you your car in the morning. Give me your keys," he motioned to Jan as the pounding on the door began.

"Quickly!" he hissed as Jan climbed into the dark gap, then onto a hidden ladder. Donny went next, then the bulldog. Albert closed the secret panel as the pounding on the door intensified, and they were plunged into total darkness, reduced to moving only by feel. Donny could hear Göring's footsteps on the wooden floor above him as he went to answer the door, but concentrated on climbing down the ladder so he didn't step on Jan's fingers, and more importantly, so the bulldog didn't crush his.

Somehow they made it to the bottom in the dark without anyone getting hurt, and found two flashlights at the bottom on a small ledge. Jan flicked one on just as Donny's right foot hit dirt, and he could see that they were in a small space lined with rock, obviously separate from the rest of the foundation. It seemed very old and he couldn't help but wonder what purpose it had originally served. A root cellar, perhaps? Then the bulldog flicked on the other flashlight and he saw the tunnel. The torch flickered, and the bulldog hit it with the palm of his hand, making it come on again, but the beam was unsteady.

"Leave that one here," Jan said in Czech. The bulldog turned it off and left it on the ledge, muttering something Donny didn't catch. He was too busy listening to the altercation that seemed to be developing upstairs.

The tunnel was low enough that Jan had to stoop to get inside. He paused at the entrance, gave them a look, then disappeared inside, taking the light with him. Donny followed him, with the bulldog once more bringing up the rear.

The tunnel, tight to begin with, was narrowing, its ceiling gradually pushing them lower and lower until finally they were on their hands and knees. This did not seem to bother Jan any, but Donny was sure he'd heard a whimper from the bulldog behind him, and he wondered if the big man was claustrophobic. The tunnel was uncomfortable even for him – he couldn't imagine how the bigger man felt.

Finally the bobbing light in front of him stopped, and his hand bumped Jan's shoe. He could see Jan checking the perimeter of the tunnel for something, then he heard a click and a groan like a heavy door opening, then fresh, cool air spilled across his face. He heard Jan move forward, up and out of the hole, and Donny scrambled after him, rolling out onto the cool, midnight grass as Jan helped the bulldog out of his temporary perdition.

There was another groan as Jan closed the trapdoor, then the rustle of brush as he re-camouflaged it. He'd turned off the flashlight, and Donny lay on his back, catching his breath, looking up at the stars. He could hear the gurgle of water, and felt more than saw a large body of water nearby, somewhere off to his left. By his reckoning, it was either the Svratka or the Svitava River. Brno sat at the confluence of the two, so all they had to do was follow the river back to town, or catch a bus, although at this time of night that seemed unlikely.

Jan quickly used the flashlight to inspect the concealment of the trapdoor, then shut it off and tucked it into a nearby hollow tree, pushing it to the back. He came back to Donny and the bulldog.

"The road should be back in this direction. Let's go," he said, gesturing in the dim light.

Walking back to Brno in the dark, only the stars lighting their way, Donny had time to think about what Göring had told him. The very idea of a weapon powerful enough to level New York made him reel. The idea that the Nazis might get it first… well, that was simply unacceptable.

The whole thing was making more sense now, though: Fighters had a much shorter operating range generally than bombers, which was why the new P-51 Mustangs were so important. For the first time, fighter escorts could accompany bombers deep inside enemy territory, and as soon as the Allies consolidated their gains in France and Italy, they could begin using former Axis airfields – giving them the range to now hit targets such as the Skoda factories in Prague, Pilsen, and Brno, as well as all of Austria.

Even the Mustangs couldn't fly across the Atlantic, however. No wonder the Germans were experimenting with parasite fighters. If each bomber could carry one or two tiny jet fighters along with them, they stood a decent chance of penetrating American airspace long enough to drop a few bombs… bombs with the power of the sun.

Not only that, but if the Germans used such a weapon in France, it would set back the invasion months, perhaps giving the German army time to recover. If such a bomb were successfully used on New York or Washington— or London, for that matter—well, all bets were off. Donny knew the key was the bombers. There's a weakness in every plan, and if they didn't have the bombers to reach the U.S., well, the crazy bastards might set one off in France, but at least America would be safe. He imagined once more New York disappearing in a firestorm and shivered, shoving his hands into his pockets.

They caught the bus to Prague in Brno, and Donny was surprised that by the time they got there, Göring had somehow managed to return the car to Elena, who also had a manila envelope for him. When she handed it to him their hands touched, and their eyes met. He felt an unexpected flash of heat, of longing for her as she looked at him, giving him a sly smile.

"Albert hopes that this will help. Let me know if I can be of any more assistance," she said.

"I certainly will," Donny said. "I look forward to seeing you again."

Elena just smiled, giving him an indecipherable look as she closed the door.

* * * *

Once back in his hotel room, Donny looked at the contents of the envelope. On a single sheet of paper were typed the names of six locations, each with the type of aircraft being produced or tested there, and detailed notes as to security. The first location had an asterisk next to it, and was located near Sankt Georgen, a small town near Linz, and the addendum noted that Eagle's Claw was supposedly being developed somewhere in the nearby area, and that a huge underground aircraft and bomb factory had been built with the use of slave labor from the large Mauthausen-Gusen prison camp complex, which included several satellite camps. This jibed with what Donny had read in the file he'd stolen, so it interested him greatly.

There were also pictures of various aircraft, so he could correctly identify them. He committed the list of airfields and factories to memory, then burned it in the ashtray. Two of the locations he was sure would be nearly impossible to get into, but some of the others were good possibilities – the first an airfield near Cologne where the Junkers 390 and "Mistel" system of piggybacking a parasite fighter were being tested. He remembered Krefeld airfield from the Eagle's Claw file. Donny decided to begin there, even though it was clear on the other side of Germany. He wanted to head straight for St. Georgen and Gusen, to the underground facility, but he needed time to figure out a plan, plus he didn't know exactly where it was. Bumbling around in the woods near a top secret facility would just get him shot. Besides that, how was he going to get inside to verify the intel? In the meantime, he could check out one or two of the less dangerous sites – the airfields. He looked at the clock. If he hurried, he could catch the 1:00 p.m. train…

34

Moeller's Journal, August 31st, 1944

I am afraid of being caught in my first lie. I'd told Gephardt that I "strongly suspected" the killer would try and infiltrate the Skoda Works to find out more about the Skoda parasite fighter, but in truth I had no idea. I was grasping at straws. Desperate to free my family from Mauthausen, I planned on visiting each facility mentioned in the research papers he'd stolen from the lab. Prague, and by extension, Skoda, was the closest, so I decided to start there.

In Prague, the Skoda representative suggested I go to the Brno office with my request – they professed no knowledge of the parasite fighter project. Perhaps once they saw my new SD credentials, they decided to pass the responsibility up the chain to Brno. I didn't trust their motives, so I asked around in Prague and was recommended to SS Obergruppenführer Karl Hermann Frank, the General of Police in Prague. A tall, leathery, unsmiling man, Frank had become infamous for the "liquidation" of the village of Lidice in retribution for Reinhard Heydrich's assassination June 4th, 1942, by British-trained Czech and Slovak Resistance fighters. I didn't relish the thought of meeting such a brutal Nazi, but if anyone had any ideas about whom I should speak with, or have information about the Skoda Works, it would be him, so I went.

Franks was as unpleasant a man as his reputation suggested, and I could see that, SD credentials or not, he was not impressed with me. Perhaps if I had been wearing a leather coat, Gestapo-style, and better clothes? But I have no time for clothes shopping, and was never much of a clotheshorse anyway. Marie always bought my clothes, and I wore whatever she gave me without complaint, save for one loud yellow shirt that I absolutely refused to wear.

Truthfully, I think now that she bought it as a joke, just to see if I were paying attention.

Franks was not much help, but he pointed me to a gauleiter named Sauckel, who was in charge of labor conscription for the Reich. His office sent me to Field Marshal Erhard Milch, who kindly helped me with a list of likely targets that the OSS agent might find attractive.

I've set up a temporary office in my quarters at another cheap hotel, which still feels luxurious after nearly a year in Fuhlsbüttel prison. I requisitioned a corkboard, a small pile of index cards, and some thumbtacks and have set up my "murder board" in my new "office." Unlike our proud party officials and gauleiters, I care nothing for ostentation – it will serve. I am like a hunter chasing a fox. I will find him, pin his hide to my wall, and free my family. Gephardt has agreed to get a letter to Marie, in Mauthausen-Gusen. This quest is all that I live for. Hold on, Marie, my love. I'm coming to get you.

35

September 14th, 1944, near Cologne, Germany

Donny lay in the tall grass on a small hill overlooking the airfield. Ostensibly he was taking a break from the heat, the bicycle on its side in the long grass, just off the road far enough that he was pretty sure he wouldn't be seen. He knew if he were caught with the binoculars, checking out the airfield, that he'd be shot as a spy… but hey, that was the job.

There were several aircraft on the field, including one of the new Me262 jet fighters, which was getting some sort of armament modification from what he could tell – a huge cannon that he couldn't believe they intended to put in it. He recognized a Fiesler Storch, an He111 converted for passenger transport, and two other aircraft – the ones he was there to see. The first was a Dornier Do217, with an odd, tripod-looking mount atop it, mounted over the wing, which Donny recognized from the blueprints he'd stolen and the model in the lab as the mount for a parasite fighter. The Mistel program, they called it, *Mistel* meaning "mistletoe" in German; an odd name, but apropos he supposed. Even the Germans apparently had a sense of humor.

The other aircraft took his breath away. It was the largest airplane he'd ever seen, with six huge radial engines and a wingspan nearly as wide as the airfield. From where he was, he could see someone moving in the cockpit, which looked tiny in comparison with the rest of the plane. From the few photos he'd seen from the lab, he was fairly sure it was a Junkers 390 – the plane he'd come to see. That the Germans were actually able to build this plane—along with another long-range design, the Messerschmitt 264 "Amerika Bomber"—this late in the war, despite the privations caused by air raids, spoke volumes about their commitment to long-range bombing.

Albert had told him he'd heard from his brother that there'd been developmental problems and delays, most of them caused by the Allied bombing effort, but they'd still managed to build two prototype 390s and this, an operational, final design with improved range. In Augsburg, at the Messerschmitt facility near Munich, they'd also succeeded in building two prototypes, and had another design for a six-engined bomber that was even bigger. Göring had told him that his brother Hermann had once, in his cups, told him the war would be over as soon as the bombers were ready and the Eagle's Claw V-weapon was tested.

Donny knew he'd likely get nowhere near the top secret bomb program itself – no one had any clue where it was, although smart money said either somewhere around Prague or Peenemunde, where the V2 research and development program supposedly was. Donny could imagine the devastation even a small atomic weapon delivered by V2 rocket on London would cause. The Blitz would seem a field day in comparison. He was so deep in thought he didn't hear the footsteps behind him until it was too late.

"RAUS. SHOW ME YOUR HANDS," the German soldier shouted from behind him.

Donny rolled slowly onto his back, raising both hands, the binoculars in the weeds behind him. The soldier was young, but clearly experienced, keeping his distance so Donny couldn't rush him; his Kar98 pointed steadily at Donny's gut.

"Up," the soldier said, gesturing with his rifle. Donny got to his knees, then to his feet, keeping his hands raised. The soldier gestured with the rifle, indicating Donny should walk past him, backing up to keep his distance so Donny couldn't grab the gun. Donny's mind raced as he moved slowly forward, the German now behind him.

They walked past his bicycle and approached the road, where Donny now saw another young soldier, this one carrying an Mp40 submachine gun. Just the two of them – and on foot? Donny knew now why he hadn't heard a vehicle – there wasn't one. They must be a roving security patrol from the airfield. He silently cursed his bad luck. Or was it stupidity? Of course they had patrols, it was a secret airbase. Donny just didn't think he'd run into one this far out.

"Was ist? I was tired from riding up the hill," he said over his shoulder. "Is there any law against taking a nap?" If he could get them in closer, he stood a good chance. Otherwise…

"Do you normally take naps with field glasses, Herr?" the German behind him said. Donny turned enough to look at him. The soldier was holding up his binoculars. "You will be shot as a spy. *After* you are interrogated," the soldier said. The sound that had been getting slowly louder in Donny's ears resolved itself; a truck was grinding its way up the hill. He saw the field radio at the feet of the soldier with the Mp40 and knew that this was it. More soldiers would be here in minutes. Unless he killed them both in the next few seconds, he was lost.

He'd been tortured by the Germans before, and he wasn't going through *that* again, no sir. When he got closer to the radio operator, he'd rush him, and the one behind him would shoot him in the back… or maybe Donny would get lucky and he'd miss. If Donny could just get hold of that Mp40 the radio operator was carrying loosely in one hand…

They were about seven yards away when the radio squawked and the German knelt to answer it, setting down the submachine gun to use the radio. *Just what I need,* Donny thought, as a grey-green transport truck preceded by a BMW motorcycle with sidecar rolled around the bend below them. *More Germans.* The truck was towing a Flak 38 20mm gun: a lethal, four-barreled monstrosity that Donny had once seen in action in Greece: the gunner had absolutely shredded a group of Greek partisans with it. Another truck followed it, grinding in tandem up the long hill, and he then realized it wasn't a truck sent for him, but just an armed convoy passing through.

Three yards now. The other soldier was speaking into the handset, the convoy just 200 meters or so away now, and Donny cursed his luck again. Should he wait until the convoy passed and hope the military police sent up the hill to pick him up weren't right behind it? If he were wrong, he'd never get this chance again. *It's now or never,* he thought, launching himself at the soldier using the radio.

36

The German looked up in surprise and blinked as Donny plowed into him. Donny heard firing and waited for the bullet that would hit him in the back, ending his run, but it never came. He realized as he tackled the radio operator that the firing was too fast for a Mauser, and the shots were coming from somewhere else – further down the road. He knocked the German on his ass and focused on snatching up his submachine gun, grabbing it off the ground as he somersaulted over the radio. The soldier recovered quickly, dropping the radio handset and reaching for his weapon, but it was no longer there. He looked at Donny with horror, scrabbling for his sidearm, and Donny put a short burst in him from where he lay on his back on the ground, knocking the German backward. He raised himself enough to see the other soldier facedown in the road, wondering who his saviors were, the sound of firing loud now, as an invisible force attacked the German convoy. Suddenly a hand fell on his shoulder, and he recoiled. A teenage girl with her blonde hair in braids, wearing a jungschaftsjacke—a sort of anorak favored by youth groups—was shaking him.

"WE HAVE TO GO BEFORE THEY DEPLOY," she yelled over the gunfire, then dove for the radio operator's ammo pouches and canteen, cutting them from his field gear with a practiced hand. She glanced at the column just below them, then darted out into the road to secure the first German's Mauser and ammo, this time unhooking the belt, but slicing the braces free. Running low, she gave Donny the meanest look he'd ever seen from a teenage girl. "Are you coming or not?" she said, then turned and ran toward the tree line. Donny saw Germans pouring out of the transport trucks and decided to follow her.

37

The girl moved through the woods so quickly and expertly that Donny had trouble keeping up. The sound of firing was sporadic now, and Donny hoped it was just the Germans taking potshots, and not executing wounded Resistance fighters.

The trail led downhill, through lush woods – a lichen-covered cliff rising on their left, and what looked to Donny like huge rhododendron bushes on the right, the canopy overhead gradually darkening their path until they were in a magical, Hansel and Gretel forest. He almost fell following her as she danced effortlessly across a moss-covered log, looking back over her shoulder briefly to make sure he was still there.

Another cliff face rose on their right – not very high, but old rock, covered with moss, small trees clinging to narrow ledges. The trail skirted the huge boulders, then dropped off precipitously to the left, the trail oddly sandy here. Donny watched his footing as he followed her carefully around a rock outcropping, hugging the rock, then she was gone – into thin air, it seemed.

Donny looked around, surprised, but there was no sign of her, and the trail seemed to end where he was standing. Suddenly someone grabbed his ankles, jerking him off his feet, and he was falling off the narrow cliff trail, totally off balance. He hit the sand, then was being dragged backwards, which his mind told him was impossible – his senses told him he was being dragged into the cliff. It was dark, and he rolled over, kicking at the hands around his ankles. He saw a flash of a face, then someone hit him, hard, and everything went black.

38

Donny came to laying on sand, head aching. He heard low voices, could smell wood smoke, and had the presence of mind to only partially open his eyes, still feigning unconsciousness. About ten feet from where he lay were five teenagers: three boys and two girls, one of them the one who'd saved him, sitting around a small fire, cooking what looked like rabbit or a small hen. Donny hadn't eaten all day, and the smell was intoxicating.

He opened his eyes wider, and saw that he was in a small cave, dim light filtering in from somewhere above – the smoke from the fire following the light out. A few decrepit bolt-action rifles, one of which he recognized as an old Steyr carbine, two Mp40s, one likely the one he'd been carrying, and a Mauser which he was pretty sure was the one the girl had taken off the dead soldier, were leaned up in a pile against the rock face.

He rolled over and groaned, pushing himself up on one elbow, causing two of the boys to scramble from their places at the fire and approach him. One of them wore the same sort of anorak the girl wore, the other, a taller blond boy, wore a simple leather hunting vest with large, deep pockets over a checkered shirt and an alpine-style climber's hat. He also held a Walther P38 and kept it pointed at Donny as if he meant to use it.

"Who are you? You aren't from around here," the older boy with the pistol said.

The other three had come to stand behind him, all looking at him curiously.

"My name is Carl Strausshind… and who are you?" Donny replied, using his current alias.

"We are the Ehrenfelder Navajos, and we saved your sorry ass from the Nazis. Tell us who you really are, or I'll shoot you right here."

"Don't do that, Hans – we'll have to drag him down the trail to bury him," the girl who'd saved him said.

Donny decided enough was enough. He quickly swung his leg around, hooking the youth with the gun behind the knees with his kick, collapsing his legs, and was on him before he hit the ground, tearing the Walther out of his hands, then pointing it at the others as he got to his feet.

"Believe me, I don't want trouble," Donny said. "I appreciate your help, but I had everything under control."

"Right. You mean when you were about to get shot in the back?" The tall boy the girl had called Hans spat from the ground, fire in his eyes. Donny had to admit it: these kids had spunk. He smiled.

"Well, okay. Maybe that wasn't part of my plan," he said, clicking the safety on and transferring the pistol to his left hand, holding it backwards so it was clearly no threat. He offered his right hand to the boy on the ground, who, after a second's hesitation, took it, allowing Donny to pull him to his feet.

"I can't give you my real name. Strausshind will have to do... but I'm American OSS," Donny said, offering the pistol butt first to the tall youngster, who took it back and stuck it in his belt, nodding.

"I'm Hans, this is Pieter, the girl in the green hat is Dana, that's Geoff with the submachine gun, and you met Katherine on the road."

"How many of you are there?" Donny asked.

Hans looked at him. "Here now? Just us five, but there are thousands of Edelweiss Pirates in Germany, hundreds in our group alone."

"It's none of his business, Hans. Don't tell him any more," Katherine said.

"Shut up, Kat," Hans said, clearly used to being obeyed.

Donny tried not to grin. These kids were tough, and smart. "Let me get this straight. You attacked an armed German convoy? Just the five of you?

This time it was Katherine, or Kat as Hans had called her, who responded.

"It was just a diversion. Saved your sorry ass, didn't it?" she said. He figured she was about fifteen, Pieter looked fourteen or so... maybe. Hans seemed oldest, but still had to be younger than seventeen – when military conscription would take him.

"Mein Gott," he said. "You are all either very brave or very foolish. Thank you. Thank you for saving me," he said, which seemed to please them, although they did their best not to show it.

"I managed to grab your field glasses," the young woman named Kat said, as she stepped forward to hand him the binoculars.

"Danke," Donny said, not knowing what else to say. Despite their bluster, the kids were right: they'd saved his bacon.

"You were watching the airfield, ja?" Hans said.

"I'm sorry, I can't tell you," Donny replied.

Hans looked disappointed in him. "You are interested in bombers, ja? You think we are just children who cannot be trusted."

"I think it would be better for you, and for me, if when the Germans catch you and interrogate you, that you don't know anything important," Donny said.

Hans shook his head. "Nein. We know of others as well – A jet bomber with two jet engines, but looks like a Heinkel 111, with a greenhouse cockpit, but smaller, almost a fighter. Its wings are like this," he said, making a slight V-shape with his hands.

"You're sure of this? A jet bomber?" Donny said. "You don't mean the Messerschmitt jet fighter?"

Hans was shaking his head. "Nein. We have seen that plane also, but this is different. We can show you... except you have to promise me to try harder not to get caught this time," he said.

"I'll do my best," Donny said, while suppressing a smile again. "Now, can you take me to this plane?"

39

Albert Göring was one of those people it was simply difficult to dislike. Aristocratic, erudite, gracious and well-dressed, he projected power in a way that was hard to resist, although he had kept me waiting.

Hermann Frank had warned me of his openly anti-Nazi politics, something I found quite curious in the brother of Reichsführer Hermann Göring, and which raised him in my estimation considerably, since I despise hard-core Nazis like Frank, despite my current position as an SD investigator, tenuous as it is.

Although Göring was solicitous and cautiously polite, he gave me no information worth having, which frankly, was about what I'd expected. He had no reason to help me, and every reason not to. Still, he *was* export director for Skoda Works and verified that Skoda had been working on a "parasite fighter" for use with bombers, but told me the program had been shelved months earlier in favor of the Messerschmitt 328.

His eyes flickered a bit when I asked him if he'd ever heard of a program called Eagle's Claw, and I was sure he was lying when he said no. Likewise when I asked him about the Junkers 390 – he told me he'd heard Junkers was working on a long-range civilian transport plane for after the war, and we both knew he was lying, but he seemed not to care a bit. I suspect he even knows that one of his secretaries, Fräulein Hertha Auer Von Radenstein, is a Gestapo informant, according to some records I'd accidentally been given.

Albert Göring is nothing if not shrewd, although from what I read in his file, he was somewhat fearless in defying the Nazis – refusing to salute, even taking off his jacket and getting down on his hands and knees to scrub the cobblestones alongside a group of older Jewish women assigned the task as punishment. I nearly laughed aloud when I read the file, imagining what the SS troopers charged with overseeing the work detail must have thought at the time, although most of the damning evidence against him was regarding his penchant and ability to save Jews from the camps – actually getting them released with the help of his powerful brother, Hermann Göring.

He had done this not just once, but to my surprise, on several occasions, with no apparent regard for his own safety. In fact, he'd been arrested several times by the Gestapo… yet each time his brother had come to his aid, and Albert literally laughed off the arrests, which, according to his file and Hermann Frank, had placed him squarely in the Gestapo's sights. They hated him, but couldn't touch him without incurring his powerful brother's wrath, and as Reichsführer Hermann Göring was still Hitler's heir apparent, he was not to be trifled with, no matter what his brother Albert did.

Recently in fact, he had shown up at a concentration camp with several trucks, demanding prisoners for a work detail at Skoda. Once well away from the camp, he'd reportedly stopped the trucks and released them all into the woods – an audacious and inherently dangerous plan, even for him. Of course, he claimed the trucks had broken down, and the prisoners escaped, but everyone knew the truth. Albert Göring hated the Nazis and the Nazis hated him.

As I was leaving his office at Skoda, he shook my hand and gave me a shrewd look. "Herr Moeller, may I ask you something personal?" he said.

"Certainly," I replied, surprised.

"You seem a decent sort – not the usual SD type. Why do you work for those animals?"

My estimation of him rose even more. He was truly fearless to put such a question to an SD agent.

"I'm not really SD. I was a Kripo investigator for many years. I'm investigating a murder."

"But why? What are they holding over your head?" he said.

"Why would you think that?" I replied, frowning.

"Oh, come now, Herr Moeller. You look as if you recently got out of prison yourself. Thin nearly to the point of emaciation, needing your hair cut

– you have the look of a haunted man about you. And your limp – did they beat the soles of your feet? Cut them?"

I looked at him, shocked that he'd seen so much. Clearly I'd underestimated the man. I didn't know what to say.

"Come, tell me what the bastards have on you. Political dissident? Using your family against you?"

I couldn't help but flinch – he'd struck a nerve.

"That's it, isn't it? They're holding your family until you finish your little errand for them. One of their favorite, and most despicable ploys. Where are they keeping them, do you know?"

I felt lost. This man, the brother of one of the most powerful Nazi generals, had guessed my secret. Could I trust him with all of it?

"Mauthausen, I am told. They are in Mauthausen," I said quietly.

I saw a brief look of concern cross his face – a mere wrinkling of the brow before an encouraging smile replaced it.

"Mauthausen? Why, that's one of the better camps, really. Practically a vacation resort," he said. I knew he was lying, but appreciated it. "What are their names?"

I described my wife, Marie; lovely fifteen-year-old Anna, the apple of my eye; and of course, Sascha, my brave, five-year-old little man. As I did, I realized I was crying. Mein Gott, what must he think?

"Do you have a picture of them on you?" he said gently.

I nodded, pulling out the ragged photo of them I kept in my wallet. It was all I had left of them. He took it gingerly and smiled at me, placing a hand on my shoulder.

"Let me see if the blueprint department can copy this. Please, compose yourself while I check. Write down any other pertinent information for me and I will look into their whereabouts. I assume you've not heard from them in some time?"

I shook my head. "I was in Fuhlsbüttel police prison for eight months. I've made inquiries since I got out, but…" I said, wiping my eyes with the back of my hand.

He smiled at me encouragingly. "It's not unusual for people to get lost in the system. I will check with my contacts. Make sure you write down where or how I can get in touch with you."

I must have looked alarmed, because he put his hand on my arm. "Trust me, I'll be discreet. We'll talk more when I get back. Please, have some Kaffee from that carafe and pull yourself together. We'll find your family," he said with a wink, then let himself out and closed the door. *Mein Gott!* I thought. *What have I done?*

40

September 16th, 1944

The kids were smart. They left the weapons in the cave, telling Donny it was just one of many such caches. They knew better than to attack the Nazis directly, but would occasionally if there were a prisoner they wanted to free, and had once bombed a Gestapo office in Dusseldorf, but explosives were hard to get, and Donny got the sense they weren't comfortable with them. He couldn't blame them – he'd *had* demolitions training, and the damn stuff *still* scared him.

They mostly did stuff like puncture tires on untended trucks and staff cars, painted anti-Nazi slogans in train stations and over Nazi propaganda, and beat up the Hitler Youth whenever they got the chance – in other words, making as much of a nuisance of themselves as possible. Of course, nothing they did made it into the newspapers like *Das Reich*. Nothing like that happened in a perfect Reich. Donny could tell that this recent raid – the hit-and-run that had freed him – was a pretty big deal to them, although they tried not to show it.

Hans told him they rode the trains all the way across Germany sometimes, and were always nice to German soldiers, pleading ignorance of not having the right stamp or rail pass. Kat and Dana were particularly good liars, and charmed the soldiers—many of them not much older than themselves—with stories of a last camping trip before military service and subtle bribes of fresh apples and cheese from Katherine's uncle's farm.

He said Katherine aspired to be an actress, and Donny had a front row seat to witness her thespian abilities when she took his arm to help her "uncle" to his seat on the train. He was still sore, and limping slightly from his misadventure at Hohensalzburg Castle, so not much acting was required on his part. They'd even grayed his hair slightly with a paste made from wood ashes and water. Once safely ensconced on the train, he asked where they were going, and Hans told him Sankt Georgen.

St. Georgen. Back to Austria. He asked Hans how some kids from Cologne knew about a top secret project in Austria, nearly an entire day's travel away. Hans told him the constant bombing had disrupted the regular school schedule, and many kids just stopped going, as was their right at fifteen, so they spent their days riding the trains, exploring their country before it was completely turned to rubble.

Dana chimed in and said there were literally thousands of Edelweiss Pirates, as they called themselves, but only a few dozen who dared ride the rails the way they did. He asked them if they weren't afraid they'd get bombed themselves, with the drone of Allied bombers overhead nearly constant now, day and night, but Pieter piped up and said the Allies seemed to be concentrating on bombing the cities, and the war industry there, and they had a theory that the Americans wanted to save most of the railroads to use themselves once they moved inland.

Kat added that they'd been strafed a few times by American fighters, but that was just part of the thrill. What she didn't like was when the engineer would stop the train inside a tunnel to wait for a bomber group to pass over. She had a fear of being buried alive in one of those damn tunnels someday, but the others laughed it off the way kids do. All of them had seen horrible things by this point in the war, and they seemed inured to it – fatalistic even. Donny just hoped they'd never get to see the worst of it.

What scared Donny far more than Mustangs strafing the train was his lack of a legend. These kids might laugh off not having the right papers or stamps, and could talk their way past a checkpoint, but Donny was clearly still of service age, and although a businessman centered in Essen, with contacts in Prague and Vienna, he had no real reason to be in Austria, and hadn't had time to appraise Dulles as to where he was. Every time they came into a station he feigned interest in an old copy of *Das Reich* someone had left on the seat next to him, hoping no one would notice the grass stains on his trousers, or his lack of a briefcase.

While he read the dreck and propaganda in the weekly rag, his guides were seemingly holding a meeting: heads folded together over a seat back, their voices low and urgent, and by the way one or the other would glance at him from time to time, Donny was pretty sure they were discussing him.

Finally the confab broke up, and Katherine came over and sat next to him, her mouth grim and set. She looked around the car surreptitiously, but they'd picked the car because it'd been nearly empty, and the last two passengers not in their group had gotten off at the last stop.

"Do you have any recent wounds or scars?" she asked him sub-rosa.

"Other than the leg? A few," he said, surprised. "Why?"

"Any on the head?"

Donny gingerly touched the side of his scalp where it'd been torn by the grenade they'd dropped out the castle window onto him. It was still tender, and he winced.

"Let me see," she said, roughly grabbing his head and turning it this way and that to get a better look.

"Oww! Stop that. It's still healing," he said, annoyed.

"Perfekt. Now listen carefully. You are a veteran coming home from the front. Your head wound prohibits you from continuing service to the Reich. You aren't all there, so put that stupid paper down – you aren't fooling anyone. Now listen to me. I'm your niece, so if you speak, call me Kat, not Katherine… in fact, it'd be better if you didn't speak at all. Now give me your best vacant stare – as if you're brain damaged."

Donny tried, but she just shook her head and clucked. "Terrible. Listen to me. Your brains have been scrambled. You aren't right in the head, get it? Here, put this on," she said, raising the ribbon of a Ritterkreuz – a Knight's Cross over his head and arranging it on his chest.

Donny stared at her in amazement. "Where did you get this? They'll shoot me for wearing this," he hissed, moving to take it off.

She stayed his hand with hers. "That's exactly why this is going to work. Now give me your papers, we don't have much time. Practice looking brain damaged – it should come easily to you. If you could drool a little out of the side of your mouth, that would be good."

Donny opened his mouth to say something, but didn't know what to say.

"Better. Leave your mouth open a little like that, and stare at the seat in front of you vacantly. No, blur your focus a little. Listen, you'd better practice this, we only have a few minutes until the next stop and they'll be checking papers."

"They'll be expecting me to have a military pass," Donny said. "This isn't going to work."

"Better than a businessman from the other side of Germany with no briefcase and grass stains on his pants. If you could stumble and fall getting off the train, that would be good. I'll help you, 'Uncle,' because your balance is off. Now, keep your mouth shut and try and look like a war casualty," she said. "Let me handle the soldiers. Just look damaged."

Donny did his best to look battle-scarred as the conductor came back through the train, staring blankly out the window at nothing, mouth slightly agape, doing his best to effect the look he'd seen on far too many valiant young men on both sides of the war who were shell-shocked and broken.

The conductor frowned as he compared the picture on the military ID and pass Kat had lifted off the same soldier she'd "borrowed" the Iron Cross from when flirting with him earlier. Apparently he was having trouble with the resemblance.

"He doesn't look like his ID," he said to Kat.

"Well of *course* he doesn't. If you'd survived a Russian rocket attack and had been sewn back together in a field hospital, I doubt you would either!" she said fiercely, taking Donny's hand. He pretended not to notice – continuing to stare out the window.

"I'm taking my uncle, a *Knight's Cross winner*, home to be with his family. Do you have nothing better to do than harass war veterans?"

Suitably chastened, the conductor stamped both their passes without even looking at hers, gave her a smile, and with a last sideways glance at Donny, continued down the aisle.

"I told you it would work," she whispered to Donny, letting go of his hand as soon as the conductor had left the car, the door sliding shut behind him.

Donny looked around slowly. It was just the six of them in the car for the moment. Hans leaned over the back of their seat, smiling. "No one messes with Kat," he said.

"I just hope this airplane of yours is worth all this," Donny said. "That could have ended badly."

"Oh, it is, trust me," Hans said.

"Hans wanted to be a pilot before the war," Kat said.

"I *still am* going to be a pilot… just not for the damn Nazis. They'll need pilots after the war too, just you wait," Hans said.

Another passenger was coming in from the car ahead of them as the train began to move out again, and Donny went back to staring out the window vacantly – once more the damaged war veteran, but although his eyes stared blankly ahead, his mind raced, trying to put together the puzzle, fearful that he already knew what it meant – an atomic attack on America.

41

The next morning, Donny found himself once again atop a small hill, laying prone in thigh-high grass, peering through field glasses at the rear of the Mauthausen-Gusen concentration camp complex below, sure now that this was the same underground manufacturing facility as in the file Albert Göring had given him. Hans lay on his left, Kat on his right, with Pieter, Geoff and Dana as lookouts, watching their flanks to prevent a repeat of last time.

If the Germans had this small jet bomber, and the other huge plane he'd seen outside Cologne as well, which he was pretty sure had been a Junkers 390, then the Allies were in trouble. He'd hoped for a glimpse of the Messerschmitt 264 – just the name "Amerika Bomber" sent chills down his spine when he'd read it in the documents he'd taken from the lab.

He lowered the glasses. "I don't see any jets down there, but they could be inside the tunnel, I suppose. Amazing really, how they built it into the side of the hill... wait, the doors are opening."

They watched silently as two airmen trundled the huge camouflaged doors in the side of the hill open – the effect being as if they were literally opening up the side of the hill itself, revealing a dark, gaping maw beyond.

After a time, Donny saw the nose of a plane he was sure was an Arado Ar234 jet bomber—the plane the kids had told him about—emerge from the darkness, being pulled out into the morning sunshine by a small tractor-like crawler hooked to a long cable.

The plane was black and sleek, with a huge jet engine tucked beneath each wing. The one-man cockpit reminded Donny somewhat of an He111, with a clear dome built out of vacuum-formed plexiglass – but smaller. Four fork-like antennae stuck out of the front, looking very odd, and Donny made a mental note: they obviously had some sort of useful purpose or they wouldn't be there. There were German crosses painted on the rear of the fuselage, about halfway to the tail, and a red swastika with white trim on the tail itself. What he assumed was a radio wire ran from the fuselage up to the tip of the tail.

The wings and engines were still detached, on separate skids, obviously to be installed later… or was there an airfield nearby? Several trucks were lined up to deliver parts; the remains of a war materiel convoy, obviously. Donny had never seen anything quite like it. Clearly it was too large to be a fighter, approximately the size of a British Mosquito, but with the jet engines obviously much faster. "I need to get in there," Donny said quietly, more to himself than them.

"That's just crazy. An underground factory full of guards—surrounded by a *prison camp*—and you think you're going to get in there… not to mention back out again?" Hans said. "Sorry, but we can't help you with that."

Donny looked at the boy, too soon becoming a man, and smiled. "Don't worry, I know just what to do. Right now, though, I need to get back to Linz. What I really want to know more about is the bomb load on this thing," Donny said.

Kat frowned. "I don't understand. A bomb is a bomb… some are just bigger than others. A miserable invention, if you ask me," she said.

"An invention of misery," Hans agreed.

Donny couldn't share classified information with them, nor did he want to. If the atom-splitting bomb the Germans were working on was as powerful as he'd been led to believe, well, it could change the course of the war, despite the current success of the Allied invasion. He was hoping that Fuhrmann's papers had been returned to his widow in Linz and that he'd be able to recover them and use them again to have duplicates made. For that matter, if they hadn't gotten too much blood on them, maybe he could just use them as is. He cursed again his decision to plant them back on the body. He took some more pictures with the Minox and took one more look at the airfield, wondering where this smaller jet bomber fit into the picture, then began sliding backwards, crawling out of his nest.

"Let's go," he said.

42

Moeller's Journal, September 16th, 1944

I left Albert Göring's office scared but hopeful. He claimed to have contacts inside several camps, including Mauthausen, and assured me that if my family was there, he'd find them, and let me know how they were.

The entire thing has me feeling conflicted, I must allow. I had never failed to finish an assignment – had never let a killer go free... but now that I was sure that the ice pick murders were not the work of a madman, but that of an Allied agent, I wondered if what he was doing would shorten the war. Was I, by extension, helping the Nazis lengthen it?

Still, despite my dislike and distrust of Eberhardt and Hermann Frank, I *am* still a representative of the Reich, like it or not, and although I despise the Nazis and everything they stand for, as a loyal German, I do not want to see such an agent succeed. An OSS agent at large in Austria and Germany could possibly affect the outcome of the war, and despite my antipathy to the current regime, I am still a German patriot, and old enough to remember Germany's sad fate after the First World War. I do not want to see it happen again. Like many, I hope for an armistice... but at this stage of the war I doubt the Allies will settle for a draw.

If we could hit them at home, in New York, Washington, London—hit them hard enough to take the fight out of them—perhaps then we could sue for peace. What scares me is the article I read in the *Völkischer Beobachter* a few days ago, an editorial by our great madman himself, and I quote: *"Not a German stalk of wheat is to feed the enemy, not a German mouth to give him information, not a German hand to give him help. He is to find every footbridge destroyed, every road blocked – nothing but death, annihilation and hatred will meet him."*

This sort of rhetoric scares me. Would Hitler destroy the country simply to keep it out of the hands of the enemy? At this point in this madness, I'm afraid I have little doubt that he would do just that.

More than anything, I simply want my family to be safe. My particular fate is of no importance. I just want Marie, Anna, and my little Sascha to be safe and happy. The one sure way I know to do that is to catch the OSS agent. I would like to trust Albert, but I don't have the luxury of time – my family is at risk. I pray that they are still alive wherever they arc, warm, not sick, and have enough to eat. Please, Lord – I beseech thee. Watch over my family. Help me find the enemy agent. Bring me my fox so I can nail his hide to the barn.

43

September 20th, 1944

Donny sipped a Pilsner and stared moodily out the tall, ceiling-high windows of the Café Slavia. It was raining, and across the Vltava River, Prague Castle slowly disappeared then reappeared out of the mist, and he wondered idly what Prague had looked like in 880 A.D., about the time the castle was being finished. Charles Bridge eased in and out of the mist as well, and all the history represented by the ancient city weighed on him. Would all this be destroyed now that Prague was in range of American bombers? Would what he was doing actually help defeat the Germans, or was he just kidding himself?

Donny didn't get melancholy very often – he was a pragmatist. He did his job and tried not to look too deeply at circumstances – that was someone else's problem, and way above his pay grade. Still, this new technology could change the outcome of the war: the idea of a bomb or bombs with the power of the sun, being dropped on New York or London from an advanced, long-range German bomber gave him chills, but losing Prague in a firestorm caused by American bombers would be every bit as tragic… and of course, he worried about Elena.

Once he'd reported in, he'd wait in Prague for new orders, but he was already sure he knew what Dulles would want: verification that such a weapon existed, that it was indeed a viable threat, and, of course, a location so that they could target it with bombers or a raid. What if the project was centered here in Prague? Then Donny would essentially be responsible for the destruction of the city – a city he'd come to love during his many trips here. It had to be done, however. How he would find out the location of such a top secret program, though, he had no idea.

He looked up and smiled as Elena came in, her slim form moving lithely between the tables as she came over to him. She gave him a dazzling smile as she came closer, and he remembered the feel of his arm around her as they walked, and the lilac smell of her as she raised her face to his to be kissed. *Too bad it was just an act,* he thought. This woman had awoken something inside him that clearly needed to be fed.

He stood, and she stepped into his arms, put a small, soft hand on each side of his face and kissed him. Donny tried not to be surprised, and slid his hands down to her narrow waist, but he knew his performance was a bit wooden, despite a stirring in his loins. He pushed the images of Prague, London, and New York as burning pyres out of his mind.

"What's wrong? Aren't you glad to see me?" she whispered in his ear in Czech.

He drew back and gave her a genuine smile. "Yes. Yes, I'm *very* glad to see you," he said, looking her in the eye. He saw her eyes change momentarily, softening into something else, and for a second it was real. Then she turned away from him to wave at the bartender, whose name he did not know but knew he should, making the sign for a beer with one finger, then glancing at the table and seeing what he had left in his glass, shook her head and changed it to two, the barman nodding his assent.

"Please, sit. It really is wonderful to see you. You look beautiful," Donny said. They both sat, close to each other, fingers tangled together, knees touching, just two lovers who hadn't seen each other in some time.

"You really should have let me know you were coming, darling. I'm supposed to be at work," Elena said.

"Truthfully, I was in Vienna and heard *'La Vie En Rose'* on the radio, and decided that I simply must see you, so I came straight here," Donny said with a smile.

"How sweet," Elena said as their drinks arrived, and she pulled her hand loose and slid back to give the bartender room to set them down on the table.

"Thank you, Yuri," she said in Czech.

"Yes, thanks, Yuri," Donny said. The bartender gave him an indecipherable look and turned back to the bar.

"I don't think he likes me," Donny said in a low voice as she fished out a cigarette, then took a sip of her beer. He pulled out a lighter and lit it for her, and she took a deep drag then blew it at the high ceiling.

"Oh, it's not that. He's just overprotective," she said. "He doesn't trust anyone I meet."

The idea of her meeting other operatives—other men—disturbed Donny for some reason, even though he knew there was nothing between them. Jealousy would be silly. *This is just a game we're playing,* he thought, but there was something about her, something in her ready smile and the way she laughed that drew him in—a moth to her flame—and he found himself yearning for her in a way he hadn't yearned for a woman in years. It was more than simple lust – he wanted to get to know her, to hear her secrets… to make her laugh.

"I haven't heard *'La Vie En Rose'* on the radio in ages," she said, letting him know she got his reference to using her radio, and that she wasn't sure whether it'd be possible.

"Perhaps they'll play it while I'm here. It would mean so much…" he said.

She raised an eyebrow, giving him that wry smile that made the gears in his heart slip a cog. "Perhaps. I haven't danced in ages," she said, her eyes on his, and for some reason he felt as if they were no longer speaking in double entendres.

Elena's apartment was as he remembered it, sans the goon stepping out of the darkness to clobber him. They'd taken a roundabout route there, just as they had the last time, just in case someone followed them, but he sensed something different in her this time. It felt less as though she were treating it as a job to be done, and almost like a real date. Donny had to admit, walking around Prague in the evening, with a vivacious young woman on his arm, was pretty damn wonderful. For a little while, he nearly forgot the war.

He looked around again as she closed the door – the apartment was small but clean, with a kitchenette in one corner, and a Murphy bed folded up against one wall. Elena pulled off her sweater and tossed it over the back of an overstuffed chair with the easy familiarity of someone in their own home. She put water on to boil, and pulled two old, but lovely cups down from the simple shelf over the sink.

"Tea or acorn coffee?"

"Whichever, is fine," Donny said.

"Fine. Eichel-kaffee it is. I'm nearly out of tea," she said. "We'll have to drink it black – cream is not easy to find these days."

He smiled at her. "That's fine," he said.

As she was lighting the stove, he came up behind her, placing his hands on her hips, his face in her hair, so he could smell her. She didn't resist, but instead leaned back against him, the soft swell of her buttocks against his groin as he pulled aside her hair with his right hand to kiss her slender neck, his left sliding around to cup the soft, gentle swell of her belly as she shut the gas off, tossed the unlit match aside and turned to him, meeting his lips with hers, her arms now around him, her fingers playing at the back of his neck, his need pressing against her now as he pulled her closer.

She let out a small mewl of pleasure as his mouth explored hers, her hands in his hair, on his back, then finally, grasping at his belt, tearing at his trousers as he shucked up her dress to get his hands under it.

Donny felt ready to explode. Both her hands were on him now, stroking, cupping, teasing, but as he picked her up by the buttocks she pulled her hands away, wrapping her legs around him, her arms around his neck again. She pulled back from the torrid kiss a moment to look at him. "I don't think you're going to make curfew," she said.

"How do we get the bed down?" he asked, but instead of answering, she unwound her legs from around him and stood briefly, taking his hand, first pulling him down to the floor, then straddling him.

"Later," she said. "This first."

44

Donny awoke early, to the gentle weight of Elena's head on his chest, her slim arm slung across his waist possessively, her breathing deep and slow. They'd made love several times, the intensity of it a little shocking. They'd taken a break after their lovemaking on the floor to eat some cheese and grapes, drinking wine out of heavy, green-stemmed Roemer glass goblets she told him had come down through her family, Donny wearing nothing but his trousers, Elena in nothing but his button-down shirt, her pretty, naked legs tucked demurely under her, which for some reason he found incredibly erotic.

He told himself that it was the fact that the Gestapo might burst in at any minute and haul them away—that the risk of what they were doing added spice to an undoubtedly temporary relationship—but when he looked at her, popping a small piece of Muenster with a grape perched atop it into her pretty mouth, he felt happier than he could remember being in years.

He wanted to know everything about her – wanted to stay right there with her, abandon the OSS, the war, his duty… just disappear with her somewhere they'd never find the two of them… but he knew he couldn't. He kissed the top of her head gently and breathed in her scent, allowing himself to fall back asleep – a short reprieve from what he knew was coming.

When Donny awoke next, she was gone, and as he blinked away the sleep, he could hear her moving quietly around the corner in the kitchen, doing something. She came into the room carrying two cups of what passed for coffee these days, really just acorn or chicory-flavored hot water, and handed one to him as he sat up on the bed. Donny smiled at her, but she looked away. She was fully dressed, and no longer wearing his shirt.

"Albert wants to see you. He says he has someone you need to meet."

"I need to send a coded message to Operations first."

"Not until you talk with Albert. Jan came by this morning on his way to work to tell me."

"Wasn't Albert arrested?" Donny asked.

"He's been arrested before. They can't hold him – not with a brother as powerful as Hermann Göring."

"So, we're going back to his house in the country, I assume?"

"No. *We're* not going anywhere. *You're* going to the Skoda Works to meet with him. I'm to give you this," she said, handing him a folded slip of paper. It was a gate pass for the Skoda plant, with instructions that Herr Strausshind was to be brought directly to Albert Göring for a meeting at 9:00 a.m. "You'd better wash up, you're going to be late," she said. "I heated some water so you can shave." She seemed colder, withdrawn – a completely different woman than he'd known last night. Donny grabbed her wrist, wanting her to sit next to him, but she pulled away.

"No. We're both likely to be dead soon. I just… can't," she said, turning her back to walk back into the kitchen. "You'd better get up."

Donny understood. Love and intelligence work was a poor mix. He sipped his coffee for a minute, the spell broken, the grey light of reality seeping in the window. He got up.

45

The scientist Albert Göring had wanted Donny to meet turned out to be a tall, bearded fellow whom Göring simply referred to as "Viktor." He seemed a bit nervous to Donny, clearly not cut out for intelligence work, but he had to give him credit for placing his neck clearly on the chopping block, which is where it would be should the Gestapo find out about his involvement.

He had a thin, leather satchel, which he gripped with white knuckles, as if it contained the secrets of the ancients. Donny didn't know *what* was in it, but it made him curious as hell. They were in Göring's office at Skoda, which Albert claimed was as secure a place as any. He told Donny that the Gestapo followed him everywhere these days, that anywhere else would look suspicious, and he wouldn't be able to control the environment. He had Jan sweep for bugs every morning, and again prior to the meeting, and assured them it was safe. Albert met Donny at the door, and once inside made introductions.

"Professor, this is Herr Strausshind. Herr Strausshind, Professor Herr Doktor Schauberger," Goring said, as Schauberger rose from his chair, clutching his precious briefcase.

"Heil Hitler," Schauberger said automatically, beginning to raise his hand, then looking immediately distraught at his gaffe.

Donny smiled as he extended his hand. "Very nice to make your acquaintance, Professor. Thank you for meeting with me," he said.

"You must forgive the professor – he has been spending quite a bit of time in meetings with the high and mighty lately, haven't you, Professor?" Albert said. The scientist nodded affirmatively.

"Please, gentlemen, sit. I have Kaffee and tea on the way. By the way, the lady bringing it is a Gestapo informant, so try not to say anything incriminating while she's in the room, won't you?"

This made the professor a shade paler, but Albert put his hand on his forearm, reassuring him. "Don't worry, Professor. Jan will warn me when she's on her way. Until then we can speak normally. Why don't you tell Herr Strausshind what your specialty is?"

The nervous academic looked at Donny. "I work in the new field of quantum physics – more specifically, at the moment, in nuclear reactions, or as some people refer to it, fission. I was forced into working for the Nazis, first in designing liquid cooling for aircraft, now at Mauthausen, doing this."

"He's helping make an atom bomb for the Nazis," Albert Göring said calmly.

The professor looked at him sharply. "I had no choice. I've tried to put it off as long as I could… delayed them as much as possible, but there are other scientists in the program who are becoming suspicious."

"How close are you to completing a bomb?" Donny asked.

"As soon as enough fissionable material arrives from the other programs, we'll be ready to test, now that my fuse design is 'finally ready,' " he said wryly. "We will likely test within the month."

Suddenly the intercom on Albert's desk buzzed loudly, making the professor jump – two short buzzes and one long one. Albert leaned over from where he was perched on the corner of his desk, his back to the door, and pressed a button on the intercom once.

"She's on her way," Albert said. Shall we discuss something else? Herr Doktor, *please* put that satchel down before you tear it in half. Please, this is a simple business meeting. Now, I don't think that Skoda can produce the kind of numbers of the VC-38 pillow block bearings you require in time, Herr Strausshind. They are needed for our own production, specifically the secondary spherical axle housings on the Hetzer…"

There was a polite knock on the door. "Come in," Göring said.

A rather stern, middle-aged woman, wearing what looked like a permanent look of disapproval on her face, entered with a tray holding two carafes, three cups, and a smaller glass bottle of milk, half full.

"I'm sorry, Herr Göring. There is no sugar left, and no fresh cream, but I found some milk," she said, setting the tray on the desk as he got up.

"Danke, Fräulein Von Randenstein. I'm sure that will be fine," Albert said.

"Will there be anything else, Herr Göring? Do you require me to take dictation?"

"Nein, Fräulein, danke. It is a minor meeting over our current bearing shortages."

"Sehr gut," she said, looking at Donny out of the corner of her eye. "Please don't hesitate to call me if you require anything further."

"Of course. Thank you," Göring said.

"I could pour the —"

"I will attend to it. Danke, Fräulein."

As she closed the door behind her, Albert held a finger to his lips and went over to the radio. "As I was saying, mein Herr, if I were to allow your company any of the VC-38 pillow block bearings, it would negatively impact our Hetzer medium tank production... for which I'd likely be hung."

As he spoke, he turned on the desk radio, but there was nothing but static. Three more buzzes came from the intercom, this time two long and one short. Holding up a finger, he slowly waved each of the items she'd brought into the room closely in front of the radio while continuing to speak – first the coffee carafe, then the tea, the cups...

"I'd like to hear your thoughts, Herr Strausshind," he said as he finally waved the tray itself near the radio, causing a sudden burst of louder static. Donny wasn't sure what to say, but he knew bullshit when he heard it.

"I'm quite sorry to hear this, Herr Göring. Skoda was our last hope in acquiring the necessary number of bearings for our project," he said as he watched Albert flip the wooden, rectangular tray upside down and search it thoroughly. Finally he smiled and pulled out his penknife, using it to pry apart one corner of the high-walled tray, exposing two wires: one red, one brown.

"Perhaps in a few more months we can help you with your requirements, Herr Strausshind," he said as he tore the red wire loose with the blade of the tiny knife, then hammered the corner of the tray back together with the heel of his hand. "But I'm afraid at this time it's simply impossible," he said, holding the tray close to the radio once more, this time without any burst of static.

Göring smiled at them and set the tray back on his desk. "It's a little game we play. The Gestapo tries repeatedly to bug my office, and I tear them out. Now, who wants Kaffee and who wants tea?"

46

"May we speak openly now?" Donny asked. Albert nodded, and made a motion with his hand for the scientist to speak.

"Although I am just a scientist, I have attended a few meetings where Eagle's Claw was discussed... and have overheard a few things," Schauberger said. "Operation Eagle Claw actually has two components: a long-range attack on the American East Coast, and the fire-bombing of London."

"Please, go on," Donny said.

"A flight of Arado Ar234s will attack London as a diversion, while a single, long-range bomber slides past at high altitude, headed for New York. They have been working on extreme long-range bombers since 1941 – bombers capable of hitting New York and Washington. Several planes have been developed; the Junkers 290 and 390, the Heinkel 177 and 277, and the jet-powered 274... which fortunately hasn't flown yet. Most recently developed is the Messerschmitt 264 'Amerika Bomber'."

Donny nodded. "I've seen a couple of these bombers. They're absolutely huge. What's stopping them from bombing America?"

Dr. Schauberger raised his eyebrows at this. "If you've really seen any of these planes and lived, you are either very lucky or very skillful. There are several technical reasons for the delays, but it boils down to two things: despite their size, the planes simply don't have the range to bomb America *and return*. The second reason is, the V5 and V6 weapons weren't ready yet, so they felt they had more time."

"Explain the range problem. Planes fly the Atlantic all the time," Donny said.

"Not fully armored against attack, carrying 5,000 kilogram bomb loads, armament, plus possibly 'parasite fighters.' They were very close to solving the problem through mid-air refueling... then the Allies invaded, pushing back any possible launch points even further. Nearly all the long-range bombers have been moved to an airfield in Norway, near Oslo. It's not as close as the coast of France, but closer to America than Germany."

"You said *almost* all the bombers…" Donny prodded.

The scientist nodded. "A few of the Junkers have been modified for transport – long-distance transport. Lightened in this way, with a nominal load of say, passengers and a reasonable amount of luggage or freight, even without with midair refueling, they could likely reach Brazil with no issues."

"Brazil! Why, that's—" Donny said.

"About 9,500 kilometers, yes. There is also at least one Me264 bomber left that has been modified with additional drop tanks. Coupled with in-flight refueling, its range could be as much as 14,000 kilometers. It's only about 6,300 kilometers to New York, so—"

"Wait. Let's go back. Are you saying that the Nazi High Command could possibly use the long-range Junkers transports to escape to South America?" Donny asked.

The scientist looked at him oddly. "Ja. This is what I'm saying. There are rumors that they've already begun moving gold by submarine."

"Okay… I want to talk about that some more later," Donny said, taking a deep breath. "But let me ask you, why keep just one bomber here? Why not send it to Norway with the others?"

Schauberger shrugged. "Perhaps because they have a limited amount of U-235. Even then, it takes time to build the larger device. We only have two larger devices available at the moment. One finished, one in the final phases. We have enough U-235 for a third device, then we will need to make more. I have heard a rumor that the Japanese are also building one, and have asked us for uranium and fuses to complete it.

The smaller, thermobaric version of the *Fritz X* bomb, the V4 vengeance weapon, is a different story. We have a number of them already, about 40, and they were tested in 1942 against the Russians. At a distance of 500 to 600 meters, everything was destroyed. The blast covered an area of over 4 kilometers, and flattened trees up to 12 kilometers away. This through the simple addition of coal dust to the device. If we had more of them during the

Russian campaign, things may have been very different. Of course, this is nothing in comparison to the atomic device, which itself will be ready for testing next month."

"Next month?" Donny said, a chill going up his spine.

"Ja, Herr Strausshind. It will be the first test of an atom-splitting bomb in history," he said sadly. "Then all bets are off."

47

Moeller's Journal, September 21st, 1944

I don't mean to sound prideful, but I'm very good at what I do. It's not very often I'm caught unaware. So I must confess, when the courier delivered the blow-ups of the security photos from the Fortress Hohensalzburg—the ones of everyone who entered the castle that night—I was genuinely surprised, so much so that I doubted my initial judgment… but the more I stared at the photos, the more certain I became that I *knew* this man – or had at least met him. I grew positive that it was indeed the fellow who had shared his meager lunch with me on the train from Pilsen to Prague.

Herr Straum… no, Strausshind. That's it. Carl Strausshind. Mein Gott, the look he gave me… I wonder if he realized that I'm a policeman? A cool character, I must give him that. Well, first thing tomorrow I will contact my old friend Ernst Meyer, the best criminal sketch artist I've ever known, and between the photos and my memory, we should soon have a good likeness of you, "Herr Straushind." That, plus two names: Buschausen, the name he used when passing himself off as an oberstleutnant, and Strausshind, the name he used with me on the train. I've sent Fuhrmann's new papers found on the body to his widow – a common enough mistake, even likely. The bloodstained ones were sent back to the RSHA. The killer took the temporary papers, which are still missing, so he knows replacements are likely in the mail. I'll put a couple of men on it to watch the house, just in case.

Correctly stamped papers are hard to come by, so I think it's likely you'll try for Fuhrmann's new papers, before she sends them back, and with the big brass balls you have, I have no doubt you would then try and pass yourself off as an officer, likely Luftwaffe, at a top secret facility again… but before then, I'll have you. Finally, a break! It's only September. If I can find you soon, I may be able to spend Weihnachten—Christmas—with my family… but no, I mustn't think like that. It's bad luck. Still, I've got the spoor now. It's just a matter of time, you bastard, just a matter of time.

48

September 25th, 1944

L inz was an old city, having been established originally as Lentia by the Romans, the name changing to Linz in 799 A.D. Full of four-story cut stone and brick buildings, it was the town of Adolf Hitler's childhood, and as such, it had done well during the war years, although some of its residents were less than thrilled at the Führer's plans to completely renovate the city – reforming it to match his vision with the help of Albert Speer, the famous architect. Still, many of the local gauleiters were rubbing their hands in glee at the thought of tearing the old town down and starting over. Perhaps if they'd known how all-encompassing Hitler's plans really were for their city, they'd have seen Linz, or at least much of it, as being sacrosanct.

Linz's best feature, in Donny's opinion, was that it straddled the lovely Danube River. Wide and slow moving, it was a natural highway, and the reason for Linz's very existence. Barges and tour boats plied its waters, although as of late lack of fuel had brought river tourism virtually to a standstill, although even now there was still a fairly steady stream of the faithful wanting to see Adolf Hitler's hometown.

Donny wasn't there to sightsee. He was there to see Fuhrmann's widow and recover the documents. He wished now that he'd simply held onto Fuhrmann's original papers instead of planting them back on the body, but the intent had been to make it look like a simple robbery, divert suspicion away from his activities, and create a dead end for investigators. He had wanted nothing tying Fuhrmann's death to his break-in at Hohensalzburg, although in retrospect, due to his dramatic exit from the castle, it hardly seemed to matter now. This might even better. Fuhrmann had temporary ID on him, which meant that proper identification was likely in the works and was sent either to his apartment address in Salzburg, or to his home. Sine Fuhrmann was obviously on a tight leash, Donny was betting it was the latter. Fresh identification was suspicious, but it was genuine, and the resistance people would 'weather' it and add stamps to make it look used. He figured it was a 50/50 proposition the ID was sent to the house, well worth checking out.

Still, as he approached Fuhrmann's house, a solid, sober, stone structure just three blocks from the river, he wondered if he was doing the right thing. It would simply take too long to get new papers, and he could no longer use the Buschausen papers—that cover was blown, so this seemed the best plan— but what if the RSHA had already recovered the documents? Would they even return them to his wife? Donny wasn't one for self-doubt, but he had a bad feeling about this for some reason. He was carrying a decent knife, instead of just the ice pick for this particular task, but it didn't make him feel any better.

As he strolled down the street, he realized that he should have taken a cab – no official of the Reich would show up on foot, as he had. He cursed and turned around to walk back uptown, when the door opened. He stopped and pretended to light a cigarette as Fuhrmann's wife came out the door, with her son in tow. She wore black, with a veil, and her son wore a starched Hitler Youth uniform. She turned to close the door behind her as her son aimed a kick at the cat crouched on the stoop, perhaps hoping to get inside on this cool autumn day. The cat dodged the kick successfully, but knocked over a small flower pot with a dead plant in it on the way down the steps. Fuhrmann's widow cuffed the boy in the back of the head and said something terse to him, pointing at the broken pot, undoubtedly telling him it would be his chore to clean up the mess when they got home.

They went out the walk and turned away from Donny, headed toward the bus stop, and Donny decided the direct approach was best. He waited five minutes, then crossed the street, walking at a normal, casual pace toward the Fuhrmann residence. As he walked, he canvassed his surroundings surreptitiously out of the corners of his eyes, checking the upstairs windows of houses opposite and keeping an eye out for moving curtains upstairs or down. He saw nothing. There were a few parked cars on the street, but they looked empty, and in any case, most were nearly a block away.

He turned onto the walkway, around a short, wicked-looking, spiked cast iron fence that would have been imposing had it not reached just above his knees, with short, roman-style spear points atop each vertical, approximately a foot apart. The short, silly fence wrapped around the yard, then turned on both sides to flank the walkway up to the front door, pretty much defeating the entire reason for a fence. *Purely decorative, bourgeois bullshit,* Donny thought.

He walked up to the front steps as if he lived there and, without knocking, tried the door. Like most doors in Germany, it was unlocked, although with the war, that was beginning to change. Things were so bad now, even a formerly trustworthy neighbor might be tempted to raid your larder while you were at work. Yet the knob turned, the door creaked open, and Donny stepped inside. Down the block, two car doors opened and two men in long coats and fedoras got out and began running up the street.

49

Donny closed the door quietly and stood listening for a minute, but heard and felt nothing. Quickly, he began searching the house for Fuhrmann's papers. First the study, then the kitchen, then the master bedroom upstairs. Nothing. He was beginning to think he'd been wrong. Had the RSHA simply caught the death in paperwork and never sent the new papers... or had they sent them to Fuhrmann's pied-á-terre in Salzburg? If so, he was out of luck.

As he came back down the stairs he noticed for the first time that the heavy, dark oak table in the front hall had two drawers, with wrought iron ring pulls on hammered steel diamonds. A few letters, recently opened, lay on top. He'd looked at the letters, but had missed the drawers somehow.

The left drawer held nothing but writing paper, a few pens, stamps with Hitler's unsmiling visage on them, and some envelopes, but when he opened the right-hand drawer, the one closest to the door, he saw a manila envelope addressed in a woman's hand to the Reich Main Security Office. It was heavy enough to require more postage – a few stamps wouldn't do, apparently, and Donny smiled as he sliced it open with the knife he pulled from the sheath behind his back, and dumped it out onto the table: Fuhrmann's fresh booklet of papers and travel permits, the covers stiff and new, still smelling of the printing press.

Suddenly the door flew open and two men burst in. Donny didn't think, he just reacted, as he had been trained. Seeing the first agent's gun, he swept it aside with his left hand while lunging forward to plunge the dagger he'd opened the envelope with straight into the German's throat. He wasn't sure if he'd hit the carotid, but it stopped the first agent dead in his tracks, in the doorway, blocking the second man from getting in. Even if he had a gun, which Donny bet he did, his partner's body blocked him from using it.

Swapping the knife quickly to his left hand, Donny grabbed the first agent's gun in his, twisting the gun brutally backwards, breaking the man's fingers and freeing the gun. He tore it away, reached over the agent's left shoulder and, aiming downward, putting four bullets into the second man's chest, rapid-fire. The second agent staggered backwards and fell off the steps, the look of surprise on his face matching the first agent's when Donny stabbed him.

Donny yanked the first agent into the room and threw him aside, into the staircase, then wiped off the gun quickly with his handkerchief and threw it aside. He wiped the bloody dagger off on the first agent's pant leg and returned it to the small of his back, under his coat, the first agent too distracted by the hole in his neck spurting blood and three broken fingers on his gun hand to do anything. He just stared at him in horror, unable to even speak.

Donny snatched the envelope from the table, dove out the door, and ran down the steps, past the dead second agent, his body impaled on the iron fence, sightless eyes staring up at the sky. He ran hard for a block and a half to put distance between himself and the crime scene, then saw a bus preparing to pull away from the curb and ran after it, yelling, "BITTE, BITTE."

Somehow either the driver or a passenger saw him, the bus squealed to a stop, and the door swung open. Donny leapt aboard, the envelope in one sweaty hand, breathless. "Danke," he said, giving the driver a wide smile. He paid the fare—a few pfennigs—and found a seat.

"Rough morning?" an older gentleman across the aisle from him said with a wink and a smile.

"Yes, most certainly," Donny replied. "A *very* rough morning."

50

Moeller's Journal, September 26th, 1944

It's funny the things you remember when you miss your family. I've been plagued by the strangest memories lately – like when we recently moved from Linz to Vienna so that Marie could finish her degree in art at the University of Vienna. Anna was old enough to watch Sascha by then, so we left her with him and went back to Linz for another load, hopefully our last. Our car wasn't very big, and we reasoned that if we left the kids at the apartment in Vienna, we could use the additional space not taken up by their squirming little bodies to fit the final few boxes in that trip – the hope being we might eat dinner at a reasonable hour, although I had already informed Marie that we were splurging on restaurant food for once. She gave no argument.

We made good time and were pleased that we'd managed to squeeze every last thing into the car, even though it was tight. We even had stuff stacked on the front seat between us. We'd come back in a day or so to give the apartment a good cleaning – we had until the end of the month, after all.

We'd left Anna with another direct order: she was to begin unpacking the dishes and kitchen and piling it on the counter. She could do the same with clothes, then take all the cardboard boxes she emptied down to the curb for the trash pickup. I was somewhat amazed when we got back to Vienna and found that she'd actually done what we'd asked her to and emptied a goodly number of boxes, and had even taken them out to the curb, instead of daydreaming or reading some foolish book. The only problem was, in the process, she'd lost her little brother.

"What do you mean, *lost?*" Marie asked her in the rare tone we all hated to hear.

Anna was a wreck – seriously worried, even tearful. I would have preferred to have this conversation inside, but she was so worried she met us at the street the minute we pulled up. You just know it's not good news when your fifteen-year-old daughter comes tearing down the stone steps two at a time.

"Liebling, start at the beginning. When did you notice he was missing?" I asked.

"About twenty minutes ago. I was bringing boxes downstairs to the curb, just like you asked, but when I went back inside, he was nowhere around! I swear, I left him inside by himself for just a minute!" she wailed.

"And you looked everywhere? All the closets?" Marie asked.

"Twice!" Anna said, as distraught as I've ever seen her. Although she could be flighty, she took her responsibilities seriously, especially when watching Sascha. I, however, had noticed some movement in the cardboard boxes, and wondered if it were a rat… specifically a 43-pound, four-and-a-half-year-old rat. I leaned down toward the stack of boxes as they shivered again. I tapped on one of the boxes with a finger, and was rewarded with a giggle.

Tearing into the boxes, we found Sascha, of course, not missing, but hiding, and inordinately pleased with his deception. If Marie hadn't taken a firm hold on Anna at that moment, I may have had to arrest my own daughter for murder – the murder of the aforementioned little rat. Of course, Marie told me I had to discipline Sascha, but how do you punish a kid for being a kid? I miss that boy, as much of a handful as he is.

Enough sentiment – time for notes: I have nothing to go on now other than my intuition. Operation Eagle Claw is simply too important for the Allies to ignore. The only question is, would they send the same OSS agent as before? To think that I sat across from him on the train – even shared his lunch – God does indeed have a twisted sense of humor. At least I know what he looks like, and know that he will likely try to pass himself off again as an officer, likely Luftwaffe.

It had bothered me at first that he'd stolen, then returned the colonel's papers, then I realized that the colonel was known quite well at Hohensalzburg. The OSS agent had to use another alias, perhaps supplied by the Resistance, but he would have needed the colonel's original papers to ensure the forgeries had all the correct stamps. His plan would have worked perfectly if he had just been able to keep the killings quiet and exit the facility as he left.

Now, however, everything had changed. He hadn't planned on leaving Hohensalzburg Castle the way he had, under duress, so now, with his alias compromised, he needed fresh papers – and who better to get them from than a deceased lieutenant colonel? I was gambling my family's lives on the belief that he wasn't done, that he wanted to follow up on Eagle's Claw, and now needed new papers to do it.

The odds that Oberstleutnant Fuhrmann was well known at the other facilities he wanted to visit were astronomical, his papers perfect for an OSS agent's use. Therefore, I had put two agents on Fuhrmann's house in Linz, in case he tried to recover Fuhrmann's replacement papers. I wasn't sure he would, but as it turned out, he did just that, killing one agent and very nearly killing the other. A dangerous man, this OSS agent. You can be sure I will show him no mercy.

Thanks to Milch, I've made a likely list of possible targets… but which will he choose? It doesn't matter. I've contacted *all* the potential sites he might visit and told them I want to know if Oberstleutnant Fuhrmann shows up for a surprise inspection. I will catch him, and free my family, then we'll find a way out of here – someplace like Spain or Portugal, where we can wait out the remainder of the war… God willing.

– Part Three –

December, 1944, St. Georgen, Austria,
Mauthausen-Gusen subcamp

51

December 11th, 1944

It took Donny two months to have the Resistance, paid by the OSS, age Fuhrmann's papers and source another uniform. He had intended to simply steal one of the dead colonel's spare uniforms from the bedroom, but the interference of the two secret policemen had ruined that. Once things went noisy, he had to run for it. He considered not using Fuhrmann's papers, but he didn't have much choice, and he felt the potential payoff was worth it.

He also managed to source a staff car – stolen from and brought all the way from the Eastern front, he'd been told. He had the temerity to actually requisition a driver from the local Luftwaffe pool in Linz. He had the corporal drive him back to the Mauthausen-Gusen complex, where he and the Navajos had seen the Ar234 being pulled out of the mountain. Donny presented his papers at the gate and was ushered in. Amazing what a forged letter from Hermann Göring would do. Albert had gotten him the family stationery and helped him with the letter. It was perfect.

At the main desk, he'd been met by a captain by the name of Hauptmann, which he found amusing, because his name was literally Hauptmann Hauptmann now with his title. The young, cruel-faced captain seemed pleased to personally give him a guided tour of the facility. Donny surrendered his sidearm, with the assurance he would get it back when he left – something about the prisoners, then Hauptmann led Donny back outside to the large door in the side of the hill. He held the man door for Donny, who thanked him, and they stepped inside, into the biggest elevator Donny'd ever seen. Hauptmann lowered the gate and pressed down.

52

As Donny stepped out of the elevator into the underground cavern, it was everything he could do not to gasp. The room was immense – nearly three stories high, and longer than a football stadium. The roof was rough rock, but fairly even, with two rows of klieg lights illuminating the hidden aircraft factory.

The floor was concrete, as were the walls up to a height of about twelve feet. Two sets of rails inset into the floor, running the length of the room, reminded him of the trolley rails in San Francisco, allowing the workers, clearly prisoners from a nearby camp, to move the aircraft fuselages back and forth the length of the cavern. Donny counted at least thirty He162 frames and around twenty Arado Ar234 airframes on steel cradles perpendicular to the tracks that could be inserted into another frame-like trolley mounted on the tracks to move the plane around the length of the cavern.

"The planes begin here," his guide said, pointing. "The components are made in small, individual cottage factories throughout Germany and delivered here for assembly," the captain told him. "There are seventeen stations here – each plane you see is built progressively, with certain tasks done at each station. They move gradually up the left side, then once the fuselage is completed, the plane is set on the tracks and the engines are mounted. The five planes you see on the right, down here near the end? Those are basically completed fuselages receiving final instrumentation and inspection while they are waiting for their engines. Then they will be moved to the surface in the freight elevator for final assembly."

At the second station Donny could see two prisoners sealing and smoothing the seams between the sections of the bare aluminum fuselage. One of them, a tired-looking, middle-aged woman with a shaved head glanced at him with haunted eyes; a look of ineffable sadness that hardened into something else briefly before she looked away and returned to her task. He looked up at the rough ceiling above them, once more taking in the gigantic space. How many prisoners had struggled and died to carve out this cavern? How many might be now entombed in the concrete beneath his feet, where they'd fallen, simply unable to continue, to become part of the very structure which had consumed them?

"The workers – where do you get them?" he asked, hands behind him, white knuckled fingers clenching his gloves as he strolled casually with his guide down the line of He162 and Ar234 fuselages.

"Most of them we get from Mauthausen or other nearby satellite camps. Ostensibly this is a work camp, as you saw on the surface. We prefer women for much of the electrical work because they have small, nimble fingers – very good at working in tight spaces with the instrumentation. This entire factory, as I'm sure you know, was built by prisoner labor, and the tunnels go on for miles," Hauptmann said proudly. "There are problems, of course, but overall, it's very efficient. They don't eat much, and although we have to compete with the bomb factory near Linz for qualified labor, we do pretty well. Even untermenschen can contribute to the Reich, don't you agree?"

"Of course," Donny said, gritting his teeth.

It was cold in the cavern, even in his wool uniform, and Donny wondered what the prisoners, clad only in thin pajama-like uniforms made of what looked like mattress ticking, or in the women's case, shapeless grey shifts, must be feeling.

"These smaller planes on this side are the new Heinkel 162s, of course – the 'Volksjager,' Herr Oberstleutnant – the 'People's Fighter.' The other, larger plane I'm sure you're familiar with, being in the position you're in. Of course, you probably have never seen an Arado 234 being built."

"Yes, a wonderful plane, but I haven't been able to get a really close look at one yet," Donny said truthfully. He looked down the line of fifty some planes, many close to being finished. If they got these planes in the air before the Allies made it over the Rhine… But where were they getting the pilots? Was their training program that efficient? Weren't they running out of pilots by now?

"Coupled with the new thermobaric fuel-air bomb design, these fighter bombers will lay the Allied ground forces to waste. We'll drive those bastards back into the sea," Hauptmann finished confidently, his face glowing with his zealotry.

"Impressive," Donny commented as he walked slowly down the line of fighters to be. At nearly every station, gaunt laborers worked on assembling the advanced aircraft. The line of Ar234s were further down, and interested him much more, but intelligence is intelligence – he didn't want to stifle his guide's enthusiasm for his subject.

"The design is ingenious – the frame is mostly plywood, skinned with strips of aluminum. This reduces the need for forming presses and expensive tooling. Once the avionics are installed… here, look at this plane here," he said, pointing at a plane in progress, "That's the bundle of avionics prior to being matched to gauges hanging over the side, there. Once the gauges are in, the canopy is installed and tested for leaks with the rest of the airframe. The rear engine mounts are a simple, but clever design, making engine changes very quick and, along with the landing gear, are one of the few all-metal components in the plane.

"The only thing holding us up really are certain components such as gauges, which are time consuming to produce, and unfortunately are not produced here yet, although new workshops are being blasted out as we speak," his guide said proudly. "The He162 has a simplified control panel, but still…" He shrugged, breaking off just as three armed guards came out of the freight elevator entrance at the other end and began running toward them. Donny got the feeling that things were about to go bad.

"Tell me more about the fuel-air bombs," he said, eyeing the guards trotting toward them over the captain's shoulder.

"I haven't had the opportunity to see a test in person," Hauptmann said, "but I did see a technical film on it. They were originally round, approximately 1,100 kilograms, approximately the size of an American basketball, but much heavier, of course. Their designation is V5 – a vengeance weapon." He motioned Donny closer. "They had difficulty with the 'Magnus effect' so are working on conventional finned versions now – that's really the holdup. Supposedly there is another, slightly larger, more powerful finned version which is guided by radio control. Imagine each one of these planes with just one or two of those bombs each. The Allies would sue for peace within the week!" he said gleefully.

Imagine one of these smaller planes piggybacked onto a giant, long-range bomber carrying an atom-splitting bomb, Donny thought, as he looked at the line of He162s. The guards were getting closer, and actually slowing down now they knew he could not escape. He wondered if the Ar234 could carry a small atom bomb. He doubted it, but the thought chilled him. Even if it couldn't, it could certainly carry one or more of the thermobaric fuel-air bombs Hauptmann was so gleeful about.

The guards were only thirty or forty meters away now, hands on their weapons, which were undoubtedly cocked. They yelled to his guide, who turned to see what the problem was, and Donny grabbed him from behind, spinning the hapless officer in front of him, his arm bent up into his back as he pulled the captain's P-38 from its clamshell holster.

"Move. Over to the door," Donny hissed, pushing the captain toward the block wall, where the tools and benches of each station were located in recessed, well-lit coves where exhausted prisoners struggled with the very tasks that would ultimately kill them. Three, huge, torpedo-like bomb casings that looked recently completed sat like broken eggs in a nearby bay, bigger than any bomb he'd ever seen. He glanced down the open bay and estimated that the guards, who were running now, were less than twenty-five yards away.

As they had moved deeper into the huge work bay, Donny had done what any good agent would do and had kept his eyes open for alternate exits. He'd noticed that the serrated wall which held the head of each individual work station ran in a line a solid ten feet away from the natural wall of the cavern, forming a long, flat ledge approximately ten feet wide and ten feet high – a ledge which ran the length of the left side of the huge bay. A single guard patrolled on top of it, overlooking the entire work area, and Donny had seen a large, double door built in herringbone style, with *Eintritt Verboten* on it, approximately a third of the way into the bay, and reasoned that there was a tunnel, likely for use by German personnel in case of an emergency.

It was built out of large stone blocks – why would the Germans go to all that trouble if not for a tunnel? It was too big to just be a raceway for electrical conduits and compressed air lines. He extrapolated that there'd be at least one more door approximately two-thirds of the way to the end of the cavern, for emergency egress. It just made sense. He'd bet the farm on it, and when he'd seen the second door, he'd stopped in front of it.

The problem was, he couldn't allow the guards to cut him off inside the tunnel by getting to the first door before he got past it, so he had to wait and draw them closer to this end first.

Now the single guard on the ledge over the tunnel began running toward him too. Another minute and he'd be too close. Donny pulled the officer down by the collar so he could peek beneath the tail section of the nearest plane fuselage. The guards were nearly on them.

Donny pushed the captain toward the door.

"It's locked," Hauptmann said.

"But I bet you have a key, don't you?"

"I'm not giving it to you."

"Then I'll have to just shoot you and take it," Donny replied calmly. "Now give me the key. SCHNELL."

The officer produced a large key from his pocket, but in a last pique of duty, threw it across the floor, where it skittered beneath a stool on which stood a young female prisoner—a girl really, about fifteen years of age— who would have been quite lovely if her head were not so roughly shaved.

Donny smacked Hauptmann on the head with the pistol and dove for the key, the sound of hobnailed boots running on concrete loud in his ears.

With a surprising burst of alacrity, the young woman slid off the stool and picked it up, holding it aside to expose the key, which Donny snatched up. As he stood, their eyes met, hers liquid and deep, communicating greater pain than he'd ever seen in a human being before.

"Good luck," she said, then smiled.

Donny was taken aback – he didn't know how to respond. "Thank you," he said, turning toward the large double herringbone doors, the guards nearly upon him now, and slid inside just as the two guards rounded the end of the plane and turned toward him.

53

The inside of the tunnel was pitch black, and Donny spent precious seconds after relocking the door from the inside searching for a light switch, but with no luck. He had no choice. The guards likely had their own keys, so he began a stumbling run down the pitch black tunnel, the Walther in his right hand, his left hand on the wall, really appreciating for the first time the plight of the blind. He just prayed the Germans weren't using the tunnel for storage also, because if he ran into something in the dark, it was going to hurt.

He heard scrabbling at the door behind him and ran faster, thinking he'd really screwed up this time. They shot or hanged spies, usually after a good beating and maybe pulling out a few fingernails, of course, and Donny just hoped if it came to that, that he could goad them into shooting him. At least it'd be quick. Actually, if it came to that, he still had the P-38... but would he be able to use it on himself when the time came? Donny didn't know, and frankly didn't intend to find out. He ran faster, totally blind, just hoping there were no walls directly in front of him. Someone finally triggered the alarm, and sirens and a klaxon began howling – normally a bad thing, but the lights in the tunnel came on at the same moment – just in time for Donny to see the pallet of wiring harnesses directly in front of him.

He tried to sidestep them but failed, catching one toe on the pallet and going head over heels. Partially landing on the harnesses didn't hurt any, but bouncing off them onto the concrete floor did. He heard the door open down the tunnel and rolled to his feet, ignoring the pain in his knee, first hobbling, then forcing himself to run again as the guards pushed their way into the tunnel and began firing at him.

Donny saw the alcove for the first door just as the shooting began, and threw himself into it as 9mm bullets began whizzing and ricocheting down the tunnel. He flipped open the deadbolt and flung the door open, his pistol at the ready, but all the guards had been drawn to the other end. He ran for the freight elevator, the sirens loud in his ears.

The guard on the roof of the tunnel spotted him and began yelling, "THERE HE IS – HE'S BACK IN THE BAY," then began firing his Mp40 at him. Fortunately, he was nearly at the other end of the cavern, and they were obviously frantic, because although bullets chipped the concrete around Donny, none hit him. A cool hand with an Mp40 would have easily cut him down at seventy-five yards, but Donny doubted the guards got much practice, and probably still had the stock folded. His luck was holding. He dove into the elevator bay, punched the up button, then yanked open the door marked "Office" and ran up the stairs instead, nearly out of breath.

He met another guard at the top of the stairs and shot him, immediately erasing the boy's look of surprise. He couldn't have been more than nineteen. Donny caught the body as it fell, snatching the Mp40 out of the young man's hands as he twisted, and pushed him away, dropping the twitching body on the stairs below him.

There were two officers in the control room, and Donny caught a brief glimpse out the windows at the cavern below – just enough to see the two guards who'd been chasing him burst out of the tunnel and begin running for the elevator, the third guard from atop the tunnel slinging his weapon to climb down an access ladder to reach ground level.

One of the officers in the room produced a Luger from somewhere, and Donny put a short burst in him, then looked pointedly at the second officer as his coworker's body slumped against the base of a high desk, knocking over a metal stool, then falling across it.

"WHERE IS THE EMERGENCY ESCAPE TUNNEL ACCESS?" Donny demanded. The man's eyes involuntarily slid over Donny's shoulder, and he turned to find a red door marked "Emergency Only" as the officer threw himself at him, grabbing the barrel of the submachine gun and pushing it aside… but it was hot, and he immediately let go with a screech. It was all

Donny needed, and he punched the German in the face with the rounded butt of the receiver, knocking him back, then brought the muzzle of the Mp40 around as the man on the floor held up a hand against the bullets.

Donny could hear boots on the staircase now. He'd used about half the magazine, he figured. He needed more time, and didn't have any. There was a shadow under the door, and Donny did the only thing he could – he yanked it open with his left hand to find two surprised guards just below him on the stairs. He emptied the rest of the magazine into them, adding their bodies on the stairs to the first guard's, then slammed the door shut, throwing the now empty submachine gun to the floor. He blocked the door as best he could with a tilted chair, then opened the red emergency door to find a concrete tube with a metal ladder staked to the wall, leading directly up.

The hatch came out in a small room, empty save for a desk, a chair, and a telephone. Windows showed the entrance parade ground outside, and what looked like an armored convoy, mostly trucks, lined up at the front gate. He took a deep breath, straightened his uniform, tucked the Walther into his holster after replacing the magazine, and stepped outside.

54

Donny closed the door behind him and strode confidently across the open ground, hands behind him, as if he had all the time in the world, although in reality his heart was beating out of his chest. The klaxons were still sounding, and although groups of soldiers and officers assigned to the convoy still stood talking, it was clear that there was much consternation as the camp guards ran to reinforce the perimeter, while some ran toward the large freight elevator that had initially taken Donny underground.

He looked around surreptitiously for a means of escape – a vehicle preferably, but the metal gate was closed, manned by more soldiers than had been at the main gate when he'd arrived, and he doubted his ability to bluff his way past them during such an alert. Clearly this area was more important than the camp itself. He was trapped. Not knowing what else to do, he continued walking toward the head of the column, wondering if he could somehow sneak aboard one of the Kübelwagens or perhaps a half-track or truck, knowing that his chances were slim to none, and getting worse the longer he was there.

At the head of the column, behind a pair of motorcycles and a Schwimmwagen—a sort of amphibious version of the Kübelwagen—was a sort of light tank, a weapons carrier really. It was one of the most unusual weapons platforms Donny had seen in his travels: it looked like a bigger, heavier version of the British Bren carrier in a way, but mounted a fully automatic 20mm flak cannon on the rear deck behind a heavy bent shield to protect the gunner. A narrow well with slitted shielding forward and on the sides held the driver. The commander stood or kneeled on the rear deck, and helped with reloads, although sometimes a third or fourth crew member would be tasked for reloads and flank security… but the Wehrmacht, it seemed, was running short on soldiers, having lost close to two million in Russia.

As Donny walked up to it, he could hear it idling like the rest of the vehicles, the gunner kneeling next to his gun, the barrel of which was pointed in the air, talking with the driver. Obviously the convoy had been preparing to leave when the alarms went off. Donny saw a group of officers talking near a command Kübelwagen two vehicles back and figured one of them was in charge of the Flakpanzer. He had to do it now. 2:1 odds were the best he'd get.

The only things in front of the Flakpanzer were the Schwimmwagen and two motorcycle escorts on their kickstands, one with a sidecar, one without. He doubted they were running – of necessity, motorcycle fuel tanks being what they are. The closed, heavy metal gate stood just beyond them: the only way out that he could see.

He adjusted his Schirmmütze again, and stepped between the Flakpanzer and the Schwimmwagen to put the Flakpanzer between him and the group of officers. Once on the other side, he stopped and patted his pockets for cigarettes casually, his heart beating out of his chest.

Placing a cigarette in his mouth, he patted his pockets again, then looked around, as if for a light. Donny always carried cigarettes, but never matches. Cigarettes were useful for getting close. He stepped over to the flakpanzer, where the gunner was still crouched on the rear deck above him, discussing something with the driver – likely the meaning of the alarm klaxons.

"Bitte. Do you have a light?"

The gunner turned at Donny's voice and, seeing it was an officer speaking to him, began checking his pockets frantically for matches.

"Ja, Herr Ober—" he began, as Donny stepped forward, quickly stabbing him in the neck twice with his ice pick. The gunner gave him a look of horror, grabbing his bloody neck with both hands, trying unsuccessfully to stanch the substantial blood flow, then fell back against his gun, turning it slightly.

The shocked driver opened his mouth to yell and Donny shot him with his P-38. Things had gone noisy, and as Major Fairbairn had told them, *"En it goes noisy, git yer arse out of there. Don't hesitate or yer det."*

Donny didn't have a choice, because when the driver's body fell back into the driver's well, his dead body knocked the gearshift forward, into gear. There was a brief grinding of gears, then the Flakpanzer began slowly lurching forward, toward the gate.

55

Donny leapt onto the deck of the moving Flakpanzer, hoping the 20mm cannon was loaded. There wasn't much protection, just the bent shield on the gun to protect the gunner from the front, and a simple rectangular plate mounted to the edge of the deck on each side and to the rear. As he pushed the gunner's body off the vehicle and grabbed the grips of the 20mm automatic cannon however, his back was exposed to fire.

The Flakpanzer lurched again as it hit the Schwimmwagen ahead of it, then began pushing the much smaller vehicle forward, toward the motorcycles, whose owners were frantically trying to start them, only one of them succeeding in time – the bike with the sidecar and Mg34 roared to life just as the front of the Schwimmwagen touched its rear tire.

He roared away as Donny found the safety on the big gun, flipped it to FEUER and swung it around rearward to face the rest of the motorized column. The second motorcyclist wasn't so lucky – as he tried to kick the BMW to life, the Schwimmwagen, beginning to crab sideways now, climbed up over the motorcycle's rear wheel, pushing it to the ground and pinning the rider's leg beneath it.

Donny couldn't hear him scream as the Schwimmwagen crushed him because of the sound of the 20mm gun punching fist-sized holes in everything he pointed it at: first the group of officers screaming at their men to attack, who disappeared in a pink mist, their shredded bodies dropping like bowling pins, then the trucks directly behind him, which the 20mm sliced though like butter, blowing apart the engines and causing small fires and explosions.

The soldiers sitting in the rear of the transports didn't have a chance against a weapon designed to punch holes in planes and tanks. A man suffering a direct hit from the 20mm was simply torn in half, and when the fused rounds exploded, it was like a grenade going off. Screaming, fires, total chaos.

The gun ran dry with a click and Donny looked behind him. The gate was buckling under pressure from the Flakpanzer pushing the Schwimmwagen and was about to tear open. Donny grabbed one of the spare magazines out of the open ammo box – it looked to be only about twenty rounds, but they were huge, and the magazine was heavy. He yanked the empty mag out and threw it aside as the soldiers in the compound, finally getting their wits about them, began returning fire.

Using both hands, Donny snicked the big magazine into place as bullets began pinging off the armor, then once more looked through the odd, rectangular optic atop the weapon's receiver, this time focusing on an Mg42 team who had set up on the open dirt and was firing tracers at him, the rounds reverberating off the shield protecting him. He was mad now, and made an example of them, eviscerating the two men where they lay. Then he began picking off individuals whom he could see firing at him, taking one soldier off at the waist with the powerful weapon.

There was another lurch, and Donny looked behind him, to the front again, just in time to see the gate crash open. He was through, and the Flakpanzer was now pushing past the Schwimmwagen, the left track climbing over the rear quarter of the little car until he was sure the Flakpanzer would flip over sideways, then the sheer weight of the vehicle crushed through the thin, pressed steel body of the amphibious car, crashing back down.

A bullet whizzed past his head, and he realized the gate guards were now shooting at him, so he spun the big gun around and began punching fist-sized holes in the concrete block gatehouse until they stopped, then turned the gun back to the compound and emptied the magazine. *Now what?* he thought. His luck wouldn't hold forever. He needed a getaway vehicle.

As he passed the gatehouse, he saw his answer – another motorcycle with sidecar, tucked back behind the tiny structure, surrounded by pieces of dead Germans. He prayed the bike hadn't been damaged by his firing as he leapt off the Flakpanzer, which continued grinding slowly ahead, a dead man at the controls.

Donny rolled when he hit the ground and came up running. He threw himself onto the bike, saw the key was in place, turned it, then kicked the

Zündapp to life with his first try, silently thanking whoever had maintained it.

He pulled it around in a tight circle, cutting in front of the still-moving Flakpanzer, which was amazingly, still on the road, and gave it everything the bike had, hunching low over the tanks and shifting rapidly up through the gears, using the bulk of the Flakpanzer as a temporary shield to cover his retreat as the firing in his direction grew heavier. He'd gotten away… for now, at least. A damn miracle really, but they'd be after him in minutes, and this time there would be no interrogation. Donny looked back at the burning supply convoy behind him and saw another motorcycle with sidecar—likely the one that'd narrowly escaped being crushed—pull out and around the Flakpanzer, which was finally headed over the ditch, and into the field. There was a soldier in the sidecar, manning the Mg34. A Kübelwagen of soldiers followed it. They were coming after him.

56

I was staring tiredly at the blurry picture of the killer again when the phone rang. It was a shock – not just because it was late, but because I'd never heard it ring before; apparently there was no one who wanted to talk with me… until now.

I picked up the receiver gingerly with my wounded hand.

"Hallo?"

"This is Gephardt. There's been a development. A man dressed as a Luftwaffe Oberstleutnant just infiltrated then escaped from a top secret underground facility in Sankt Georgen, near the Gusen prison camp. What is particularly interesting is that he stabbed a Panzergrenadier manning a Flakpanzer in the neck with an ice pick."

I was immediately wide awake.

"Get up there and check it out. Oh, and Moeller?" Gephardt said.

"Ja?"

"I have a letter for you – from your wife. I will send it along to you. It's the best I could do, but I assure you, she's doing fine."

"And the children?"

"There's a child's drawing in the envelope also, but I really don't know much. Do you think I'd read your letter?"

I swallowed my answer and accepted the carrot.

"Danke, Herr Gephardt. I appreciate it," I said.

"Now get to Gusen and do your job. Find this OSS agent, or whoever he is, and *stop him*. Du verstehst?"

"Ja," I said, as he hung up on me without a word of goodbye. What a prick. If I left right away, I could be there by morning, I thought, hanging up the receiver. I could sleep on the train. My eyes became blurry with tears – a letter, finally! I ached for it, but knew I'd have to put it out of my mind or I'd never catch this killer, and the unspoken message was clear: Catch the OSS agent, or your family dies.

57

Donny checked the gas tank. It was half full, probably enough to get him to Linz. The problem was the soldiers behind him. They'd gained a little, but just a little. He was lighter and a little faster than the bike chasing him since he had no passenger, but the bike with empty sidecar didn't handle as well, and they gained a bit on the turns. Sooner or later they'd get some people in front of him, and that'd be it. He needed to get off the road.

It was mostly farmland here, with some rolling hills, and he'd seen several good places for an ambush, but how? The Germans were about 800 meters back, but gaining slowly, and he had no doubt they'd radioed ahead to set up a roadblock. It's what he would do. It was just a matter of time.

A sign for a town, Luftenberg, flashed past. Were there already Germans in the town waiting for him? He sped around the curve, the sidecar's wheel coming off the ground, then he saw a narrow farm lane drop off the road to the right. He slowed the bike and carefully eased it off the road and onto the lane so as not to leave any tracks, staying on the short grass ridge between the tire tracks. He hunched down as much as possible and drove slowly into the tall grass, hoping he wouldn't be seen.

The lane curved around to the left, following the base of a gentle hill and, once out of sight in the shallow swale, he shut the bike off to listen, coasting to a stop. Immediately he heard the sound of his pursuers. Would they notice where he'd turned off, or would they continue into town?

The sound of the motorcycle slowed, then stopped, but he was sure it was at the turn-off to Linz, not at his hidden drive. The sound of a Kübelwagen whining up the road soon caught up, then they stopped also, and he could hear the sound of the two vehicles idling, and the murmur of voices, then one obviously in command yelling something – he couldn't tell what.

Donny was too far away to hear much at all, but he caught the final command: "MACH SCHNELL," then both engines revved again and tore off in what sounded to him like two different directions… but he wasn't sure.

For the moment he was safe, but it wouldn't last long. They wouldn't stop until they caught him. He needed other clothes, and to get out of the damn uniform. They wouldn't be looking for a civilian.

Leaving the bike where it was, he took out the P-38 and checked the chamber, then began walking down the narrow cart path toward the roof of a barn sticking up over the next small rise.

58

The farmhouse was ancient, built of stone with an old saddle-backed roof that looked about ready to collapse under its own weight. The small barn next to it matched the house in both appearance and age. Both had been clearly built to last, to resist the elements, and, by the look of the small windows and stout design, to keep its occupants safe during time of war. Even if the roof burned, it could be easily rebuilt, and Donny wondered idly how many wars the old farmstead had weathered.

A pair of goats were tethered in the backyard and were munching contentedly on the weeds as well as everything else within their circle, and behind them, on a line just out of reach of the goats, waving gently in the wind, were several pairs of pants and some shirts. Surely they wouldn't miss one set?

Donny waited, watching and listening for movement, but the place was quiet except for the soft clucking of a few chickens doing their best to keep bugs out of the yard, and of course an occasional comment from one of the goats. He saw no dog, but knew most farms would have one. He had no choice, he couldn't afford to wait any longer. As silently as he could, he crept closer, keeping the clothesline between himself and the windows of the farmhouse.

The clothes were well-worn, but looked as if they would fit. Silently, he unclipped a pair of pants and a grey serge shirt from the line. One of the goats noticed him and bleated, then bleated again.

The real problem was his shoes. Any German soldier worth his salt would recognize the highly polished officer's boots right away. He needed something else, even if they didn't fit. Creeping to the back door, he peered in through the window, and sure enough, on the floor of the mudroom were several worn pairs of shoes – both men's and women's, along with a pair of wooden clogs and two pairs of rubber boots in different sizes.

Ever so gently, he tried the doorknob, breathing a sigh of relief when it turned. Donny eased open the door just wide enough to reach in and grabbed the nearest pair of worn, men's brogues, then straightened up – to a sharp pain in his back.

"Caught you in the act now, didn't I?" the farmer said, shoving the shotgun into Donny's back again for effect.

Donny winced. "There's been a mistake…" he began, not sure what to say.

"Oh, yup. There's been a mistake made, all right. Your mistake was thinking you could come rob me alone, without your friends. Let yourself right in the door, didn't you?"

"Wait, let me explain. I'm an officer in the Luftwaffe…" Donny began.

"Oh, I think I know what you are. You're a deserter… and a thief! Bastards like you took my son – put him in a uniform and sent him to be killed at Stalingrad. Bastard officers like you took all my pigs for bacon… now you come here stealing my clothes too? Deserting now, are you? Oh, yes. I know who *you* are," the farmer finished, pointing the shotgun at Donny's belly. He had no other choice.

"Actually, I'm an American OSS agent, on the run from German troops. We don't have much time. Look, the war is nearly over. Help me end it sooner."

"Son, I grew up on a farm. I know a load of bullshit when I smell it."

Donny looked him in the eye. "I *am* an OSS agent and I have critical information I need to report," he said, edging closer to the farmer.

"Why should I believe you?" the farmer said.

Donny batted the shotgun aside with his left hand, then tore it from the farmer's grasp with his right in a reversal so fast it was a blur – a reversal Fairbairn had shown them, albeit with the caveat: *"Sometimes it doesn't work. Then yer det."*

The farmer blinked, gaping at Donny, who was now pointing his own shotgun at him. Donny smiled, broke open the double-barreled gun, removed the shells and handed the gun back to the farmer.

"I really am OSS… will you help me?" he said.

59

Moeller's Journal, December 12th, 1944

I arrived at the underground manufacturing facility near Sankt Georgen the next morning. Some pioneer engineers were busy repairing the front gate, which looked like a tank had run into it. The bodies were gone, but the blood pools remained, and women prisoners were busy dumping dirt into the blood to clump it, then sweeping it into bins that were carried away by male prisoners. My heart went out to them. What had they done to deserve such a fate? They were all terribly thin, nearly to the point of horror, the men dressed in ragged, striped uniforms which reminded me of bed ticking, the women in horrible-looking dresses made of coarse grey cloth, their general demeanor one of despair and exhaustion.

I found that I couldn't even look at them, just as they avoided all eye contact with me. I felt like a monster – complicit somehow in their degradation simply by being there. My God, could Marie and the children really be in similar straits? It was as if my worst fears had come to life. I knew they must be nearby as this was one of many of the Mauthausen-Gusen subcamps… could they actually be *here*? I kept my eyes open but did not see them. I knew that to ask for them would be to seal their fate, so I said nothing, but my heart ached at the thought. My chest literally hurt. I was taken to an administration building, shown into an elevator, and taken down into the depths of the underground facility. I tried to keep my mind on the matter at hand, but I just couldn't focus. Was Marie at this very moment sweeping up the remains of someone's life into a dust pan? My God, I have to find this man, this OSS agent, soon. It's my family's only chance.

60

Not only did the farmer loan Donny his clothes, even with the certainty that he'd never see them again, he actually loaned him better-fitting clothes; his son Josef's, as it turned out. His son, who would have no more use of them, who had been lost on the Eastern front in 1942. His dress shoes even fit, and looked good. He told Donny his wife, who was currently visiting her sister in Linz, had cleaned them and polished them with a little fat on a soft cloth so that her boy would have decent-looking shoes when he came home. There was a girl a few kilometers away – she'd hoped they'd eventually wed...

The farmer, whose name turned out to be Franz Geller, also fed Donny and told him he should stay the night, then catch the bus in Luftenberg in the morning, which would take him to Linz and the train. He wondered if the farmer would double-cross him and turn him in, and there was a bad moment when a Kübelwagen came up the lane – they'd found the motorcycle, but the farmer professed no knowledge of it, and told them to go ahead and search, proudly showing them the picture of his son he kept on the mantel. "Anything for das Reich," he said to them.

Donny, hiding in the crawlspace beneath the floorboards, could hear every word. His life was in the farmer's hands. Finally the patrol left with a final exhortation to report anything suspicious. "Of course!" the old man agreed. "Heil Hitler. Guten Abend," and Donny finally breathed a sigh of relief. He slept that night in the boy's room, which was decorated with a purloined poster of a brave SS tank commander with a map in his hands, a Panzer tank and command car behind him, with *"Panzer Deine Waffe!"* across the bottom in red. Clearly life on the farm had not been exciting enough for him. *Well, you found plenty of excitement, didn't you, you young fool?* was Donny's last thought before he passed out into a deep, exhausted, dreamless sleep.

61

Donny left his uniform and gear, along with his Walther, with Geller, knowing that the sense of security the pistol gave him was false and that it was more likely to get him killed. Instead, he asked the farmer for a small paring knife and made a crude, but snug sheath for it out of a scrap of leather and some twine old Franz provided. Tucked into his right boot, beneath his pant leg, it was invisible.

He was a bit surprised when the old man presented him with an egg sandwich and some carrots and cheese in a small cloth bag for his journey, but accepted them gratefully. Geller told him where he could catch the bus, and asked if he had enough money. Donny told him yes, and told him to burn the uniform and dispose of the gun as soon as possible. The old man said he would, but Donny had the odd feeling that the farmer had some other use in mind for the P-38, the way he looked at it when Donny gave it to him.

They shook hands, and Donny thanked him again. The old man told him to be careful, and Donny said he'd come back to see him after the war, but Geller just smiled and shut the door.

He followed the narrow path Geller had indicated, through a meadow on the opposite side of the house from the way he'd come in, down a short hill to a gate in the fence that he let himself through, then across another field, this one smaller, and up to the road, which he approached cautiously. Donny crept from the brush and looked both ways but the road was empty for the moment. He turned right and picked up the pace. If he was going to catch the bus, he had to hurry.

The town was small, and old, red roofs on whitewashed buildings with a mish-mash of cobblestones, dirt, bricks, and occasionally newer concrete paving the tree-lined streets. Donny could see several German army transports parked on the main thoroughfare and cursed silently. This couldn't be the same convoy he'd shot up back at the facility, could it? Would they recognize him? He pulled the peasant cap Geller had given him down and lowered his gaze to hide his face as he walked into town.

He could see the small square with fountain the old man had described to him, and a muddy, blue and white bus that looked as though it'd seen better days parked in front of a small outdoor café. There were two soldiers checking the ID of the people boarding the bus. An officer with a bored look on his face stood nearby, his hands clasped behind him.

The bus was out of the question now. He looked around, stepping behind the last truck in line just as the officer swiveled his head his way.

The back of the transport was open, the canvas tied back on each side, tailgate down, and was full of crates – likely armaments and ammo. The motorcycles stood silently nearby, and as Donny peered around the other side of the truck, he could see a group of enlisted men smoking and laughing, making the most of the brief break just as any soldier would. He considered stealing a motorcycle briefly, but then had a better idea, and slid silently beneath the truck.

62

Letter from Marie Moeller, dated November 5th, 1944

*M*y *Darling,*
They said I could write you, so I am writing you to let you know that we are all well, although Sascha has developed a slight cough. I'm sure it's nothing to worry about. Both Anna and I have been fortunate enough to have been given tasks that will serve the Reich. She sorts electrical parts and I do the assembly. For now, they have allowed Sascha to play at our feet, although there was mention of a Kinderhausen several times. I'm unsure as to what they really mean by this.

They took our luggage, and issued us the most hideous uniforms – solemn grey dresses buttoning down the front with wide collars that would make Marlene Dietrich look like a cow. Ours have upside down black triangles on the breast, where the Jews have yellow or sometimes yellow and black stars. Others have different color badges – the homosexuals, for example, have pink triangles, the gypsies black like us, Soviet prisoners red, and so on. I understand the need for conformity and cleanliness, but shaving our heads and delousing us seems a bit much. If their true goal is cleanliness, a decent laundry facility for prisoners and a change of clothes would be a big improvement.

Not to worry – our hair is already growing back. It is a bit crowded in the sleeping quarters – it seems new prisoners come in every day. Mauthausen has subcamps and there is talk of sending us to one. The Aufseherin in charge of our Kommando told me it's a newer, bigger facility. The main thing is that we are still together, and the other women in the barracks have adjusted to give us our own bed, which is more of a sacrifice than you might think.

The food is terrible, and there's not much of it, but I don't know of many people in Germany who are eating well these days, do you? It will suffice. I do not want you to worry. We are safe, and I'm sure that they will release us once they realize a mistake has been made. I hope this letter finds you well, my love, and I hope that you have not suffered too greatly for my transgressions. I will try and write you again – they don't allow the Jews to write letters, but political prisoners apparently have it a bit better. I miss you so much.

–All my love, Marie.

Moeller's Journal, December 13th,1944

My hand shakes as I write this. I returned to my hotel to find the promised letter and a drawing from Sascha. It's the first I've heard of my family in months, and it's made me emotional, I'm afraid. I will try not to read too much into it, but Sascha with a cough? The little minx has a propensity for picking up whatever bug is going around. It's a relief to me that they are still all together – many families get split up, but I just can't imagine my wife without her lovely, auburn tresses. I just can't see it in my head: she and Anna with their heads shaved like convicts, like the women at Gusen sweeping up blood-clotted dust. God, please keep my family safe, and give me the strength (and luck) to find my quarry, arrest him, and save them all from that horrible place.

63

Donny's back and arms were killing him already, but he had no choice but to hang on and wait. He had taken off his belt and used it to sling himself underneath the chassis of the last truck, propping his heels up on a brace running across the rear of the truck in front of the rear axle. He had cinched the belt up as tight as he could, and had wrapped his hands overlapping the frame of the truck, there being just enough room for his fingers between the frame and the bed.

The truck was nearly new, so he got a little dirt in his mouth, but no rust in his eyes as he had the last time he'd tried this stunt. He knew they typically checked trucks coming in and out of facilities with mirrors and dogs, but he hoped for once they'd bypass that bit of security, seeing as the convoy was already on the road.

He looked at his watch. It was two minutes to three. The guards going on the convoy were probably eating, although the trucks were still well guarded. Every few minutes a guard would walk slowly up one side of the truck and back down the other.

He watched the black boots as they passed. One particular soldier had toes splayed out to the side and waddled like a duck. Donny grinned at the picture in his head of a duck wearing a German helmet, then remembered that this particular "duck" was still carrying an Mp40 submachine gun.

Finally he heard the clomping of boots as the soldiers forming the column came back from their break, joking and laughing, ribbing each other good-naturedly as all soldiers do when they aren't in immediate danger. They shuffled around the trucks, adjusting weapons, double-checking tie downs on the canvas tops, finally climbing into the trucks. He counted two in front of his truck and two in the back. Obviously the crates he'd seen them loading into the transports took up too much room for any more soldiers.

Still, there would be a motorcycle with sidecar behind them for security, and now he wondered if they would be able to see him hanging underneath the truck, in which case they'd simply stop the convoy, haul him out from underneath, and shoot him. He was sweating now between the thought of being so exposed and the effort of holding himself up beneath the chassis. Finally the trucks started up with a huge puff of diesel that billowed around him and it was everything he could do to keep from coughing or sneezing. Then Donny heard the whine and bark of a dog as it strained at its leash and cursed under his breath. He heard a sergeant tell a corporal to check under the trucks with the dog.

Donny sighed. This was it; he was as good as caught. He almost rolled out from under the truck, but decided to wait, hoping the dog wouldn't bite. He could hear the dog sniffing as it was walked down the right side of the trucks, the side he was hanging under, of course. He looked down to his left, waiting for the mirror, but it never came. Instead he saw the dog, head down, sniffing the spare tire at the side of the truck. Please God, don't let him attack, he thought, as they came closer.

He was looking right at the dog when it stuck its head under the truck, looked up, and saw him. Their eyes met, and Donny wasn't sure why, but he smiled at the dog. The dog paused, and Donny knew this was it. He was about to pull his feet off the brace holding them up when the dog turned and continued down the side of the truck without giving any alarm. Why, he didn't know. He just breathed in with relief, then realized that was the wrong thing to do: the fumes from the idling trucks were horrible. At this rate he'd have brain damage by the time they got to where they were going, or worse, pass out from the carbon monoxide and be dragged beneath the rear wheels. He suppressed a cough as the engines revved, then with a jerk the truck began to move.

The trucks wound around through the German countryside. The trees bordering the fields were silver, the mid-winter light filtering down through the clouds, making them ethereal at a distance, as if they were merely ghosts of trees and not real to the touch.

Donny gritted his teeth and held on for dear life against every jounce and bump, and with the condition of the wartime roads, there were a lot of them. Twice he was burned by the exhaust pipe, and the huge drive shaft spinning just inches from his head was disconcerting. He was afraid that one of these times he would catch some hair or a piece of clothing in it, and that would be all she wrote. His muscles had stopped merely aching with the tension of holding on miles ago and now burned constantly. His back was on fire, despite the heavy belt supporting him, and he honestly wasn't sure how much longer he could hang there. His fingers were cramped, another bad sign. He was beginning to think this had been a really, really bad idea.

He had been thinking about how to get out from under the truck without being seen and had come up with a plan, if you could call it that. It was rapidly getting dark, and the trucks had switched on their lights and were going slower now, since the lights did little to light the way, blacked out as they all were to prevent the convoy from being bombed. Several times in the last couple of hours the motorcycle at the back would pull out and pass the trucks, going up to the front of the convoy, whether to provide additional security, clear the road of refugees, or just to communicate with their comrades, he didn't know.

How the two soldiers manning the motorcycle with sidecar hadn't seen him from behind Donny didn't know and didn't care, but he was hoping his luck would hold a little while longer. All he knew was that would be his only chance. He figured it was dark enough now that the two guards in the back of the truck might not see him when he let go. There was a better than even chance that the huge dual wheels would run right over him if he didn't land just right. He knew he didn't have the strength to support himself and undo the belt, as he had when he first climbed under the truck, so he'd decided to just cut the belt loose with his knife, which in and of itself was going to be a tricky, one-handed operation. He just hoped he had enough strength left to hold on while he cut himself loose.

It was nearly full dark and Donny was gritting his teeth to hold on when he heard the motorcycle rev its engine. When he opened his eyes he saw the dim glow of the headlight on the ground beside the truck and heard the engine blat as it went past. He grunted, shifting his weight to the left hand, reaching down into his boot for the paring knife with the other. There was a moment of desperation when he nearly dropped it, his hand was so numb, but then the blade was out and he began sawing at the leather belt as the truck slowed.

He had to keep his weight from breaking the belt somehow, but at the same time keep enough tension on it to cut it, meanwhile holding on with just the one hand, which he could feel was slipping. He tried not to think of the consequences. He stopped and moved his feet so that he was pushing against the crossbar with the soles of his feet, not with his feet above the crossbar as he had been riding. If his ankles were caught on the crossbar when the belt let go, and he couldn't catch himself, his legs would be caught in the loop of the crossbar and the rest of his body flipped backwards as the truck rolled over him, breaking probably not only his legs, but his back, and likely his neck as well.

"Don't try this at home, boys and girls," he muttered to himself, perched under the rolling behemoth, tensioned between the bar, the belt he was cutting through, and his left hand which gripped the frame of the truck. Suddenly the belt gave way and he felt his hand slip. He was falling! He tried to drop straight down, pushing off with his legs against the bar so his feet wouldn't get caught in anything. He hit the ground hard and bounced, then something hit him in the head and it all went black as the big truck rolled over him.

64

December 12th, 1944, 5:00 a.m.

When Donny awoke, he found himself lying in the middle of a dark, deserted road and every muscle in his body hurt. He raised a hand to his head and felt a little blood in his hair, and a small lump. The rear drive axle must have clipped him as it passed over him. A couple ribs felt as if they might be cracked, but his arms and legs seemed to work, so the wheel hadn't hit him. It was a miracle, but boy, it didn't feel like one. Obviously the soldiers in the back of the truck had not noticed him rolling out from under the rear, because the convoy was gone. Where he was now? was the question. How close to the American lines was he? He knew they hadn't crossed the Rhine, although they'd passed over the Danube and through Linz what felt like eons ago, so he was still in Germany, but where?

He lay on his back for several minutes until it occurred to him that lying in the middle of a road, especially with everyone using blackout headlamps, might not be the best idea. He forced himself to sit up, supporting himself on one arm, then he heard it. It was clearly a motorcycle, approaching quickly. At first he thought it was the Germans coming back, then he realized that it sounded different, and besides, they would have already shot him. He focused his eyes in the direction of the sound and could barely see a dim, wavering headlight making its way toward him. He still couldn't get up, so he decided to try flagging the bike's rider before he ran over him. To tell the truth, he didn't really care if it did run over him, as he had already been run over once by a truck. Being run over by a mere motorcycle should be a piece of cake.

As the dim light fell on him Donny waved his arm weakly. He didn't have to act. He was all in. He saw the headlight stop, then tilt as the rider dismounted but kept the bike running for light. There was a shadow in front of him, then a woman's voice in German.

"Mein Gott! Are you all right? What happened to you?"

"I was thrown from a truck," was all Donny could think of to say.

"Scheisse! Here, let me help you up. I will give you a ride to my village and you can report it."

"Nein, Fräulein. I do not wish to report it."

She squinted at him. "Fine. I will take you home, we will look at these ribs, maybe get you some hot soup, then you can go jump off another truck for all I care."

Donny smiled despite himself. "Danke, Fräulein. That would be fine."

"My name is Lilli."

"A beautiful name."

"And yours?"

Donny decided against using Carl Strausshind at the moment. They were undoubtedly looking for him. She might read a notice and decide a reward would be a nice thing to have.

"Schultz. Just Schultz."

"All right, 'Just Schultz,' let's get you out of the road."

She helped him climb onto the bike, which he did with difficulty, every muscle in his body sore, refusing to work properly. She unfolded the rear foot pegs and helped him find them, then climbed onto the bike in front of him. She brought the still-idling bike upright, kicked the stand back out of the way, then took his arms and placed them gently around her middle, well below her breasts. He could feel her slim waist beneath the heavy wool men's coat she wore.

"Hold on, Schultzie, don't fall off," she said as she kicked the bike into gear and gave it some gas. Donny leaned against her, unable to hold himself upright, afraid in his dizziness he would fall off the bike. He thought he could smell apples in her hair. Not a bad way to travel, he remembered thinking before he passed out.

65

Donny woke up in a small, low-ceilinged room. There was light coming through the windows, and someone had removed his shoes, socks, and shirt, and unbuttoned his trousers. The quilt atop him was warm, but the room cold. He could feel the chill on his face. It hurt to breathe, and when he reached to touch his chest he found that it had been bound expertly with strips of linen, probably from some old sheets, serving as bandages. Another bandage was around his head, which throbbed constantly.

Other than being sore everywhere he felt pretty good, and couldn't help smiling to himself. *Another safe landing, Donny boy,* he thought. Things could be worse. He lay there a few more minutes, reveling in the softness of the bed he'd found himself in, then forced himself to sit up, swinging his legs over the side of the bed to the cold floor. He pulled the handmade quilt around his shoulders, shivering. There was a pitcher of water and a glass on the bedside table, and he poured a glass, hands shaking with the effort, and drank it thirstily, following it immediately with another, then a third glass, which he consumed more slowly. Finally he put the glass down, got unsteadily to his feet, and went to the door.

The main room looked ancient, with a low ceiling held up by large, rough-hewn beams that looked as though they had been set in place around the time of the Vikings, with rough, whitewashed plaster now brown with age filling the spaces between. Huge upright timbers punctuated the room, supporting the beams and, Donny assumed, possibly an upper floor.

A somewhat modern kitchen ran along the opposite wall, clustered around a gigantic black and chrome monster of a wood cook stove. His eyes were drawn to a large butcher's block on which lay a large sharp knife, some turnips and potatoes. Someone was making dinner. Suddenly Donny realized how hungry he was. He hadn't had anything to eat since the previous morning, and the egg sandwich the farmer had given him, and his stomach growled loudly at the thought of food. He thought about stealing a turnip from the table, but he didn't want to offend his hostess.

To his right there was a low fire going in the rough stone fireplace, so he shuffled over, his feet cold on the ancient wood planking, except where the floor was covered with modest but colorful rag rugs. He sat down in a faded, red brocade chair, well worn at the ends of the arms and the edges of the cushions, but as he pulled the quilt more tightly around him he could see why the chair was so well loved. Despite its ragged appearance it was simply, incredibly comfortable, one of those rare chairs you never want to part with or change, no matter how they look. With the heat from the fireplace on his face, swaddled in the heavy quilt and ensconced in the old, soft chair, Donny soon returned to the world of dreams.

He woke to the sound of a knife chopping vegetables. Once he could focus, he turned his head to find the woman who'd pulled him off the road standing at the chopping block, giving the bad news to the turnips. She looked up at him and their eyes met for a moment. Her eyes were a green-hazel, and a tiny smile flitted across her lips.

"Just Schultz! You're awake, mein Herr. How did you sleep?"

"Gut. Danke. Danke schön."

"That's…was, my grandfather's favorite chair."

"Your grandfather?"

"This was his house," she said, with a general wave of the knife. "Now it's mine…but I'm having trouble changing it. It's still his, you see. His smell, his soul is still here, I think…" she tapered off, smiling sadly. "I painted the main bedroom, the one you were in, yellow, just before the war started, thinking I'd sell the place, but it's hard to get a good price during a war."

She shrugged. "It's not bad here, though. I have a garden, a few chickens the soldiers haven't stolen yet, and I trade eggs for wood… and other things."

"You're fortunate to be here. There are many refugees on the roads these days," he said.

"Such as yourself?" she said with a hard look. He wondered what the look meant. He shrugged noncommittally.

"Thing is, Schultzie, I don't believe you're a refugee. You're dressed like a farmer on his way to town, but I've known farmers my whole life, and you are no farmer. Your hands are too soft for one thing, although that doesn't mean by itself... but you're too well fed as well. I have half a mind not to feed you."

Donny's eyes must have widened in alarm, because she laughed.

"Oh, don't worry. There'll be a bowl of soup for you. I hope you like turnips."

Her soft laughter filled the room, and it warmed Donny every bit as much as the fire had. Not much laughter found in Europe these dark days, he thought.

Dinner was even better than he had hoped – not just soup and black bread, but some real cheese in the small omelette she'd whipped together, and he tasted onion and garlic in it as well as some spices he couldn't identify.

She kept pushing food at him, and he'd obliged her, unable to help himself, hungry as he could ever remember being, and unsure of when he'd eat again. He noticed she didn't eat much, just sat there smoking her hand-rolled cigarette, watching him eat, that wry smile trying to force its way out of the corners of her mouth again. Finally he pushed his plate and bowl aside and sat back with his mug of ersatz coffee in both hands, looked at her, and smiled.

"That was delicious. Danke."

"You're quite welcome," she said.

She was attractive, but not conventionally pretty, with high cheekbones and unruly brown hair coiled like a bird's nest. A high forehead rose above intelligent hazel-green eyes, which framed a very Polish nose. A small, pretty mouth above a noble chin, leading to a thin porcelain neck rising from a rough peasant's sweater, a sweater obviously too big for her, even with the sleeves rolled up, and he realized that this had given him the impression that she was more petite than he had first thought. She was confident, and he found himself comparing her to Elena's petite frame. She was attractive, but

Elena held his heart. He couldn't wait to see her again. His heart ached for her.

Frankly, it kind of pissed him off – he seemingly had no control over it. Still, he couldn't stop thinking about her, even in the company of another attractive woman. Would he ever see her again? Donny set his mug down and got up, realizing just how sore he was from his truck ride. Everything hurt. Everything.

He carried his dishes to the sink, where she was running water.

"Can I help?" he asked.

"Can you wash dishes?"

"I believe I can," he said.

She bowed to him with a smile, sweeping her arm at the sink and throwing the dishtowel over his shoulder. "I will leave you to it then, Schultzie, while I make some more coffee."

Donny finished filling the sink with water drawn from the boiler mounted on the side of the woodstove, adding just enough cold water from the hand pump at the one corner of the sink to avoid getting burned. He liked it as hot as he could stand it, and found a rough cake of soap made from lard and lye and lathered up the dishes. It was a strange feeling, standing here at this sink, in a different country, with a different woman, one he barely knew, doing the dishes like any good husband. For some reason he found himself wondering what such a life would be like with Elena. Would it be like this? Totally incongruous to his mission. He felt the bite of conscience. He would have to go, very soon now.

Lilli came up to him to draw water from the pump at the sink, standing next to him, and she smelled like the sun on a garden in June, so different than Elena's scent.

"You saved me on the road out there, nursed me, fed me... Thank you. Please, tell me about yourself. I know nothing about you," he said.

She set the kettle on the stove, then checked and stoked the fire through one of the round lids on top. She added a couple of sticks of wood from the copper boiler at the side of the stove where she stored her kindling, making the fire crackle and leap from the hole devilishly until she slung the lid back on with a practiced hand, hanging the handle back on the wall next to the stove, on the nail where it lived.

"I could say the same about you, Schultz, or should I say 'Herr Strausshind'?"

Donny stiffened at the sound of his cover name. How stupid he had been. Of course she had gone through his papers and wallet while he was asleep. Who could blame her? She would want to see just who it was she had brought into her house – anyone would.

"Somehow I get the feeling that Strausshind isn't your real name, either. You speak German very well, but you are not German."

"Then what am I?" he asked without turning, the dishes rising from the sudsy hot water almost of their own volition, clinking softly as he rinsed them and laid them on a towel, his hands working automatically, wondering if she was going to pull a weapon on him and he was going to have to kill her.

She sat back down at the kitchen table – a simple, sturdy ark of a table, a no-nonsense table with no pretensions of being what it was not, and it fit her perfectly. In fact, as he glanced back over his shoulder at her she seemed to be one with it; one bare arm slung across it as she sat beside it, chair turned to watch him at the sink, a new cigarette between her fingers as she pulled a tiny, stray piece of tobacco from between her teeth. Even this she did gracefully, but without any drama, with just such a simple, common-sense way about her that he knew instinctively that she was not one of those who panic easily, but rather simply does what needs to be done in an emergency. Solid as a rock, this one, he thought. And what was worse, she knew it.

He finished the dishes, reaching in to let the water out, letting it gurgle down the drain, then turning and standing with his back to the worn enamel drainboard, his hands in a dish towel. Their eyes welded together for a moment and that was when he knew he was going to tell her. He'd never make it to the American lines without her help. He just simply had to trust her…but he couldn't tell her everything. He spun a wild yarn about new parts for U-boats being on those trucks, and although he was a consummate liar, as you had to be in his business, he could see the doubt in her eyes.

"I have some discretionary cash on me. I'd be happy to pay you for your time, and the gas, of course."

He could see right away that it had been the wrong thing to say, and that whatever she did, it would be out of her hatred for the Nazis, and because she wanted to, and for no other reason. Once again he found himself marveling at her strength. She looked away, her profile illuminated by the weak winter light coming in the row of kitchen windows over the counter. She stubbed her cigarette out angrily and looked at him.

"Fine. I will help you, and you will pay me. Just as you would a prostitute."

"Listen, I didn't mean it like that..." he began.

"Herr Schultz, or whatever your name is... Do you think I picked you up off the road with the hope of getting *paid?* That I washed your wounds and fed you for a few Reichsmarks? Does no one in America ever do anything for anyone without recompense?"

"I'm sorry," Donny said. "Please forgive me."

"I'll help you, Schultzie, but only because someone has to. Someone has to stand up to the Nazis, no matter what it costs. They took my father just as they've taken others, and only for speaking the truth as he saw it. He's in a camp somewhere. I haven't been able to find him yet, but I got close enough to see one of their damn work camps, and you cannot believe how bad it is. My father has a bad heart. In a place like that..." she trailed off, her gaze not on the table, but out the window as if looking back into the past, or trying to imagine the man who raised her, vibrant and alive instead of a naked skeleton in a lime-filled pit. She looked at him again and there was fire in her eyes, and not a little sadness.

"So I will help you, my Schultz, but not because of your money. I will help you because the Nazis are monsters who load men, women, and children onto cattle cars until there is no room to move, let alone sit down, then haul them off to hell. I will help you because I must."

She got up and went to the back door of the kitchen, the one which led to the backyard that had been turned into a truck garden, the plants brown and withered as if tired of the war, a few rows still covered with burlap and straw to keep the remaining vegetables warm, spotted here and there with tiny explosions of dark earth where she had dug for their dinner. Donny had seen it through the window as he'd washed the dishes, embarrassed for eating so much.

"I'm going to the privy. We'll leave in the morning. I'll get you as close as I can, but I'm not getting killed for you, verstehen? The weather hasn't turned yet. We'll take the motorcycle. It does better with gas."

"Thank you."

"Don't thank me, Schultz. I'm not doing it for you," she said, flinging a brown scarf around her neck and going out.

66

2nd letter from Marie Moeller, Dated December 10th, 1944

*M*y darling. How I long to see you, to hold you, to have you take me in your strong, loving arms. This world seems so bleak lately – you must forgive me my mood, but it is hard even for me to maintain my optimism lately.

I'm afraid to tell you this – no father should have to hear such terrible news in a letter, but our Sascha, our precious little Sascha, is gone. They took him from me a few weeks ago, and assigned him to a "Kinderhausen." What kind of monsters would think of separating young children from their mothers and putting them in a separate facility?

His cough had gotten much worse by then, and he'd been running a fever. I asked for medicine for him several times, but even food is hard to get enough of, and what we do get— stale bread with weevils and a bit of thin gruel of unknown substance once a day—is simply not enough. I gave him my share, but he refused it, even when I was stern with him.

When they took him from me I begged them to make sure he got treatment, and the Aufseherin in charge of our section assured me he would, but I didn't believe her. She's not only a liar, but cruel. She cares for nothing but the sharpness of her uniform and how her damn hair looks. At least she has hair! Three weeks later she told me he died of pneumonia. Whether it was that, or something simply more evil seems not to matter… our little angel is gone.

Anna has been a real comfort. She held me when I cried the evening they took him as if it were she who were the mother, and I the child. She is also suffering from lack of food. She looks far too thin, and her complexion, so beautifully clear previously, is showing signs of malnutrition. What concerns me most, however, is I caught her eating an apple the other day and asked her where she'd gotten it. She didn't want to tell me, but finally admitted that a guard had given it to her, and *that he'd been giving her small gifts of food – a piece of cheese, a turnip, even a bite or two of Scho-Ka-Kola chocolate now and then.*

I told her flat out that nothing is free in this horrible place, that he had something unspeakable in mind for her, and to never accept another gift, but she sees the world through the eyes of a fifteen-year-old girl, and despite the privations of this place, retains her youthful optimism, even after they tattooed numbers on our arms. Normally such optimism in her would encourage me, but I can find little hope for the future in this place.

I'm so sorry to be the bearer of such bad things, my love, but I simply have nothing good to report to you. Sascha's death seems an omen to me; an omen of our own destruction. I got your letter, and am glad at least that you are well, and I pray for your success in catching this killer – not just selfishly for myself and Anna's salvation, but so that we might be together once more as a family, to grieve our little Sascha together. Take good care of yourself, as I cannot be there to make sure you eat, and remember us in your prayers, as we remember you in ours.

– All my love, Marie.

67

Moeller's journal, December 13th, 1945

I've had plenty of time to think in my hotel room, and unfortunately, they are not good thoughts. It's been six months since I began this quest, and although Gephardt continues to assure me my family is fine, sustenance and warmth is difficult for *any* German to find these days, let alone those in a prison camp. I have always been a bit prone to melancholy – Marie was the eternal optimist of the family, and I have no doubt I married her because of it. Her nearly constant joyfulness lit up the space around her, her laughter always lightened my mood, and after coming home from my chosen work as a murder investigator, it was as welcome to me as sunshine.

There is no sunshine today. I worry about them constantly, especially since receiving Marie's recent letter. Poor little Sascha; the report of his death has been all I can think of, and at the moment this entire manhunt seems futile to me. Still, how can I stop? Gephardt's recent telegram made it clear that he considers the investigation a failure. I have no illusions that he will spare my family in light of my efforts – we had a deal, and I've been unable to hold up my end. These Nazi animals understand nothing of human decency. It's all about manipulation and your usefulness to the Reich. It seems now my usefulness is at an end. I have a few more Reichsmarks left, so I will defy his orders on the crazy, outside chance that the OSS agent will try to get pictures or other information on some other top secret facility, and that I can catch him doing it. The odds are simply not in my favor, but I just can't give up while there's still a chance – for my family's sake, I simply can't.

68

Donny drove the motorcycle, which did all right, despite the snow, as the road was fairly clear due to the brief warm spell and the passage of so many vehicles, either fleeing the war, or heading towards it. The sun was shining where they were, but there were dark clouds on the horizon, where they were heading, and it looked like snow.

Lilli held onto him from behind, directing him with her hand as they came to crossroads. When they reached the main road, however, he found to his surprise that it was as busy as any roadway he'd ever seen, with German troops moving west, and refugees already moving east. The troops were impossibly young and fresh, in obviously good spirits, and Donny realized that he was looking at the mobilization of a major offensive. He couldn't believe it. Where did they get all the tanks and troops? He realized with a chill that the Allied forces were about to get a lesson about overconfidence.

Everyone knew the war was nearly over… but here was the evidence that it was not. Entire armored divisions moving to the west, their ultimate destination unknown. Donny said goodbye to Lilli, telling her he could find the front from here – he'd just follow the German army. She shrugged and turned the bike over to him, walking off toward the train station, nearly all the money he'd had left in her pocket. He felt it was the least he could do for her, despite her protestations. At the very least it would help pay for the loss of the motorcycle. He began weaving slowly through the crowds of refugees, against the natural flow, just another civilian trying to get home to his family. He wasn't the only one.

The Wehrmacht pretty much ignored the refugees unless a staff car or Kübelwagen needed to get through, then the opposite lane was cleared immediately. He nearly lost sight of the convoy he'd picked to follow several times because of this, but always managed to catch up. He realized with a chill that they were moving toward Belgium, perhaps Antwerp. Donny was no strategist, but he knew if the Germans broke through to Antwerp they could very well drive the Allies back into the sea. The British and Americans were stretched thin along a long front stretching from northern France up to northwestern Belgium. If the Germans succeeded, they could trap entire Allied divisions by cutting off their means of resupply.

Donny gritted his teeth, wondering how he could get a hold of a radio to warn command. If the Americans were caught with their pants down, the entire front could collapse. He would follow the convoy as far as he could, then try and work his way back to the American lines as soon as possible, rather than trying to sneak through or around them. He figured it was the only choice. If he got shot trying, well, he took this job knowing the risks. He had to let someone know about this troop movement.

Village by village, the Germans moved closer and closer to the Rhine. The Americans were on the other side somewhere, and Donny realized that the hardest part was going to be getting across the river. The bridges would be heavily guarded, and he cetainly didn't have any papers allowing him travel to the other side of the river. He couldn't imagine who would. In fact, if he was caught here, with the papers he did have, specifying Linz as a destination, he would likely be shot as a spy. Linz was clear on the other side of the country, and even an idiot wouldn't believe that he had simply gotten lost.

Night was falling and the motorbike was nearly out of petrol as another village appeared. The sign said Gemünd and he recognized it as being on the river. It looked as though some of the troops were turning toward the Rhine, while others continued northward, undoubtedly to other bridges further on. He shut the motor off and walked the bike, pushing it slowly, not having to pretend he was tired. It was getting colder, and the wind bit through his thin coat.

When he reached the center of the village, he could see the convoy stretched out in a line waiting to cross the bridge. He lit a cigarette and leaned the bike against the wall to take a break. He was still working on a sleep deficit even though he'd slept the night before, and his eyes were gritty, the lids heavy. He knew if he closed them just for a minute he would be lost. His head nodded, the cigarette burning down in his fingers…

He jerked awake just in time to see the last motorcycle in the column disappear down the street he was sure headed toward the river, the column inching forward. He stubbed out his cigarette, field-stripped it, and put the remains in his pocket. The Germans were fanatical about cleanliness, and it wouldn't do to be arrested for littering. Leaving the motorcycle where it was, he crossed back across the street, sticking his hands into his jacket pockets, the collar turned up against the cold. He wished he had a heavy coat, but there had been no time. All he had on was what the farmer had lent him.

He worked his way slowly down the narrow street, surprised to see so many people out, then turned down the street the column was inching down, on their way to the bridge. The diesel exhaust fumes were so thick here between the buildings from the idling tanks and trucks he nearly retched. Donny turned left down a narrow alley, calmly walking away, as if he had lived there all his life.

The cobblestones were wet, with rainbows in the puddles left from oil leaks from tanks and troop carriers, dirty snow lining the streets. He lit another cigarette as he walked, trying to figure out a way across the river. Somehow he had to get across the river and through the German lines, then through the American lines without getting shot, or worse yet, captured. His mind raced as he looked at the steel grayness of the wide river, almost like something alive in its slow, deliberate, repeated movement. It slid past coldly as he tried to think where he might find a boat, as the snow began lightly falling.

69

December 15th, 1944, late afternoon, the American forward lines

Nearly every night there was a dance in Hosingen, cold or not, and the Americans danced with every woman in town, married or not. Most of the husbands didn't mind at all, so glad was everyone that the war was nearly over. Champagne and red wine had flowed like, well, like wine, generals toasted each other, entire units had been sent on leave, most choosing to go to Paris, which took in the Americans with open arms, while bands played and children waved tiny American flags.

New troops brought into the area were told these were technically the front lines, but that the Germans were on the run. Mostly they stood guard duty and practiced patrolling the dark, empty woods and gently rolling farmland. Eisenhower's decision to stop here was simple logistics – the forward elements of the 1st and 3rd armies had advanced so far, so fast, that they were having trouble getting resupplied. He knew from Napoleon's mistake not to overextend his supply lines. As it was they were stretched perilously thin, and although German units attacking their flanks were generally small and unorganized, Ike knew better than to go any further without consolidating his positions. These days he was spending more time dealing with the bickering between Bradley and Montgomery than anything else, it seemed.

New replacements flooded units decimated by the push across France. The war was pretty much over, and from what everyone was saying, they'd be in Berlin by Christmas. The terror of the Panzers and the German "zipper" gun, the Mg42, had been replaced by the welcome monotony of guard duty and an occasional patrol in the dark, empty countryside, the gently rolling fields reminding many a GI of their home. Men leaned against their artillery pieces and command cars, smoking cigarettes and talking, wondering if this would be their last Christmas away from home. The way the Germans had been running, most of them thought so.

First Sergeant Thomas Franklin of the 110th Infantry was sitting on a packing crate in the tent he shared with three other NCOs, feeding broken shards of ammo crates into the little drum stove he'd traded three days' leave for. He was content with the trade – he'd be seeing Paris soon enough. He'd met a bosomy blonde-haired beauty by the name of Annette in Bastogne, and they were getting along fine, despite Annette's lack of English and his lousy French. Their bodies did all their communicating for them, and they were slowly learning each other's language.

Franklin personally hadn't seen a German since Arnhem and hoped to never see another one. If there was any fighting to do, as far as he was concerned, the new guys could do it. He'd had his fill of it after North Africa, Italy, Holland, and now France. It was someone else's turn, the way he saw it. Oh, he did his duty, but he had no intention of going home in a box at this stage in the game. His CO, who had been his commanding officer since Africa, saw it the same way, and found their unit a cushy security job walking patrols through the fields around Hosingen, which was one of the loveliest little towns Franklin had ever seen. The countryside was beautiful that fall, as were the people, and if it wasn't for the recent cold spell, he'd be quite content to spend the rest of the war in this place. The tent flap moved and a helmeted head was thrust through.

"Sergeant Franklin?" It was Captain Hillary, Franklin's CO. Franklin didn't rise, just nodded. They two men had spent too much time in trenches together for formalities when alone.

"Sir. Please come in." Hillary came in and stood over the stove with his hands out.

"Warm in here. Hell, this is nicer than my quarters. Not bothering you, am I?"

"No, Sir. Just drying my socks."

"I gathered as much," Hillary said, wrinkling his nose.

"I'm sure officers have much better smelling socks, Sir."

"Of course we do," Hillary said with a grin. "Hate to take you away from your fire, but I'd like you to take a squad up to the line tonight and poke around. We've been getting reports again of tanks and trucks moving through the woods east of here."

Franklin shook his head. "Sir, we both know it's just those phonograph recordings the Germans use to try and psych us out. I mean, we've captured them, Sir. I doubt Jerry has many tanks left at this point."

"I know, Bob. Even brigade thinks it's just psy-war, but they still want us to check it out. Being the officer, I'll make it my duty to stay here and keep your fire going while you take some of the FNGs from Charlie Company up to the line. It'll be good experience for them. Take that kid Johnson – I don't think he ever saw a tree until boot camp. Maybe you can find one of those German phonograph players so we can have some music," he said with a wink.

"Yes, Sir," Franklin said, pulling a dry pair of socks from the clothesline he'd strung through the tent, close to the little stove. He brought them to his nose, sniffed them lightly, and grimaced, looking at his commanding officer. "Captain, you wouldn't by any chance be able to get me a couple pair of those odorless officer's socks, would you?"

Hillary smiled as Franklin pulled on his socks and boots.

"Christmas is coming, Sergeant. Anything's possible."

70

December 14ᵗʰ, 1944, East side of the Rhine

Donny lay on a hillock watching a constant stream of German tanks and troop carriers pass on the road below. Just beyond was the Rhine; the great, wide river which guarded Germany's western borders. On the other side lay the Ardennes, a mixture of field and forest, Hosingen and Kiischpelt, then beyond that, as far as he could figure, Bastogne. Somewhere out there lay the American forces Donny was trying to reach.

He looked down the hill and wondered if the Allied forces knew there were entire battalions headed in their direction, then looked at the low, grey cloud cover, the kind of heavy clouds that usually carried snow, and decided probably not. The low clouds of the last few days had most likely grounded any reconnaissance aircraft. They undoubtedly knew the Germans were to their east somewhere, and were reinforcing the Rhine, but what Donny was seeing was more than mere reinforcements; there were entire battle formations on the move.

Somehow he had to get to the other side of the river and hook up with the American forces. Unarmed, with no supplies of any type, wearing clothes and shoes meant for a night on the town, not tramping around in snow and mud-covered fields, Donny had no idea how he was going to do it. First thing was to somehow get through the Germans to the other side of the river. If he lived through that, then he'd decide what to do. Nothing to it but to do it, as his grandfather had been fond of saying. Donny sighed, pushed himself back from the edge, stood up and brushed himself off, and started walking back to the motorcycle.

The side street where Donny had left the motorcycle had filled up – a tide of refugees blocked from the roads by incoming German troop columns sat or stood around, miserably clutching their meager possessions. Donny felt bad for these people, but he had a job to do. He pushed his way through the crowd to the motorcycle, took hold of the handlebars, and was about to throw his leg over it when someone tapped him on the shoulder.

Donny turned to find a man about his age and height, but much better dressed in a heavy worsted wool suit, wearing a snappy fedora and a dark burgundy leather jacket. Gestapo.

"Excuse me, mein Herr. Your papers, bitte," the man said pleasantly, holding out one gloved hand for them.

Donny had no choice. He let go of the motorcycle, smiled, and said, "Of course." He gave the Gestapo agent his papers – his Strausshind papers, fairly confident they were still searching for Carl Buschausen. As the Gestapo agent looked through them, comparing the photo in the booklet to Donny's face, a pair of Gestapo goons joined him – they'd clearly been canvassing the crowd for someone. Donny felt a cold bead of sweat run down the back of his neck.

Herr 'Burgundy Coat' put Donny's paperwork in his left pocket and at the same time pulled a folded piece of paper from his right, unfolded it, and compared it to Donny's face. Donny smiled as if he didn't know the man was comparing him to a wanted poster. No wanted poster or police photograph ever showed the subject smiling. They'd taught him that at Camp X, when he'd first become an agent. Simply smiling changed the face's proportions and the way it looked to the eye. It wasn't good that the Gestapo agent had kept his papers, but you never…

"Take him," Burgundy Coat said, and before Donny could react, the two big goons were on him, each pinning an arm, wrenching them together painfully behind his back and handcuffing him. Burgundy Coat stepped closer to him, close enough that Donny could smell his aftershave, and this time smiled widely.

"Herr Strausshind, or should I say, *Herr Buschausen,* it is a pleasure to meet you," he said pleasantly, then suddenly punched Donny in the stomach, doubling him over.

"Not smiling now, are we, Herr Strausshind, or is that another alias?"

Donny didn't respond – *couldn't* respond.

"Put him in the car," Burgundy Coat said, and the two goons bent him back upright and began hustling him through the crowd.

71

They quick-marched him around the corner, pushing their way through the crowd, using Donny as a battering ram. The crowd parted silently. They knew who these men were, and what they did. No one would even make eye contact with Donny, although he caught a few fearful side glances – as if he were contagious in some way.

The car was a huge, dark green Horch, with suicide doors in the back. One of the goons cuffed Donny's hands in front of him for the car ride, while the other goon held a gun on him. Donny looked at the handcuffs. The bracelets were substantial, likely Krupp steel, with a short piece of stout chain joining them. He'd picked handcuffs before, but doubted he'd get the opportunity this time. He was as good as dead, he thought, already hardening his mind against the pain to come.

The goon who'd cuffed him searched his pockets, then opened the left rear door and pushed him into the car. Donny turned to attack, but the goon with the gun still had it pointed at him through the window – open despite the temperature. Donny moved to seat himself better, as if that's what he had meant to do all along, and stared out the windshield morosely, trying to think of a worse time in his life… then began crying. The Gestapo men just looked at him smugly.

"Biermann, stay here and continue looking for the deserters," Burgundy Coat said. "We'll take him to headquarters and call this Moeller fellow who's looking for him, then come back. If you see them, don't try and apprehend them until we return, verstehen?" The goon with the gun finally tucked it back into a shoulder holster and nodded, then said, "Perhaps you should sit up front. It'd be safer."

Burgundy Coat turned to look at Donny, his face in his hands, sobbing openly, and smirked. "Nein. I have nothing to fear from this one. Look, he's broken already. It's the stress of operating clandestinely for so long. Just look at him. I bet he's secretly glad that it's over. I'll be fine sitting in back," he said, as the other goon, the one Donny had begun thinking of as "Handcuff Man" got in the front and started the big car's engine.

Burgundy Coat, clearly the boss, got in beside Donny, as Donny turned his head away.

"Don't feel bad, Herr," he said, slamming the door and rolling up the window. "Stronger men than you have cracked right away. Perhaps if you cooperate, we can forgo the worst of it eh?" Burgundy Coat said as the big Horch staff car began easing forward, through the mass of refugees, the driver using his horn liberally to encourage them to move aside.

72

Donny figured they'd take him deeper into town, but instead they headed out of town, the local Gestapo headquarters obviously being somewhere else. He kept his head turned away from the agent seated next to him, which suited them both. He'd stopped sobbing, but kept his face averted, sniffling or wiping his eyes with his hands occasionally. "If you *do* get caught," his first instructor at the OSS farm had told them, "put them at ease. If there is absolutely no way to get away, then capitulate entirely. You won't get a chance to escape later if they believe you're really dangerous."

The OSS even brought in a team of thespians to teach them to cry on cue – something Donny had found incredibly difficult, but was able to do after putting his mind to it, despite his doubts that it'd ever be useful to him. Yet here he was. He was happy to see that his act had worked, and even more relieved to see that he had only two men to deal with instead of three. Fate was smiling on him.

They were in open country now, only the occasional group of refugees on the snowy road, and they leapt out of the way immediately upon seeing the huge Horch staff car with red flags on its fenders flying toward them. Donny could see the Rhine out the window to their right, brown and glassy, reflecting a brief ray of sunshine during this respite from the snow. The snow clouds filling the grey sky, however, promised more to come.

There was a curve coming up, and no refugees in sight. Donny could see what looked like a town in the distance and decided that there was no time like the present. He lunged forward, looping the handcuffs over the driver's head like a garrotte, yanking back hard, then rolling onto his back effectively crossing his hands in an X, now facing Burgundy Coat—in his lap now really—and simultaneously yanked hard on the handcuffs again. He used them to anchor his shoulders against the seat, as he kicked right with his left foot, catching the surprised-looking head Gestapo agent squarely in the right temple with the toe of his left shoe, knocking his hat off and rolling his eyes up into his head as the car swerved across the road.

Not confident that the blow had killed him, Donny used his feet, the back of his right foot in front of his throat, his left hooking in back, and broke the Gestapo agent's neck with a quick, practiced move as the car swerved back the other way, the driver scrabbling at him with desperate hands.

Rolling back over now, Donny concentrated on the driver, putting his knee against the back of the seat and pulling as hard as he could against the man's windpipe, doing his best to yank his head clean off his neck. The car swerved yet again, and Donny, seeing that they were headed straight for a large tree, braced himself for impact, closing his eyes instinctively against flying glass.

73

Donny shook himself awake and found that he was now in the front seat, his handcuffs still tangled around the driver's neck. It took him a few minutes to extricate himself and find the key in the driver's pocket. He'd been taught by his instructors to pay attention to such things, and he knew Handcuff Man kept the key in his left trouser pocket. The problem was, the impact had thrown the driver sideways and left him upside down – his head in the passenger wheelwell, his feet twisted around into the driver's side. If he wasn't dead before, he was now.

Donny could hear steam escaping somewhere, but he couldn't seem to see out of one eye, and realized he had a minor head wound, which he gingerly touched. It hurt like hell and was bleeding freely, as head wounds will, but his brain bucket seemed intact – no brains showing… that he could tell. Then, with his one good eye, he noticed a flickering gout of flame from the hood. The car was on fire. Wonderful. It was a real pain to get to the driver's left pocket – he was lying on his left side, his legs bent backwards like a broken chicken-wing, locking him in place against the seat. On top of that he was a big man, and Donny was wearing handcuffs.

Donny could hear crackling now… the fire was spreading. He figured he had no more than a few seconds. Frantically, he struggled with the body, practically standing on his head to reach, and was just about to leave it and figure out some other way to get the handcuffs off, when his fingers found the key. It caught on the inside of the driver's pocket, then there was a loud WHOOSH as the entire front of the car caught fire.

Donny tore the key loose, fought open the driver's door, and pulled himself outside onto the ground. He didn't stop to unlock the handcuffs; he just got up and ran like hell, trying to put distance between himself and the burning staff car.

He was still close enough that, when the fuel tank finally blew, the pressure wave knocked him to the ground. He covered his head with his arms as he was showered with small, burning pieces of the vehicle. After several long seconds he raised his head. The car was still there, but now burning merrily. He looked around. He was still alone on the road, but had no doubt that would change soon. He unlocked the handcuffs and threw them as far as he could, then began jogging down the road toward a nearby farm.

74

December 15th, 1944 somewhere east of Hosingen, Luxembourg

Sergeant Tom Franklin led his squad of newbies across the quickly whitening fields toward another stand of trees. The snow had started an hour earlier, and he was glad he'd worn his heavy, long, army greatcoat, thinking it was the best thing the army had ever given him. Most of the men, however, didn't have any winter gear yet due to multiple snafus in supply chains. The Army had outrun its supplies, and they were only now beginning to catch up, thus no clean socks and no winter boots and coats for the new guys, who shivered behind him as the wind shifted and the snow began slanting in from the northeast. Visibility was getting worse by the minute, and he didn't want these guys to freeze to death out here. Hell, *he* didn't want to freeze to death out here. Enough was enough already. He thought of his warm tent and gritted his teeth. The light was failing, his feet were turning into Popsicles, and the Garand he carried felt like a railroad tie in his cold fingers, despite his half-gloves.

Suddenly he heard something. He held up his fist to stop his tiny column just 200 yards from the tree line.

"What is it, Sarge?" one of the new kids asked.

"Shut up and listen!" he growled fiercely. They stood there in the twilight silently as the snow coated their shoulders, straining their ears against the silence. Then he heard it again, the squeal and slap of tank treads. It was unmistakable; once you had heard that sound you never forgot it, much as you wanted to. Nothing strikes fear into the heart of an infantryman quite like a tank, especially those big goddamn Tigers. It didn't sound like a phonograph record to him; in fact, it was getting louder, and it was coming from the trees ahead of him. Franklin felt a cold chill run up his spine as the sound grew louder yet. It filled him with dread, the light fading, nearly dark now, the sound of not just one, but multiple tanks by the sound of it, crashing through the woods straight toward them. It grew louder and louder, then Franklin felt the earth trembling beneath his feet and knew for sure it was no damn recording.

"Jesus. Fall back now, dammit! MOVE, MOVE, MOVE!" He turned and followed his men back across the field, glancing back over his shoulder every now and then as they stumbled through the dirt clumps and snow, his frozen feet temporarily forgotten. He tried not to think of it, tried not to give in to the raw fear that ran through him, but if those tanks caught them out here in the open…

They'd barely reached the hedgerow where they had taken their last cigarette break when he looked behind him just in time to see the huge cannon of a Tiger tank thrust itself through the brush with the crash of breaking limbs, the trees no match for the gigantic, tearing machine. A second, then another, then yet another tank burst through the line of trees next to it as the squad went to ground. Sergeant Franklin counted six Tiger tanks from behind his tree before he saw the German troops following after them as they broke through the trees, then ran ahead of the great war machines to draw fire. There were hundreds of them.

"Time to go! RUN," he yelled.

"But, Sarge—" one young idiot began.

"I SAID HAUL ASS. We'll radio command from a safer position. Now MOVE."

75

Donny found a small punt with a pair of decrepit oars leaning up against an ancient, gray barn and had "borrowed" it to cross the Rhine. From the looks of it, and the way it shipped water, he figured he was probably doing the owners a favor. The boat had been half-frozen into the ground and looked as though it hadn't touched water since he was a boy. Due to a flat keel it was hard to keep pointed in the direction he wanted, but it floated, and that's all he could hope for. Donny didn't try to buck the strong current of the Rhine in full flow, but let it sweep him downstream, concentrating on just making it to the other side intact. It was snowing in earnest now.

By the time he made it across his feet were wet and his shirt soaked through from perspiration, but there had been no way he could have stopped and removed his coat. The current had swept him a good two or three miles downstream by his estimation, but he was on the other side of the river now, and still breathing.

Now, crossing the interminable snow-covered fields, his feet felt like clubs, having lost all feeling hours before. At least it seemed like hours. It had grown colder and the sweat from his exertions was freezing on his skin, the thin sweater he wore over his shirt and under his coat no longer enough. He knew he was going hypothermic, and if he didn't find warmth and shelter soon, he was going to die of exposure.

The snow was coming harder and thicker now, blanketing him in white, coating his eyelashes so he could barely see. He had no hat or gloves, and he silently cursed the Germans, Allen Dulles, the OSS, and whoever else came to mind as he stumbled across the frozen stubble of the fields, no longer knowing if he was even going in the right direction, no longer caring who saw him. It was nearly dark, and he could hear a low rumbling all around him, which he assumed was German tanks or transports, or both. One way or another, it didn't look good for Mrs. Brooks's little boy. Either he would freeze to death in this godforsaken field, or get caught out here in city clothes going in the direction of the Allied lines and shot as a traitor or spy. Getting shot as a spy was beginning to sound good to him, as long as he could get warm and have a coffee and cigarette first.

He'd crossed the last two fields in a numb stupor, then suddenly another hedgerow loomed magically before him, He wasn't sure which he hated worse, the open fields and the feeling of being in someone's rifle sights, the wind beating at him, or struggling through the treacherous, snow-covered tangle of the hedgerows bordering the fields, snow plopping from the trees, going straight down his neck, the wet bushes slapping at him, soaking him in preparation for the wind's torment on the other side. Maybe he'd get lucky and step on a mine…

"Halten Sie!" came the command in German. Donny stopped, the shivering uncontrollable now, realizing that he was beyond caring what happened. He just wanted to be warm. A dim, helmeted figure wearing a long coat rose out of the bushes in front of him like a ghost. "Hands up!"

Donny had raised his hands before he realized that the figure had spoken to him in English. He had found the American lines.

"Sproeken zee English?" the figure said in a poor parody of German. Donny opened his mouth to speak, but all that came out was a croak. He cleared his throat and tried again.

"Yes. Yes, I speak English. I'm American."

"Sure, and I'm Jayne Mansfield," the figure responded, the rifle pointed unerringly at Donny's gut.

"No, really. I have to speak to your CO immediately. The Germans are attacking!"

The dim figure gave a wry laugh as several other snow-covered ghosts rose from the ground to stand next to him. Sergeant Thomas Franklin looked at the miserable figure in front of him and sighed.

"We *know* the Germans are attacking. We just outran a whole tank regiment. Put your hands down, you're coming with us."

"Thank you."

"Don't thank me, as far as I'm concerned, you're a prisoner. Hammond, search him – make sure he doesn't have a weapon."

"I have a kitchen knife in my coat pocket," Donny said helpfully as the young soldier began frisking him.

"So, what the hell are you doing out here, Fritz?" Franklin asked, his suspicions clear.

"I told you, I'm an American. OSS if you must know, but my mission is classified. I need a field telephone immediately."

"Tell it to the officers, pal. Now let's go. Those tanks are going to get ahead of us if we don't hurry. Mason, try to raise HQ on the radio again."

"Trust me, Sergeant, those tanks are the least of our worries if you don't get me to secure communications."

"Shut up and walk," Franklin said, gesturing with his rifle. Donny started walking... again.

76

Donny sat wrapped in a blanket and sipped hot coffee while a group of officers decided what to do with him. He had given them his bona fides: a telephone number they could call to get verification he was who he said he was. It was a convoluted structure, with a series of false fronts leading back to Dulles's office, so it was taking a while. He fumed, glad to be warm, but wanted nothing more at the moment than to make his report to Dulles, then take a damn nap. Finally the telephone rang, a harsh, blatting sound that scraped his nerves even further. A lieutenant answered it, said something low into it, then covered the receiver with his hand and called out.

"General?"

General Anthony McAuliffe looked up from where he stood at his desk, conversing with two lower-grade officers over a map.

"Sir, I have OSS on the line. Bern office. About…" he threw his head in Donny's direction as if Donny couldn't hear or wouldn't notice. The general gave him a sharp look and rose, crossing the low room to take the phone from the lieutenant's outstretched hand.

"This is General McAuliffe. Whom do I have the pleasure of speaking with?" he said, one hand on his hip, his body language anything but polite. He caught Donny's eyes as he listened.

"Can you describe this man to me?" he said into the phone, never taking his eyes from Donny's. "Right. Okay. I don't know. I said I don't know. Things are bad here right now, the Germans are on all sides of us. We're afraid we're being cut off. I'll do what I can to help him, but I've got my hands full right now. No promises." He took a breath, nodded to himself, and waved to Donny to come over to the phone, which he held out just as the lieutenant had done.

"I believe it's your boss," he said, giving Donny a look of fresh appraisal, as if he'd misjudged him, then returned to his map.

"Hello?" Donny said into the phone.

"Where in hell have you been? What in blazes are you doing in France in the middle of the German offensive?" It was Dulles, all right.

Donny quickly told him what he knew, of barely escaping the factory near Mauthausen, then making his way across Germany.

"All right. The general said he'd try and get you out of there. Get your ass to Paris and report."

"You're in Paris? Any champagne left?"

"No champagne yet, hero. This isn't over. Now get your butt back here," Dulles said and hung up.

"He says I need to get to Paris, General. ASAP. Can you loan me a Jeep?"

"Don't we all," McAuliffe said under his breath, signing a form and handing it to his adjutant. "Ned, get this man a Jeep and a driver. He'll just get lost without one, and I want the damn Jeep back."

"Right away, Sir," Lt. Colonel Moore said, sticking his head out the door of the room and calling for a staff sergeant. McAuliffe gave Donny a less than friendly look.

"I hope whatever you know is good intel, son. I have a feeling we're going to need it," he said as Donny heard another artillery shell go over. *Screw this,* he thought. *Paris, here I come.*

77

Moeller's Journal, December 16th, 1944

As I stand here by the great Rhine River, watching the water slide past, I know that it is my fault the American agent has likely crossed the river and is attempting to make contact with forces friendly to him. He has proven to be a formidable foe; to be arrested by the Gestapo, yet be able to kill the two men in the car with him, even while in handcuffs, tells me how dangerous, yet resourceful he is. I have lost the battle, I think, and it's my fault again for not catching him, just as it was my fault my family was put in that hideous camp in the first place.

My dear, gentle wife you see, is an artist, a genius with any form of media. She sculpts in clay, wax and even creates beauty out of detritus she finds on the street. Our house in Vienna was full of the craziest, wild-looking things… and it makes me a bit sad to contemplate the fate of her body of work – no doubt thrown in the trash by the new tenants. Mostly though, Marie loves to paint.

People who don't understand Picasso look at his work and scoff, perhaps not aware of his classical training, of early works of realism every bit as good as the Dutch masters – but Picasso was not satisfied with following a path created by others. He had to break the mold, defy convention, dare to be different. Marie is much the same that way, which is why I fell in love with her. This is the true beauty of art.

I first became aware of her in Linz. I was a young Kripo investigator then, not yet a murder detective, and I fell in love not just with her squirrel's nest of red hair, her lovely high cheekbones and grey-green eyes, but also with her ability and her passion.

I came across her one day sitting in the park near the river where I often took my lunch. She was drawing the most amazing sketches of passersby in mere minutes. It helped pay her rent, and I would stand a little behind her, watching her work while I ate. It seemed a harmless enough pastime, but one day she simply turned around, looked at me, and waved me over. I don't know how she knew I was there, watching her work, but when she asked me what I was eating, I told her what kind of sandwich it was, although to this day I don't recall what it was, and I have a very good memory. All I could see was her.

What I remember is offering her the other half, and watching her take that first, big bite, then wiping her lips delicately with one perfect, slim finger. I found the courage after a week of bringing her lunch to ask her out, and we were married six months later. I cannot think of those years without smiling. We were young, and in love. She said yes when I asked her to marry me, but warned me that she'd never give up her art, and would require time to pursue it. I would have to understand this. She was so serious about it that it made me laugh. *Of course* I understood. I fell in love with her brain, as odd and slightly twisted as it could be at times. Anna was born a year and a half later, and our "little arrangement," as Marie sometimes called our marriage, flourished.

Anna turned ten the day Germany invaded Poland, and Sascha was born eight months later, with the fall of France. There seemed to be restrictions on everything by that time, and although we were not Jewish, we had many Jewish friends and had heard horror stories of people being deported – where, no one was really sure. We sheltered a female friend of Marie's for several weeks, in fact, until she could find transportation out of the country to Switzerland. How naïve we were then.

The Nazis had quickly expanded their book burning into other areas: other forms of art, banning certain music either because the composer was Jewish, or because it was "degenerate." Mahler, Mendelssohn, Irving Berlin, even George Gershwin, and, of course, any sort of jazz music was prohibited. That's to say, pretty much anything worth listening to. These were all types of music we enjoyed, and had many banned albums ourselves, but we were of a like mind on this, and didn't get rid of them. It seemed ludicrous, and we told ourselves that such silly rules would eventually be rescinded, but we were wrong.

Then they began confiscating "degenerate art." Works by Paul Klee, and other modernists like Max Beckmann and Oskar Schlemmer, Pablo Picasso, and even Van Gogh were confiscated. By 1944 we were living in an artist's hell. Marie did not respond well to this, and volunteered a couple of her stranger paintings to an avant-garde underground exhibit without telling me. It was a collection of Gaga-inspired works that would have made Man Ray or Salvador Dali proud, but someone reported it, the show was raided, and all the works confiscated.

I can only remember seeing Marie really angry a handful of times, but her normally sunny disposition was nowhere to be found when she went down to the local office of the Reich Culture Chamber to demand that they return her paintings. She was furious that morning, and I pleaded with her to let it go for now. I had to go to work, there had been a murder, but I swore I'd find a way to get her paintings back. She seemed calm when I left, but a few hours later I got the call that she'd been arrested.

It took everything I knew about the system, every favor I'd accrued over the years, plus a healthy bribe, to get her released. When we got back to our house, all of her art had been taken, plus our precious jazz albums, and of course, the record player. She was furious, as was I, but I think she understood by then that she was powerless against the will of the state, that it was dangerous to oppose the Nazi Party, even in such seemingly minor matters.

It lasted two days, then children's services showed up to investigate allegations that Marie had abandoned the children, left them alone for an unacceptable period of time. It was a lie, of course—by this time Anna was 14, and well able to take care of little Sascha—but it caused us a lot of grief.

I identified myself as a police detective, and managed to mollify them for the moment. Ten minutes after they left, the SD showed up to arrest Marie for "crimes against the state." I had had enough. There was a vociferous argument, then a struggle when one of them grabbed Marie's arm, intending to cuff her. Then I was attacked and pulled my weapon instinctively, as any good police officer would, and the SD agent lunged for it.

Although I wish I could somehow rewind the film in my head and stop Marie from going downtown to the Reich Culture Office to demand her paintings back, I do not regret shooting that prick of an SD agent. He represented everything wrong about Germany these days: the pointless persecution and brutality, the lack of the true democracy the Nazi pedagogues promised us, or even simple compassion, for that matter – the horrible inequalities we see each day, with powerful party officials and gauleiters living like kings while the rest of Germany scrabbles for mere existence... Yes, I wish that I could rewind this film, in the interest of a happier ending for us all.

– Part Four –

February 1945

78

#10 Downing Street, London – the Prime Minister's study

Winston Churchill stared blearily through a cloud of cigar smoke at his two closest advisors: General Hastings Lionel "Pug" Ismay, and Frederick Lindemann, the noted scientist. Churchill was exhausted – he'd been up all night, and while he still wore his favorite, tattered dressing gown, he'd switched from coffee to brandy an hour ago. After this morning's meeting, he'd get a few hours' sleep, then rise, compose his notes, and address Parliament – a job, frankly, that he'd have much rather left to someone else.

"What do we know? Is the threat real?" he asked. "Pug, if you would?"

General Ismay set down his tea and looked at his longtime friend. "As you know, Winston, we've been paying particular attention to any *Ultra* grade messages regarding an atomic bomb. The problem is, the program is so secret, the Jerries don't speak of it in open radio transmissions."

"And rightly so, because they haven't accomplished a bloody thing," Lindemann broke in. The brilliant, but prickly head of the MD1 experimental section was considered obstinate and outspoken, even a bit pompous by many, but Churchill trusted him. His scientific knowledge and practical advice had guided him through many difficult decisions.

"The new Arado Ar234—a jet bomber of unparalleled design—is overflying Britain on a nearly nightly basis," Ismay went on, nonplussed. "At this point they are only photo-reconnaissance, but they are undoubtedly planning something. According to *Ultra*, their bomber arm, KG76, centered in Achmer–Hesepe has fifty-one of these planes. Surely they are not *all* there simply to take pictures," Ismay finished.

"Rubbish," Lindemann said. "Even if they had an atomic device, the Arado is too small to carry it."

"*Ultra* messages maintain that they also have developed a thermobaric weapon: a fuel-air bomb. Although the atomic device would require a larger bomber obviously, the smaller, guided bomb could almost certainly be carried by the Arado," Ismay replied.

"Pah. Again, there is no proof that the Germans have achieved fission, or built a thermobaric weapon. There is no reason to dedicate valuable resources to such a ridiculous idea. It shouldn't even be under consideration," Lindemann said forcefully.

Churchill held up a hand. "Gentlemen, please. Now, not being familiar with this Arado 234 light bomber you speak of, can one of you please tell me *why* the Germans are able to fly the damn thing anywhere they want, such as over our beloved isle?"

Lindemann looked at Ismay, the chief military advisor, clearly not wanting to attach himself to any perceived military failure.

Ismay sighed. "It's simple, actually. The damn thing's simply too bloody fast. By the time we get planes in the air, or fire our antiaircraft guns, it's already gone. Imagine something about the same size and radar signature of our Mosquito, but much, much faster. The Americans are testing a new jet interceptor to counter the Me262 and this plane, but they say it's not ready."

"So, potentially, even if they don't have an atomic device, they could still bomb London with incendiaries or this new fuel-air bomb, correct?" Churchill said. "Would you both say that's a fair statement?" he said, puffing a cloud of smoke into the air as he peered at his advisors shrewdly.

"Well, of course, that's not my area of expertise," Lindemann said.

"That's never stopped you from sharing your opinion in the past," Ismay said, earning a dirty look from the scientist.

"Pug, what say you?" Churchill demanded.

"Yes. They have the capability to bomb London, basically unopposed, as long as it's a small flight. A larger force would, of course, show up quite handily on radar."

Churchill slammed his fist down on the ornate, 18th Century table, rattling its contents. "Then *why* haven't they?" The two men looked at each other uncomfortably.

"We simply don't know. Perhaps they are waiting for something," General Ismay said.

"Oh, I think it's pretty bloody clear they're waiting for something, but what?"

"Now wait a minute. The Arado jet bombers *are* being used. They bombed Belgium with nine of them during the Battle of the Bulge. It was the first time we'd seen them, in fact. Also, they are gathering photo reconnaissance..." Lindemann began

"Are you deliberately being obtuse? Fifty-one bloody jet bombers sitting there, not retreating deeper into Germany, and you don't think England is in danger? Don't be a fool, Lindemann!" Ismay exclaimed, beginning to get angry.

Lindemann opened his mouth to reply, but Churchill raised his hand again. "Gentlemen, please!"

He pushed himself tiredly from his chair and began pacing in front of them, the ever-present cigar clamped between his teeth, his brow furrowed.

"The Americans have information that there is not only a fleet of bombers that have been moved to Norway, but also that a single, huge bomber with additional wing tanks and in-air refueling capabilities is currently stationed at either Achmer or Hesepe airfield along with the Arado 234s under KG76's command. *One bomber,*" he said, giving them each a meaningful look. "Also, according to a deep cover OSS operative, not only may have the Germans tested a small atomic device in October, but they are preparing a simultaneous attack on both London and New York or possibly Washington. In fact, from what we've received via *Ultra,* the Germans are preparing a long-range attack on America, using an attack on London as a diversion."

"Utter rubbish! I'm telling you, Winston—" Lindemann began, standing up from his chair.

"Frederick, do shut up and let me finish," Churchill said, eyes blazing.

Lindemann sat back down. "I'm sorry if I overstepped, Prime Minister."

Churchill nodded, then said. "The Yanks have come up with a rather audacious plan to steal the bomber, hopefully with the atomic device on board. At the same time, they'll attempt to sabotage any operational Arados, or, at the very least, verify their efficacy and plant radio beacons our bombers can use to pinpoint their locations on the airfield, at which point we'll simply bomb them into oblivion.

"Two agents, both American, one of them a pilot, will be dropped into Germany. They have requested that the SOE run the operation, since we have so much experience with this sort of thing, and that we share any *Ultra* graded information about possible dispersal of the bomb or bombs, specifically in regards to KG76. I have decided that we will help them in any way possible."

"But... *two* agents? How are just two agents, only one of which is a pilot, going to steal a heavy-lift bomber right from under the Luftwaffe's nose?" Pug Ismay said. "For that matter, how are they going to even get near it? This pilot... what man would be crazy enough to do such a thing?"

Churchill smiled at his primary military advisor. "I'm told that the primary agent has posed as a Luftwaffe lieutenant colonel not once, but several times, and has actually penetrated several of their top secret weapons facilities. It was he who received the information about the atom bomb in process firsthand, directly from a scientist involved in the research."

Pug Ismay raised an eyebrow.

"As far as the pilot goes, Pug," Churchill said, "you're quite correct. No *man* would be crazy enough to attempt such a thing... which is why, I suppose, it's in our favor that the pilot's a woman. She'll be impersonating the famed German aviatrix, Hanna Reitsch. Their plan is to waltz right into the airfield using a forged letter from Hitler himself."

"Rubbish. Absolute, bloody insanity. What makes the Americans think they might possibly succeed?" Lindemann said.

"What makes you so sure they can't?" Churchill replied, his eyes twinkling as he puffed another cloud into the room. "And if they *do* manage to steal a plane, I suggest that it might be in our best interest not to shoot it down, eh?"

79

February 14ᵗʰ, Valentine's Day, 1945

Paris was alive again in a way it hadn't been since the Germans had invaded. Women once again wore their best dresses, the Americans had brought food and money with them, and it seemed everywhere Donny went, people were smiling, and bade him *bon jour*. The sun was going down, and with no fear of bombers any longer, the lights were coming back on, turning the city back into the magical refuge for lovers it had always been. Despite the cool weather, couples walked slowly through the city arm in arm, most of them American servicemen with their new, French sweethearts on their arms, enjoying the evening the way you only can with the one you love.

As Donny crossed the Avenue Duquesne he could see the Eiffel Tower glowing in the cerulean dusk, lit once more with white lights, like a symbol of redemption. He didn't understand why Allen Dulles wanted to meet at a café instead of at his temporary office, his suite at the Hotel du Louvre, but he didn't mind – he was hungry and Dulles was known to be a bit of a gourmand, so he was assured of a good meal, at least.

Although Donny had returned with much valuable intel, Operation Eagle Claw was still in motion as far as they knew. He looked around at the city – so alive and vibrant this evening, then pictured jet bombers dropping thermobaric incendiary bombs on the city. It made him frown. Well screw it. He had a ton of leave coming, and he intended on spending it right here in Paris. He'd rented a small pied-à-terre in the sixth arrondissement, stocked it with a record player and booze; now all he needed was Elena.

He wished that she was here with him tonight, right now, walking with him as they had in Prague, her arm tucked into his like all the other happy couples, and he wondered if he'd ever see her again. There was a couple kissing passionately beneath an ornate lamppost, and Donny turned away, down a long, dark cobblestone street, toward the café. It was Valentine's Day 1945, and for the first time in his life it bothered him to be alone. He just couldn't stop thinking about her.

The Aurora was small but well lit, with large windows out front that had miraculously survived the German invasion unscathed; the trim rich gold against a dark green background, the awnings clean but slightly tattered and sun-faded. The name was painted in a circle on the window in front in matching gold with black shadowing. There were four small tables out front, with no more than twice that inside, from what he could see past the low curtains.

Light spilled out the open door, the brightly lit interior a celebration of sorts in itself; the polished espresso machine and row of bottles lined up at the rear of the bar, sparkling and inviting. Soft music reached him from inside... so why did he feel so melancholy? Despite the growing chill, there were a number of people at the outside tables, and Donny saw Dulles sitting at the far table, with a woman in her late twenties or early thirties. Not his wife, surely. His mistress? Dulles didn't seem the type, but you never knew. A waiter wearing an apron stood by the door, hands folded before him, looking bored.

Allen Dulles smiled as he approached and raised his wine glass. "Donald, there you are! Care for a libation? This Pinot is wonderful. Please, have a seat – have some cheese," he said, referring to the cutting board in front of them, holding a sampling.

"Jackie, this is my colleague, Donald Brooks. Donald, this is Jacqueline Love. She's a pilot in the WASPs," Dulles said.

Donny took the diminutive brunette's hand with a smile. "Call me Donny, please. The only one who ever called me Donald was my brat of a sister," he said, sure that Dulles must know this and was deliberately baiting him.

She laughed politely, exposing straight white teeth and a comfortable sense of humor. "Donny, it is. Please, call me Jackie – everyone does. Have a seat," she said, turning to the waiter and holding up her glass. "*Garcon!* A glass for our friend, please?" she said in excellent French, clearly a woman in charge of her own destiny and comfortable with it.

Donny sat as the waiter brought an empty glass and poured Donny some of the Pinot Noir they'd been drinking. Donny sipped some. Dulles was right, it was very good.

"Anything else?" the waiter asked.

"Would you please check on our table? *Merci*," Dulles said.

"*Oui. Un moment, s'il vous plaît,*" the waiter said, turning back to the door.

"The *foie gras* here is amazing," Dulles said. Donny couldn't care less, really. He was in a foul mood for some reason, when he should be enjoying this. The war was nearly over, Paris was free again, and despite the chill in the early evening air, it was a beautiful night.

"I wanted you to meet Jackie, since you two will be working together," Dulles continued.

Donny paused, the wine glass halfway to his lips. "Bullshit. I'm on leave until I decide otherwise."

Dulles shook his head. "I'm afraid not. I need you for a job."

"I'm not going anywhere. I just spent over six months in enemy territory. My ribs are still healing. I'm taking a damn break from this madness."

"How convenient for you. Shall I call up Herr Hitler and see if he can put the war on hold for you?"

"Would you?"

"Don't be insufferable."

"Then don't say stupid things, like you want me to go back into the field."

"This is important or I wouldn't give it to you."

"You mean it's a shit job and no one else is stupid enough or expendable enough to do it."

"It could change the war."

Donny Brooks snorted from behind his glass. "I want two weeks."

"You can have a week off when you return."

"Gee, a whole week?"

"Look, Donny, I don't have time to fence with you. You already know about their tests – the Germans have successfully set off a small… device, and we have it on good authority that they plan to attack London and the East Coast of the U.S. soon with atomic and thermobaric weapons. Now, one of the thermobaric weapons by itself might not turn London into a smoking pile of rubble, but I expect fifty of them might."

"Look, I told you, I'm not interested. I've had enough of this damn war," Donny said, pushing his chair back and standing up. He drained what was left of his wine and turned to leave.

"We're bombing Prague tonight," Dulles said, stopping him in his tracks. Donny turned back to see him look at his watch.

"They should be approaching the target about now. Of course, it will be reported as a mistake – one bomber tasked to the raid on Dresden that went slightly off course – they're practically the same longitude…"

"You bastard. Have you warned the Czech Resistance?" Donny said. "Those people are our allies."

"Is that what we're calling it now? Elena's her name, right? No, we couldn't risk it."

Donny placed his hands on the table, leaning toward Dulles, murder in his eyes. "If she's hurt in this raid, I swear, I will kill you with my bare hands."

Dulles was nonplussed. "You think I came up with this? Oh, no. You can thank Wild Bill for this one. Got FDR's and Churchill's approval, so you'll have to kill them too, I suppose."

Donny stood there for a moment, then slumped back down into his chair, poured himself half a glass of wine, and drank it down in a few gulps. He looked at Dulles, who looked back at him.

"All right, what do you want me to do?" he said.

"Steal a plane. If you can't steal it, blow it up," Dulles said.

"Why do I have the feeling this isn't just any plane?"

"It's not. It's a long-range bomber loaded with an atomic weapon the Germans are planning on dropping on New York or Washington, we're not sure which. Worse, they're going to cover up the attack with a fire-bombing of London using a new fuel-air bomb delivered by jet fighters. The bomber is the linchpin. We steal or destroy that, there's a good chance the attack on London will be abandoned or delayed while they get another bomb, and plane, ready."

"And just how do you propose we do this?" Donny asked.

"Jackie here is a consummate pilot. She's a WASP – an air transport pilot. She can fly anything. She also happens to look a great deal like the famous German aviatrix, Hanna Reitsch. You have had such great luck impersonating Luftwaffe officers in the past, we think the two of you could penetrate the airfield at Hesepe where the bombers are staged, and steal or alternately blow up the long-range bomber."

"You're out of your mind," Donny said.

"On the contrary. It's just crazy enough to work," Allen Dulles replied.

"I mean, yes, she looks like her, but you really think they're just going to let her fly the damn thing?"

Dulles shook his head. "The backup plan is simple sabotage – you'll be close enough for that. We just need you to plant transponders on key targets, such as the bomber, so that our boys can get a good fix on it from the air. Even if the bomb isn't loaded yet, without a delivery device, it'll be useless with no way to deliver it... although clearly we'd like to destroy the atom bomb itself. It should be a piece of cake for an operative of your experience."

Donny snorted. "It's suicide, is what it is." He looked at Jacqueline Love. "Doesn't this bother you at all? What if one of them has met Hanna Reitsch before? What if you can't fly the damn thing?"

"I can fly anything," she said confidently.

"How's your German?"

"Perfekt, mein Herr."

"Well, shit. I think you're both nuts," Donny said.

"Is it any crazier than what you've been up to so far?" Dulles said. "You'll be inserted by the Carpetbaggers again, in a pinpoint night drop. A car will be waiting."

Donny snorted again. "Pinpoint night drop? No such thing."

Dulles sighed, emptying his glass. "Fine. I suppose I'll have to go myself then," he said.

"You? You've got to be kidding me," Donny began.

"I've done it before, I'll do it again. Sorry for wasting your time," Dulles said. "I just thought you'd want a chance to stop Operation Eagle Claw before they destroy New York and London. I see I was wrong about you."

"Just wait a minute," Donny said, holding up his hand. "If I do this, I'm not coming out through France."

Dulles looked at him. "What do you want?"

"Clean papers and enough money to get me to Prague, and through the remainder of the war. This is my last mission," he said.

Dulles looked at him and smiled. Donny hated that smile – it meant that he'd been had.

"Fine. I'll draw something up and we'll look at it in the morning, all right? Well then, let's eat. I'm positively starving," Dulles said, rubbing his hands together in anticipation. "Have you ever had duck l'orange?" he asked as they followed him inside.

Cooked goose is more like it, Donny thought, as he held the door for the woman with whom he was going to steal or destroy the Luftwaffe's latest, most powerful weapon.

80

Eleven days later, Donny found himself in another repurposed B-24 bomber with most of its armament removed to save weight, flying nap of the land despite much of what they were flying over now being recaptured territory. Both he and Jackie were wearing the same camouflaged jumpsuits the SOE and Jedburgh groups had used so effectively. The suits were baggy, designed so they could wear their German uniforms beneath them; Donny in the uniform of a lieutenant-colonel in the Luftwaffe, and Jackie, or "Hanna" as he'd been calling her for the last several days to ensure there wasn't a slip-up, wearing a replica of Hanna Reitsch's custom uniform she had designed for herself, as an honorary Luftwaffe Flugkapitän.

Her hair had been cut and dyed ash blonde, to match a recent picture, and they both looked the part, he had to admit. MD1 had done an amazing job producing spot-on papers for them both, as well as a forged letter from Hitler. Whether they could pull off the masquerade was something else entirely.

Donny had insisted on weapons this time, even though he knew they were likely safer without them. They'd be extremely vulnerable when they first hit the ground, and could stash the guns later, so they both carried Welguns – an odd, but extremely compact folding submachine gun with a strange receiver that was open on both sides. Donny'd had his doubts at first, but after thoroughly testing the little gun, had come away impressed.

He also carried a small Mauser P14 pistol in a clamshell holster on his uniform belt, and a new Fairbairn-Sykes fighting knife in the small of his back, along with a package of civilian clothes, fresh papers in yet another name, and enough cash to hopefully get him and Elena through the war in style… well, in relative comfort, he hoped.

They'd spent the last two weeks giving Jackie a crash course similar to the extensive training that Donny had received at Camp X in Canada years earlier.

There was no way to fit everything he'd learned in six months into a couple weeks, but they'd left the comforts of Paris for the utter misery of the Scottish Highlands in winter, the location of the SOE training facility they were taken to hidden even from them, as there were no windows in the C-47 that delivered them.

While the SOE handled Jackie's training, Donny received some updated weapons and radio cryptography training. The time went quickly, and Donny spent their meager evening hours off together trying to impart enough of what he'd learned over the years as an agent in the field to keep her alive – to keep them both alive, for if one of them were caught in a lie, then they were both dead.

The two of them spoke nothing but German, and he impressed upon her the fact that out of his class of fifteen operatives at Camp X, seven had died, none of them with their fingers intact. This was no game, he told her. They didn't share much personal information, but he had learned that she'd grown up on a farm in Iowa, and her father had been a barnstormer in the 1920s, which was where she'd gotten her love of flying. She'd first flown a plane at the tender age of ten, with 2x4 blocks strapped to the pedals, and hadn't looked back.

They eventually lost the farm, her father being a far better pilot than farmer, and by the time she was fourteen their family was chasing the carnival circuit. Her father was killed in a flying exposition in Kansas, and her mother had immediately moved them home to Iowa, the strain clear on her face: a simple farm girl who'd fallen in love with a dreamer.

Jackie was far more like her father than her mother, however, and got her pilot's license as soon as she was able, then left home to see the world. When the war came along, she wanted to help, but the Army Air Corps wasn't taking women pilots. Then the Women's Auxiliary Ferrying Service came along in 1942 and she joined up immediately, to her mother's dismay. In 1943 the service was joined with the WFTD—the Women's Flying Training Detachment—to form the WASPs: Women Airforce Service Pilots. She'd been flying ever since, and had flown everything from B-25s to Spitfires. She'd even ferried captured German planes from the mainland back to England,

and not just a few times. She spoke and read German fluently, having taken it in high school, and had an ear for it. It was these dual skills, as well as her physical similarity to Hanna Reitsch, that had gotten her nominated for the mission.

The B-24 lurched again, and Donny grabbed the netting to avoid sliding, holding the Welgun across his lap with the other hand. He looked across the narrow bay at Jackie, but she was asleep. Goddamn pilots. The copilot of the B-24 banged the bulkhead with his fist to get Donny's attention. "TWO MINUTES," he yelled over the loud drone of the engines and the rush of air outside. The B-24 was the same sort they'd used to fly him from Italy to Austria when this whole mess had started, and had been stripped of most of its gun turrets, with the waist turrets replaced with smooth aluminum, then painted matte black. The belly turret had been changed over to a simple, round hatch lined with aluminum, and a plywood floor added with hard points near the jump hatch for static lines so SOE and OSS agents could drop out the belly. The pilots were Carpetbagger Air Force, the same unique volunteer force of crazier than normal pilots who had dropped Donny into Austria. You had to be crazy to fly a B-24 at low level at night over enemy territory.

Suddenly someone was throwing rocks at them – big ones. They came tearing through the fuselage and out the other side. Donny looked over at Jackie – awake now, with a look of concern, although not panic, on her face. He was glad—he hadn't been sure how she'd be under fire, but now he saw that she'd be okay—as long as the antiaircraft rounds didn't hit either of them on their way through the plane.

More rocks were thrown, impacting the plane with a THUNK… THUNK, THUNK. Donny heard the pilot say a word he was positive his mother hadn't taught him, which is almost never good, then the left engine blew, and Donny could see a huge gout of flame eerily reflected on the inside of the cockpit glass. The green jump light came on as the "dispatcher," a former waist gunner, yanked the folding plywood door from the hole in the floor.

"YOU HAVE TO GO NOW," the dispatcher yelled at them, the cockpit illuminated by the fire on the wing.

"Are we over the—" Jackie began.

"GO NOW," the copilot screamed back from the cockpit as the pilot fought to keep the plane in the air. The crewman gestured to Jackie, who jumped into the open hatch and was gone. Donny heard the pilot yell to the copilot, "TAKE 'ER UP. WE'LL HAVE TO DIVE TO PUT THE FIRE OUT," then he dropped out of the belly of the plane into the darkness, the wind hit him like a fist, and he was tumbling through the night, somewhere over Germany.

81

It was a low drop, so Donny had no time to get straightened out. He just tried to time pulling the ripcord with the tumble so the chute would deploy properly, mentally crossing his fingers as he did so. If he pulled at the wrong moment, the chute would open beneath him, wrap itself around him, and at such low altitude, become his death shroud.

The massive jerk on his shoulders told him he'd gotten lucky, then he was swinging down through the night, wondering how close they were to their original drop zone. He could make out dim forms in the darkness and realized they were trees. A huge, dark shadow suddenly loomed up before him, and he braced himself and tried to cover his face as he hit – harder and faster than he'd anticipated. This time it didn't just knock the wind out of him, it knocked him right out.

Donny awoke surrounded by branches, with a knot on his head where he must have hit a particularly large one. He was hanging in a tree, but couldn't tell how far up – it was dark as sin. Then he heard a tearing sound and dropped a foot or two lower, realizing that's what had awoken him. Whatever his chute was hooked on had torn it. He looked down, but still couldn't tell how high he was off the ground. If he landed wrong and broke a leg, he was done for.

He got his hand around a branch, but it wasn't very big, then there was the sound of ripping cloth and breaking branches and he was falling uncontrollably, hitting every damn branch on the way down. Finally he was spun by a big one near the bottom, nailing it squarely with his torso, arms over the top, feet dangling below, and he fought to pull himself up, but he was sliding off.

He scrabbled for a better handhold, but he slid off, smacking his chin on the branch, biting his tongue, then he was falling backward, through the air, hitting the ground hard, knocking the wind out of him yet again.

This is getting really old, he thought as he lay on the cool grass, fighting for breath, wheezing in the night air, which smelled of grass, and dew, and... manure. Always stepping in the shit. *Just once,* Donny thought. *Just once I'd like a normal goddamn insertion.*

Once he'd caught his breath, Donny stood cautiously and took stock. There was blood in his mouth from when he'd bitten his tongue, his chin was a bit scraped up, and the rib he'd broken climbing down the side of Hohensalzburg Castle hurt like a bastard, but other than that he seemed whole. He quickly stripped the parachute harness, rolling the whole thing up in his arms and stuffing it into some brush – the best he could do at the moment, but he expected to be miles away by morning. He dumped his jump helmet as well, but kept the camo coveralls on over his uniform to keep it clean. He took a compass bearing, but had no idea where he was relative to their intended drop zone, or where his jump partner might be. Saying a quick prayer, he extended the stock on the Welgun, cocked it, and began slowly moving east, through the darkness.

82

Jackie had been stressing about the jump for days. Like all pilots, she'd had parachute training, but this was her first live jump, and in the dark yet. She'd been lucky and landed in a field. She'd banged up her left shoulder a bit on a rock, but it didn't feel too bad, and although she'd been surprised at the violence of the impact, she was on her feet almost immediately, her first thought being German patrols, even though their chutes had been dyed OD green, and the moon wasn't up yet.

She took a compass bearing, wondering where Donny was, and used the signaling cricket, the same brass and tin toy the Allied airborne troops had used during D-Day to identify each other, but got nothing in return. They'd discussed the likelihood of getting separated during the jump, however, so she wasn't worried yet. She removed her helmet, then shook out her hair as she'd always done when riding motorcycles—another passion of hers—only then remembering there was nothing to shake out anymore: her hair had been cut short and dyed blonde to match the real Hanna Reitsch's hair. Jackie had been a bit rueful about it at the time—she'd always been proud of her hair—but truthfully, now she kind of liked it short. It was very freeing.

Jackie shrugged off the harness, ran her fingers through her short hair a couple times, then scooped up the chute, jump harness, and helmet in her arms after making sure the Welgun was slung over her right shoulder where she could get to it quickly, and began moving east, toward the tree line. She'd hide the chute, then keep moving east until she found the road to Osnabrück. Hopefully Donny wasn't far away, and they'd meet up at the crossroads as planned.

It was dark, but there was a moon playing hide-and-seek with some fast-moving clouds, so Jackie could see well enough to navigate. She came to a small stream and went right, which, according to the small, luminous jump compass she wore like a wristwatch, was east. She had a map but didn't dare risk a light, even the small, red penlight she carried, as she had no idea where the German lines were. She remembered seeing a bridge near the crossroads where they were supposed to rendezvous, so she followed the stream, hoping she was in the right place.

A half hour later her nerves were shot, the moonlight turning small trees into SS troopers, the murmur of the wind sounding like murmuring voices as every stray branch seemed to reach out to grab her, making her want to shriek each time it happened.

Her route seemed strewn with rocks put there intentionally to make her stumble, and she very nearly shot a small calf that bolted from the hedgerow in front of her, then trotted back to the safety of its mother. The stream eventually fed into a larger one, running east and west, and although she couldn't tell how large, it seemed like a river or perhaps a canal, hopefully the Mittelland Canal.

The moon slid behind another cloud, and she nearly walked straight into a stone wall... a wall? Jackie ran her free hand over it, the mean little submachine gun they'd given her in the other. She could hear the burble of water to her left, and looked up as the moon slid free, realizing she could see the top – the low arch of a bridge. If she was right, the crossroads should be about twenty-five yards or so from the other side of the bridge. If not, then she was hopelessly lost.

She went right, climbing up the slight slope to the road, then, crouching low, she looked cautiously both ways, taking the time to listen carefully as she'd been taught, but heard nothing. She rose to her feet and stepped out onto the road, going left, over the bridge. It was a big canal, and a good-sized bridge, big enough to easily hold a large truck. She continued down the other side, a gradual ramp, until she reached the crossroads, sighing with relief as she felt more than saw the signpost with crossed indicators. She slid closer and took hold of the square post, peering up at the sign, waiting for the moon to reappear.

Finally the moon emerged from its bed in the clouds and she found she'd been right – the left road was clearly marked Achmer. Chuffed, she turned around to go back the way she came to wait for Donny, but found herself face to face with a German soldier pointing a rifle at her, just ten feet away.

83

"**H**ände hoch! – Hands up! NOW," the soldier told her in German. Jackie slowly let go of the Welgun, letting it droop on its sling beside her, raising her hands as another German soldier shouldered his way out of the brush. Was it just the two of them, or were there more? She'd had a crash course in self-defense and silent killing taught by a short, insane Scotsman that, as tough as it was, nevertheless had left her feeling confident – a real femme fatale. Now, however, with two soldiers pointing rifles at her, she was wondering if she could really take them.

If she could get closer, inside the swing radius of the rifle, she felt confident that she could kill at least one of them with the Fairbairn-Sykes dagger strapped to her right jump boot, but the other one would likely shoot her. Still, she knew she had no choice. She couldn't be taken: the Gestapo would torture her, then they'd either shoot or hang her… and who knew what else first? This was her last and best chance. *It's now or never,* she thought, as she edged closer.

Suddenly Jackie heard the stutter of a submachine gun and was blinded by flashes to her immediate left, from the crossroads. She threw herself to the ground, then rolled left, bringing the Welgun up to bear on the falling Germans, breathing a sigh of relief when she realized they were already down. Not knowing who her benefactor was, she stayed on the ground, not moving, until her hearing, dulled by the gunfire, returned.

It was quiet once more on the bridge, and she heard rustling in the bushes on the other side of the road to Achmer, then heard the cricket-like clicking of the D-Day signaling device, a rectangular, brass box operated with your thumb. She scrambled to pull hers from her pocket and returned the signal, in the agreed-upon pattern of clicks. The other "cricket" signaled back and she smiled, getting to her feet. It was Donny.

Jackie tucked the stamped metal toy back in her pocket and moved to meet the shadow that was running through the intersection toward her. It looked as though he was limping a little.

"Are you all right?" Donny asked her as he came closer.

"You're limping."

"Twisted my ankle in the landing. It'll be fine. Looks like it's just these two. Help me drag their bodies off the road. They have a Kübelwagen on the other side. We'll ditch this stuff and drive into Osnabrück," he said, already moving toward the dead Germans.

"Thanks for saving my bacon," Jackie said.

"No sweat, sis. That's what I'm here for," Donny grinned in the moonlight, then made sure both soldiers were dead, dispatching the one he found still breathing with a flash of his dagger. Jackie helped him drag the bodies into the woods, then they both stripped off their jump smocks, revealing their German uniforms beneath. Donny waited while Jackie changed out of her jump boots and into more appropriate Luftwaffe lightweight flying boots, then they wrapped the Welguns and everything else incriminating in the smocks and dumped everything that wasn't German into the canal.

Then Donny changed his mind and decided the soldier's bodies should go into the canal as well, neater that way, he said, so they spent an additional five minutes dragging them down to the water and rolling them in. The only thing American they kept were their OSS daggers, which they tucked inside their tunics, just in case. Jackie set her rakish Flugkapitän's cap at a jaunty angle over her short, ash blonde hair.

"How do I look?"

"Flugkapitän Reitsch, you look ready to steal a bomber," Donny said. "Now let's get out of here before another patrol comes along."

"Jawohl, Herr Oberstleutnant. Right behind you," Jackie said as Donny moved off into the dark.

84

The Kübelwagen's tank was half full, likely enough to get them where they were going. Since Jackie was the celebrity, despite his ostensibly greater rank, Donny got in the driver's side. He started the little four-door Jeep, paused, then shut it off again.

"What is it?" Jackie said.

"I was just thinking. The only reason we involved the French Resistance in this mission at all was for an appropriate vehicle to get us to the airfield. Why don't we just take this?" Donny said, indicating the Kübelwagen with his hands. "It would save time and reduce risk, both for us and the Resistance."

"But we aren't supposed to reach the airfield until early afternoon."

"We'll stop for lunch."

She gave him a look, making him laugh.

"Seriously – give me one good reason we should drive in the opposite direction simply to change cars. Plus, then either we or our Resistance contacts will have to dispose of this thing somehow. Let's just take it and go."

Jackie shrugged. "You're the one with the experience. I'm just the pilot."

Donny grinned at her, his wide smile white in the dark. "All righty then," he said, starting the light Jeep again.

Thirty minutes later, Donny saw a German convoy speeding toward them in the opposite direction, led by two motorcycle outriders. "Heads up," he said.

Jackie looked up from the map she was holding. As they came parallel to them, she suddenly stood up on the seat, hanging onto the windshield with one hand and waving wildly with the other, nearly giving Donny a heart attack.

"HALLO, JUNGS," she yelled, giving them a wide smile.

252

The soldiers in the open trucks of the convoy responded with whoops and waves; unsmiling just minutes before, they were transformed back into the young boys they really were, smiling and waving at the pretty girl.

Once past the trucks, she dropped back into her seat with a final thrown kiss and wave at the receding convoy.

"I believe that could be construed as giving comfort to the enemy," Donny said wryly.

"Oh, shut it. I'm Hanna Reitsch, remember? I'm here to boost morale."

"Well, don't boost it too much, the damn war'll never be over."

85

3rd letter from Marie, dated February 12th , 1945

*M*y love,
     This may be the last letter I am able to write. Lack of sustenance and the cold has taken its toll, I'm afraid. There is so much sickness here, that it is impossible to avoid, and I believe now I have pneumonia as well. Not only is there no medicine, but all supplies have become so dear that the Aufseherin and the guards seem to resent even the meager portions of gruel they distribute. It's as if they resent us for being here, and are simply waiting for us to die. The overall feeling of gloom and desperation in the camp is a palpable thing – you can feel it everywhere.

*   I have more bad news. Anna was offered a "position" at one of the "relaxation centers" and the fool girl took it, not realizing the position offered would most likely be on her back. I hesitated in telling you this, but we have always shared the truth, good or bad, as husband and wife, and I thought you should know. She came to see me just before they took her, and looked happy for the first time in months… at least for the moment. My God, she's just a child – she has no idea of the cruelty of men, or what new ugliness awaits her.*

*   I feel as though I have failed completely as a mother; my children gone, all vestiges of our family destroyed. I don't know where you are – I've had no word other than that first letter in which you outlined the conditions of your temporary release. Please, my love, come get me! Take me away from this horror. We'll find Anna and escape this madness. Please, it's just too much to bear anymore. –All my love, Marie.*

86

Moeller's Journal, February 25th, 1945

This may very well be the final entry in this journal… not that anyone will ever read it. I have been ordered back to Salzburg, where I have no doubt my sentence will finally be carried out; the cost of my failure. Shot or hanged, does it really matter? What matters is that I have failed miserably. No sightings of the OSS agent in the last six weeks – nothing which could be construed as his handiwork. Frankly, it's dispiriting. My family has been suffering in that damn camp for months, now Sascha gone from sickness… how long will Anna and Marie manage to survive in that miserable place? Marie's most recent letter took me past the gates of despair; it broke my heart.

I care not that I will likely be shot upon my return, but only that my darlings are still held behind barbed wire, with little to eat, sleeping three or four to a bed, and the sanitary conditions, or rather lack of them, according to Marie's last letter, dated over a week ago – unbelievable. What a monster Hitler is! His minions as well. Though I know most of the German people and German soldiers are inherently good folk, there is a cancer in our country; an evil, spreading cancer, insidious and most foul, which must be eradicated, and I am not referring to the Jews, as Herr Hitler has maintained. I mean the Nazi Party itself, and all it stands for.

So, I have chosen to disregard my orders to return to Salzburg and visit just one more top secret facility: an airfield in northwest Germany, near Osnabrück, where, I'm told, bombers carrying the new vengeance weapons are preparing for an attack. I will not divulge how I know this—who my source was—as it would just cause another senseless death, but if "Herr Strausshind" is still operating in this country, and is as good as I think he is, then this is a nearly irresistible target.

As far as putting my family at risk for disobeying Gephardt's orders, how could they be more at risk than they are already? For all I know, Marie and Anna are already gone – although I do not want to believe that – cannot believe that. On the other hand, any chance of success at this point is worth taking, in my opinion. What do I have to lose? Well, everything. However, if Herr Strausshind *does* show his face at the airfield, once again impersonating a Luftwaffe officer, I will arrest him and free my family.

Once more I beseech thee, oh Lord. Keep my darlings safe and guide me in this time of darkness. Please, please bring the OSS agent to me – if only for their sake.

87

They had to go through three levels of security to reach the airfield proper – an outer checkpoint on the main road, then two inner gates. The airfield was surrounded by a hurricane fence, cleverly woven in and out of the surrounding trees and hedgerows to diminish its signature from the air.

The repair hangars were built into the ground, for the most part, and operational planes were simply pushed into the trees and covered with camouflage netting. The only buildings in the open were fairly nondescript, brick buildings, unremarkable and un-military in appearance, and by the time they reached the inner gate, the Kommandant of KG76, Oberstleutnant Robert Kowalewski, was waiting for them wearing a wide smile.

"Miss Reitsch, what a pleasure to finally meet you! I am sorry, but we had no idea you were coming," Kowalewski said, extending his hand to help her from the Kübelwagen.

"Oh, but it is I who am sorry for just dropping in on you like this, Herr Oberstleutnant, but the Führer thought a quick tour of the forward airbases at this difficult point in the war might be encouraging," Jackie said, taking his hand, which he brought briefly to his lips, clicking his heels in a very proper, Prussian bow.

"Of course! A wonderful idea. How is our beloved Führer?" he asked.

Jackie wrinkled her brow a bit, as if discussing a friend in distress. "As strong as ever… but I worry about him. He has a great deal on his mind these days," she said.

The Kommandant gravely nodded his understanding.

"This is my companion for the trip, my 'watchdog,' if you will, Herr Oberstleutnant Fuhrmann," Jackie said.

Donny clicked his heels and raised his chin, saluting Kowalewski smartly. "Heil Hitler. It is a pleasure to meet you, Oberstleutnant. I do hope that this is not too much of an intrusion."

"Nein! Of course, this is a forward area now, so I must warn you both, both Hesepe and Achmer airfields have been receiving a great deal of attention from American bombers lately, so if you hear the air raid siren, please do not disregard it."

"It can't be worse than Berlin, eh, Hanna?" Donny said to Jackie with a wink, and they all laughed. *So far so good,* Donny thought.

"Oh, Colonel – der Führer asked me to give you this," Jackie said, handing the colonel a sealed envelope, which he took gingerly. He carefully opened it and quickly read it, then returned it to the envelope.

"It would be an honor to show you around. Please, walk with me. Are you hungry? Have either of you had breakfast?" Kowalewski said.

Donny opened his mouth to speak, but Jackie beat him to it.

"As a matter of fact, no. All we've had is a bit of muddy water dipped from a roadside ditch," she said.

The Kommandant of KG76 looked at her in horror, then realized by her wide grin that she was joking and laughed loudly. "Ah, well I think we can do a little better than some muddy ditch water, Miss Reitsch… or do you prefer Flugkapitän?" he said, referring to her honorary rank in the Luftwaffe.

"Actually, among friends I prefer Hanna," Jackie said, giving him a wink to go with her smile.

"Hanna! Not too familiar? Very well then, Hanna, and…"

"Jakob. Please, I could use a bit more muddy water as well, Herr Oberstleutnant," Donny said. "Preferably hot, mixed with brandy."

The colonel laughed again. *So jolly, aren't we?* Donny thought.

"Then you must call me Robert. But please, not in front of the men? Now, I'm afraid we are fresh out of ditch water. Would Kaffee and some scones be acceptable?"

"That sounds wonderful," Jackie told him as they followed the colonel to his staff car for the ride across the airfield.

88

After a gracious but rather plebeian breakfast of blackberry scones and ersatz coffee, and far too much chit chat for Donny's taste, they once more piled into the staff car for the tour of the airfield. It was warm for February, and the colonel had the driver put the top down so they could see better.

Donny had been surprised by Jackie's skill as an actress. Everywhere they went she smiled and asked questions, laughing and joking with officers and enlisted men alike. He knew she'd had some theatrical training, but she nearly had *him* believing she was Hanna Reitsch, the famed aviator. She was completely natural, and he found himself relaxing into his own role. His greatest fear was that they'd run into someone on the airfield who'd met Hanna Reitsch during a previous tour, perhaps at another airfield, and they'd recognize her as a fake. It was one of the flaws in the plan, but there was no way to control it – they just had to take their chances.

They took a break for lunch: sausages and fresh bread with sauerkraut, and an unusual, but filling tomato basil soup. The colonel had pulled out all the stops. During lunch Jackie mentioned that their time was limited, and she was anxious to inspect the planes mentioned in the Führer's letter. Kowalewski's initial response made Donny wonder if she'd pushed it too far; he simply gave her a shrewd look, as if deciding something, then acquiesced with a wide smile. It made Donny nervous.

The bomber was absolutely huge, the largest plane Donny'd ever seen, other than maybe an Me323 *Gigant*. It was covered with camouflage netting and was being worked on – clearly not ready to take off. Donny was getting the sinking feeling that they'd come a long way for nothing. There was nothing he could do: Jackie was the lead here, and he simply followed "Hanna" around—just part of her growing entourage—while he tried to figure out a way he could sabotage the huge plane in such a way as to prevent it from taking off.

"It's the latest of four prototypes, and the only one with *both* jet and conventional propeller engines. The men have nicknamed it *Der Adler* for obvious reasons," Kowalewski said. "Note the large drop tanks specifically designed for her," he said, pointing at four large, teardrop-shaped tanks that looked more like bombs mounted to the wings. The two inboard ones were bigger than the other two. "When all four tanks are full, they add an additional 3,500 kilometers to its range. Coupled with in-air refueling, it gives *Der Adler* a range of nearly 14,000 kilometers."

"Mein Gott, it's huge," Jackie said admiringly, saying the words all men love to hear. "Please, may we see the inside?"

"But of course," Kowalewski said with a smile, leading the way.

"I didn't realize it had both normal prop engines and jets. How well do the two engines work in concert? I have flown the Dornier 335, so the idea of a pull and push prop is not new to me, but I cannot imagine how they work together with jets. Are they only used at cruising speed? Are the props feathered?"

Kowalewski laughed. "I am a fighter pilot, myself. Perhaps the pilot could explain better," he said, indicating a dashing officer in flying gear standing nearby. "Flugkapitän Hanna Reitsch, may I present Flugkapitän Johann Koch."

The pilot took her hand, fawning over her like all the rest. Donny was using the time to inspect the outside of the aircraft, wondering what a good fire would do to it.

"Flugkapitän Reitsch, it is an honor," Koch said. "I missed meeting you some years ago when you visited JG54, but Walter Nowotny told me all about you."

"Oh, how is dear Walter?" Jackie said.

Koch gave her an odd look. "Walter was killed in action in November. I'm surprised you didn't know," he said.

Jackie looked shocked, and Donny was fairly sure it didn't require much acting on her part. This is what he'd been afraid of. A simple slip-up could get them both killed.

"MEIN GOTT. *I didn't know…* oh, I am so, so sorry," she said, taking his hands in hers. "I have been so busy, between traveling and testing new aircraft… I've lost track of so many friends. So many good people gone. I feel horrible… some friend I am, eh?" she said miserably, and Donny could actually see tears in her eyes. *Damn, she's good,* he thought.

Koch placed his hands over hers. "I completely understand, Miss Reitsch. These last few months have been difficult for us all," he said.

"Ja, very difficult… but we must continue, eh?" she said. "For the Reich, for the Führer, for all of Germany," she said, wiping her eyes with the back of one hand.

"Miss Reitsch—if I may call you that—*this* plane, and its bomb load, will change the course of the war. With the Arado Ar234 firebomb attack on London as a diversion, we'll simply be lost in the chaos, flying overhead at high altitude. The Americans will never know what hit them… at least until the Führer announces it over the radio," Koch said vehemently.

"Show me," "Hanna Reitsch" told him.

The inside of the plane was as impressive as the outside. Donny had been inside a Heinkel He111 once, and the cockpit, a domed, "greenhouse" design, reminded him a bit of it, but much bigger. The entire front end from the inside reminded him oddly of a huge antiaircraft gun sight, with curved windows in a concentric pattern, meeting the domed ribs like pieces of a pie when viewed from inside. A tall instrument pod stood in the center, with the forked wheel of the control yoke extending out over the pilot's seat in an odd, 90-degree arrangement.

The copilot's seat had been removed, and a technician was lying on his stomach, working on something in the nose of the aircraft. A large, floor-mounted control panel covered with switches, gauges, levers, and lights filled the space between the seats. How the hell anyone could fly this behemoth was beyond him, but Donny was pretty damn sure it was going to take more than one pretty WASP to get the job done, and he was no pilot. Didn't even like flying, for God's sake, and how many times had he jumped out of a damn airplane now? This last one on fire as well. Give him a car any day…

To the right, on the fuselage wall, were two odd-looking, wall-mounted units with a simple gauge, a switch, and a large hose attached and mounted into clips set in a U-shaped configuration. The pilot noticed him looking at them curiously and smiled.

"You're not a pilot, are you?" he said.

Donny smiled back and shook his head. "Nein. Just a simple adjutant," he said.

"Well, these are the oxygen units for the flight engineer and forward gunner to use at high altitude," the pilot said, unclipping the hose and holding it to his mouth to demonstrate, flipping the switch on, then off again. "You'll find them in two-man pods throughout the plane," he said, reattaching the hose to the wall. "The hose clips into the oxygen mask. It's a long way to America," he said with a grin.

If he's this confident, Donny thought, *then they must have solved the range problem. It's only a matter of time before they finish building more atom bombs. Seventy or more bombers on a field outside Oslo...* He imagined for a minute every one of them armed with an atom bomb, running up their engines, just waiting for the signal to bomb America. Even so, this single bomb dropped on New York or Washington would stop the Allied war machine in its tracks. Coupled with a firebombing of London by fifty-one jet bombers faster than Spitfires or Mustangs, and the Germans might well get the time they so badly needed to concentrate on just fighting the Russians and consolidate their war production.

Of course, Donny knew it was ludicrous to imagine the Germans would ever produce more than a handful of atomic bombs, but from the animations he'd seen in London recently, just one of the damn things was too many.

"How large a crew?" Jackie asked.

"Der Adler requires a crew of nine. Well, three to fly it: pilot, copilot and navigator, who doubles as radio operator, plus five gunners. I'll show you their positions."

"How does she fly?" Jackie asked.

This prompted a long, technical discussion between the two pilots about wing-loading, take-off weight, and something called RATOs, which made Donny's eyes glaze over.

As they began moving toward the rear of the plane, on the left wall, behind the pilot, Donny could see a load of complicated electronic equipment, likely the radio, compass, and radar equipment, with a simple, padded metal seat bolted to the floor in front of it. Several of the boxes had *SCHUTZKAPPE ERST BEIM EINSETZEN DES GERÄTES ENTFERNEN!* or "Close lid before activating equipment" in red on the cover.

They followed the pilot through a narrow, arched access hatch, duck-walking to get through. The compartment they were now in was dark, and Koch flipped on a ceiling-mounted light.

"The bomb bay," he said, pulling a tarp off a huge bulge on the floor.

In the middle of the bay was the largest bomb Donny had ever seen. It was cylindrical, like a fat torpedo, painted bright, Nazi red, with black stripes on the finned rear housing, built like a box kite, with the six fins meeting the structure at each corner. On each side, in a large, white circle, a black swastika had been painted, as if there were any doubt as to its ownership.

The nose was painted black as well, the welds done perfectly, with large, oddly shaped brackets around the circumference of its middle. Donny recognized the housing as the same huge "broken eggs" he'd seen piled in the underground workshop. *Jesus, how many of these are they thinking of building?* he wondered. Then he wondered how many they already had. Supposedly there was just this one… but what if there were more?

Donny had already come to the conclusion that there was no way they could fly the bomber out of there. Just having it covered with camouflage netting and being tied to ground electrics was an insurmountable problem. He knew from his briefing with the scientists at MD1 that it was theoretically possible to destroy an atomic device without setting it off, but in truth, no one knew for sure.

Still, he and Jackie had both agreed to the mission knowing full well it was likely a one-way trip. Right now he was racking his brain, trying to figure out where he could get the explosives to destroy the damn thing. Suddenly he heard the air raid siren winding up – so loud that you couldn't mistake it for anything else.

"Quickly – into the bunker!" Koch yelled at them, leading the way out of the aircraft. As they climbed out the access hatch, Donny could hear the roar of antiaircraft guns firing all around them, as well as a loud, droning noise getting louder by the minute. Then came the CRUMPH and rumble of bombs impacting nearby, as they quickly dove into a small bunker already crowded with technicians and flight crew, a few of which, mostly the younger ones, had looks of abject terror on their faces, while the older, more experienced hands seemed to take the bombing with equanimity. One of them saw Donny eyeing the roof supports and sand bags warily.

"Don't worry, Herr Oberstleutnant. If it's a direct hit, you'll never feel it," he said with a grin.

Donny had been through several bombing raids, but always in deeper bunkers. This was the worst he'd experienced. He looked at Jackie, squatting next to him. She had her eyes squeezed shut, hands over her ears against the constant cacophony. She was not taking it well. He put a hand on her back, startling her, looking into her eyes and sending her a mental message: *Hold it together.* His next thought though was: *God, I hope they hit the plane,* even knowing that it would be the end of them. Finally the rumble and roar of detonations slowed, and the drone of the bombers seemed to lessen as the antiaircraft fire slowed as well, then stopped. The all-clear signal came, and they all scrambled out of the bunker, a bit shaken but no worse for wear.

89

The bombing had done surprisingly little damage, although one of the three runways, set in an overlapping triangular pattern, had been hit twice. The other two, however, had been untouched, and repair crews were already working to repair the damage.

Miraculously no planes had been hit, although one ammunition bunker close by had been destroyed. Colonel Kowalewski, who had sheltered in another nearby bunker, told them it was partly due to the excellent camouflaging, and partly due to the phalanx of over 500 antiaircraft guns surrounding both Achmer and Hesepe airfields, forcing the bombers to drop their bombs from higher altitude.

"Hanna" reiterated her desire to fly one of the Arado Ar234's, and demanded that it be armed with one of the new fuel-air thermobaric bombs they would be using on London, stating that without it she couldn't get a feel for how the plane performed with such a heavy bomb load – something the Führer had specifically asked her to evaluate.

"But Miss Reitsch, this is a very dangerous bomb load, particularly upon landing. We have no more dummy bombs as we have used them up in training runs," the kommandant of KG76 said, his concern plain.

"Really? More dangerous than flying the Me163? It doesn't even *have* landing gear – just skids. Have you flown one? What about the Fieseler Fi103? The entire aircraft is basically a big, flying bomb. Have *you* flown one of those? Well? Have you? Have *either* of you flown either one of those planes?"

The two men looked at each other.

"Now, Colonel, you received direct orders from the Führer, did you not?"

"Yes, Miss Reitsch, but…"

"But nothing! I was sent here by Adolf Hitler to evaluate these planes and this unit prior to the mission being given its final approval. If I were you, I should not be too anxious to receive a failing grade from me. Am I making myself entirely clear, *Herr Oberstleutnant?*"

She was bluffing, of course, but only she and Donny knew it. The combination of a pissed-off woman who happened to be (as far as they knew) the best known test pilot in Germany, not to mention a personal friend of the Führer, did it. After conferring with a number of other officers, a decision was made that brought a smile to Jackie's face. As the others were given their orders, Jackie came over to Donny, her eyes fairly sparkling with glee.

"They're going for it. They're going to let me take one up!" she said sotto voce to Donny.

"Fully armed?"

"Not only is it fully armed, but get this – those smaller bombs we saw with the fins like fish?"

"Yeah?"

"The boys at MD1 were right – they're thermobaric. Big, BIG boom. The best part is, they're apparently based on something called a *Fritz X* bomb that was designed for attacking shipping."

"So?"

"So, it's a *guided weapon*. The bombs ride a radio signal to the target. Of course, you have to maintain line of sight to the target until the thing detonates, or you at least get close…"

"How will you see the bomber with the camouflage nets over it?"

"Well, I'll have to come in low… really low."

Donny shook his head. "No way. It's too crazy, too dangerous. We'll figure something else out. If we can just set the fuse on one…"

"Typical man. A woman comes up with a plan, it's not good enough. Now, if you had thought of it, and were piloting the damn plane…" she began angrily.

"You could be killed. In fact, it's *likely*," Donny said.

"What'd you think I volunteered for, an ice cream social? You wouldn't give this a second thought if I were a man, would you?"

Donny had to admit, she was right. "I still think it's a bad idea," he said.

"It's the *only* idea. Here comes the Kommandant our way again. It'll take about an hour to fuel and preflight the plane. Koch's going to check me out on the controls. I suggest you leave soon, and get as far away from here as possible. Once I hit that bomber it's going to be like kicking over the proverbial hornet's nest," Jackie said, then indicated Kowalewski with a nod of her head.

"Is there a problem?" the colonel asked as he came up to them. He seemed hopeful.

"Nein, Herr Oberstleutnant Fuhrmann just agrees with you that this test is dangerous. Too dangerous for a *woman*, isn't that what you were saying, Herr Fuhrmann?" she said angrily.

"I just don't know what I would tell the Führer if you were to get hurt, Hanna," Donny said.

"Perhaps testing the plane without armament would be the best compromise," Colonel Kowalewski said.

Jackie Love looked at him coldly. "Haven't we already had this discussion, Colonel?"

He took a deep breath. "Ja, ja. The plane will be ready for preflight in a few minutes. They are removing the netting and will begin fueling it."

"Danke, Herr Oberstleutnant. I will join you in a moment." She turned to Donny. "Since you do not wish to see me hurt myself, Jakob, why don't you go into town and get some supper?"

"It's too early for supper," Donny said.

"A drink then, perhaps two. It won't take me long to evaluate the plane – less than an hour, I should think. Why don't you go enjoy yourself and come back then?"

"It's a good thing your title of Flugkapitän is honorary, Fräulein," Donny said, giving Kowalewski, his "fellow officer," a knowing look. "You're a bit too impertinent at times to people who are technically your superiors," he said, playing his role.

"I suppose so," Jackie replied. "Of course, *I'm* following the Führer's orders, whereas the two of you are simply trying to prevent me from doing my duty to the Reich!" she said, stomping off to the plane.

"Is she always like this?"

"Just when she doesn't get what she wants," Donny said. "And you know, she's right. Truthfully, I find all this airplane business incredibly boring. Would you mind if I drove into town for a drink?"

"Of course not. I understand completely. I would join you, but I have to stay here and deal with… this," the colonel said. Donny couldn't help but laugh. "I'll have one of my men bring your vehicle around."

"Danke, Herr Kommandant."

90

Moeller's Journal, February 26th, 1945

I have to say that it's heartbreaking traveling through western Germany these days, not to mention difficult. The train stopped several times, once in a tunnel, to avoid strafing by American warplanes. It seems like the entire countryside is pockmarked and divoted with bomb and artillery craters, and the wreckage of tanks and other military vehicles from both sides litters the sides of the roads and the fields, especially around major cities or towns, such as Cologne; a literal skeleton of its former self. It's very depressing to see. Can Germany ever fully recover from this?

I have had to hire a taxi to take me from the station to the twin airfields of Hesepe and Achmer – a decrepit, wood-alcohol-powered Borgward that looks like some mad scientist's crazy fever dream. It has a burner and a smokestack cobbled onto the back, where the trunk would normally be. I don't understand how you make gas from wood, but apparently it's possible.

From what I understand, the Arado 234s are stationed at Hesepe now with KG76, with mostly Me262 interceptors working out of Achmer – the 262s doing their best against the seemingly endless tide of bombers the British and Americans send day and night.

The jets are amazing. I've seen the specifications and blueprints of both planes—as well as some others—and if it weren't for the war, I believe Germany would lead the world in aviation technology.

We should be getting close to the airfield. The cost of this taxi will nearly wipe out what little money I have left, although I should be able to get a room in Achmer for the night simply by showing them my SD credentials. I hate using them this way, but I will do what I must. This may very well be my last night of freedom, if… ah, here's the first gate now. I will finish this entry later.

91

It took longer to fuel and preflight the plane than Jackie expected. The Germans were sticklers when it came to safety procedures, and rightly so – the fuel-air thermobaric weapon slung under a recess built into the fuselage, although fairly small, was too big to hang on the wing, and by weight was still one of the most powerful bombs in their inventory… which is what Jackie was counting on. If she could just drop it close to the big bomber…

The other thing that took a lot of time was her briefing on the new *Fritz XII* guided bomb, based on the *Fritz X*. The design, like everything the damn Germans came up with, was ingenious. It wasn't a missile per se, but the rate and spin of its descent were carefully designed, and the thing was remarkably stable for something of its type – and somewhat steerable, which she found amazing. Small servo-powered fins had been added to help stabilize and steer it, and the technology of the guidance system was so complex as to be indecipherable by your average pilot. All she had to know, though, was to hold down the firing button while she kept the sights on her target, and the complex radio-controlled mechanism would do the rest.

The cockpit was large for a plane its size, but still only designed for one person, and she could tell Koch was enjoying being squeezed into such a tight space with an attractive woman, so she used it to her advantage, pressing her breasts against his arm, or touching him lightly on the leg when asking him a question. It seemed to have the desired effect, and she learned more about the plane in an hour than she'd expected.

He warned her that the Jumo 004 jet engine liked to occasionally flame out, although he felt personally that it was an issue of fuel quality and not an issue with the engine itself. He went over the emergency restart procedure and made her repeat it back to him. The truth was, this was her first time in a jet. *If Hanna Reitsch can do it,* she thought, *Then I sure can.* Nevertheless, it was a bit intimidating.

After Koch was confident that she understood the controls sufficiently, they crawled out and went through the preflight checklist, with her instructor leaning close in over her shoulder, pointing out critical details on the checklist. Then Koch showed her the thermobaric weapon up close, and they inspected the attachment hard points carefully. He showed her the safety pins, which he said would not be removed for this flight. This gave her pause – she couldn't drop the bomb with those pins in place – then the Kommandant called Koch over to ask him a question and she was left to continue the preflight. It was a simple matter to pull the clips and stuff the safety pins in her pockets. Hopefully no one would notice they were gone until she was in the air.

Finally it was time. Koch helped her into the cockpit, strapping her in as Jackie buckled her leather flying helmet: a well-used German one she'd brought with her just as Hanna would've done. He closed and locked the hatch, then tapped it twice with his fist, giving her a smile and a thumbs-up, which she returned.

Jackie plugged in her headphone jack and contacted flight operations, receiving the go-ahead for engine start. She consulted the cheat sheet Koch had taped to the firewall. Fuel on, electrics on, full flaps. She gave the thumbs-up to the start crew and they engaged the external starter they'd rolled up on a cart to crank the jet turbines over. She felt a shiver of anticipation as the port-side turbine began spooling up, finally reaching its operating rpm, and the crew leader gave her the hand signal for start. She punched the left igniter button and the jet engine roared raggedly to life, smoothing out as she throttled up a little bit, feeling the plane pushing against its port-side wheel chock.

The start crew ran to disengage the starter cables, then rolled the cart efficiently to the right side of the plane and repeated the sequence. She soon felt the second engine roar to life, and for the first time she forgot the mission, forgot the danger, simply thrilling at the big Jumo 004 jet engines vibrating the entire airframe. For the moment she was just a pilot, about to take off in a jet plane.

The jump crew gave her the all-clear and pulled away. She watched the flag man to her forward left, and, more importantly, his flags. He would let her know when the wheel chocks were pulled, and she was clear to taxi. The German signals were a bit different than the American and British flag signals, but she'd actually sat in a dead plane on a runway in Northern England and worked with a ground control flag man to memorize the German signals, so there'd be no surprises.

The chocks were pulled away and the signal was given to taxi, as the command came through her headphones. She fed power to both engines and released the brakes. There was a slight lurch, and the plane began slowly moving forward as the flag man stepped out of the way.

Jackie followed the control center's directions to one of the undamaged runways, which, it had been explained to her, were set up in an overlapping triangular pattern that corresponded to the prevailing winds in the area. The plane rumbled over what looked like recent asphalt repairs, the wings flexing as it rolled, her stomach full of butterflies.

Finally she was told to turn left onto runway #2, line up, and stop. It was explained to her that she'd be taking off into the wind, which was currently from the southeast, and that the radar showed slight cloud cover at 3,000 meters but no planes at the moment, and there were no flights expected in or out of Hesepe or Achmer for thirty-six minutes. She had a bad moment as she waited for the all-clear to take off. *Why's it always seem to take so long?* she wondered.

Finally, in her ear: "Flight 715, you are cleared for takeoff. Have a good flight, Miss Reitsch."

"Danke," she said into the mike, settling her goggles snugly over her eyes. "I will."

92

The base wasn't easy to get into; three layers of security told me that whatever was going on there, it was strictly top secret. We were on the road approaching the final checkpoint when I saw the Kübelwagen headed the other way. The driver was a tall, dark-haired officer. I couldn't believe it. I was sure it was Strausshind, the OSS agent.

"Turn the car around!" I shouted. "SCHNELL," I yelled at the driver as we approached the checkpoint. "I SAID, TURN THIS DAMN THING AROUND. Follow that Kübelwagen!" I was beside myself. All this way to find him, only to lose him here? Unacceptable.

The driver did as he was told, pulling a quick U-turn, and I leaned over the seat, exhorting him to drive faster. "The Kübelwagen we passed – it's being driven by a criminal posing as an officer. Faster! MACH SCHNELL."

I could see the Kübelwagen clearing the second checkpoint – the one we'd just passed through. As we came tearing up to the guard shack, the gate came back down. I was yelling at the idiots out the window to stop him, but they didn't know me. *Mein Gott!* I thought. *He can't get away! Not now - not when I'm so close...*

I leapt from the car, yelling at the guards, which was clearly the wrong thing to do, because they pointed their weapons at me as if *I* were the criminal. *Dummkopfs!*

It took precious minutes to get things straightened out, with the inner checkpoint telling them on the field phone about our sudden U-turn, me showing my SD credentials and yelling for them to stop the Kübelwagen at the final checkpoint, but the idiots called their officer and the fool told them to hold me until he got there.

I've never been so angry in my life. I threatened, cajoled, pleaded with them. *Just stop the Kübelwagen!* But by the time we got things straightened out, the morons had already waved him through the last checkpoint. He was gone, along with my family's salvation.

I made them hold the final gate open, and told the officer if I were stopped there, that I'd come back and execute him personally, which actually worked. I threw more money at the taxi driver, and either because of that or my SD credentials, we blasted through the last checkpoint as fast as the old taxi could go, which, in its sorry condition, felt rather dangerous.

The Kübelwagen was nowhere in sight, for despite having very low gearing for off-road travel, they are still pretty fast in their upper gears, certainly faster than the wreck I was in. When we came to a tee in the road, the left fork leading to Achmer, the right towards Halen. I had the driver stop a few meters short.

"Wait here," I said, leaping from the car. I ran forward to the crossroads, my eyes on the packed dirt. I found what looked like the most recent tracks and it looked as though they went left, to Achmer, although I wasn't completely sure. I ran back to the car and climbed in, slamming the door.

"Go left at the tee... what are you waiting for? SCHNELL."

93

Donny couldn't help but be nervous as he passed through the checkpoints, remembering his last narrow escape from a top secret facility, but everything went smoothly. He passed one car on the way in; a decrepit Borgward, with a wood-gas boiler hanging off the back – likely a private taxi. Other than that all he saw was Luftwaffe eldgendarme bored with their jobs.

He hadn't wanted to leave Jackie, but the AR234 was a single seat aircraft, as large as it was, and he knew she'd been right; blowing up the '*Amerika Bomber*' with the thermobaric weapon on the AR234 was the only realistic way to accomplish their mission. He figured he had around an hour before she was in the air, so he stopped at a small store in Achmer; a Tante Emma Laden which reminded him of the the one in Salzburg for some reason, planning to get a sandwich or something he could eat later. He didn't plan on stopping again until the Kübelwagen's tank ran dry, and he'd had the tank filled at the airfield. He parked in front, on the street, and went inside to find provisions, wondering how Jackie was doing.

94

The Arado 234 jet bomber trembled as Jackie ran the engine up to take-off speed. Despite her headphones, the roar was loud in her ears this close to the ground. She checked flaps for the third time, looked at the checklist taped to the control panel a last time, and released the brakes. The aircraft began rolling forward, slowly at first, then faster and faster, until the sides of the runway were a blur and she felt the sense of anticipation she felt each time she took off. She pulled back on the stick smoothly, and the Arado left the ground behind.

The rumble of the wheels was gone now, along with much of the engine noise, now that she was airborne. She watched the altimeter, and when high enough, raised the landing gear and pushed in the levers for the flaps, retracting them. The plane immediately smoothed out, and she let it climb, enjoying the smooth push of the jet engines at her back. She'd flown Mustangs and P-38s, and they were fast, but from the specifications they'd shown her, she knew this plane was faster by at least 20 mph, and without any visible prop spin outside the cockpit, it felt even faster, and slightly surreal. The Me262 was faster yet, they told her, but definitely not a bomber, no matter how the Führer felt about it.

As she climbed she fed in some stick to roll the plane, spinning upward in a corkscrew maneuver, just as a pilot testing the plane would, then straightened the plane out, rolling it over on its back in a gentle loop to begin her descent.

For the first time, she got a good look at the airfield, with its overlapping runways, set in the triangular pattern they'd told her about. To the south she could see Achmer airfield – nearly a twin of Hesepe, but with its triangular runways set in a slightly different orientation, so that between the two airfields, nearly every possible take-off or landing was covered.

She pulled out of her descent at 3 kilometers, or about 10,000 feet and cleared her altitude with the control center – a simple, but stout brick building with a short tower she'd been shown during the tour. The plane was so fast that, despite taking careful note of possible landmarks, she had trouble identifying the bomber's location under its camouflage netting – the Germans really were good at hiding things.

She reduced power, and on her third time over the airfield was sure she'd identified where it was. She decided on a low-level, full-power pass to make sure, then she'd swing around one more time and get the job done. This was the dangerous part – she wasn't cleared for a low-level pass, and rightly so – ground effect, wind shear, and other issues made low-level passes dangerous. They were not going to like this in the tower one bit.

She fed in more power, banking around the airfield with the Arado stood up on its left wing tip. *Hell of a plane,* she thought, then straightened it out as she lined up her approach, dropping down to her practice run at only fifty feet off the deck.

95

My heart was in my throat as we sped into town as fast as the beat-up old car would take us. All I could think about was Marie and my sweet Anna. Failure at this point was unacceptable. This was their last chance. It was *my* last chance.

I had the driver slow to normal speed as we came into town – a good thing, because the shock absorbers on the ancient car were shot, and the cobblestones rattled my teeth. My concern, however, was not in my comfort, but in possibly spooking the suspect. We approached the center of town slowly, as I would with any dangerous criminal. The buildings were old— mostly stone or timber frame—and most had survived the Allied bombing attacks fairly well, although I saw several people sorting through the rubble of one building desultorily for salvageable material.

I told the driver to slow at the center of town so that I could look both ways. I looked right and saw nothing, then looked left and saw a Kübelwagen parked in front of a small store. My heart leapt in my chest. Could it be him? Would he stop so soon? I knew I had to check, so I told the driver to pull straight ahead, park, and wait for me. I leapt from the car, ran to the intersection, then slowed as I approached the corner, walking as casually as I could manage, my right hand gripping my pistol inside my raincoat pocket so hard that I thought I might break it. I peered in but could see nothing. I pulled open the door to the small "Auntie Emma Store" with my left hand and stepped inside.

96

Jackie's first low-level run was close, but the approach was a little off – just a couple degrees, but it would make a difference. She caught a glimpse of the nose of the bomber peeking out from under the camouflage netting as she flashed over, and made a mental correction. She'd only get one chance at this, then they'd be scrambling jets – and the Me262s could catch her. Of that, she had no doubt.

The radio began squawking in her ear as she pulled out, rolling back around for her final run, but she just said "Ja, ja," and paid attention to her flying. The next approach looked perfect, and she engaged the radio targeting system at just the right time, keeping the plane steady, with the bombsight on the bald spot on the field she now knew was her indicator to where the bomber was located. She flipped up the safety covering the bomb release, and as she came up to the bomber, held the button down.

Once more she flashed over "Der Adler" at over 400 mph, pulling up once she'd passed her target. Nothing. She checked her rearview periscope, but there was nothing, no explosion. Then she noticed the light flashing on the panel before her. The release mechanism had jammed! She flipped the safety back over the button and pulled around in another tight turn, the screaming in her headphones loud now.

Jackie yanked the headphone plug from the dash and cursed. Koch had explained the arming and safety mechanisms carefully, and she'd paid close attention, so she was sure she'd done everything correctly – she'd pulled the retaining pins during preflight, disengaged the safety… then she remembered him saying the hydraulic bomb release had been designed for lighter bombs, and would sometimes stick due to the bomb's weight, which made sense.

She knew she'd only get one more chance to take out the bomber – they were likely scrambling Me262s from Achmer at this very moment. If it didn't work this time, she was finished... or was she? The Japanese destroyed battleships with slower planes and less powerful bombs. Jackie knew she couldn't let them drop that terrible weapon on Manhattan. If she couldn't shake the bomb loose on this run, she'd go around one last time and ride it in. *One way or another, that bomber is toast,* she thought grimly.

97

The interior of the store was like a hundred "Auntie Emmas" I'd been in before, except now, in early 1945, the shelves were mostly bare, the prices on what remained, exorbitant. The spy had his back to me as I came in, yet I was immediately sure it was him. He was ordering a sandwich, and the proprietor, a woman, was telling him she had nothing but a little liverwurst and onion, but the bread was fresh, which likely meant fresh sawdust at this point in the war.

She looked past his shoulder at me and said, "Hallo." I raised an arm in greeting, ducking behind a line of mostly empty shelves and bins. I wondered idly how long it had been since the meat slicer and butcher's scale had seen any real use.

"Is there anything I can help you find?" she said to me over the shelves, as if there were anything to find.

"Ja. I'm looking for a pot roast, a bag of potatoes, and some glühwein," I replied.

She laughed. "Oh, ja, ja. We have plenty… perhaps a liverwurst sandwich instead?"

I came around the other end of the shelves with my tiny pistol in one hand, my handcuffs in the other. I was close to the spy, but not close enough for him to disarm me. He looked up from the *Völkischer Beobachter* he was reading, in shock.

"Herr Strausshind, I presume?" I said. "Or should I call you Oberstleutnant Fuhrmann today? Put these on, or I will shoot you," I said, tossing him the handcuffs. He clicked them on his wrists and I smiled, knowing my family—what was left of it—was finally safe.

98

As she turned in on what she hoped would be her final run at the bomber, Jackie decided she'd made a mistake in unplugging her headphone set and plugged it back in. Immediately her ears exploded with a cacophony of German – the control tower was talking to Achmer airfield, explaining the situation, and requesting that Me262s be scrambled.

"Hallo? Hallo? Can you hear me?" Jackie said into her mike.

"Miss Reitsch? Can you hear us? Flying that low over the airfield is *verboten!* Please respond."

"I am having trouble with my headset… I am practicing low-level bombing runs with the *Fritz XII* bombsight, do you copy?" Jackie said, grinning.

"NEIN, this is NOT ALLOWED. Please come to zero–two–zero and land the plane on runway three."

"Your… is… garbled," she said, making static noises into the mike. "I… nearly done. Do you read me?" It was a trick used by many an Allied pilot when they didn't want to obey orders, but it didn't fool anyone – well, maybe it *would* fool the Germans. She doubted if German pilots ever did it – Germans tended to follow their orders.

"Miss Reitsch! Bitte, DO NOT OVERFLY THE FIELD AGAIN."

"Hallo? Hallo? Can you hear me?" she yelled into the mike as she lined up the plane for her bombing run.

This time she reduced power a bit, even though it was more dangerous this close to the ground. She fed in a touch of flaps and the plane trembled, so she reduced power until it went away. Her airspeed was still quite high for such a low-level pass, but it felt more stable than the first run. She set her sights on the patch of bare ground she knew was right in front of the bomber and went in. Things happen quickly at nearly 400 mph, and Jackie had mere seconds to arm the bomb. Then she jinked the aircraft quickly left and right, waggling the wings, which would hopefully free the jammed hydraulic plunger so it'd release. It was dangerous this close to the ground, but she had no choice. At the last second she straightened out, armed the weapon, and pressed the bomb release.

This time there was no light blinking on the dash, and she felt the Arado lift slightly as the three-thousand pound bomb released. She held the sights on the target as long as she dared, holding down the targeting button, then as she flashed past the "Amerika Bomber" once more, she released the button, pulled back, and climbed, feeding in power as she went. The plane trembled again, but this time it was from the huge shockwave from the explosion of the fuel-air bomb below her. The light filled her rearview periscope, and lit the cockpit glass in front of her. She rolled the plane over to get a better look.

The explosion was the biggest one she'd ever seen – a gigantic yellow and orange fireball, black around the edges, with secondary explosions going off on each side as the fire set off fuel tanks and ordnance on the Ar234s flanking it. The yelling on her intercom had changed to manic screaming, so Jackie yanked the comm cord out again.

She circled higher, knowing she should head for Allied territory, but unable to take her eyes off the huge mushroom cloud the fireball had turned into. She wondered for a moment if she'd set off the atomic bomb, then discounted it. From the briefings she and Donny had received, she knew that if she *had* set it off, she wouldn't be able to think about it – she would have been vaporized instantly… then she wondered if the bomb had been destroyed – or worse, just hadn't gone off yet. It was time to go.

The aircraft was still trembling, and somehow it didn't feel like turbulence anymore. Then she remembered that she'd fed in some flaps for her low-level run! She jammed the flaps' levers forward, but it was too late – the warning buzzers began shrieking at her, telling her the left engine had just flamed out.

99

Moeller's Journal, February 26th, 1945, early evening

Now that I'd captured the OSS agent, I needed a place to hold him temporarily. I didn't want to involve the local Polizei, as the entire operation was classified. Instead I walked him back to the wood-gas taxi in handcuffs and asked about a hotel. The driver said he knew of a decent one a block away (from whom he received a kickback, no doubt), and I told him to take us to the telex office, then to the hotel.

I sent two telegrams: the first to Gephardt, indicating my success and asking for additional funds and transport. I also asked him to begin preparations to release my family immediately, and that I would return to Salzburg with the prisoner as soon as funds arrived. The second telegram I sent to Albert Göring, care of Skoda Works, again detailing my success, but asking his help in ensuring my family's prompt release, and thanking him for his efforts on their behalf. I hadn't heard from him as to whether he'd located them or not, but he would have no idea where I was at the moment until he received this telegram. I don't trust Gephardt, and it's always good to have a back-up plan. Their welfare is all that matters now.

Now, seated in the hotel room I commandeered using my SD credentials, I sit across from the American agent who is indirectly their salvation. I remember him from the train – he is clever, and I haven't slept, so I must be on my guard. More later. Thank you, Lord, for sending me my quarry.

100

Koch had explained the emergency restart procedure to her and made her go over it several times; shut down the fuel, drop the nose to increase airspeed, cold-fire the igniter twice to clear the turbine of excess fuel, then turn on the fuel again and hit the igniter. The only problem was, she hadn't been that high to begin with when the engine flared out, and that meant very little time before she augered into the ground. She only had one chance at it. She pointed the plane down and began picking up speed.

Jackie cold-fired the turbine once, then twice, then a third time for good measure. The ground was rushing up at her, warning buzzers screaming, the altimeter spinning crazily, then the right engine faltered, making her heart jump, then came back online. She waited for the airspeed, the ground getting uncomfortably close now, then flipped the fuel back on and hit the igniter. She heard the engine whine, then stumble, run raggedly for a few precious seconds, then it caught, and she fed in full power, now in a powered dive, heading straight for the ground at 461 mph.

Pulling the Arado out of its dive took all of Jackie's strength, but she somehow tapped into reserves she didn't know she had, pulling back on the controls until the plane finally flattened out a mere fifty feet off the ground. She breathed a sigh of relief, then realized there was a plane in front of her – another Arado jet just lifting off the ground, heading straight for her. She didn't think about it, she just flipped the safety up on her guns and fired a burst into it from her pair of MG151/20 cannons. The other plane disintegrated and fell to the ground in flames as she flew through the fireball, pulling up, climbing out of there.

Time to get the hell out of here before they scramble more jets, she thought, then smiled. *Three more, I'll be an ace!* Then she wondered how many Arado

Ar234s she'd destroyed on the ground. Would that count? She had no witnesses, dammit, and no cameras. A smile pasted on her face, she pointed the jet west and fed the coal to it.

101

Donny perched uncomfortably on the edge of the bed as Moeller sat in the chair, near the door, his pistol pointed at him, an indecipherable look on his face. Donny could tell that Moeller was not one to let down his guard, despite looking exhausted... but he had to try.

"What if I told you that I am actually Luftwaffe intelligence, working undercover?" Donny said.

Moeller smiled. "I know who you are, and what you are doing in my country, Herr Strausshind, or whatever your name is. Please, we can make this easy, or make it hard. If you persist in talking, I will gag you. You will be interrogated in due time. Until then, we have nothing to say to each other. Of course, there's no reason we can't listen to the radio to pass the time," Moeller said, getting up to turn on the radio.

Donny noted that his eyes and the gun barrel never wavered. "Goebbel's latest bullshit speech? I bet you're one of those guys who have swastikas on their damn boxers," he said, trying to get Moeller mad, but Moeller just smiled at him and turned on the radio. It was a French station, and the orchestra sounded live. So close... He'd nearly gotten away with it—nearly got to Elena—but now everything was lost. At least Jackie had succeeded – at least he thought she had. Walking from the taxi to the hotel they'd heard a huge explosion, and seen a gigantic fireball rising from the direction of the airfield. Donny just hoped the bomber at the least had been destroyed, and hopefully, the atom bomb with it.

A knock came on the door. Moeller opened it, but kept his eyes on Donny. "Yes?"

It was the hotel manager. "I'm sorry to disturb you, sir, but this telegram just came for you."

"Danke," Moeller said, taking the telegram. "I've been expecting this," he said, and closed the door, then tore the telegram open. He scanned it quickly, and it was clear to Donny that whatever it was in the telegram had hit Moeller hard.

```
Telegram:
Herr Moeller. I found your family. Words cannot
express my regret. You have my deepest
condolences. - AG
```

"Are you all right?" Donny asked his captor. He couldn't help it. Hardened Nazi or not, the man had clearly just gotten some bad news. He was staring at the wall blankly, the telegram clenched in his hands, his mouth slightly open as if someone had just told him something he couldn't quite believe. *Now is the time to attack,* the voice inside Donny said, the voice that had kept him alive all this time. He clenched his hands in preparation to spring, but something stopped him – he wasn't sure what.

Moeller looked at him. "My family..." he said, and Donny knew then what had shocked him so. Something hardened in Moeller's face. "Stand up and turn around," he said harshly, standing up himself. Donny stood slowly. Moeller had his hand in his pocket.

"If you're going to shoot me, you'll have to do it facing me, you Nazi pig," Donny said as he stood, getting angry now, but knowing with his hands manacled behind him, this was likely it.

Moeller nearly smiled, pulling the handcuff key from his coat pocket. "Don't worry, Herr Strausshind, I have no intention of shooting you. Please turn around so that I can remove your cuffs. Oh, and please don't call me a Nazi. I've never been a party member. Please don't lump me in with those assholes," he said, as Donny turned around, not knowing what to think.

Donny looked out the window as Moeller moved to uncuff him. It was dark, but with no overhead drone of planes, no artillery lighting the horizon with false lightning – just a small, dark town at the edge of the war, the combat having passed them by as it moved inland, north and east, toward Berlin and Prague. He couldn't help but feel that the war might be over soon.

He felt the cold steel around his wrists release and turned to face Moeller again, rubbing the circulation into them.

"You are free to go," Moeller said, slumping back into his chair again, his attention no longer on Donny.

"Why? Tell me," Donny said.

Moeller looked at him sharply, then at the room's dresser where the proprietor of the hotel had left him half a bottle of Calvados and two small glasses. He got up and poured two healthy shots, and handed one to Donny, looking at the man who just minutes before had been his adversary.

"To my family," he said.

"Your family," Donny said, raising his glass. They clinked glasses and threw back their shots.

"Tell me about them," Donny said.

Moeller looked at him for a long minute, then refilled both their glasses and sat back down heavily.

102

The Arado Ar234 was faster than it had any right to be. Jackie was enjoying the brief flight and knew she'd be approaching the Allied lines in a few minutes, but the possibility of Me262 fighters having already been scrambled while she was making her final pass over the airfield nagged at her. The 262s were faster than the Arado, and it was possible they'd—

Suddenly tracers stitched past the cockpit and she checked the rearview periscope for the hundredth time. This time it was filled with the image of two sleek jets with barrel-shaped engines under their wings. 262s. They'd come out of nowhere, and they were close.

She threw the plane left, then right, then rolled the plane over and dove, but the German 262 pilots were the best of the best, many of them with over 200 kills, and they stayed right with her. A combat pilot she was not.

Cannon fire again – this time clipping her right wing. She pulled up, climbing in a tight roll into the grey February sky, feeling the drag on the damaged wing. She looked out of the cockpit and could see where the 30mm cannons of the 262 behind her had torn up her control surfaces. It made the plane sluggish – a bad thing in a dogfight. It also slowed the plane, making the 262s reduce power to stay with her.

"Well, at least I took out that damn bomber," she said to herself, rolling the Arado onto its back to level out, then rolling upright again, the torn aluminum of the wing flapping loudly now as it tried to tear itself loose, making the plane shudder. She checked the periscope to find, unsurprisingly, that they were still there.

Suddenly two P-51 Mustangs blew past her in the opposite direction, hauling ass, close enough to her that it shook the Arado. She'd already tuned the radio to the agreed-upon frequency, and keyed the mike.

"Hello, Mustangs, this is Eagle Flight… I repeat, Eagle Flight. I am an

American flyer being targeted by Me262s. Authentication is as follows: Six, niner, five, two, Murphy, Foxtrot. I repeat, this is Eagle Flight, do you copy?" she said into the mike, desperately hoping the Mustangs had been briefed about her; otherwise she had two more problems. There was a pause, then a response.

"Copy that, Eagle Flight. Are those Me262s friends of yours?"

Jackie had been speaking German so long she nearly said "nein."

"Negative. Could you help me out with them?"

"See what we can do, Eagle Flight," came the response as cannon fire ripped past her again, despite jinking back and forth to present a more difficult target. There were more thunks as they hit the wings again, making the Arado even more sluggish, and she knew it was just a matter of time before the plane's slower response time got her killed. She saw two specks in front of her, getting rapidly larger – it was the Mustangs, making another head-on pass.

This time the cannon fire came from in front of her, streams of .50-caliber tracers whizzing past her cockpit like a snowstorm as she tried not to flinch. The P-51s flashed past in a roar, nearly hitting her, rocking the plane again, and she checked the rearview periscope in time to see the first Me262—the one directly behind her—explode in a ball of flame and black smoke, suddenly cartwheeling downward, out of her line of sight. She saw the second Me262 roll over and dive, and a flash of silver wing as the Mustangs followed it down. She was safe… well, if she could just land the plane all shot up, she was. She checked the wings again. The piece of torn aluminum flapping on the right wing was larger now, making a racket, and looked as though it was about to tear off. She just hoped the flaps were all right. Her airspeed was reduced to well below 400 mph now as a result.

"Eagle Flight, Eagle Flight, this is Red Five, do you copy?"

"Copy, Red Five," she replied.

"We're rolling up beside you now. Your wings are looking pretty bad, but I don't see any fuel or oil leaks. We're coming up beside you and we'll guide you in."

"Roger that, Red Five," Jackie said, easing up on the throttle a bit, hoping one of the engines didn't flame out again.

The Mustangs pulled up on each side of her, their shining silver bodies contrasting with their red nose and black-and-yellow-checkered tail sections and black wing identification bands. Even though they weren't jets, with a top speed of 437 mph, they were fast as hell, although not nearly as fast as the Me262. Jackie guessed the other German pilot hadn't liked the odds and had beat feet.

"Your right wing doesn't look good, Eagle Flight," the Mustang pilot said.

Jackie grimaced. "Tell me something I don't know, Red Five," she said into the mike.

"All right, come to three-zero-zero and follow us home. You're safe now."

"Thanks for the assist, boys. See you on the ground," Jackie said, smiling despite the persistent shudder in the airframe.

– *Epilogue* –

Moeller's Journal, Vienna, July, 1945
(One year later to the day of Moeller's release)

L ike many of the Nazi criminals who helped destroy our beautiful country, Gephardt went into hiding. The country was a mess right after the war – everyone, including myself, was simply trying to survive. Because of this, it took me quite a while to find him.

He was working for the Americans now, as a minor functionary in the reconstruction government, pushing papers as always. What people don't understand is the damage done by mere bureaucrats. It's my belief that pencil pushers killed more civilians in the war than soldiers, yet most will never stand trial for their crimes against humanity.

I followed him for a week, until I knew his schedule cold. It was easy – Gephardt was a creature of habit. Every day he would ride his bicycle six blocks to work at the Brigittenau administration building. He usually ate a simple sack lunch in a small park across the street, then rode home slowly, the only variance in his schedule being Thursday, when he would stop at a small Tante Emma Laden for groceries, which he packed into panniers on the bike, then rode straight home. Oh how the mighty have fallen.

He didn't socialize, or go to bars or cafés. He was polite but abrupt with neighbors, and I got the impression they didn't like him much. No great surprise, I didn't like him much either. He lived in a second-floor walkup, and his first-floor neighbor didn't get home from work for two hours after he did. It was perfect.

Like most Germans, he was punctual, and that Thursday, instead of being in my usual observation post across the street, I was walking up the adjacent street on the south side of his building. I would be hidden by the building until I turned. I rounded the corner just as he let himself in, and he was busy fighting the bicycle with its full panniers of food through the doorway as I came up behind him. I held the exterior door, which was giving him so much trouble, and smiled at him when he looked back at me, no doubt surprised to find someone there. He said "Danke," and pushed the bicycle forward into the small foyer, then turned to face me with a smile.

He didn't recognize me at first—I've gained some weight since he last saw me—but then his brow furrowed, his eyes widened, and his mouth dropped open. I gently closed the door behind me, not taking my eyes off him.

"Moeller," he breathed. "Please, I did everything I could to save—" he began, but I hit him in the throat with a gloved fist. I didn't want to hear his excuses.

He dropped the bike, which fell over against the wall with a crash, then turned, trying for the stairs, one hand at his throat as he gasped for air. I pulled the garrote from the pocket of my coat and flipped it neatly over his head, pushing him down against the stair's worn runner by jamming my knee abruptly into his back, breaking his spine, which I suspect hurt a great deal.

I strangled him as slowly as I could, letting up on the pressure a couple times to let him get a breath. I wanted his pain to last as long as possible, and for that reason had decided against using piano wire for the garrote, nor did I tie a knot in it to crush his larynx as the Thuggees did – it was just a simple piece of parachute cord attached to wooden handles. I wanted him to die slowly and painfully.

Finally it was over – his body went completely limp. I unwound the garrote and checked his pulse. Gephardt was dead. By my watch it had taken him twenty minutes to die. Twenty minutes of agony hardly made up for the many months of pain you and the children experienced, but it was the best I could do, my love.

I realize you wouldn't approve—the policeman turned killer— but this was the only justice he would ever receive. There are many out there like him – minor functionaries who were "just doing their jobs." The courts in Nuremberg are far too busy with the Görings, the Himmlers and Speers, the Franks, and others of their ilk to bother with minor bureaucrats… but me?

Well, I have a new hobby. I'm going to track down as many of the rotten Nazi bastards as I can and send them to hell. Think of me as a 'Special Prosecutor.' I love you, Marie, and I miss you and the children. My heart is yours always. – Friedrich

Prague – March 1945

Donny couldn't wait to see Elena. The last time he'd seen her she'd been all business, cold and aloof the morning she'd dropped him off in front of the big Skoda factory for his meeting with Albert Göring, as if the night before had never happened. He figured it was her way of putting distance between them. They were in a dangerous business, and he guessed she didn't want to feel anything if he were killed. *This is what war does to us,* he thought.

The Café Slavia was bright and well lit as usual, the bartender, Yuri, at his usual place behind the bar. He looked up from washing glasses as Donny came in, and when he recognized him, got an odd look on his face.

Donny sat down at the bar instead of his usual table and ordered a Pilsner. Yuri brought it to him, his brow furrowed. Donny pulled out his money clip, but Yuri held up one hand. "It's on the house," he said, surprising Donny. Yuri being nice? He could get used to it. He took a sip gratefully.

"Thank you. I'm looking for Elena," Donny said. "It's good to be back in Prague—" he began, but Yuri was shaking his head no.

"What? She doesn't want to see me? Listen. Tell her I understand, but now the war's over. I came as soon as I could, just to see her… to be with her, you understand?"

Yuri looked at him with pain in his eyes and suddenly Donny knew what he was going to say before he said it.

"The Gestapo has her. They found her radio set last night as she was transmitting. A radio car finally tracked her signal. I'm sorry."

Donny set his beer down on the bar, staring into its yellow effervescence for a moment, then he looked up at Yuri.

Donny sat back, mouth open like a fish, too shocked to think clearly. All his hopes, his dreams, nearly within reach, now shattered. He tried not to imagine what the Gestapo had done to the woman he'd fallen in love with, but he was well familiar with Gestapo interrogation techniques, having experienced them himself. He felt a cold rage growing inside him – a hatred so strong it demanded retribution. He waved Yuri back over.

"Where would they take her? Do you know?"

Yuri nodded.

"Tell me," he said, his eyes filled with a terrible light.

* * * *

Donny staggered outside, into the late afternoon, the spring wind harsh and cold, whipping leaves and the occasional wrapper across the cobblestones. He crossed the street without looking, then turned and crossed the other street to stand by the railing, staring at the steel-grey Vltava River sliding past. A pair of ducks argued about something below him at the edge of the river. He felt empty, completely devoid of thought for once, totally unable to function. He'd envisioned their reunion several ways, from tearful to ecstatic, but he'd never envisioned *this*.

Black hatred for the Gestapo filled him. How was he going to get Elena out? *God help them if they hurt her*, he thought. He'd hunt down every one of the local agents one by one, and kill them slowly. His head hurt, the hatred was so strong.

He raised his gaze from the ducks, up to the Charles Bridge, then back along the line of ancient buildings flanking the river, to the corner where the Café Slavia stood in all its glory. The door opened, and a slim woman came out, closing the door behind her, then began walking away from him, up the street, along the river. *No,* he thought. *It can't be...* Then he remembered what business they were in: a business filled with lies, and ran after her.

He caught her halfway down the block, and as he got closer, he *was* sure. Reaching out, he grabbed her arm and spun her around to him. She'd been crying.

"The Gestapo, eh?" he said.

She stared at him in shock, then threw herself into his arms, burying her face in his chest.

"You came back – you came back for *me*!" she said.

Donny pulled her away from him so he could look at her properly, even though all he wanted to do was to hold her.

"Yes," he said. "I came back for you. Why'd you have Yuri tell me the Gestapo had you?"

She looked down. "I'm sorry. I thought you didn't care. I figured if you came back it would be either to just use the radio or because you found an easy lay in Prague…"

Donny took her face in his hands. "Do you love me?" he asked. Her tears were back. She nodded.

"Well, I love you too, and you love me, so… what? What's wrong?"

"I'm pregnant," Elena said.

Donny paused, then looked at her. "Is the baby mine?"

This time her nostrils flared in anger and she pulled back and slapped him. Hard.

"Who do you think I am?" she said.

Donny just grinned and pulled her back into him. "I think you're the woman I want to marry, Elena… my God, I don't even know your last name."

"It's Novotný. Elena Novotný," she said without a smile, obviously still a little pissed at him.

Donny got down on one knee, still holding her hand.

"Elena Novotný, will you marry me?" Donny said, watching the change come over her face. He stood up and pulled her close. She hit him on the chest with a closed fist, but not too hard. Then she hit him again.

"What? What'd I do wrong now?" he said.

"You made me cry, you bastard," she said.

"I love you and promise to never make you cry again."

"You idiot," she said, but now she was smiling through her tears.

"That's me," Donny said, first kissing her hand, then kissing her again hard, some passerby giving them a wolf-whistle of appreciation, but neither of them cared.

Author's Notes:

Although *Eagle's Claw* is a work of fiction, I wove it together using threads of truth. The German, heavy-lift bomber program began in 1941, and I believe it was no coincidence that it was named the 'Amerika Bomber' (sic) program in the same year that the U.S. entered the war. Indeed, Germany declared war on us that year, after we declared war on Japan as a result of Pearl Harbor.

The idea that the Germans had an operational nuclear weapon before us, will undoubtedly, be scoffed at by most traditional historians, yet in doing research for my previous thriller, *House of Apache Fires*, I became convinced that there's a very good chance that's exactly what really happened.

While it's true that we did successfully destroy their stocks of heavy water in Norway by sinking the ferry SF Hydro in February 1944, after several other attempts, (See 'The Heroes of Telemark' 1965, or 'The Heavy Water War,' an excellent mini-series for more information on these important top-secret Allied missions) the Nazis had more than one nuclear program, some sources say as many as five, although my personal number is three that I can verify. Remember, the Germans *invented* nuclear physics. The scientists who really made the Manhattan Project succeed were German, and any nuclear physicist can tell you that there's more than one way to enrich uranium—in fact, we did so at Oak Ridge Tennessee, using cyclotrons—the very same technology the Iranians are utilizing today.

You need three things to run a cyclotron: plenty of water, plenty of labor, and the expertise. Auschwitz stood near the confluence of the Vistula and Sola rivers, had an inexhaustible labor supply, (the camps) and supposedly, several physicists were working there. Why? From several sources I've heard that the Buna R synthetic rubber and fuel plant run by I.G. Farben produced very little rubber, some methanol, and no coal diesel until 1945… it may be reaching, but could they have been producing something else?

Then there is the U.S. Army Air Corps interrogation report dated August 19th, 1945 in which one Hans Zinsser, a pilot, details watching an atomic bomb test in the 4 corners area of Silesia, in early October 1944. He noted a mushroom cloud followed by strong electrical disturbances, making radio contact impossible. Please note, EMP does not destroy vacuum tube technology, just integrated circuits. The London Daily Telegraph mentioned in a 1945 article that Londoners were preparing for the possibility of a German 'Atom bomb attack' in August 1944. On October 11th, 1944 the Daily Mail published an article about Berlin going silent: 'BERLIN IS SILENT 60 HOURS - still no phones,' the headline read.

The testimony of Major John Lansdale, the man Leslie Groves put in charge of sourcing more uranium in Europe near the end of the war, for the Manhattan Project is also interesting. He states here: https://www.youtube.com/watch?v=pNLRmDFx8Xw that he confiscated 560 kilograms of uranium from the submarine U-234, headed for Japan, which was also carrying several tons of documents and blueprints of weapons, including the V2 rocket, an entire crated Me262 jet fighter, 5 German military officers, one an expert in air defense, as well as a couple civilian engineers and two Japanese officers. He states quite clearly that the material was used in a bomb dropped on Japan.

One of the bombs, the bomb dropped on Hiroshima, was different than the one used on Nagasaki. They had different names, and looked very different. *Fatman*, the bomb dropped on Nagasaki, was a plutonium weapon of the same design tested at Trinity… but the first, smaller bomb, *Little Boy*, was different. Now, why would the U.S. government drop an untested weapon on Japan, especially when so much relied on the result? Perhaps they knew it already had been tested? Robert Oppenheimer himself stated that the bomb dropped on Hiroshima "…was of German Provenance," or of *German origin*.

If this seems outlandish, consider this: Just in the last few years, an underground Nazi facility called 'B8' near Sankt Georgen outside of Linz, which was part of the Mauthausen prison camp complex, was unearthed. The tunnels had been filled with concrete after the war by the Allies. To the surprise of the excavators, radioactivity was detected in several of the tunnels. Why fill them with concrete? To keep them from the Russians perhaps? Why did we so readily hand over Berlin to the Russians? Allow them to enter the city first? Why was Patton and the 3rd Army sent to Prague instead of Berlin? Well, that area of (then) Czechoslovakia and the border area with Austria and Poland was the center of all the SS 'black programs.' Most of the top secret material and scientists recovered by 'Operation Paperclip' as it became known, were located in or around this area.

Let's look at the other technology in the book for a moment. The Arado Ar234 was a jet-powered, light bomber that was not quite as fast as the Me262, but actually saw quite a bit of use. It had a range of 1,340 miles, operated from September 1944 until April 1945, and was used to try and destroy the bridge at Remagen, each plane carrying two 2,200-pound bombs. Nine of them were used in the Battle of the Bulge, yet you never hear about them. 214 were built, 51 of which were stationed on the Western theater front lines at the end of the war, and were being used for photo-reconnaissance. What were they waiting for? Only a few at a time would be used in such a fashion – in fact, the last German plane to overfly London was an Ar234, which was an almost nightly occurrence, without a single loss of aircraft.

Then there was the article in the New York Times at the end of the war about 70 heavy bombers being found on an airfield in Norway after the end of the war. Seventy. Again, waiting for what? There is a report of a Junkers 390 flying within 12 miles of New York City and snapping pictures of the skyline, before returning to Europe.

Albert Speer, the famous Nazi architect and later Minister of Armaments, stopped the heavy-lift program in June of 1944, ostensibly, (as he states in 'Inside the Third Reich') to redistribute war materiel required to build more fighter planes to defend Germany against the nearly constant bomber attacks that were decimating the country. Please note that the He162, the 'People's Fighter' depicted in the book was a very real thing.

Google it and you will find pics like this: of them being produced in underground factories – this photo was in fact, the one I chose to use as inspiration for the underground factory in the book. See it here:

https://kreuzberged.files.wordpress.com/2011/09/heinkel_he_162-undergound-factory-storage.jpg These were, for the most part, located in the same area where the Mauthausen concentration camp is located, along with the B8 factory, where the radioactivity was detected recently.

So, you ask, why didn't the Germans bomb us? The answer is, even their very largest bombers, the He277, the Junkers 390 and of course, the Messerschmitt Me264 'Amerika Bomber,' did not have the range to fly fully loaded to the U.S. mainland *and return*. Plus, they had the same problem the Allies had early in the war prior to the advent of the P-51 Mustang—their fighters couldn't follow the bombers that far, leaving the bombers sitting ducks—a problem which decimated the Allied bombers before the Mustang arrived on the scene.

This was the impetus behind the "Mistel" or in English, "Misteltoe" program – to see if they could piggyback tiny fighters atop the bombers themselves, essentially 'hitching a ride.' They made it work, but it turned out to be too impractical. They considered towing a flying fuel tank behind the plane, refueling it at sea using U-boats (no one really thought *that* would work), but finally they considered refueling in the air, mid-Atlantic, from another 'tanker' flying along with it. If they refueled at the mid-point, the tanker could return to base, and the bomber could continue.

We take in-air refueling for granted these days – we see it in movies all the time: Air Force One has the capability, as do fighter jets being ferried long distances, such as across the United States. It can be a dangerous and difficult procedure, but has become fairly routine for our military.

Now what if I told you that in 1944, the Germans had four different designs to refuel planes in the air, and that in fact, the most successful design is, for all intents and purposes, the same design we use today? Now imagine those 70 bombers in Norway retrofitted with this technology – perhaps half as tankers and the other half carrying bombs? Even a conventional bomb load dropped from 35 bombers on New York or Washington would have been devastating to morale and would've done a lot of damage. Now imagine just one atomic bomb the size dropped on Hiroshima...

Imagine them being accompanied by Me262 and Ho229 fighters,

(Northrup recently came to the conclusion that the Horten Ho229 flying wing was indeed the world's first stealth aircraft. The History channel did a segment on it.) also refitted to refuel in flight, over the Atlantic.

If it hadn't been for Allied bombers smashing German production lines day and night, the East Coast of America, in particular New York, Philadelphia and Washington, could have been turned into a smoking pyre. One more year of war could have turned the tables. If we hadn't succeeded on D-day… It was a much closer thing than we can imagine, and oh – what was taken from Prague and the surrounding area, particularly anything to do with the German nuclear program? Still classified until 2045 – 100 years.

The Edelweiss Pirates? Very real. These were kids who hated Hitler, who risked their lives, who beat up Hitler Youth on a regular basis. They were real heroes, and the real 'German Underground.' When I heard about them, I knew I *had* to put them in the book.

The *'Fritz X'* bomb? Another German first: the first radio controlled, guided munition in history. It was designed to be used against Allied shipping, and was a 3,450 pound, guided missile designed in 1943 and used with some success against shipping convoys. Ever hear of one? Check Wikipedia. The Germans also apparently had thermobaric weapons, 'fuel-air' bombs, which are the next most powerful thing to a nuke you can get, apparently. There is much supposition that they were used on the Eastern Front against the Russians. I do not doubt it. Of course, I coupled the two in the book, which is purely artistic license, but I have no doubt the Nazis, being as bloodthirstily innovative as they were, would have gotten around to building one sooner or later. By the way, one of these would fit quite handily in an Ar234 jet bomber – the same bomber overflying London on a nightly basis. Would fire-bombing London with 51 of these provide enough of a diversion so that one heavy German bomber, along with its refueling tanker, would be able to sneak by overhead at high altitude?

While the particular design of the Me264 bomber in the book, (Der Adler or "The Eagle") was never built, two, possibly three Me264s were built and tested, and the design for a future model utilizing both turbo-prop and jet engines, as described here, was in the works. Anyone really interested can find a color plate of an artist's rendering of a swept wing Me264 matching the description of the plane in the book on pages 112 and 113 of Robert Forsyth and Eddie J. Creek's wonderful reference: *Messerschmitt Me264, Amerika Bomber – The Luftwaffe's lost Transatlantic Bomber.*

Finally, I want to mention the WASPs: brave women who ferried all sorts of planes around Europe during the war. Although they didn't technically engage in combat, it was a dangerous job, and I felt they should get some long-overdue credit, so I combined two of the most famous Wasps, Jaqueline "Jackie" Cochran, and Nancy Harkness Love, into one character: Jackie Love, who literally saves the day. Women pilots are today flying jets not only in support, but in combat, and these women led the way. I applaud them.

Thanks for reading, folks, I hope you enjoyed it. Please leave me a review on Amazon - it makes a huge difference. Auf Wiedersehen.

Made in the USA
Monee, IL
25 July 2020